Ladies of Disrepute

Also available from
Harlequin HQN

Castonbury Park: Scandalous Whispers

MARGUERITE KAYE
and ANN LETHBRIDGE

Ladies of Disrepute

ISBN-13: 978-0-373-77794-5

CASTONBURY PARK: LADIES OF DISREPUTE

This edition published by arrangement with Harlequin Books S.A.

For questions and comments about the quality of this book, please contact us at CustomerService@Harlequin.com.

www.Harlequin.com

Printed in U.S.A.

Contents

The *Lady* Who Broke the Rules

MARGUERITE KAYE

Prologue

Booth Plantation, Virginia, Fall 1805

It had been cold last night, the temperature dropping rapidly as dark fell. The initial pain of the whipping had passed. He was used to it, the searing heat of the lash as it ripped open his skin, the white-hot flashpoint as the salt water bit like acid into the open wounds, the sudden blackness which accompanied the soaking—which always accompanied it, no matter how hard he tried to remain conscious. Now the cycle of recovery would follow. He was inured to that, too, the throbbing which became a dull ache as his flesh began to heal, the stiffness in his shoulders and neck from holding himself upright.

Huddled into the corner of the tiny space of the cellar, Virgil was grateful for the cool air on the lacerations which crisscrossed his back. He must have leaned against the rough stone walls, for there was a raw pain tugging at the knitting flesh of his wounds this morning. It was almost impossible to avoid the walls in the confined space, which was not big enough for one his size to do anything other than crouch, not wide enough for him to lie down. He could only curl, foetus-like, on the hard-packed mud of the floor.

Tentatively, Virgil sought out the newly tender spot. His fingers came away wet. Unable to see anything in the pitch-black of what his fellow slaves called the hellhole, he sniffed. The iron tang of fresh blood reassured him. Once, when he was fifteen or sixteen, his wounds had become infected. He'd wondered, before then, whether death would be better than the life he was shackled to. No more after that, and now that there was Millie, what he wanted was not just any life but a better one.

Virgil winced, dropping his head onto his knees. He'd been so sure their strike would succeed this time. So damned certain! But even though the tobacco leaves ripened on the stalks, even though the clock was ticking mercilessly towards the arrival of the merchants' ships, Master Booth had held strong and the rebellion had been broken. He'd thought they would hang him for it, but he'd been festering so long in the dungeon now that Virgil had concluded he would be sold instead.

If it were not for Millie, this would be a victory of sorts. What would she do without him? What would he do without her? The sweet, tender moments they shared were what kept him going. Lying together under the stars in the blissful aftermath of lovemaking, they wove their dreams. His insurrection hadn't come close to making them real.

Guilt, an agony much worse than any whipping, racked Virgil's soul and wrung his heart. Millie was everything to him. Everything! He clenched his fists tight, making the cords of his sinews stand out. He would keep their dreams alive. He would make them happen and that would be his revenge. The time for trying to right the system which kept them all in chains from within was over. Master Booth and his like would never bend. No point in bloodthirsty plans for taking revenge on them either, for bloodshed only led to more bloodshed. He would have his revenge, he would triumph over them all, and he would make his dreams happen, not by physical force but by force of will. His will. He was better than them. He was stronger. He would show them, he would prove to them all that he could be better, and he would do it on *his* terms. He would win his freedom. He would win their freedom, his and Millie's. He could read and write. He knew himself smart, for he'd seen that look, fear and confusion, on Master Booth's face when he'd presented his case before the strike. And he could work. He could certainly work. No one could work as hard as he. The interminable hours he'd worked for the larger part of his nineteen years on earth had honed his body into a powerful machine.

They'd most likely sell him in one of the northern markets, for everyone in Richmond would know him for a trouble-maker. If he hit lucky, his new master would be a liberal. It was of no import. He would triumph, and no matter where he was sent to, no matter how long it took, he would win. Then he would come back for Millie. He would make sure and tell her that somehow, though she'd know—she knew him enough not to doubt that, surely? He'd come back for her. He'd tell her so. She just had to keep herself safe until then.

Deep in thought, he hadn't noticed the tiny fingers of light slanting through the hatch of the cellar. Only as the key grated in the trapdoor lock did Virgil realise they had come for him. He braced himself for the pain as he unfurled his large frame, shading his eyes against the light, taking his first stumbling step in five days.

The plantation square was headed by the master's residence, the other three sides formed by the huge drying rooms which housed the newly harvested tobacco leaves. His fellow slaves filled the space. As his eyes became accustomed to the light, fear made Virgil's skin clammy. All of them, field workers and indoor servants, were there in ranks. In front of the whipping post stood Master Booth himself. Was he to be beaten again? Anxiously, he scanned the row of house servants, looking for Millie, but she wasn't there. Fear turned to dread. The sweet, rotten smell of drying tobacco was overlaid with the sharp, tangy scent of sweat. He saw his dread reflected in the faces of his fellow slaves. A terrible premonition made him stand stock-still. Only a sharp nudge from one of the white servants urged him forward, the manacles on his ankles clanking, to stand in front of the master.

'You will be sold,' Master Booth said in that peculiar drawl which still held the faintest traces of his English ancestry. Beads of sweat dripped down his ruddy cheeks. His brown tied wig sat at its usual odd angle. 'I will not tolerate insubordination. It is time you learned your place in life, boy.'

Virgil straightened his shoulders and threw back his head, meeting Booth's gaze full-on. 'There is nothing you can teach me about my *place* in life,' he said, his voice raspy from lack of water.

In the past, such defiance had angered Booth. Today, he smiled. It was this which tightened the knot in Virgil's stomach. Following the direction of the master's gaze, he was aware of that smile broadening. His knees threatened to buckle as his stunned mind absorbed what he was seeing. Millie. Her hands tied with rope. Her eyes fastened on him. Pleading. Terrified. And beside her, Harlow. The overseer.

Virgil lunged, but the white men holding him strengthened their grip. Even so, he had all but escaped when his manacles were yanked, dropping him to his knees. Millie was crying now, loud, racking sobs that pierced his heart. Not this. Not Millie. Not this. The pride which had kept him silent all his life meant nothing in the face of this new horror. 'Please,' he yelled to Booth, 'please.'

But the master simply scowled. 'Too late.' He nodded at his overseer. Millie was struggling desperately. Regina, the cook, took a step towards her, but she was pulled away by one of the housemaids. They all knew from bitter experience that interference would only result in a more brutal assault. Virgil knew it, too, but it made no difference. He continued to struggle, his muscles straining with every last ounce of their power to free himself, to reach her.

He called her name over and over. Their eyes met across the dusty courtyard. The overseer readied himself, unbuttoning his breeches. His white buttocks would have looked absurd under any other circumstances. Millie screamed. One almighty surge of energy and Virgil was back on his feet.

The two blows fell at once.

The overseer smacked Millie hard across the mouth. Silenced but still conscious, she fell onto her back and Harlow made short work of rucking up her brown sackcloth skirts.

The cosh hit Virgil hard across the back of the head. He fell, his face biting into the hot dust, into an oblivion denied Millie as the overseer set about the brief and brutal business of punishing her for her lover's crimes.

Maer Hall, Staffordshire, 1816

'Kate! So glad you could make it.' Sarah Wedgwood pushed her way through the crowd to greet her friend. 'I was afraid you were still in the Lake District.'

Lady Katherine Montague grimaced. 'No, I returned a couple of weeks ago, just in time for my cousin Araminta's wedding.'

'I heard that your other cousin, Ross, ran off with a ladies' maid,' Sarah said sotto voce, eyes agog as she led Kate to a quiet corner of the room. 'Surely that cannot be true?'

'We don't actually know what happened. When my Aunt Wilhelmina discovered that Ross's intentions towards the girl were honourable, she rather lost the rag with the poor soul and sent her packing. Ross was furious—he headed hotfoot after her, and frankly we have no idea where they are now. Wherever it is, I do most sincerely hope they are married, for it seemed to me that Ross was quite besotted, and of course,' Kate said with a mischievous smile, 'to discover that her meddling has had the exact opposite effect of what she intended will make my dear aunt furious. She can talk of nothing but nourishing vipers in her bosom, and my father—actually, I'm not sure that Papa takes in anything much these days, since Edward and Jamie…'

Kate broke off, the familiar lump in her throat preventing her from continuing. Though it had been more than a year since Ned died at Waterloo, longer since Jamie had disappeared, the loss of her brothers still felt unreal. Both were buried in the distant lands where they fell. She wondered sometimes if that was it—with nothing to mark their passing, she could believe that they were still abroad, fighting. At times, she could wholly understand her father's desire to live in the past. Though Jamie had always been too much the duke-in-waiting for her to do anything other than spar with him, she had loved Ned.

'Sorry,' she said to Sarah. 'Things at home have become rather horribly complicated. I won't bore you with the details, but suffice to say that your invitation for tonight was most welcome, though my aunt was furious at my accepting it. But I could not deny myself *such* an opportunity. Where is your guest of honour, I do not see him here?'

'That is my fault, I fear,' Josiah Wedgwood, son of the famous potter and the owner of Maer Hall, interrupted. 'Mr Jackson was with me at the Etruria works, and I did not notice the time. He is changing for dinner, but he should not be long. How are you, Lady Katherine? It is very good to see you.' Josiah bent low over Kate's hand. 'Our Mr Jackson made his fortune in American stoneware, you know, and we plan to do some business together, but I will not bore you with the details, my dear. Tell me how the duke does?'

'Bearing up. He sends his regards,' Kate said, a bare-faced

lie, for her ailing father was not even aware that she was here in Staffordshire, and would never have thought of sending his regards to a man he would consider to be a tradesman. 'Never mind Papa, tell me about Mr Jackson. I cannot tell you how excited I am about meeting him. What is he like?'

'See for yourself,' Sarah replied, nudging her arm in a most unladylike manner. 'Here he is now.'

As the double doors at the end of the Great Hall were closed by the Wedgwoods' head footman, a ripple of excitement fluttered through the assembled guests. All eyes turned towards the man making his way down the room. Whispers, like the ruffle of a spring breeze playing on new leaves, rose to a murmur of anticipation. Silks rustled as the ladies of the company vied surreptitiously to be the first to greet him. Gentlemen edged closer to their host with the same intention.

The focus of all this attention seemed oblivious. He was tall, which was the first thing which struck Kate. And he was exceedingly well-built too, with muscles straining at the cloth of his coat, though he carried himself with the grace of a predator. There was about him something fierce, an aura of power, of sheer masculine force which should have repelled her but which Kate recognised, with a frisson of awareness, was actually fatally attractive. In every sense, Mr Jackson was different from any man she had ever met.

As his host stepped forward to greet him, Virgil Jackson resisted the urge to pull his coat more closely around him. A huge fire blazed at the end of the long gallery, but the heat it emitted radiated out to a distance of a few feet only, before disappearing into the chilly air. The copious renovations which Josiah had explained to him in detail during the tour of the hall the day before had not extended to this great gallery, which was part of the original Jacobean building. Despite the tapestries and hangings, a permanent breeze seemed to flutter around the cavernous space. The English didn't seem to notice the cold, however. The ladies were all bare-shouldered, the rich silks and lace of their evening gowns low-cut, showing an expanse of bosom that in Boston would have been deemed shocking.

The starched collar of his shirt was chafing Virgil's neck. The gathering, which his host had described to him earlier as 'a few choice friends,' seemed to consist of at least thirty people dressed in their finest. He smiled and made his bow to a stream of faces it was not worth his while remembering, relieved that he'd had the sense to visit a London tailor upon arriving in England.

Though he had nothing to be ashamed of in the quality of his Boston-made clothes, there was no denying that they were behind the times compared to English fashions. The dark blue superfine tailcoat he wore tonight was fitted so tightly across his shoulders and chest that it was frankly a struggle to put on, but the tailor had assured him that this was how it should be. His knitted grey pantaloons seemed indecently tight, and a far stretch from the formal black silk breeches and stockings worn on such an occasion back home, but the valet he'd hired—much against his own inclinations—had assured him that in the country evening dress was reserved for balls. The man had been right. He had been damned finicky, fussing over the perfect placing of a pearl pin in the cravat Virgil had been forced to allow him to tie after his own third attempt ended in a crumpled heap with the others, but he'd been right, and though it irked him that it should be so, Virgil was grateful for this small mercy. In attire, at least, he was the same as every other male guest in the room.

Of course, in virtually every other sense he was quite different. Virgil suppressed a sigh. He was grateful for the effort that Josiah and his wife had made to welcome him into their home, but with business concluded, he would much rather have avoided this soirée and the collection of influential people Josiah had invited for the sole purpose of demonstrating their support for what they perceived to be a shared cause. So many variations of that famous abolitionist medallion created by Josiah's father were being brandished under his nose—the manacled slave cast in gold and silver worn as a bracelet, a necklace, a fob or a hair ornament—that he could be in no doubt of their goodwill. But the people of Old England were as ignorant of one salient fact as those in New England. It was one thing to cut the chains of slavery, quite another to be free. No one in this room knew that better than he.

He was the only black person at the gathering. Since leaving London, Virgil felt as if he was the only black man in England. Being so distinctively different nibbled away at the edges of his hard-earned confidence. He felt as if he were constantly teetering on the precipice of some irrecoverable *faux pas*, for though his success made him accustomed to mix with the highest of Boston society, and the people in this room were rather politicians and businessmen than aristocrats, the rules seemed to be quite different. It was disconcerting, though he was damned if he'd allow anyone to see he found it so!

'Virgil, I would like you to meet our most esteemed neighbour and my sister Sarah's dear friend.'

'Surely not *most* esteemed, Josiah. That honour must go first to my father, and I have four older brothers who—I mean, two. I have just two older brothers now.'

The voice, slightly husky, lost its lightly ironic tone as the woman's smile faded. Josiah patted her bare shoulder. She flinched and tightened her jaw in response. 'Lady Katherine's youngest brother died fighting for his country at Waterloo,' Josiah said, oblivious of the fact that the sympathy he exuded was making his guest squirm, 'and her eldest brother—the heir, you know—also died fighting in Spain. It is quite tragic.'

'It is, however, of no interest to Mr Jackson, I am sure.'

Virgil, who had been about to offer his condolences, was rather taken aback by this brusque tone. Was she simply a very private person, or was she in some very English way slapping him down? Before he could make up his mind, a slim, gloved hand was held out towards him, confusing him even further, for ladies, whether old world or new, did not shake hands.

'I am Lady Katherine Montague. How do you do?'

His first impression of her was that she was rather severe. His next, that she had a clever face, with a wide brow, sharp cheekbones and a decided chin. Her eyes were her best feature. Neither blue nor grey, fringed with curling lashes, they seemed to tilt up at the corners like a cat's. Virgil took the proffered hand in his own, noting the way her gaze fell to the contrast of his dark skin on the white kid of her glove. 'My lady,' he said.

'Lady Katherine is the daughter of the Duke of Rothermere,' Josiah Wedgwood said. 'Castonbury is the biggest estate in Derbyshire, and the Montagues are the oldest family in the county. You have heard of them, I'm sure. The duke...' He broke off in response to a summons from his wife. 'Ah, you will excuse me, I must go and see—dinner, you know. Virgil, if you will escort Lady Katherine?'

A forbidding duke's daughter, who would cast her eagle aristocratic eye over his table manners. No doubt she expected him to eat with his fingers or, at the very least, use the wrong cutlery. As Josiah hurried over to join his wife, Virgil repressed another sigh. It was going to be a long night.

'Are you enjoying your visit to the Midlands, Mr Jackson?' Kate asked politely, wondering at the harassed look which flitted across his handsome face. 'Josiah was telling me that you are to go into business together.'

'Imported Wedgwood pottery will be subject to the new Protective Tariff which our government is introducing, putting it well beyond the means of your average American. We plan to introduce a new range, manufactured in my factories, which can fill a gap in the market for affordable luxury. Josiah's people are working on the design at the moment.'

Virgil Jackson's voice was a slow drawl, neither ironic nor lazy, certainly not languorous, but mesmerising. Though she was, like all the Montagues, above average height, Kate had to look up to meet his eyes. Almond-shaped and deep-set, they were an indefinable colour between tawny brown and gold. His hair was close-cropped, revealing a broad, intelligent brow. His lips were full, a sort of browny pink tone which she found herself wanting to touch. His skin was not really black, but closer to…bronze? Chestnut? Coffee? None of those did it justice. Bitter chocolate, maybe?

Realising that she had been silent far too long, Kate rushed into speech. 'You will forgive me if I tell you that I find you far more interesting than tea sets,' she blurted out. 'I cannot tell you how thrilled I am at having the opportunity to meet you. I braved the wrath of my brother and my aunt to do so, you know, and my aunt is a *most* formidable woman.'

'To brave an aunt and a brother, your desire to meet me must have been strong indeed. I'm flattered, Lady Katherine.'

His teeth gleamed an impossible white. She supposed it

must be the contrast with his skin. Despite his smile, his expression had a shuttered look, as if he had seen too much. Or perhaps it was simply that the habit of always being on his guard was so ingrained as to be impossible to overcome. Virgil Jackson was not a man who would trust easily. Or at all, Kate thought. She wondered what there was in his history to have made him so.

The fullness of his lips were a stark contrast to the hard planes of his face. She had not seen such sensual lips on a man before. The thought made her colour rise. She was not in the habit of having such thoughts. 'It is Kate, if you please—I hate Katherine. And as to being flattered—why, you must be perfectly well aware what an honour it is to meet you. Your achievements are little short of miraculous.'

All traces of his smile disappeared. 'For a black slave, you mean?'

Kate flinched. 'For any man, but perhaps especially for a black slave, though that is not how I would have put it.' She met his hard look with a measuring one. 'Every man and woman in this room is in awe of you.'

It was the truth, but he seemed quite unmoved by it. 'As they would be a performing bear, I suspect,' he replied.

Was he trying to intimidate her? On consideration, Kate thought the opposite. Unlikely as it seemed, given the kind of man he must be to have achieved so much, it appeared to her that he was actually trying *not* to be intimidated. 'We are all staring, I know, and it is very rude of us, but I doubt any of us has ever met an African before, let alone one with such an impressive story to tell. Our fascination is surely quite natural. Is it so very different in Boston?'

Virgil Jackson shrugged. 'Back home, it is not so much my colour as my success that makes people stare.'

'Unless the ladies of Boston are blind one and all, I doubt very much it is that alone,' Kate retorted. 'You must be perfectly well aware that you are an exceptionally good-looking man. Why, even my friend Sarah is sending you languishing looks, and believe me, Sarah is not a woman who is prone to languishing.'

She was laughing, not at him, but in a way that seemed to include him in a private joke. Virgil couldn't help smiling in return, even while he wondered whether her words contained a hint of the irony for which the English were so famous. 'And yet I do not see you languishing, Lady Kate. I suppose you will tell me that you are the exception which proves the rule?'

'I am afraid languishing, along with every other feminine wile, is anathema to my nature. Which is just as well, since I am hardly endowed with the feminine graces which make such wiles effective.'

The laughter faded from her eyes, which was a shame for it had quite transformed her, softening her expression, making her bottom lip look more kissable than prim. Even that white skin of hers above the creamy froth of lace on the décolleté of her gown had turned from winter snow to warm magnolia. Was she fishing for a compliment? Virgil studied the tiny frown which puckered her brows and decided most definitely not. 'That is a very disparaging remark,' he said.

She shrugged. 'Realistic, merely. My mirror tells me the limitations of my attractions whenever I look in it, Mr Jackson. I bear rather more resemblance to a greyhound than I would like.'

Her words were a challenge, but in the short space of this conversation Virgil already knew her well enough not to fall into the trap of flattery or polite contradiction. 'Yes, I can see that,' he said coolly, 'there is about you a kind of sleek gracefulness in the way you carry yourself, and your bone structure, too, has that delicate, well-bred look.'

For a fraction of a second, she looked as if she would slap him, before she laughed again, a low, smoky sound, intimate and sensual. Once more he was struck by the transformation it wrought, as if a curtain had been thrown back, allowing him a very private glimpse of the person behind the severe facade. Why would such a privileged woman require such a disguise?

Before he could pursue this question, the butler announced dinner. Virgil offered his arm, and he and the duke's daughter followed their hosts through a succession of chilly corridors to the dining room which was, thankfully, in the renovated part of the house. The petticoats of Lady Kate's gown rustled seductively as she walked. The claret velvet of her dress lent a lustre to her skin, and brought out golden highlights in her brown hair. As Virgil held her chair out for her, catching an illicit glimpse of very feminine curves as he did so, the first stirrings of attraction took him by surprise. It had been so long, he hardly recognised them.

Lady Kate sat down, leaving the faintest trace of her scent in the air, flowery and elusive. Despite the relative heat of the dining room compared to the gallery, it was not particularly warm. Another quirk of the English, Virgil had discovered, to serve their food tepid—or perhaps it simply travelled so far from the kitchens that it could not help being cool. Warming dishes were a rarity here, though kitchens built in the most inconvenient place possible were sadly common. 'Aren't you cold?' he asked abruptly, taking his place on Lady Kate's right-hand side.

She took a sip of her wine. 'A little. I forgot my wrap. It was my own fault. Polly, my maid, was offended by something the butler said to her, and for almost the entire dressing hour I had to listen to her wax lyrical about servants who were no better than they ought to be, who wouldn't know a hard day's graft if it bit them on the ankle, who lived a cosseted life wrapped in cotton, and who had no right at all to look down their noses at a working woman. My dresser used to be a working woman of a very particular kind, you see.'

Virgil replaced his glass on the table, slopping a drop of red wine onto the immaculate damask. His eyes narrowed. 'You can't mean you have a—a courtesan for your maid?'

'Streetwalker. I don't think Polly ever rose to anything so lofty as a courtesan,' Kate replied candidly.

She was expecting him to be shocked, Virgil realised. There was a defiant look in those blue-grey eyes. He recognised it, and he liked it. She was no insipid English rose. 'Did you take her on to annoy your aunt or your brother?'

'Let us not forget my father, the duke. And no, I did not. Well, only partly,' Kate admitted ruefully. 'I took Polly as my maid because she used to work the streets around Covent Garden, and since her protector was rather eager for her to continue to do so, I thought it best to remove her from the city.'

'And does she like being your maid, this reformed streetwalker—I take it she *is* reformed?' Virgil asked, torn between amusement and shock.

'Oh, I'm pretty certain of that. There is Mrs Taylor's Gentlemen's Parlour in Buxton, of course, but I really don't think Polly is refined enough for Mrs Taylor, and besides, I feel sure that I would have heard if my maid had been practicing her arts so close at hand, for it is a mere two or three miles from Castonbury you know, and we are a very tight-knit community,' Kate said, smiling once again. 'Though Polly is an extremely loyal maid, she's a little like a vicious dog, liable to savage anyone else who tries to pat her. Her taste in clothes, however, is exquisite. I can see from your face that you're thinking I am one of those English eccentrics you have read about.'

'I'm thinking that you are about as far from a typical Englishwoman as I am likely to meet,' Virgil said bluntly.

'I shall take that as a compliment. My father would agree with you, though he views my eccentricities in a rather less positive light. He would much prefer me to be what you call a typical Englishwoman, though to be fair, since I put myself beyond the pale, his efforts to make me conform have been rather half-hearted.'

Though she had not put the shutters up completely, she had definitely begun to retreat from him. There was an edge to her words. Virgil was intrigued, and a little at a loss. 'You must have committed a heinous crime indeed,' he said, careful to keep his tone light. 'And here was I thinking myself privileged to have such a blue-blooded dinner companion. Should I have shunned you? No, I have that wrong—given you the cut direct?'

'You are mocking me, but believe me, in what is termed the *ton*, I am very much a social pariah.'

She was turning a heavy silver knife over and over, not quite looking at him, not quite avoiding his eye. Hurt and determined not to show it, Virgil guessed. 'Then that makes two of us,' he said, covering the back of her hand with his. 'I know all about being an outcast.'

Kate was not used to sympathy, even less used to understanding, but she *was* accustomed to insulating herself with her flippant tongue. 'You are very kind, but I know perfectly well the circumstances are not the same at all.' The words were out before she could consider their effect.

Rebuffed, Virgil snatched his hand back. 'Temerity indeed, to compare myself to a duke's daughter.'

'I didn't mean that!' Kate exclaimed, aghast. 'I merely meant that…' But Virgil Jackson shrugged and looked the other way, and they were clearing the plates, and Kate's other neighbour was patiently waiting to claim her attention. She was almost grateful for the interruption, despite the fact that the subject would inevitably be her family, and could not be anything other than painful, given the recent developments at Castonbury.

Sure enough Sir Merkland, an old hunting friend of her father's, and one of the few who seemed either oblivious or uncaring of her tarnished reputation, asked after the duke with that mixture of morbid curiosity and smugness which the healthy reserve for the decrepit, especially when the decrepit person in question was overly proud of his superior rank. Kate abandoned her soup. The consommé was good, but the Wedgwoods' chef was an amateur compared to the genius currently running the Castonbury kitchens. Not that Monsieur André was likely to remain with them for much longer, for her father's taste, since the loss of his sons, ran largely to milk puddings and gruel.

She provided Sir Merkland with a much more optimistic account of her sire's health than Papa's frail appearance the day before merited, then listened with half an ear to the squire praise her sister Phaedra's prowess on a horse, smiling and nodding with practiced skill as he proceeded on to one of his interminable hunting anecdotes. On her other side, Virgil Jackson was discussing American politics with the wife of one of Josiah's business partners, patiently explaining the differences between the federal system and the British Parliament. That slow drawl of his was mesmerising.

The arrival of a haunch of beef and various side dishes distracted Sir Merkland, who was almost as dedicated a trencherman as he was a huntsman, tempting Kate into leaning a little closer to her right. Virgil Jackson was a very solid man. There was a presence about him, a very distinct aura of power which drew one into his orbit. He was certainly different, and undeniably the most innately charismatic man she'd ever met, and it was nothing to do with his colour either, she decided, taking the opportunity to study his profile while his attention was fixed elsewhere. There was just something about him.

She could not imagine him ever being subservient, which must have made him a rather unusual slave. Had he courted danger? She did not doubt it. Was the skin of that broad back covered in a fretwork of scars? She shuddered, for the answer to that question was almost certainly affirmative. What other scars were there, hidden deep inside that attractive exterior? For she did find him attractive, a fact which was somewhat confounding, given that she had been quite convinced that she was immune to such feelings. Was it that Virgil Jackson was in almost every way the antithesis of Anthony? Or was it, she wondered wryly, the fact that he was in every possible way ineligible, which tempted her wayward streak? Imagine Papa's reaction if she introduced him to the family. Or better still, Aunt Wilhelmina's. Oh, if only!

Finally released from his neighbour's earnest interrogation, Virgil stared down with distaste at the slice of bloody beef on his plate and decided to confine himself to the accompaniments. He was hungry, but the food seemed more designed for display than satisfying a healthy appetite. The goose in the middle of the table looked good, but it was out of bounds. Why it was that he must serve himself only from those dishes within reach he did not know, but he had no wish to repeat the shocked silence which had greeted him at the last formal dinner, when he had asked his neighbour to pass the peas.

He helped himself disconsolately to some mushroom fritters. On his other side, Lady Kate was moving her food around without making any attempt to eat. A smile played at the corners of her mouth. Her eyes were unfocused, her attention obviously far from the dining room of Maer Hall. Her skirts brushed against his leg. He could smell her scent over the rich aroma of beef. The delicate diamond and ruby drops she wore in her ears drew attention to the slender line of her neck. At her nape, wispy tendrils of hair clung. Such a tender spot. What would it be like to breathe her in, to taste her? The muscles in his stomach clenched. It had been a long time since such thoughts had occupied him. Eleven years.

Lady Kate looked up, perhaps conscious of the intensity of his gaze. Their eyes snagged. A trickle of sweat ran down between Virgil's shoulder blades. He couldn't understand how he'd ever thought her severe. He couldn't take his eyes off her plump lower lip. Moist. Pink. 'Aren't you hungry?' he asked a little desperately.

Kate gazed down at her untouched plate and shook her head. Around them the scraping of china, the clatter of silver being dropped into the clearing baskets, made it clear that she'd been wool-gathering for some time. 'You don't like the beef, Mr Jackson,' she said, looking at the slab of meat sitting untouched in front of him.

He grimaced. 'Blood. You will call me heathenish, but it puts me off.'

'Monsieur André, our very superior French chef at Castonbury, would call you heathenish. He thinks beef is overcooked if the animal's heart has ceased to beat,' Kate replied, 'but I prefer it properly dead and what he would call burnt to a crisp. Not that I would dare say so to his face. Monsieur André has a very Gallic temperament and would likely beat me with his rolling pin.'

Virgil laughed. 'I would like to see him try.'

'I wish you could—come to Castonbury with me, that is,' Kate said impulsively.

'Well, I… That's very nice of you, but—'

'It's not nice, it's selfish. I have to leave first thing tomorrow, you see, and I haven't had the chance to talk to you properly. There is so much I would love to discuss with you, I have so many questions, but there are matters—family matters—oh, why is it that family matters always arise at the most inconvenient of times?'

'I wouldn't know, since I have no family,' Virgil said.

'Lucky you!' Kate exclaimed, then was immediately contrite. 'Oh, I am so dreadfully sorry, I did not think. Have you indeed no family at all? Your parents—?'

'I was separated from my mother as soon as I was weaned,' Virgil said tersely.

'So, too, was I. Mama was not much interested in any of her children, and as a female of course, I was…' Kate broke off, covering her mouth in horror. 'Do you mean you were *sold*?'

'Family ties are very much discouraged in the plantations. It was—still is—common practice to separate mothers and children.'

'And your father?'

Virgil shrugged. 'I never knew him.' He took a draught of claret. 'As I said, family ties were discouraged. You should be grateful for yours, whatever your relationship with them.'

'I am quite humbled.'

'That was not my intention.'

'You need not concern yourself. To be honest, what I meant

was that I *ought* to be humbled. If you knew my family, you would understand why it's very difficult to be grateful for them—some of them, at least.'

He liked that hint of wickedness in her smile. She was not only unconventional but irrepressible. It was a pity their acquaintance was doomed to be of such short duration, Virgil thought. 'You are not, then, in the habit of doing as you ought?'

Her smile disappeared abruptly. 'My aunt would tell you that I am rather in the habit of never doing so. Tell me, Mr Jackson, did Weston make that coat?'

He would have taken the change of subject for a deliberate snub had it come from anyone else, but he was pretty sure that a snub from Lady Kate would be much more direct. He had obviously quite inadvertently touched upon a sore point. 'My tailor *was* Weston, though how you knew I have no idea.'

To Virgil's relief, Lady Kate laughed. 'My brothers go to Scott, being military men, so I knew it was not one of his, and I confess that I know only one other tailor. It was an educated guess, that's all. You will have the Bostonian ladies sighing into their teacups at your style, Mr Jackson. Though perhaps you are interested in the sighs of just one particular lady?'

'I am not married, and nor do I have any particular lady in my life,' Virgil replied curtly. 'As to my coat—I doubt it will see the light of day when I get home. It took that valet I hired several minutes to get me into it, and I feel as if every time I breathe the shoulders will burst at the seams. Back home, I dress for comfort.'

'I'd like to hear more about back home,' Kate said, telling herself that the fact that Mr Jackson was unattached was neither here nor there. 'May I ask how long you expect business to keep you here in Staffordshire?'

'Actually, I'm planning on heading north tomorrow while Josiah's men work on the samples for our wares. We'll meet up in London to conclude our business before I return to America, but I have other business in Glasgow to see to in the meantime, and there is a model village not far from that city which I have arranged to visit.'

'Do you mean Mr Owen's New Lanark?' Kate exclaimed. 'How I would love to see it. I am a great admirer of Mr Owen, I have read all his works, and in fact our own little school in Castonbury was established along similar lines—or at least that is what I would like to believe.'

'Your school—you mean *you* have set up a village school?'

'Do not look so astonished. Not all English ladies confine themselves to playing the pianoforte and painting watercolours for amusement, Mr Jackson. Some of us prefer to utilise our time to more effect,' Kate said stiffly.

'So you rescue streetwalkers and educate the village children. I did not mean to offend you, but you'll admit it is something out of the common way, to meet a duke's daughter who is a revolutionary.'

'You are far too modest. Rare as we revolutionary aristocrats may be, a freed slave who has made himself into one of the richest men in New England must be rarer. I wish you would tell me more about how you became so.'

Virgil shook his head. 'I am much more interested in your school. Do you teach there yourself?'

'I help out when I can, but we have an excellent mistress in the form of Miss Thomson. I rescue governesses in addition to streetwalkers,' Kate said with a smile. 'Miss Thomson tries to follow the principles which Mr Owen set down, but to see them in practice would be so much better than reading about them. I wish *I* could visit New Lanark. How I envy you. Were you serious about establishing a similar place?'

'Serious about testing its merits. Very serious about the school. Without education, it is not possible to make the most of freedom. I believe that education is power.'

'With that I wholeheartedly agree. My own education did not amount to much, which goes some way to explaining why even setting up a simple school has taken an enormous amount of effort.' Kate pulled a face. 'That, and the fact that as a mere woman I am not considered worthy of having an opinion on the subject. Being female does rather shackle one.'

Virgil bit back a smile. 'You don't strike me as being some-one constrained by her position in society.'

'I know perfectly well that there is no real comparison be-tween myself and a female slave,' she replied, disconcerting him by reading his thoughts, 'but it is nevertheless how I feel sometimes. Perception and reality are not always the same thing.'

'*That* is most certainly true.'

How had *he* come by his education? Kate was about to ask when a footman leaned over her shoulder, a huge lemon syl-labub trembling on the platter in his hands. She shook her head impatiently. Sir Merkland was clearing his throat. The change of course dictated a turn in the conversation. Port and cigars and business would detain the gentlemen until tea. She would be obliged to surrender her monopoly of Virgil Jackson to the other guests when she had barely scratched the surface of what she wanted to know about him.

'You could do a lot worse than come to Castonbury with me,' she said impulsively. 'Then you could see our school for yourself and it would give you something to compare with

Mr Owen's. You know, the more I think about it, the more I am sure it is the perfect solution.'

'To what?' Virgil asked, confused by the sudden change in the conversation.

Kate had been thinking only of her desire to know him better, so his question threw her, for though of course it was because she wished to know him better, to say so would imply something much more personal. And though it was personal in a way, it was not *that* sort of personal because she wasn't the type of female with whom men wished to be *that* sort of personal. 'The solution of your travelling all the way to Scotland without having seen anything of our true English countryside,' she said mendaciously. 'Derbyshire is the most beautiful of the counties, and though I admit to being rather biased, Castonbury is one of the most beautiful houses.'

'Are you serious?'

Determined, more like, now that the idea was in her head, but Kate thought better, at the last minute, of saying so, for Virgil Jackson looked like a man who would resist any attempt to force his will. 'Perfectly,' she said instead. 'I would love to show you our school, and I would welcome your opinion on the plans I have to extend it.'

Virgil frowned. He was tempted. A school established on the Owen model would certainly merit a break in his journey, and he had not yet confirmed the precise dates of his visit with New Lanark's proprietor. Besides, there could be no denying that a visit to a real stately pile held its own subversive pleasure. He shook his head reluctantly. 'Much as I appreciate the honour, I very much doubt your family would be as welcoming as you,' he said.

Which was, as far as her father and Aunt Wilhelmina were concerned, the truth, but that only made Kate more determined. Since those same two relatives had taken such pains to collaborate in her ruin, she would have no compunction in flaunting that ruin in their faces. 'Actually, it is rather your birth than the colour of your skin which will concern my father. According to him, there are less than a dozen other families in the country with blood so blue as the Montagues. Though since he chooses to confine himself to his own quarters, his opinions do not particularly matter. My brother Giles is acting head of the family at present and he is not at all prejudiced.'

'Nevertheless,' Virgil said, 'I do not think…'

She could see she was losing the battle, but Kate, now quite set on winning, switched tactics. 'Are you afraid you will be put under the spyglass, Mr Jackson?' She could see from the way he stilled, that she had hit home. 'How can you expect to break down barriers if you do not face them?'

'I hope, Lady Kate, that you are not thinking of using me as a weapon in some sort of private war. Are you perhaps eager to prove your reputation for being a revolutionary to your father and your aunt?'

He spoke softly, but there was an underlying air of menace which made Kate's skin prickle. Virgil Jackson was obviously not a man who could be threatened. She threw up her hands in a gesture of surrender. 'I admit, there is a part of me which relishes the notion of introducing you to Aunt Wilhelmina, but I promise you, it is only a small part. What I really want is to get to know you better.'

Her frankness disarmed him. He *was* tempted. Who would not be, by such an argument put forward by such a— He could not think of a word to describe Lady Kate Montague. Not that her personal attractions had anything to do with his decision. 'I will think about it,' Virgil said.

'With a view to saying yes?'

'I'll think about it,' he repeated, telling himself he would, though he had already more than half decided.

Two

His valet brought the note with his shaving water, proffering the folded sheet of thick paper on a sliver tray. Virgil knew who it was from the moment he saw it, though he couldn't have said how. Had he been expecting it? Hoping for it? His name was written in a clear hand utterly bereft of flourishes, starkly legible. A man's hand, he would have taken it for, under other circumstances. His valet was not taken in either though, judging from the curious looks he was casting at him via the mirror over the dressing stand.

'I'll shave myself, Watson,' Virgil said, deliberately catching the man's eye. Though he would have preferred to break the seal in private, he would not lower himself to the subterfuge of sending the valet away, nor indeed would he grant the note the importance such an act would imply.

> I was perfectly serious. I wish you would do me the honour of paying a visit to Castonbury. We have much in common, and I am most eager to further our acquaintance. I leave at ten. I have sent a note ahead warning

them to expect us, and arranged for your man to travel separately with my maid and the baggage. From what Polly has told me of him, he will have an entertaining journey! K.

Virgil smiled. Practical, blunt and wry, and leaving him with very little option but to accept. It was as well he had already resolved to go, for he made a point of never allowing himself to be coerced. Reading it again, he could picture the sparkle in her eyes as she wrote that last sentence.

'A change of plan, sir?'

From the supercilious look on his face, Watson already knew the contents of the letter. How the hell? In the way that all servants knew, Virgil supposed. It had been the same on the plantation. Knowledge was power; he shouldn't judge the man for that. He folded the note and placed it in the pocket of his silk dressing gown. 'I take it you've been speaking to Lady Kate's maid?'

Lathering his face, Virgil watched out of the corner of his eye as his valet debated between honesty and what seemed to be the English servant's custom of pretended ignorance. He was relieved when the man plumped for the truth. 'Miss Fisher did mention that Her Ladyship had invited you to Castonbury,' the man admitted grudgingly.

'And did Miss Fisher happen to share her views as to my likely reception there?'

Watson blanched. 'Miss Fisher had a— She was— The truth is, sir, that Miss Fisher is not short of opinions,' he said grimly. 'I cannot imagine how Lady Katherine came by such a female, nor indeed how such a female survives in a ducal household.'

'Like her mistress, I believe she is rather unconventional,'

Virgil replied. 'Prepare yourself, Watson, for you will be sharing the baggage coach with her.'

'You mean we are going to Castonbury? You wish me to accompany you? I was under the impression that you were journeying north alone.'

Judging from the look in his valet's eye, the invitation was even more of an honour than Virgil had surmised. 'Do you wish to return to London?'

'No indeed, sir. I would not dream of leaving you to the ministrations of another,' Watson declared.

'Nothing better to do with your time, eh?'

Watson drew himself up. 'If I have fallen short of your expectations…'

'Don't be an idiot, you know perfectly well that you've been keeping me right. I don't like to be waited on, but it seems I must be, and you do it very well, so if you wish to continue with me in the short term…'

'I do indeed, sir.'

'Then get packing. I must make my farewells to my host.'

Kate swept down the stairs with her gloves and whip in her hand, trying to ignore the fact that her heart was fluttering in a quite ridiculous manner for one of her age. It was simply that she was *interested* in Virgil Jackson, that was all. There was a lot to find interesting in him. It was nothing, nothing at all, to do with the fact that he was an attractive man.

Just as the fact that she had spent much longer than usual dressing had nothing to do with wanting to look her best. As she very well knew, even at her best, she could never aspire to beauty, though it had to be said that this particular shade of blue was becoming, and the rather military cut of her riding habit, with its silver braiding and snugly fitting jacket, draped well on her slim form. Kate made a face, chastising herself. What mattered was that *she* was pleased with her appearance, she reminded herself. What did *not* matter was what Virgil Jackson thought.

Except, as she turned the corner to the last flight of stairs and saw that he was waiting for her in the tiled hall, dressed in a plain black coat with a grey waistcoat, buckskins and top boots polished to a gleam, and she noticed that his eyes lingered on her as she made her way towards him, she found that she did care. Chiding herself for it, she couldn't help the tiniest flush of pleasure at seeing that he liked what he saw any more than she could deny that she liked what she saw too. Very much.

She held out her hand. To her surprise, he bent low over it, pressing a kiss on her knuckles. His lips were warm. The touch was fleeting, but it was enough to set her pulses skittering. In the bright light of the early-autumn sunshine streaming through the fanlight above the door, his skin gleamed. His eyes were more amber than brown. The way he looked at her warmed her, as if he saw something in her that no one else could see. 'I'm so glad you decided to accept my invitation,' she said brusquely, for it was embarrassing enough, this girlish reaction, without letting him see it.

'I could not pass up the opportunity to visit this school of yours.'

It was most foolish of her to be disappointed, for what else was there between them save such business? Kate smiled brightly. 'I'm glad.'

Virgil frowned. 'Yes, but I'm not so sure that your family will be as enthusiastic. It is one thing to test barriers, as you said last night, but another to force an uninvited guest on people who, frankly, may not be very happy to receive me.'

'You *are* invited, for I invited you.'

'Did you tell them— The note you sent—how did you describe me?'

'As a man of great wealth and extraordinary influence, a business associate of Josiah with a fascinating history.'

She had not mentioned the one salient fact that he was sure would have been the first to occur to almost anyone else. 'You don't think,' Virgil asked tentatively, 'that it would have been safer to warn them about my heritage?'

'Why should I? I look at you and I see a man who has achieved what very few others have. You are rich and powerful and you have succeeded against overwhelming odds which also makes you fascinating. Why should I tell them the colour of your skin any more than I should inform them the colour of your hair, or whether you are fat or scrawny.' Or attractive. Really extraordinarily attractive. Which, she should remember, was quite irrelevant. 'Besides,' Kate said disparagingly, 'why encourage them to judge you before they have even met you?'

Virgil drew himself up. 'I don't give a damn—begging your pardon—about what your family think of me. I was more concerned about what they'd think of you.'

'My family can think no worse of me than they already do. They are perfectly well aware of my support for the abolition laws, and I am perfectly capable of defending myself, if that is what you are concerned about,' Kate said with a toss of her head. 'I've had practice enough, God knows.'

'I don't doubt that. I suspect you take pride in being a rule-breaker.'

'Not at all,' Kate said, 'you misunderstand me. Breaking rules, even unjust rules, is far more painful than unquestioning obedience. I wish I did not have to be a rule-breaker, as you call me. Life would be so much more pleasant if what one believed and what was expected of one coincided more often.'

She looked quite wistful and Virgil found himself at a loss, for it seemed that they were speaking about two different things. He could, however, agree with the sentiment. 'I know exactly what you mean.'

Kate nodded, touching his sleeve in a gesture of sympathy he was already beginning to associate with her. 'Our cases are hardly comparable. There are a good deal of rules which ought to be broken, no matter how painful.'

She would not have said so if she knew the price he had paid for his disobedience. No matter how unconventional she was, she would likely condemn him for it, and quite rightly so. Virgil rolled his shoulders as if the familiar burden of guilt were a tangible weight he carried. 'I play by my own rules,' he answered, more to remind himself of that fact than in response to what she had said. He could see his remark confused her, but the crump of carriage wheels on the gravel kept him from saying more, and then the Wedgwoods' groom appeared at the front door and informed them that the gig awaited Her Ladyship's convenience.

Kate pulled on her driving gloves. 'I hope you don't mind the cold, but I drive myself. I hate to be cooped up in a carriage.'

'That's fine by me.' Virgil pulled on the greatcoat his valet had insisted that he would require, having been forewarned that Her Ladyship scorned the closed carriage in which any other lady of her rank would have been expected to travel. With extreme reluctance, he donned the beaver tricorn hat which Watson had also insisted upon. Hats and gloves were items of gentleman's apparel to which Virgil had never managed to become accustomed.

Kate leapt nimbly into the carriage in a flutter of lacy petticoats at odds with the masculine cut of her dress, and took up the reins. The gig rocked under Virgil's weight as he climbed in beside her. His knee brushed her skirts. The caped shoulder of his driving coat fluttered against the braiding on her jacket. The air smelt of leaves and moss, with that sharpness to it that was distinctively English. As she urged the horse into a trot, she smiled. 'I'm glad you're here,' she said impulsively.

Virgil laughed, and for once spoke his mind without thinking. 'That makes two of us,' he said.

They had left Maer village behind, and were heading eastwards along a country lane at a steady pace. The morning was bright but cool, the sun shining weakly in the pale blue sky. The blackberries which grew so prolifically in the hedgerows were past their best now. The leaves on the trees had turned from gold and amber to brown, curled and crisped by the change in the temperature, ready to float down at the merest hint of a breeze. In the distance, a bell clanged as a herd of sheep made their way across a field.

'I was about to ask you last night, before the lemon syllabub separated us, how you came by your education,' Kate said. 'I realised later that I must have sounded quite the malcontent, complaining about my lack of formal schooling when it was likely that you'd had none at all—as a child, I mean.'

'I never went to school, not when I was a slave, nor when Malcolm Jackson freed me either.'

'Jackson is the man who brought you to Boston?'

'Bought me at auction, and brought me to Boston. There's no need to dance around the subject. I was a slave. I was sold. Malcolm Jackson paid for me in gold and set me free.'

'You took his name.'

'That man placed a lot of trust in me, it was the least I could do. Besides, the only other name I had belonged to the man who sold me. It was no hardship to give that up.'

'And this Jackson, he gave you an education?'

Virgil smiled. 'I gave myself an education. Malcolm Jackson gave me a job at his factory and a place to live. He let me have books, and when I was done with his, I found more, and plenty of ideas, too, at the African Meeting House in the city. I studied hard every night and I worked hard every day so that within a year there wasn't a job at that factory I couldn't turn my hand to. Sometimes I had just two or three hours' sleep, but I didn't need any more. I discovered I had a head for figures. I found I had a mind for business, too, which is more than poor Malcolm Jackson had. He was leaking money, he was being taken for a ride by just about everyone he did a deal with, and he was missing so many opportunities that it was criminal to watch.'

Virgil had shifted in his seat as he talked, so that his knee brushed against her skirt. He was more animated than she had yet seen him. His eyes glowed. He had cast his hat onto the floor, and tugged repeatedly at his neck cloth as he spoke. The finicky valet he had mentioned had obviously tied it tighter than he was used to. He had already admitted that he could not tie such a fancy knot himself. It was endearing, though Kate took care not to let him know she thought so, judging quite rightly that he would have been horrified. 'I assume there came a time when you could no longer stand by and watch things going wrong,' she said.

'I would have interfered eventually, but I didn't have to. Malcolm Jackson didn't have the hardest business head but he wasn't a fool. He could see what was happening, and he could see I knew what to do about it. He was getting old, and he was getting tired and he had learned to trust me. In a year I'd doubled our turnover and he made me a partner. Another year, and we had just about cornered the new market for cheap, practical stoneware.'

'Was that your idea?'

'One of them.'

'And not too many more years later you are one of the wealthiest men in America. This deal with Josiah, is that going to allow you to corner another new market?'

'I wouldn't be doing it otherwise,' Virgil said with a grin.

'But you have other businesses than—what do you call it, stoneware?'

'I sure do. I have real estate—that's property, to you English. Homes to rent to the freed men coming north that are fit for human habitation. Rooming houses that aren't flea pits. I have some interest in retail—shops to sell what we make at the factories. And some other investments too. As I said, I have a head for business.'

'It must be a very ruthless one, to have achieved so much in such a relatively short time, with the odds stacked against you to boot. Your ambition knows no bounds. Tell me, do you still exist on two or three hours' sleep a night?'

'I prefer not to waste time sleeping if there's something better I can be doing.'

Kate pursed her lips, her brows drawing together in a deep frown. 'But why? Why not enjoy your success? Forgive me, but you sound almost like a man obsessed. What more can you possibly want? Aren't you wealthy enough?'

'I don't care about being rich.'

Alerted by the change in his tone, Kate glanced sideways. The light had gone from his eyes. What had she said? 'You're so used to working twenty hours a day that you can't stop, is that it?' she ventured, trying to make a joke of it.

'I'm not interested in money, Lady Kate. I'm interested in what money can buy.'

He had shifted in his seat again, to look straight ahead. His expression seemed to have hardened.

Kate's brow cleared. 'Oh, you mean schools? Your model village?'

He meant reparation, but it was the same thing. 'Power,' Virgil said. 'The power to change.'

Kate nodded. 'Yes. If I felt I could have that, I think I'd manage on two or three hours' sleep a night too. Do you ever wish you could go back? To the plantation, I mean, to show them what you have become.'

He realised, from the casual way she slipped the question in, that this was the subject which interested her most. 'No.' It was baldly stated, making it clear, Virgil trusted, that neither did he ever discuss it. He could sense her eyeing him, calculating whether to press him or not.

'I'm surprised,' she said cautiously. 'Were I in your position, I think I'd want to rub their noses in it a bit.'

'There's other ways of payback.' This time, Virgil was relieved to see that she recognised the note of finality in his voice. He never talked about that part of his past, never consciously thought about it, for to do so would be to admit the tide of guilt he had spent the past eleven years holding back. It was one thing to talk around his history, quite another to paint its picture and admit to the pain which he had worked so hard to ignore. Yet there could be no denying that her choice of silence made him contrarily wish she had questioned him more.

The miles wore on. At the border between Staffordshire and Derbyshire they stopped at a village tavern, taking bread and the crumbling white local cheese on a bench outside. It was chilly, but there was no private parlour, and neither

Kate nor Virgil wished to endure the curious eyes of the locals in the tap room who had greeted their appearance with a stunned silence.

As they continued on into Derbyshire the scenery changed. The land became softly undulating, the higher, rolling hills of the Peaks casting shadows over the valleys through which they drove. It seemed wetter and greener here. The limestone villages huddled into the creases and folds of the hills, or stretched out along the banks of the fast-flowing rivers such as the Dove, which they followed for some time, where the water mills turned.

It was beautiful, though incredibly isolated, each hamlet seeming to exist in its own world, unconnected and self-contained, Virgil thought. 'Why aren't you married, Lady Kate?'

The question startled her, for her hands jerked on the reins, pulling the horse to a walk. 'Why do you ask?'

Why? He hadn't realised, but now he thought about it he saw that her remarks over dinner last night had been niggling at him. He could not reconcile what she'd said of herself with the little he knew of her. 'You said you were a social pariah, though I saw no evidence of it.'

'Josiah's guests are my friends but they are not what my father would consider high society. Were you to see me in that milieu you would have evidence aplenty.'

The horse took advantage of her lapse in attention to stop and crop at the grass verge. Virgil took the reins and looped them round the brake. 'Why? I know I joked about you being a revolutionary, but…'

'Oh, it is naught to do with that. I have always been outspoken, but the daughter of the influential Duke of Rothermere, you understand, is given rather more latitude than, say, a mere Miss Montague.' Her voice dripped sarcasm. She threw her head back and glared at him, her eyes dark and bleak, the colour of a winter sea. 'The fact is, I am a jilt.'

Virgil searched her face for some sign that she was joking, but could find no trace in her stern expression. 'That's it? You changed your mind about getting married?'

'A mere two weeks before the ceremony, and the engagement was of very long standing. I had known Anthony all my life. I did not quite leave him at the altar, but I may as well have, according to my aunt.'

The husky tones of her voice were clipped. There was hurt buried deep there. Had she loved this Anthony? Virgil didn't like to think so. 'What made you change your mind so late in the day?'

'We didn't suit.'

'But…'

'I know what you're going to say, if I knew him so well why did it take me so long to change my mind? I knew him as a friend of the family. I thought we would suit, and when I tried to think of him as a husband I found I could not.'

The anger in her voice was raw, fresh. 'How long ago did this happen?' Virgil asked.

'Five years.'

'Did you love him?' He should not have asked such a deeply personal question. He could not understand why he had done so, for he was usually at pains to keep any conversation, especially with a woman, in neutral channels. But he knew all about the pain of loss.

He covered her tightly clasped hands with one of his own, but Kate shook him off. 'Don't feel sorry for me, there is no need. I am not wearing the willow for Lord Anthony Featherstone.'

Rebuffed and baffled, Virgil said nothing. All his instincts told him to drop the subject, which was obviously extremely sensitive and extremely painful, but there was something in her voice, in the way she had closed herself off, that he recognised and could not ignore. She was hurt and determined not to show it. He gently unfolded her fingers and took one of her hands between his. 'Then tell me,' he said. 'What happened?'

She hesitated. He could see the words of refusal forming, but for some reason she swallowed them. 'Do you really want to know?'

When he nodded, she took a deep breath. 'Anthony was—is—the son of one of my father's close friends. His family has a bloodline which can be traced back to the Norman Conquest, according to my father. Our betrothal was the result of a bargain struck by our parents when I was still in my cradle. What you have to understand is that as far as my father is concerned, my only value is in making the best marriage which can be arranged. I knew from a very early age that I was destined to marry Anthony, and since I had not met any other man I preferred after almost two full Seasons, I agreed. Anthony was far from repulsive,' Kate said, determined to be scrupulously fair. 'In fact, he was considered to be something of a beau.'

'But you were not in love with him?'

'I have never been in love with anyone. I doubt it is in my nature to feel so strongly, and in any case, love has nothing at all to do with marriage. At least, not for a Montague. People of our sort make alliances, not love matches,' she said bitterly.

Falling in love was the one thing Virgil had been free to do. He had loved Millie. He would have married Millie. Were there other forms of chains he didn't understand? Duty had weighed heavily with Lady Kate. It was not a comparison she would dream of making, but he made it. 'So you agreed to the marriage because it was what your family wished, even though you were not sure?'

'I wasn't unsure, it would be unfair to say that. I was resigned. No, it was not even that. I simply didn't question it, I suppose.'

Virgil smiled. 'I find that hard to believe. You seem to question everything.'

'As I said, life would be less painful if I did not. Would that I had questioned this match earlier. Or had the strength of will to say no when I knew what—knew my own mind better.'

'What about your mother?'

'Mama died when I was a child. My Aunt Wilhelmina is her sister, and she was most—most anxious for the match to take place. Even more so than my father, in the end. When I tried to discuss my reservations about Anthony she—she did not— She said that I...'

Her hand curled into a fist within his clasp. Her jaw clenched, her eyes were bright with tears. This was obviously the source of her hurt, or one of them. Virgil felt a momentary spasm of anger at the unknown aunt. 'And the duke?'

Kate laughed bitterly. 'My father's word is law. He made the match. As far as he was concerned, there was no question of my changing my mind, whatever the circumstances.'

'And yet you did change your mind?'

'I had to.'

I had to. It was a curious choice of phrase, Virgil thought, but the tightness in her voice, the way she held herself, as if she was afraid she might shatter, and the sheen of tears which he was fairly certain she would be mortified to shed, made him cautious. 'So you called it off?'

She nodded. 'My aunt said that I would be ruined, and she was right. Papa refused to put the notice in the paper. He left it to Anthony to do so. *"Lord Anthony Featherstone wishes it to be known that his betrothal to the Honourable Lady Katherine…"* You can imagine how that looked.'

What Virgil found extraordinary was that such an act could have led society to ostracise her, but he had discovered that there was much he found inexplicable about the English. He supposed it was something to do with her family's status, and the fact of the date having been set. 'But your father, your aunt, they are surely reconciled to your decision now, after five years?'

Kate gave another of those bitter little laughs. 'You'd think so, but you see, I have refused to do penance in the only possible way by making any other sort of match. Though, of course, my situation must have reduced my expectations significantly,' she said in a voice which left Virgil in no doubt she was quoting her aunt, 'my blood and my dowry were still sufficient to tempt a few ambitious suitors. However, I may be foolish but I am not stupid. I have no intention of repeating my mistake. I am resolved never to marry.'

'That is what you meant when you said you have put yourself beyond the pale?'

'Did I?' She smiled faintly. 'Yes, that is what I meant. So you see, as far as His Grace and my aunt are concerned, I am a failure.'

She had said more than enough to make Virgil despise the duke, though it was the aunt, who had signally failed to support her as a mother should, towards whom he directed his anger. All his reservations about the effect of his presence in the ducal residence fled. He very much hoped he *would* throw them all into disarray. He could now perfectly understand Lady Kate's desire to defy them. 'I don't think you are a failure, far from it,' Virgil said. 'To stand up for yourself in the face of such opposition took real courage. I think you are extraordinary.'

'Do you?'

She had been staring down at her feet, but his words made her look up, and the vulnerability he saw there pierced Virgil's defences. 'Yes, I do,' he said softly. Pushing back the leather cuff of her driving glove, he pressed a kiss on the inside of her wrist. 'You really are quite extraordinary.'

He meant merely to show her that he understood. That he admired her. That he had not judged her as her family had. A token gesture of solidarity, that's what he intended. But when his lips touched the delicate skin his intentions changed. Her scent, the taste of her, turned his empathy into desire.

She stilled, her eyes fixed on his when he looked up, wide, startled, but she made no move to pull away. A pulse fluttered at her neck. Entranced, Virgil could not resist touching it. The diamond drops in her ears glinted in the sunlight. He pressed his lips to her skin. It was cold and smooth. She breathed in sharply, but did not pull away. 'Extraordinary,' Virgil repeated softly. The air was still, save for the contented sound of the horse champing on the grass by the wayside. There was no one else in sight. He shifted on the narrow bench, his knees pressing into her thigh. Still she didn't move. Her scent, flowery and already imprinted on his mind, made him think of summer meadows. His heart was beating in time to that fluttering pulse of hers. 'Kate,' he said, thinking that her name suited her precisely.

Admiration leached into wanting. He covered her mouth with his own, pausing just a second lest she protest. She did not. Her lips were so soft. She tasted of peaches or apricots or strawberries, sweet and lush. He slipped his arm around her back and pulled her closer. So long it had been since he had kissed a woman. His other hand he used to push back her hat and his mouth shaped hers so easily, so naturally, that he forgot to think about whether he could remember what to do, and sank into her kiss as if he had been waiting to do so from the moment they met.

Kate closed her eyes. Such a gentle touch he had. And the look in his eyes, as if he could see the feelings she kept parcelled up deep inside her. His mouth was warm. His kiss made her feel as if the sun had strengthened. His lips moved over hers slowly, tasting her, seeming to want nothing but to savour her. It made her skin tingle. It made her want. Just want. The purity of it gave her a pang. The simplicity of it, the ease of it, as if their mouths were made for each other, made her wonder. The gentleness made her want to cry.

But as she reached up to touch his hair, as she nestled closer, as she sank into the sensual haze of his kiss, Virgil pulled away. 'I guess I should apologise for that.'

Kate blinked and touched her fingers to her lips. He sounded singularly unrepentant. She ought to be insulted, but in fact this realisation was pleasing. 'Mr Jackson…'

'I wish you would call me Virgil. Hardly anyone does.'

It was a relief to see that he looked slightly dazed, because that was exactly how Kate felt. Or was it dazzled? Were kisses supposed to make you feel like that? Not in her experience. 'Virgil,' she said. 'I like it. Your name, I mean. I like your name.' And his kisses. She didn't want him to think she didn't like his kisses, but she couldn't very well tell him that. She fanned her cheeks.

Virgil took her hand, stroking the pulse at her wrist with his thumb. 'I haven't wanted to kiss anyone in a long time.'

'Then that makes two of us,' Kate said with a husky little laugh. His touch was making her even hotter.

'How long?'

'Not since Anthony.' Had she ever wanted to kiss Anthony? She must have done, else she would not have… 'What about you?'

Virgil shrugged. 'A while.'

'Days? Weeks? Months?' Kate persisted. 'Years?' she squeaked, disbelievingly.

'A while.'

He dropped her hand, moving away from her, as far as the gig's limited seating allowed. She wanted to probe, but she knew better than to do so. Whatever *a while* was, it was surprising. Astonishing that a man as attractive, as assured, as Virgil had kissed no one. Though not as astounding as the fact that he had kissed *her*! She wanted to know why. Or did she? Perhaps ignorance in this case truly was bliss. Kate untangled the reins from the brake. 'I hope it was worth the wait,' she said, resorting to her customary glibness.

'Have we much further to go?' Virgil asked some time later.

Kate shook her head. 'We've been on Montague land for the past couple of miles. The farmers here are all my father's tenants.'

'Good God, I didn't realise he owned so much.'

'Well, it's not really my father but the dukedom. The land is all entailed, so he can't sell it, and he can't bequeath it to anyone other than Jam—I mean, Giles. Giles is the heir. Or at least he is at the moment. That may well all be about to change.'

'How so?'

Kate grimaced. 'It's complicated. I should have told you. I've invited you into a hornet's nest, but I so wanted you to come with me. I didn't really think about it last night, but—oh, God, the truth is that we're actually in a bit of a mess,' she said. 'Are you angry?'

'How can I be, when I don't know what you're talking about?'

'Yes. Of course. Sorry. Well, it seems that my brother Jamie took a wife in Spain just before he—he died. We knew nothing about it until a few months ago, when my father received a letter from the woman demanding that we do right by her son who is, she claims, Jamie's heir. You can imagine the uproar that caused. My brother Giles suspects the whole thing is an elaborate fraud but Ross—he is my cousin—met the woman, and seemed fairly convinced by her. So now Giles, who is the heir at the moment but might not really be the heir, has sent my brother Harry—who is the next in line to Giles but of course is further out if this child…well, anyway, Harry is off to Spain to see what he can discover, and in the meantime my father, who is most anxious to detach his grandson from what he has called the scheming wretch, has insisted that they both come to Castonbury.' Kate drew a breath and laughed at Virgil's expression. 'I told you, it's complicated.'

'Extremely,' Virgil said, amused by her method of recounting the tale, dismayed by its content.

'The reason I had to come home today is because Giles has demanded a sort of family counsel of war.'

'And knowing all this, you still insisted I accompany you! Surely your time will be quite taken up with these matters, and my presence in the midst of it all can only be an inconvenience at best.'

Kate slowed the horse down as they rounded a bend in the lane, pulling the gig to a halt at a large wooden gate. 'You *are* angry. I'm sorry, I ought to have told you sooner, but I so wanted you to come to Castonbury and I was afraid that you would not, and that is the truth.' She transferred the reins to one hand, placing her other on Virgil's sleeve. 'I'm glad that you're here.'

He covered her hand with his, and smiled crookedly down at her. 'Thank you, but I think perhaps I should not make it such a long visit.'

'We'll see,' Kate said, deciding wisely not to push her luck. 'Now, look over there.' She pointed her whip. 'That is Castonbury Park.'

The field by which they had stopped was on a rise, looking down on the house. Behind them, the trees which bordered the lane through which they had been driving would provide a pleasant perspective. The house itself was perfectly symmetrical with matching wings set to the east and west. In the centre of the building, a domed roof gave it a distinctive appearance, more like a classical Roman villa or place of worship than a family home. Though it was difficult to see the detail at this distance, it looked as if the architect had been an admirer of the classical style, for there were pediments and pillars, the rustic stonework of the ground floor giving way to the smooth finish on the *piano nobile*, from which a grand staircase curved down to the neatly manicured lawns. He had expected something flamboyantly grand, but the perfect proportions were so beautiful that he could not but admire them.

'What do you think?' Kate asked.

'It's not what I thought it would be. I thought the home of a duke would be more…showy.'

She gave a gurgle of laughter. 'Just wait. There is gilt and gold aplenty in the state rooms.' She urged the tired horse into motion once more. 'The prettiest part of the grounds is to the north, which is where the main lodge is. The smaller one you can see leads to the Dower House. And through those woods there is a path to the village, where Lily, Giles's betrothed, lives in the vicarage.'

'Let me make sure I have this right. Giles is your eldest brother now, and you are next in age?'

'No, I come after Harry. Ned was next after me,' Kate said, ignoring the familiar lurch in her stomach as she spoke Ned's name, 'and then there is my sister, Phaedra, who is twenty, four years younger than me. Since my spectacular failure to make a good marriage, all my father's hopes are pinned on Phaedra making her debut next Season but I suspect they are misplaced, for though my sister has the potential to be quite dangerously attractive, she has very little interest in anything but horses, and none at all in either parties or clothes, much to my aunt's despair. My Aunt Wilhelmina,' Kate explained, seeing Virgil's puzzled look, 'is a widow, my mother's sister and has been at Castonbury since Mama died. Oh, and then there is my cousin Colonel Ross Montague, the one who has met Jamie's wife. He also grew up at Castonbury with his sister, Araminta, but she is lately married. And Ross has returned to India…and very possibly ran off with his sister's maid! And that,' Kate said, laughing, 'concludes the current history of the Montagues. I can see from your face that we have signally failed to live up to your expectations, and I haven't told you half the skeletons we have in our closet, believe me. Why Papa thinks himself superior, I have no idea.'

'Nor indeed have I,' Virgil replied, wondering what the devil he'd let himself in for, but unable to resist returning her smile, all the same.

It was late afternoon by the time they turned into the main entrance to Castonbury Park. Virgil watched with increasing unease as Kate tooled the gig through the iron gates, waving her whip at the gatekeeper. She continued at a smart trot along a well-kept carriageway through pretty parklands where two lakes, the larger with an island in the middle, were divided by a rustic bridge, before coming to a halt in front of the main entrance of the house.

Close up, the building looked far more imposing, the central structure fronted by a colonnaded portico worthy of the Roman senate, flanked by two curved galleries sweeping out to an east and west wing. Rows of windows gazed watchfully down. As he leapt lightly onto the gravel and held out his hand to assist Kate, Virgil told himself that it was purely fancy to think that they looked disapproving.

Inside, a rather gloomy hall dominated by a number of stone pillars and four huge empty fireplaces.

'Lumsden, I trust you received word that I was bringing a guest,' Kate said to a superior-looking grey-haired man.

'Indeed, Lady Kate, I have prepared the Blue Room.'

'Excellent. Mr Jackson's man is travelling with Polly. I don't expect they will be too far behind us. This is Mr Jackson, Lumsden. Virgil, this is Lumsden, our butler, who has been at Castonbury longer than any of us care to remember.'

'Pleased to meet you....'

The butler stopped in the act of executing a bow.

'Mr Jackson is an American,' Kate explained.

The butler made a huge effort to pull himself together, but his protuberant eyes remained fixed on Virgil.

'From Boston,' Virgil corroborated, more amused than offended, for the man was looking at him as if he were about to pounce.

'Boston,' the butler repeated.

'In Massachusetts. That's New England. Though obviously I'm not originally from there,' Virgil said helpfully.

'Indeed, sir, I had gathered not.'

'Oh, do stop staring,' Kate said impatiently. 'Mr Jackson is not going to bite you.'

'Well, not yet, at any rate,' Virgil said. 'I've just been fed.'

Taken aback, for she had not thought him a man given to teasing, Kate suppressed a chuckle and cast Virgil a reproving look before turning back to Lumsden. 'I take it you know about this counsel of war that Giles has called?'

'Indeed.' The butler looked as if he himself bore the burden of the Montagues' woes. 'A difficult business, my lady. Lord Giles wishes to discuss the matter in the drawing room before dinner. If I may suggest, perhaps Mr Jackson could take sherry in the library, since it is a family matter. We have the London papers there.'

'That will suit me fine,' Virgil said, smiling reassuringly at Kate, who was looking troubled.

'If you're sure? Then I shall see you in a couple of hours. Lumsden will show you to your bedchamber.'

Kate disappeared into the gloom of the vast hall, leaving Virgil alone with the old retainer, who made more stately progress in her wake. The guest rooms were in one of the wings which adjoined the main body of the house, connected by a curved corridor lined with ancestral portraits, where Lumsden slowed to a crawl, intoning: 'the fourth earl who became the first duke'; 'his first duchess'; 'his second duchess'; 'her second son'—as if he were introducing them at a party. Virgil wondered if he was expected to make his bow to each one. Their eyes followed him as he passed. He was pretty certain he could hear their affronted muttering.

Alone at last, staring out the window of the Blue Room at the lakes, he felt a wave of homesickness. This house was steeped in the kind of history he could not begin to comprehend. Though the current building was less than a hundred years old, Kate's ancestors had lived on this land for centuries. A direct line, as Lumsden had informed him, fluffing his feathers like a proud cockerel, going back to the first earl, who had been raised from a mere baronetcy by Queen Elizabeth. The Montagues had roots so deep they were entrenched in the very soil of England. Their customs and traditions, their bloodline and heritage, hung around Castonbury like a protective cloak.

Virgil had not thought of himself as rootless until now. Gazing around the Blue Room, at the tapestry depicting a naked woman bathing surrounded by nymphs and exotic creatures, at the Chinese porcelain on the carved mantel, at the rich silks of the bed hangings and the thick oils of the paintings in their heavy gilt frames which hung on the walls, and the soft pile of the rug which covered the polished wooden boards, he felt as if all of it was conspiring to remind him that he had no place here. The antiques screamed of wealth and position, of traditions so well established as to be inviolable.

He ran his hand over the embroidered coverlet. Black skin on celestial blue silk. His being here was a violation of something entrenched. Though Kate did not think so. She had welcomed his touch. The contrast of his skin against hers seemed to fascinate her. In another world, the differences in their skin colour would not matter. Virgil stared at his image in the long mirror which stood by the nightstand. 'Not another world, another planet,' he muttered.

A gentle tap on the door made him snap to. He was here now, and he was damned if he would allow these blue-blooded aristocrats and their haughty servants to look down on him!

'Ah, Katherine. So good of you to join us. Finally.' The Honourable Mrs Landes-Fraser swept into the drawing room, the puce feathers in her turban waving majestically, the demi-train of her evening gown swishing violently, while the fringes of her shawl caught on the crook of a Dresden shepherdess perched atop a card table, causing the maiden to skitter across the polished rosewood before coming to rest just short of the edge.

Deigning to accept her customary glass of very dry sherry, a libation ideally suited to her extremely dry humour, Mrs Landes-Fraser disposed her wraith-like person upon one of the large blue damask sofas. The sofas, ornately scrolled and gilded, were adorned by a blatantly naked sea creature on each arm, a feature at which Mrs Landes-Fraser took personal affront each time she sat upon them. With a flair born of practice, she flicked her shawl expertly over the exposed bosom of a mermaid. 'I am sure,' she said, looking down her Roman nose at her niece and speaking in a tone which made it clear she was no such thing, 'that your hasty visit to Staffordshire was necessary, but it was most ill-timed. Though I am aware you do not think so, I believe that your family have first claim on your time, particularly in a crisis. I cannot quite believe that you have, under the circumstances, inflicted a guest upon us. Really, Katherine, it is most thoughtless of you. You must get rid of the person as soon as possible. Giles will agree with me, I know.'

Her nephew, who was leaning his tall frame against the mantel, shrugged impatiently and sipped on his Madeira. 'This is Kate's home—she's perfectly entitled to invite guests.'

'But this man is apparently an American,' Kate's aunt said with a shudder. 'Bad enough we have to put up with one outsider…'

'If this woman's claim proves to be true, then she is not an outsider but family,' Giles said shortly.

'Well, I, for one, have no intention of treating her as such until her claim *is* proved,' Mrs Landes-Fraser declared.

Giles shrugged. 'I expect she'll find a friend in Kate. Aside from her tendency to support the underdog, my sister will most likely form an alliance, if for no reason other than to oppose our father,' he said, casting his sister a sardonic glance.

'You do me an injustice, brother dear,' Kate retorted. 'I would support any downtrodden female. As to Papa—I believe my refusal to consider that old goat Sir Nathan Samuelson as a husband set me well and truly beyond the pale.'

Giles gave a harsh crack of laughter. 'I told him it was a bloody stupid idea. I'm glad you gave it short shrift.'

Kate smiled. She and Giles were almost always at outs, since he would never deign to explain or discuss anything and she regarded his reticence as arrogance, but they shared a dark sense of humour. 'I gave him shrift so short it was barely detectable,' she replied.

'And you will rue the day, Katherine,' her aunt said witheringly, 'for you have now quite firmly confined yourself to the shelf of spinsterhood.'

'Oh, for goodness' sake, Aunt, the man is a buffoon,' Giles said, throwing back the remains of his Madeira and thumping the glass onto the marble mantelpiece. 'We have far more important matters to discuss than Kate's matrimonial prospects.'

'My niece has no matrimonial prospects, thanks to her imprudence,' Mrs Landes-Fraser intoned, always determined to have the final say. 'Were it not for her lineage, even Sir Nathan would carp at taking on soiled goods.'

'Aunt Wilhelmina! Whatever do you mean?' Phaedra, who had been sprawling on the opposite sofa, flicking through a stud book, looked up. Seeing her aunt's pursed lips, her brother's scowl and her sister's blush, her interest, normally reserved solely for horses, perked up. 'Kate? What does Aunt Wilhelmina—'

'Damn it! This is no time to go raking over *that* matter.' Giles glowered at his aunt. 'Lumsden will be ringing the bell for dinner before we know it. Just for once, can we discuss something in a civilised manner without squabbling like cats?'

'Civilised, Giles? That will be a first for you,' Kate said softly.

Her brother had the grace to smile, but as he threw himself onto the sofa beside Phaedra, his expression darkened once more. 'This is serious. Our father is—to be frank, I fear our father has become slightly deranged.'

'Giles! His Grace—'

'Aunt Wilhelmina, His Grace has more or less suggested that we separate his purported grandson from his mother by force if necessary,' Giles interrupted in clipped tones. 'He is willing to bring the full weight of the law to bear in order to do so, and if that fails, he talks of kidnap.'

Mrs Landes-Fraser clutched at her meagre breast. 'I feel sure you exaggerate.'

'And I feel sure he does not,' Kate said tersely. 'Behind that feeble front he uses to his own advantage, our dear papa has a will of iron. This woman—what are we to call her, Giles?'

'Until proved otherwise, I suppose she is the Dowager Marchioness of Hatherton,' her brother responded with a shrug.

'Lord, we can't call her that,' Phaedra piped in, 'she's no older than you, Kate. Her name is Alicia. Ross says she's very pretty.'

'I fail to see what that has to do with anything,' Mrs Landes-Fraser said acerbically.

'Knowing Jamie, it has everything to do with it,' Kate retorted. 'If she were fubsy-faced and plump, we could at least be certain that she was a fraud.'

'True,' Giles agreed, 'but quite beside the point.'

'No, the point is that our father seems to believe his title puts him above the law of the land,' Kate agreed. 'What is to be done, Giles?'

'She's agreed to visit, though of course I didn't invite her on the terms our father suggested, which was that she deposit the child into the hands of a nanny and disappear.'

'There is no nanny,' Phaedra interjected.

'Because I won't be party to my father's ridiculous conniving. He's had the old nursery redecorated in preparation, can you believe it? Yet he won't contemplate having a room prepared for the mother—though what he thinks we are to do with her, I don't know. Suggest she sleep in the stable block, I suppose.'

'There is no room there, unless she shares a bed with old Tom Anderson, and I don't think he'd be best pleased by that,' Phaedra exclaimed. 'In fact, I don't think it's a good idea at all. I don't want to upset him because that would upset the horses and—'

'And of course there is nothing so important as keeping the horses happy,' Kate said, laughing. 'He was joking, Phaedra.' She turned back to Giles with a frown remarkably like her brother's. 'It seems to me that we ought to do nothing precipitate until we can prove the claim—or disprove it. Assuming what this Alicia says is true…'

'Which seems more likely than not,' Giles interjected.

'Then we must act accordingly and offer them a home. There can be no question of separating them.'

'I don't see why not.' Faced with three disapproving faces, Mrs Landes-Fraser twitched at the fringe of her shawl. 'Provided she knows that her son is being cared for, what possible objection can the woman have?'

'You don't perhaps think that the child—who is a mere two years old—would prefer his mother to a complete stranger?' Giles asked incredulously.

'Aunt Wilhelmina, how can you say that to us?' Phaedra said indignantly. 'Do you think we would wish the poor little boy to be raised as we were?'

'What can you mean?' her aunt asked, bristling. 'Your mother was no absent parent.'

'She was to me. She died before I could even remember her.'

'Well, I remember her,' Kate said. 'Mama may have been a presence at Castonbury, but she was not a presence in any of our childhoods. Were it not for the fact that we were no longer paraded in front of her in the drawing room once a week, I doubt very much that we'd even have noticed she was gone.'

'Katherine! How dare you slander my sister in such a way? Your mother—'

'For goodness' sake, Kate, leave it,' Giles interjected. 'Not but what she ain't right,' he added, looking pointedly at his aunt, 'but we have once more strayed from the point and we are no further forward. I should have known better than to try to get some sort of consensus. Let us just forget it, I shall think of something. I always do.'

Struck by the weariness in her brother's tone, Kate felt a pang of guilt. With their father living in cloud cuckoo land half the time, the weight of managing the estate fell on Giles's shoulders, a burden he was very far from welcoming despite what Papa and Aunt Wilhelmina might think. She cast her mind around desperately for something to help him out, and it came to her that she had actually pointed out the solution to Virgil that very afternoon. 'I have it,' she exclaimed, 'the Dower House. It's been empty since old Cousin Frederica died, save for the dratted cats she left behind.'

Giles's brow cleared. 'Do you think it will suffice?'

'It's perfect. It will give the poor woman independence, and it will bring her into the bosom of the family without suffocating her. She may bring the child to visit Papa, but her living separately will ensure that he doesn't become too attached, should matters prove—well, we shall have to wait and see how matters prove once Harry has done some digging.'

'It will be a considerable amount of work to get the place fit for habitation. I am not sure how I am to find the time, with all my other duties.'

'You may leave the detail of it up to me, Aunt Wilhelmina,' Kate said. 'I will look over the place tomorrow.'

'And His Grace?' Mrs Landes-Fraser demanded. 'Am I to tell His Grace that his arrangements have been overset?'

'You may leave our father up to me,' Giles said brusquely.

'And you may leave the ordering of a pony for the boy up to me,' Phaedra said, bestowing one of her naughty smiles upon her aunt.

'The child is but two years old,' Mrs Landes-Fraser blustered.

'If he is a Montague, that is long past the age of throwing him onto a saddle,' Phaedra retorted.

Her aunt's opinion of this was lost, as the butler made his stately entrance. 'Dinner will be served in fifteen minutes, my lord.'

'Excellent timing as ever, Lumsden.' Giles beamed. 'Best fetch my sister's guest now.' He poured himself another Madeira, and turned to Kate. 'An American businessman, eh? What on earth does he hope to find of interest here at Castonbury?'

'You know what these New Worlders are like.' Though Mrs Landes-Fraser had never, in fact, met anyone from the New World, American or otherwise, her complete ignorance did not prevent her from holding an opinion—it never did. 'More than likely he wishes to boast to all his friends of his rubbing shoulders with a duke's family. They have no aristocracy over there, you know. It is one of the many things which makes them an inferior country.'

'Actually, Aunt, I believe that America is likely to prove a most superior country in the very near future,' Giles said. 'You only have to look at the way the cotton trade is going to see—'

'Trade!' Mrs Landes-Fraser wrinkled her nose. 'Money cannot buy rank.'

'Yes, well, if we don't sort out our family finances soon, we will be living in genteel poverty, and frankly I'd rather be wealthy than well-born,' Giles muttered.

'Actually, Mr Jackson is more interested in our village school than our family tree,' Kate chipped in brightly. Looking around the room at her relatives, she felt the first flicker of serious doubt. Lumsden had obviously said nothing. Perhaps she should have mentioned it, after all, but then that would have implied that it mattered to her and it did not, save that she liked the way Virgil looked. What must he be feeling? Had she allowed her determination to shock to overrule her judgement? Jumping to her feet, she was at the door of the drawing room just as Lumsden threw it open. Virgil stood on the threshold, his tall, well-built figure immaculate in evening dress, quite dwarfing the butler.

'Mr Jackson.'

Lumsden's tone was funereal. Thinking that Virgil must be feeling horribly like a gladiator cast into the lion's den, Kate stepped towards him as if to shield him, but he shook his head, tilted his head back proudly and stepped into the drawing room.

The effect of his entrance was almost comical.

'I thought you were magnificent. I confess, when you walked into the drawing room last night, I felt dreadfully guilty for putting you through the agony of a family dinner, but you were wonderful.'

It was not yet nine of the clock the following morning, but having decided, after the endurance test which had been last night's repast, to spare Virgil—and, if she was honest, herself—the ordeal of breakfast *en famille,* Kate had used the need to investigate the Dower House as an excuse for an early start. It was a pleasant day, the air crisp with autumn, the grass mossy and soft underfoot as they made their way along the lower lakeside.

'It was hardly an ordeal. Your sister doesn't care who she talks to as long as it's about horses, and your brother…'

'Yes, what were you talking to Giles about? You sat forever over the port.'

'Business.'

'My father's investments, you mean. Don't worry, you are not breaking a confidence. I know his imprudence has left the family coffers sadly empty. Were you able to advise Giles?'

'I need to understand more about the situation first. In my experience, there are always loopholes if you know where to look. If that doesn't suffice, your brother has a number of other ideas for raising funds. The problem is,' Virgil said with a grin, 'that they are all too safe. Low risk is what Giles calls them, and I can understand why—it's not his money. If it were down to me—anyway, I said I'd take a closer look and let him know what I think.'

'That is very generous of you.'

'Business of any sort interests me.'

They stepped onto the rustic bridge whose three arches spanned the cascade between the two lakes, and which Kate claimed gave one of the best views back to the house. They stopped at the centre, leaning side by side on the lichen-covered parapet. A silver fish leapt dramatically in pursuit of a fly, landing with a loud splash which sent ripples eddying out over the greenish-brown water. Blades of grass stuck with the dew to Virgil's top boots. The skirts of his coat brushed against Kate's gown. She wore a dark green habit today, with another of those tight little jackets which clung to her slim form. Her hair was gathered into a heavy chignon at the base of her neck. She wore neither hat nor gloves.

'Giles strikes me as most unhappy with his situation as heir apparent,' Virgil said. 'I got the impression that he would much rather be back in the army than here.'

'He's a dark horse, my brother. There are depths to him which I confess I did not realise until recently. Lily, his betrothed, is of Romany origin, you know—though Giles has been at pains to keep *that* fact from our father. Romany blood is no blood for a future duchess in our father's eyes. And you're right, he would much rather be back in the army. Giles never had any expectations of inheriting this place.'

'It is quite a place.' Virgil gazed back at the house across the parkland; it seemed to nestle in the line of trees to the south. The symmetry of the building was most pleasing from this angle. 'It looks as if the landscape has been designed for it.'

'It was,' Kate said with a brief smile. 'None of this perspective is natural—it was all designed by Robert Adam, the man who built the house. Even the lakes have been dammed to give a more pleasing prospect. Nothing here is as nature made it, though I'll admit it has been very well done.'

'Very well indeed,' Virgil exclaimed, 'it all looks as if it has been here forever.'

'Yes, that is rather the intention, to make it seem perfectly natural. In order to reflect the perfectly natural right of centuries of Montagues to exploit Castonbury villagers,' Kate replied caustically. 'If my father had his way, none of it would change. Educating the serfs, you must know, is in his eyes nothing short of anarchy, for it will only give them aspirations beyond their proper place in life.'

'It is a view I am unfortunately extremely familiar with,' Virgil said.

Kate turned to face him, leaning back against the stonework of the bridge. 'You mean my father shares his outlook with the plantation owners. I shall make a point of telling him that.'

'Do you enjoy being at outs with him?'

Her smile faded into a small frown which spoiled the smooth arch of her brows. 'It's not that I do it deliberately, but we have so little in common. He doesn't really know me. I don't think he knows any of his children very well. We are not exactly a close family, nor have we been raised to expect affection from one another. I used to think it would have been different if Mama had lived, but actually I don't think it would have been. I don't recall her being in the least bit maternal. Of course, I care for my father in a dutiful way, but I don't like him any more than he likes me.'

There was hurt there, behind that fierce expression that made her eyes more slate-grey than blue. It was there, too, in the way she crossed her arms over her chest, in the defiant tilt of her chin. 'Shall I meet him while I am here?'

Kate chuckled. 'I hope so, and if you do, I beg you do not let the fact that he is nominally your host constrain you. He is bound to be just as offensive as Aunt Wilhelmina, so you need have no qualms. She was quite crushed by the end of dinner last night. I could have kissed you.'

Immediately the words were out, Kate wished them back. 'I mean, I thought you put Aunt Wilhelmina down beautifully. I did not mean I actually wanted to kiss you. Not in the dining room.'

She could feel the hot flush prickling up her back and prayed it would not reach her cheeks. Why had she mentioned kissing? She had been trying so hard not to think of kissing Virgil ever since he had kissed her and now… Much too late, Kate bit her tongue.

'Not in the dining room,' Virgil mused. The pulse was there again, just below her ear. He touched it. He could not resist touching it, feeling it flutter under his fingertip, fascinated by the soft warmth of her skin, by the contrast of his skin on hers. 'If not in the dining room, then where? I wonder.'

He hadn't meant to touch her. He hadn't meant to kiss her again, but he could not resist her. Eleven years, and he had never had any real trouble in repressing his desire, but there was something about Kate. He forgot to be on his guard with her. 'What about here?'

Virgil curled his fingers into the thick bundle of her hair and covered her body with his. She was pliable as a willow. Her thighs brushed his. His blood stirred and heated. His desire for her unfurled sleepily, slowly, but surely all the same. He knew he was playing with fire, but still he leaned closer to her. Her breath clouded the air between them. 'Will you kiss me on the bridge, Kate?'

'Virgil, I'm not very good at this sort of thing.' Her heart was hammering in her breast. Her body was tingling where it met his, and aching where it did not. She wasn't the type of woman who even wanted this sort of thing, whatever it was. Except that she did want it.

Virgil pulled her towards him, bracing one hand on the parapet, the other sliding down from her hair to the small of her back. He smiled, a slow smile, as if that, too, was unfurling from a long hibernation, stretching sensuously, sinuously. 'You're not good at this sort of thing, and I'm out of practice, and yet we managed well enough yesterday.' He nibbled at the lobe of her ear, then tasted the skin behind it, the fluttering pulse. Sweet and heady. His hand settled on the curve of her bottom. He had forgotten what curves could do to him.

'Virgil.' Kate touched his face. She ran her fingers over the springy crop of his hair. His head was beautifully shaped. His body was so solid. So very different from hers. So very different from…

She closed her mind on that thought. The scent of him was so different too. She leaned in to him, nipping his ear in imitation of what he had done to her. He shuddered in response. She wanted more. She wanted to know more too. Why was he out of practice? How long had it been? Why her? She opened her mouth to ask him, but something stopped her. A warning in his eyes? His hold on her slackened. Unable to bear it, Kate stood on tiptoe and kissed him.

He was startled into stillness. His lips were cool with the morning air. He tasted of the coffee he'd had at breakfast. It was not so much his intriguing abstinence or her own far from satisfactory experience, but a simple desire to merge and to mingle with another, to be no longer alone, which made Kate move her lips more insistently against his. His body was so big compared to hers, so powerful, yet it was a potent contrast, exciting and reassuring rather than intimidating. She felt infinitely female against his blatant maleness, then he gave a little groan and his arms went round her like a cooper's hoops around a barrel, yanking her almost off her feet, and she stopped thinking about anything at all.

He was not gentle. His kiss was neither untutored nor timid. It was a harsh kiss, his mouth hungry, ravaging hers in a way completely unlike their kiss of yesterday. Heat flared between them. Kate felt as if she could not breathe and did not want to breathe, squeezed tight and breathless, lightheaded with it. His lips pressed against hers, his tongue licking its way inside her mouth in a shockingly intimate way, his teeth nipping and biting, the pressure too much and yet not nearly enough.

Her back was pressed against the stone of the bridge. Her breasts were pressed against Virgil's chest. Her nipples were tingling. The solid length of his manhood pressed between her thighs. She had forgotten. She had not quite forgotten, though she did not remember this…this urgent need, ache and throb. Her hands clutched at his head, his shoulders, his coat. A strange guttural sound came from deep in her throat.

And then she was free, panting, staring up at Virgil, who was staring out across the bridge towards the house, his eyes narrowed. 'What…?'

'I don't know. A gardener. A groom, perhaps,' Virgil said, moving away from her.

Kate peered across the lake. The figure was some distance away. She could just about make out that it was male. 'Do you think he saw?'

Virgil shook his head. 'I doubt it.' He blinked and looked down at Kate. She was flushed. Her lips looked like crushed berries. He was uncomfortably aware of his erection, and was relieved that he was wearing buckskins and not those ridiculously tight-knitted pantaloons. Though Kate must be perfectly aware—he swore under his breath.

'You must have very keen hearing. Or eyesight.' Kate's own eyes had been closed. Hadn't Virgil, then, been as carried away as she? 'Which was it?' she asked, striving and completely failing to sound light, as if kissing a man on Robert Adam's bridge was an everyday occurrence for her.

'Both. Neither. I don't know.' Virgil realised he was rubbing his forearm, caught himself and self-consciously tugged the starched cuff of his shirt. 'Instinct, I suppose,' he said. 'It was a stupid thing to do.' Here, he meant. Or anywhere, he should have meant, though he was too coiled, tense, wound up with the soaring heat of that kiss, to wish it had not happened, quite yet.

'Yes, it was,' Kate said, mortified.

Her eyes were overbright and Virgil, who had made his own opaqueness of character a trademark over the past eleven years, found he did not wish this particular woman to misunderstand him. 'Kate, I don't care who sees us, but you ought to. This is your country, your home. People will talk.'

'I doubt it,' Kate said drily. 'They will think they have imagined it, it is so very unlikely. It doesn't even seem real to me.'

'That a duke's daughter should kiss a freed slave, you mean?'

She shook her head impatiently. 'That someone like you would find someone like me even remotely kissable. I am not the type of woman men want to kiss, I know that. Besides, what can I ever be to you? Your life is so different from mine you may as well come from another world. You are here to see our village school. Castonbury is but a stopover on your route north. It is known that I have an interest in abolition. Why should people put any other construction on our being together? It is ridiculous, that is what I meant.' Kate nodded, quite satisfied with this explanation, now she came to think of it.

'Ridiculous,' Virgil repeated slowly. 'Ridiculous that we could possibly mean anything to each other, is that what you mean?'

'Well, I suppose so.'

'Though that doesn't stop me finding you extremely kissable.'

'But that's probably why you do. Because it's so unlikely.'

'You have a very low opinion of yourself, Kate.'

'A very accurate one, Virgil.'

'No. You are quite unique.' He caught her hand and pressed a kiss on her palm. 'But you are quite right too,' he said, smiling down at her. 'It is so impossible that it is almost laughable. You think that's why we are attracted to each other?'

Was that relief in his voice? Was he, then, just as confused as her? It was true, Virgil being the antithesis of everything her family would deem eligible added a frisson to their kisses, but it wasn't all there was. 'Each other,' she said with relief, only just realising what he had admitted. 'It's not just me?'

'I thought that was pretty obvious.'

She was going to blush again. She was twenty-four years old, and quite beyond blushing. Kate consulted the little gold watch which she wore on a fob at her waist. 'We must get on. I promised Giles I'd set whatever must be done to the Dower House in motion this afternoon. Our new sister-in-law—if that is indeed what she is—is expected within the week.'

She was right, again. It was just a kiss. An aberration for both of them, and they now had a perfectly reasonable explanation. No point in discussing it further. It couldn't mean anything. It was just a kiss. Virgil nodded to himself and made haste to follow Kate off the bridge.

Four

The path they were following went round the side of the house, joining another, wider but overgrown, which led in one direction back to the disused gatehouse where they had stopped yesterday, in the other to a copse of trees, behind which the mellow sandstone of a building could be glimpsed. They made their way through the copse of oak trees, and onto the approach to the Dower House. Kate walked quickly, her arms swinging out by her sides, easily keeping pace with Virgil's long-legged stride, the skirts of her habit flying out over the weed-strewn gravel.

The Dower House was built of mellow sandstone, with a pillared portico, two stories under a very low roof and very long windows in the old French style reaching almost to the ground. It was shuttered, and had about it an air of neglect, with weeds clogging the approach and a fretwork of ivy working its way along one of the side walls up into the eaves. Several large shrubs were so overgrown as to make the path which wound round to the north-facing garden impenetrable.

'These will need to be cut back,' Kate said, producing a

large iron key from the pocket of her habit. Though it fitted easily enough into the lock, it would not move. Kate swore under her breath as she wrestled with it in vain. 'I don't think anyone has been here since Cousin Frederica died.'

'Let me try.'

'It needs oiling,' Kate said stubbornly.

Nudging her aside, Virgil turned the key easily. She glowered, caught his eye and was forced to laugh. 'Very impressive,' she said sarcastically, though, in fact, she *was* impressed, and shamefully excited by his strength. She wondered what he would be like naked, and gave a little shiver which she quickly covered up, pushing the door back on its protesting hinges. A sensible woman would conclude that kissing Virgil again would be extremely foolish. Dangerous, even. So why was she thinking that the very impossibility of kissing Virgil again was what made it—well, possible. Safe? Not that, but…

Like swimming naked, as she sometimes did under cover of the night. It gave her a vicarious thrill to know how appalled her aunt would be, how outraged everyone would be, a thrill she could savour all the more for knowing she was highly unlikely to be caught. Kissing Virgil would be that kind of safe and a whole lot more exciting. Too exciting. She had to stop thinking about it and concentrate on the task in hand.

Shafts of sunlight pierced the gloom through the fanlight above the door. Their boots rang out on the chequered marble of the reception hall. Dust motes danced, stirred up by the sweep of Kate's skirts. The place smelled musty, though there was an acrid undertone. 'Cats,' she said, wrinkling her nose. 'Cousin Frederica had at least a dozen of them. They get in and out through the stillroom window. At least it should mean that there won't be any mice.' She stirred the pile of leaves and twigs which filled the hearth of the large fireplace with her boot, disturbing the remnants of a bird's nest. 'We'll need to have all the chimneys swept. And if this is anything to go by,' she said, gazing up at the cobwebs which swung in silver threads from the wrought-iron chandelier, 'it will take an army to clean.'

The room to the right was the drawing room. Virgil threw open the creaking shutters which guarded the window, flooding it with light. The furniture was draped in Holland covers, the carpets rolled in one corner, but the room was pleasantly proportioned, the plain wall panelling and cornicing painted in pale shades of green. 'At least it doesn't smell damp.' A cloud of dust flew out of the window hangings when Kate shook them, making her sneeze.

Across the hall again there was a dining room and a small music room. To the rear of the ground floor, the windows of the study, another salon and the breakfast parlour, which opened out onto the wilderness of the garden. Virgil opened the catches and walked out into the late-morning sunshine. The fountain was clogged with ivy. A mangy brindled cat eyed him malignantly from the muddy basin. Another was washing itself perched atop a stone lion which guarded the entrance to what had once been a rose garden. 'I hope your new relative likes felines,' Virgil said, as yet another of the furry creatures twined itself around his legs.

'They seem friendly enough,' Kate said, 'and she's going to need some friends. Should I arrange to have the guttering cleaned, do you think?'

'You're going to a lot of bother for this woman. I thought you said she was just coming for a visit.'

'If her claim is proved, her son is my father's heir. Castonbury Park will be her home.'

'Unless she marries again.'

'Well, I suppose—I hadn't considered that.' Kate looked thoughtful. 'She is only just widowed, but I believe she is quite young, and according to my cousin Ross she's pretty so—Lord, that really would set the cat amongst the pigeons.'

'How so?'

'My father wants his heir here at Castonbury. He certainly won't tolerate the child being raised by another man. Giles says he's already set his lawyers onto sorting out a legal guardianship for the boy. If his mother is not careful, she will find that she has signed away her rights to her child.'

'Surely she would not be so foolish?'

Kate shrugged. 'Since Jamie did not see fit to inform the family that he was married, there was no settlement made for her. She is wholly dependant upon my father's goodwill, and he can be very ruthless when he wants to be. I intend to ensure she has her own legal advisors. It's the least I can do.'

'So she will have at least one friend who is not feline,' Virgil said with a faint smile.

'I sincerely hope that she does not have cause to have to rely on me, however,' Kate replied. 'I would not like to wager on her success should the might of the Montagues be brought down upon her head.'

They made their way back into the Dower House and ascended to the first floor. It was darker here, with only the light from the landing window to guide them. Kate's arm brushed against Virgil's coat sleeve as they turned into the long corridor, where doors stood closed on either side. The largest of the six bedrooms contained a fantastically carved bed, the four posts a mishmash of gryphons and dragons and other strange fairy-tale beasts.

'It was meant for the main house,' Kate said, laughing at

Virgil's expression, which was a mixture of astonishment and horror as he traced the form of a voluptuous siren-like creature, 'but even for my grandfather, it was a step too far. Cousin Frederica thought it profane and would not sleep in it, despite the fact that this is the best bedroom.'

'What are the carvings supposed to represent?'

'A confused mind?' Kate replied flippantly. 'Actually, the key is in the central carving up there in the support for the canopy.'

She leant over the mattress to peer up, explaining the various myths which the artist had chosen to entwine. The bed was high. Though he tried not to notice, Virgil couldn't take his eyes off the way her bending over brought attention to the roundness of Kate's rear, the indent of her waist, the length of her legs. She wore riding boots. Did they stop at her calves, or were they longer? Perhaps the leather fitted snugly all the way up to her thighs. Though the skirts of her habit were full, he had already noted that her long, graceful stride seemed to be unimpeded by layers of petticoats. He realised he had no idea what ladies such as Kate wore for undergarments. It hadn't occurred to him to wonder, until now. Lace and silk? Practical cotton?

He was hard again. He had already, in his imagination, taken the short leap from underwear to skin, from looking at her curves to imagining his shaft sinking into the pink, moist heat of her. He had taken a step towards her in the process, ready to cup and to mould and to stroke. So long it had been since he had shared such intimacies. He thought he had forgotten, but looking at Kate, he discovered he knew in astoundingly lurid detail exactly what and where and how he wanted to touch her. She had stopped talking, was looking at him, lips parted. Just looking at him, as if she could read the turn his mind had taken.

She was not shocked, that was what he thought first. There was something, a heat in her eyes, a recognition or a reflection of what he was thinking. That was his second thought. That it was wish fulfilment was his third. Just because no one else would ever guess, just because it was so outrageous it could not be anything other than fleeting, did not mean that he planned to indulge in this attraction which sparked between them.

Virgil stepped to one side of the tempting display of curves, careful to keep a distance between them, and leaned over on the mattress, looking up at the carving as if that, and not touching her, stroking her, sheathing himself in her, had been his intention all along. 'Charybdis, the daughter of Poseidon, you were saying,' he said.

'You *were* listening?'

'"Zeus turned her into a monster because she ate some sheep she stole,"' Virgil repeated, relieved to discover that he had, on some other level, been taking in what she'd said, after all. He wasn't touching her, but he was a breath away from doing so. They were on a mattress. On a bed. His body was very well aware of this, though Virgil tried not to be. He could smell her scent. Lavender? No, more complex than that. More female.

'Charybdis made whirlpools to wreck ships,' Kate said. 'There is her accomplice, Scylla, on the post there.'

Virgil had the impression that what she was saying and what she was thinking were quite different. He thought this because it was the same for him. Kate pointed at the post on the left side of the bed at the top, though she continued to hold eye contact with him. The movement made her wobble, but she steadied herself before he could help her. He adjusted his weight so that he was propped on his side. 'So the bed does tell a story,' he said.

'Several, all tangled up.'

She was not whispering, but her voice was low, husky, sensual. Did she know it? Did she mean it? There was a speck of dust on her cheekbone. Virgil brushed it away with his thumb. The pulse was there, just discernable, under her ear. He ran his hand down the length of her spine, into the dip at the base, over the swell of her bottom. He hadn't meant to do that. He couldn't stop himself. 'All tangled up,' Virgil repeated, imagining just that.

Kate made that strange little noise he remembered from earlier on the bridge, a breathy growl which seemed to connect directly with his groin. She leaned over and repeated his own action, her hand trailing down his back, to the base of his spine, to his buttocks. His muscles tightened under her fingers. His coat, the silk back of his waistcoat, the fine lawn of his shirt, the leather of his buckskins—he resented every stitch of expensive, fashionable clothing he wore.

He was so unaccustomed to a woman's touch he had thought himself immune. The agony of loss had established a physical shield long ago. Celibacy gave him strength. In eleven years, he had never had the slightest problem in maintaining it, but Kate broke through all his defences with just this whispering touch. Virgil rolled onto his side. 'Turn around,' he whispered.

On her back beside him on the bed, her eyes wide, her skin delicately flushed, her mouth soft, she watched him. He touched her, traced her shape through her clothes, enthralled, fascinated by the shallow rise and fall of her breasts, by the fluttering of the pulse below her ear. When he flattened his palm over her belly she pulled it tight. When he cupped the slope of her breasts, she gave a tiny moan. Her eyes never left his face. When he tugged up the hem of her skirt, she made no move to help or to hinder. Her riding boots were almost as long as her legs. Like the boots worn in ancient times. Like the boots in one of her family portraits. He wondered if that was where she'd taken her inspiration from. He could hardly breathe, running his hands up the soft leather to her narrow flanks.

He ached to have her touch him, but it would be too much. Far too much. What had happened to his self-restraint? Think. Think! His scars. No one had seen those. Not since—and not even Millie…

Too late, he wished he had not invoked her ghost. Why had he needed to? It was done now. It had worked, that was the important thing. Virgil rolled over and got to his feet, turning his back on temptation in a pretence of examining the post where Scylla was carved. The silence, a few moments only, seemed to stretch and stretch. 'Unless you wish to give your new relative nightmares, I think you should have a different room prepared for her,' he said.

Kate got up, slanting him a puzzled look. He knew before she spoke that she was not going to follow his lead. 'What happened?'

'Nothing. I'm sorry.'

She straightened her jacket and gazed out of the ivy-clad window at the carriageway below. 'Sorry you touched me or sorry that you stopped?' Which was she? She didn't know. Both. Kate rested her hot cheek against the thick glass. The panes were diamond-shaped, criss-crossed with lead. Some of them were loose. She would have to get someone to re-solder them. William Everett, the estate manager, he would know who. She must make a note to speak to him. He would deal with the chimney sweep too. And a gardener. And she'd have to get some help from the village to do the cleaning. Three women? Maybe four, with—

'Both,' Virgil said, making her jump. 'Sorry that I touched you. Sorry that I stopped.'

Having her own thoughts so exactly articulated confused her. He confused her. What he made her feel confused her. This whole situation confused her. Anthony had put an end to her nascent desire—or so she had thought. Anthony had said it was her fault, her lack, and she had believed him. But what she felt for Virgil, it was so different. Did that mean that Anthony was wrong? Or she had changed? Or Virgil was different? She had no idea, and he was waiting for her to speak and she could not think straight enough to prevaricate. 'I don't know what to say. I'm not like this. I thought I wasn't like this—wasn't capable of being like this.'

'Not capable!' Virgil exclaimed, quite taken aback. 'Kate, you can't possibly mean…'

'I don't know what I mean,' she said wretchedly. 'You confuse me.'

Another thing they shared, but Virgil was too much in the habit of keeping his own counsel to say so. He ought to say they should forget it, but could not bring himself to do so. Did Kate really believe she was frigid? The idea was preposterous. He was struggling to find a way of saying so, when a movement in the carriageway below caught his eye. 'Who is that?'

'Oh, it's Charlie!' Kate declared. 'The boot boy, you know. I wonder what he wants. I must go and see.'

She was already heading for the door, obviously relieved. He ought to feel the same. Virgil eyed the bed resentfully, wishing he could blame its confused mythology for what had happened. But it wasn't the bed or the bridge or the carriage.

He sat down on the edge of the mattress and stared sightlessly down at his boots. He had come so far in eleven years. He had the means to put his past to rights now, thanks to a decade's worth of single-minded, sheer bloody hard work. The relentless pursuit of success, the need to be better, stronger, sharper, quicker than anyone else had been exhausting, but he had never tired. He had reached the pinnacle, just as he'd always known he would. He couldn't help but see Malcolm Jackson's death as symbolic. The passing of the old. That his patron's dying request had coincided with the opportunity to do business with Josiah Wedgwood, Virgil could not help but interpret as an omen. When he returned he would finally make a start on paying his debt to Millie.

He would make his new world, and in it he would finally be free. Virgil got to his feet and looked out of the window, where Kate was talking to a small boy. That she had come into his life at such a crossroads perhaps explained, even more than the impossibility of it, why he had let down his defences. She was the apex, the turning point, nothing more.

Satisfied now that he understood himself, Virgil turned from the window. How could someone who kissed like Kate imagine herself cold? As he made his way downstairs, he couldn't help wishing for the opportunity to prove her wrong.

'Polly sent me.' Charlie, an irrepressible twelve-year-old, stood at the bottom of the shallow flight of steps clutching a large wicker basket to his chest. 'She said as how you would be busy and would more'n likely forget to eat and even if you was hungry she wouldn't blame you for not coming back to eat with the old tartar Mrs Landes-Fraser 'cause one look at that face would put anyone off their grub.' Remembering too late that Polly had also threatened him with a clip round the ear if he repeated her remarks, Charlie employed his most winsome smile. 'There's game pie and cheese and bread and chicken. And wine. And apples. Polly said you might give me an apple if I didn't drop anything and I didn't, so I ate it on the way 'cause the basket was awful heavy.'

Kate couldn't help laughing as she took the picnic from him. 'Very sensible.'

Charlie lowered his voice to a whisper. 'Polly says you've got a gentleman friend here what's come all the way from Africa.'

'It's America, Charlie.'

The boy's face fell. 'So it's not true, then? What they said, Mr Lumsden and Mrs Stratton and Joe and Daisy and all?'

Kate, who had been rummaging through the basket for another apple to give to the boy, instead gave him a sharp look. '*What* have they been saying?'

Charlie took a quick step back. Everyone in the big house knew that Lady Kate was one of the better ones, even if she was always banging on to him about practicing his letters, but he didn't like that look in her eye. It was the same look his mum had when she was thinking about clouting him. Not that Lady Kate would actually hit him, but he'd been on the receiving end of one of her set downs before, and even if he didn't know half the words she used, he got her drift all right. 'Nothing,' he said, taking another defensive step away from her.

'Charlie, what did they say?'

Her tone made it clear that he would be better to come clean than make something up. Besides, she always knew when he was fibbing. 'They said he had skin the colour of coal, if you please, my lady. And Agnes, she said that it would make the sheets black. And Mr Lumsden, he said that he most likely wouldn't have been allowed to stay if His Grace wasn't ill and wouldn't have cared if the devil himself was visiting. Then Mrs Stratton, she said we oughter remember that whatever else he might be, Mr Jackson was your guest and so he must be a gentleman. I dunno what Daisy said but Polly clipped her ear. And that's when Joe said—Joe said...'

Virgil appeared in the doorway and Charlie let out a squawk, his mouth falling open in astonishment. 'Well? What did Joe say about me?'

'He said you had a tail.'

'Charlie!'

But Virgil gave a shout of laughter. 'What do you think?' he demanded, moving with impressive speed to catch the boot boy as he made to run, and spinning round in front of him.

'I think I'll plant a facer on Joe Coyle for making game of me,' Charlie muttered.

'Fancy yourself in the ring, eh?'

Realising that he had not, in fact, brought the wrath of the muscular giant down on his head, Charlie's spirits quickly recovered. He put up two very small and grimy fists.

Virgil tutted, and repositioned the child's arms. 'Like this,' he said, 'unless you want a bloody nose. And those feet, do you want to trip over them? Look at me. See. It's as much about balance as punching.'

'I reckon you'd strip down mighty fine,' Charlie said, staring with new respect at Virgil. 'Do you box, sir?'

'No. No, never.'

'You must have, else how would you know how to stand. I bet you were good. Were you good, sir?' Charlie asked, too excited to notice that his questions were making his newfound hero extremely uncomfortable.

'I told you, I don't,' Virgil said shortly.

'Did you fight anyone famous? What about that one, you know, my dad told me all about it. Molly—something. He was like you.'

'He means Tom Molineaux,' Kate said, giving Charlie a reproving look.

'I know who he means.'

'Good grief, *do* you know him?'

'Do you, sir?'

Virgil dug his hands deep into the pockets of his coat. 'I met him.'

'Did you—did you *fight* him?'

Charlie's eyes were wide as saucers. Kate's expression was more…arrested. Inside his pockets, Virgil's fists were clenched painfully tight. Inside his head, he could hear them. The shouting. The jeering. The smell of blood and dust and sweat. Baying at them, just as they did at the dogs they set to scrap, at the cockerels they put at each other in the pit.

'Did you fight him? Molly—Molineaux. Did you, sir?'

'No! I told you…'

'Charlie, that's enough.'

Kate's voice was sharp, enough to silence the boy instantly. Virgil blinked. She cast him a look, equally sharp, but it was one of concern, not reprimand. And though she couldn't possibly understand, he knew that she'd sensed enough. He wasn't sure whether to be angry or relieved. She was chastising the boy gently for his questions, and at the same time slipping him an apple. Charlie was looking sullen as he made for the path back to the main house. It wasn't the boy's fault, those memories, but how could he explain? He could not.

Charlie ran off down the carriageway. Virgil picked up the hamper. 'This looks good. I'm hungry. Where shall we go?

I noticed a little arbour with some benches in the garden.' Without waiting on a reply, he set off with the basket, pushing his way through the overgrown bushes.

'Virgil!' Kate called.

'The sun isn't exactly warm, but it will be nicer than sitting in that dusty dining room.'

'Virgil!'

He whirled round on her so suddenly that she stumbled. His face was set, his jaw clenched. 'I don't discuss that part of my life. Ever. It's over.'

It was not the threat in his voice, nor even the frightening stillness of him, but the coiled-up pain, the bleakness which dulled his almond-shaped eyes, that made her back down. His expression had closed over completely earlier, at the mention of the prizefighter's name. He had retreated, to somewhere dark, frightening. Though she desperately wanted to know because she desperately wanted to help, Kate suspected that whatever part of his past Virgil was remembering, it was something quite beyond her ken. 'Yes,' she said. 'I'm sorry.' She reached for him, meaning only to touch his arm in a gesture of—what?—pity, sorrow, understanding, empathy?

She wanted only to comfort him, but he flinched, and then so, too, did she. He made to speak, but seemed to be at a loss for words. Instead he took her hand, and led her silently through the wilderness of the garden to the arbour. She sat down abruptly. Her hands were shaking. Her legs too. She couldn't understand it. Such a strong reaction, but she wasn't quite sure what it was she was reacting to. She clasped her hands together, watching her knuckles tighten.

'Kate.'

He was sitting beside her. He seemed to have the ability to move silently. She smiled wanly.

'I hope you're hungry,' Virgil said. 'Polly's packed enough to feed an army.'

They spent the rest of the day examining the house in more detail, from attics to cellar, taking pains to stick to the task in hand, taking even more pains not to touch as they did so. As they made their way back to the main house, the sun was already sinking.

'A cook, a butler, two footmen, say three maidservants, a scullery maid,' Kate muttered, biting the end of her pencil, frowning in concentration as she looked at the close-written pages of her notebook. 'The nursery maid and her own lady's maid I'm sure she will wish to manage herself, but I think we'll need two—or do you think three other menservants besides whatever occasional help she needs if she chooses to entertain, of course?'

She looked enquiringly at him. Virgil's own house, while not the grandest in Boston, was by no means one of the smallest, and was run by one housekeeper, one maid and one manservant. Wealth was power, power was what he needed to pay for his sins, but he had never felt the need to flaunt success with the trappings of wealth. He preferred to speak for himself. 'It's just one woman and a child,' he said.

'She is the Dowager Marchioness of Hatherton—or at least she will be, if her claim is validated.'

'Does a dowager marchioness, then, take more looking after than a mere miss?'

'That's not the point. It's not about her needs but her consequence.'

In the short space of time he had known her, Virgil had

come to think of Kate's views as similar to his own. He had forgotten that she belonged in this other world, where consequence must be evidenced in the quantity and quality of servants, amongst other things. 'I don't even have a valet.' He was suddenly bone-weary. 'The man I brought with me, I hired him in London. He was offended that I wouldn't let him shave me. What does that make me, in your world?'

'Self-sufficient. Crotchety, for some reason.' Kate sighed. 'Don't you see, you carry your consequence with you, Virgil. There is an authority in the way you walk, the way you look, the way you talk. It's not about how many servants are necessary to run a household—were it mine I would certainly do with considerably less—but it is not mine. My father is dead set upon wresting this woman's child from her at any cost. Giles doesn't want to believe her claim, despite the fact that it would relieve him of the burden of this stately pile, because it would mean admitting that Jamie is dead. My aunt—well, I don't have to tell you what my aunt thinks. This woman, Alicia, she has no one to speak up for her. She has no idea what she's risking, coming here. She most likely thinks we're giving her sanctuary, when, in fact—oh, heavens, I don't know what will happen. Surrounding her with just a little of the pomp due to her position may not be much, but it's all I can do. Do you see?'

'I guess.'

Kate wrinkled her brow. 'What does that mean?'

'I reckon so. Would you really do things differently if it were your household?'

Kate shrugged. 'I guess,' she said, smiling faintly at the way the phrase sounded in her English accent. 'It's a moot point, since I'm never likely to have a household of my own.'

'Can't you just move out?'

She laughed, but not pleasantly. 'Apart from the fact that it would give both my father and my aunt an apoplexy, I don't have any money.' Seeing the look of disbelief on his face, she laughed, this time with genuine amusement. 'Don't let all this fool you.' Her sweeping gesture encompassed the house, the parklands, the Dower House. 'It has nothing to do with me, a mere daughter. All I have, save whatever pin money Papa allows me, is my dowry. And if I don't marry...'

'I know your father has financial troubles, but he has more than enough to set you up if he wished.'

'But he doesn't wish, because it's not the way things are done here in England.'

'In America, it is not exactly common, but it's not frowned upon for a woman of independent means to have her own establishment.'

'Had I independent means, then America is where I'd go.'

'You'd like it there.'

'I don't doubt it, but I'll have to take your word for that.'

Kate spoke lightly, but he knew her better now. That was just her way. 'It's our loss,' Virgil said, and realised as he did that he meant it.

With a date set for the arrival of Jamie's widow at Castonbury, and Aunt Wilhelmina declining to have any part in the overseeing of the mountain of work required to make the Dower House habitable for a confidence trickster, Kate found herself without any time to call her own. As she suspected he would, Virgil suggested that he cut short his visit and continue north to New Lanark. Utterly frustrated by her family commitments, furious at Aunt Wilhelmina, who, she was certain, had made herself unavailable precisely to achieve this very outcome, Kate was relieved and astonished when her brother Giles came to her rescue.

'I'd be happy to take Virgil out and about a bit, show him some of the countryside,' he said. 'To be honest, I'd be happy for any excuse to get me out of here for a while. I'm sick of this whole damned mess, what with our father carping on about taking sole guardianship of his grandchild as if the boy does not already have a mother, and hiding his head in the sand over the mess he's got us into with his investments. There's not been a word from Harry for weeks, and I still have no idea where Ross is, and—in short, Kate, I'm in need of some uncomplicated male company and your Virgil seems like a most interesting chap.'

Though she was delighted with the solution, for over a week Kate met Virgil only at dinner, when they were separated by the expanse of the dining table and Aunt Wilhelmina's determined efforts to keep her nieces from any personal conversation with 'the American,' as she called him.

Wishing to consult the housekeeper on the details of some of her arrangements for the Dower House one afternoon, and having no desire at all to take the chance on her aunt sticking her oar in, Kate decided it would be safer to seek Mrs Stratton out in the servants' hall. As she opened the heavy green baize door at the end of the kitchen corridor and stepped through onto the gallery from which Lumsden and Mrs Stratton were accustomed to keep a beady eye on the staff working below, she was surprised by a loud burst of laughter.

The huge Castonbury kitchen ran the full length of the house, with windows facing to the north and south. Heat emanated from the massive black range. On the long, well-scrubbed table was an orderly line of basins and bowls and kitchen utensils whose use was a complete mystery to Kate, but the main kitchen itself was empty. She made her way down the stairs and headed for the servants' hall, which was on the opposite side of the room from the warren of pantries and stillrooms over which Lumsden presided. Another burst of laughter greeted her, and made her pause. Surely the servants would not be so noisy in the presence of Lumsden or Mrs Stratton? Perhaps those two were taking tea elsewhere.

She was on the verge of heading for the butler's pantry when a slow drawl stopped her in her tracks. Kate crept towards the open door and peered into the servants' hall. The table was set for tea, with bread and butter, a large fruitcake and several pots of jam, but the tea in the cups was half drunk, the bread on the plates half eaten, the majority of the wooden chairs pushed back and abandoned. Virgil sat in the middle of the table, shuffling a pack of cards. Lumsden was on one side of him, Mrs Stratton on the other, a smile crinkling her normally austere face. Clustered behind Virgil were Daisy the chambermaid, Polly, and Agnes the scullery maid, of all people. In all the years she had been working in the Castonbury kitchens, Kate had never once managed to elicit a smile from the dour maid and here she was, not just smiling but giggling.

Across the table, young Charlie was squirming in his seat, straining to get a better view. Beside him, Joe Coyle was looking decidedly out of sorts, while Watson, Virgil's valet, was by contrast looking decidedly smug. Of the senior servants, only Smithins, her father's valet, and Monsieur André, the chef, were absent.

'Do another one,' Charlie implored, his eyes fixed adoringly on Virgil.

'Haven't you seen enough yet?'

She hadn't heard that teasing note in Virgil's voice before. He looked completely at ease as he shuffled the deck expertly, his neck cloth loosened, his coat unbuttoned, sprawling back in his chair and seemingly quite at home. When Kate took tea in the servants' hall, which she tried to make a point of doing once a month, she was always horribly conscious that they were all on their best behaviour. Teaspoons tinkled against the cups. Conversation was muted. Only Polly ever laughed freely at her jokes, and even then, it was a kind of defiant laughter.

'Go on, Mr Jackson, just one more,' Mrs Stratton said, and to Kate's astonishment the housekeeper actually tapped Virgil on the hand.

The plea was taken up by all around the table save Joe Coyle, and Virgil laughed, a much more carefree laugh than Kate had ever heard; it was almost boyish. He spread the cards into a fan. 'Take a card, Mr Lumsden. And you, Agnes. I'll close my eyes while you let everyone see what you've chosen.'

'No cheating now,' Polly said, and outrageously leaned over to put her hands over Virgil's eyes, flicking a knowing look towards the open door as she did so, making it clear that she, if no one else, was aware of Kate's presence.

'Right, put them back in the deck, anywhere you like,' Virgil said. 'You done? If the lovely Miss Polly will free me from her clutches?'

Kate caught her breath at his smile, and noticed she wasn't the only one. Agnes and Daisy, blushing and nudging each other, were obviously quite smitten, and she couldn't blame them. She longed to join them; she felt quite excluded and, yes, if she was honest, the tiniest bit jealous, hovering here in the doorway. But she knew that one step forward would have them all jumping awkwardly to their feet.

'Now, then.' Virgil made a show of shuffling the deck and frowning, selecting first one card, consulting it, shaking his head and putting it back. His audience craned their necks, anticipation and excitement writ large on their faces. They wanted him to succeed, Kate could see. All except Joe Coyle, that is. Charlie was kneeling on his chair, sprawled across the tea table in a way that would normally have earned him a sound box around the ears, but Lumsden and Mrs Strattton were far too engrossed in watching Virgil to chastise him.

'Well, I don't know. I think you have me beat this time. I just can't find either of the cards in this deck. Won't you check for me, Mr Lumsden?'

The butler took the cards and began to look through them, shaking his head. By the time he had finished, his face was a picture of bewilderment. 'But I put my card in myself,' he said plaintively, 'you all saw me.'

'And me,' Agnes agreed breathlessly.

'I wonder.' Virgil reached into the pocket of Daisy's apron and pulled out one card. He reached behind the housekeeper and seemed to retrieve another from her cap. Holding them up, he received a spontaneous burst of applause.

'But how…?' Lumsden spluttered.

'It's magic,' Charlie breathed, his eyes glowing in admiration.

'It's a trick,' Joe Coyle said sullenly. 'Go on, show us how you did it.'

Virgil grinned and shook his head, pushing back his chair. 'It's easy enough. Even a monkey could do it, if he knew how,' he said pointedly.

The footman turned a dull red and glared furiously at Charlie, but the boy was too intent upon begging Virgil for just *one* more trick to notice.

'No more,' Virgil said, ruffling the boy's hair. 'Your tea is quite cold, and we've kept Lady Kate waiting long enough.'

All eyes turned towards the doorway, and exactly as she

had predicted, there was a scramble to push back chairs and straighten aprons and make curtsies and bows. 'Please, I didn't mean to disturb you,' she said. 'Finish your tea. I merely wanted to ask Mrs Stratton—but it can wait.'

Five

'Kate, what's wrong?' Virgil caught up with her as she started to climb the stairs to the kitchen gallery. 'I know it's not exactly the done thing for guests to take tea with the servants, but I'm not exactly a typical guest. If I've offended you somehow, I'm sorry. After the way young Charlie described the reaction in the servants' hall towards me, I wanted to meet them for myself. I didn't think you'd mind.'

'Of course I don't mind.' Kate hurried on through the baize door and back along the dim kitchen corridor.

'Then what is it?'

She stopped, leaning against the cool of the tiled wall, embarrassed. 'You'll think I'm being foolish.'

'Try me.'

'You're supposed to say that you could never think me foolish.'

'I never lie.'

Kate was obliged to laugh. 'You seemed so at home there and I felt like an intruder. I've never seen Lumsden so—so *unbent*! And Agnes! I thought that woman didn't know *how* to smile. It *was* foolish of me, I know it was, but I was jealous,' she confessed. 'I try, you see, to make friends with them, and though they are always polite enough, they are always on edge too.'

'You are their master's daughter. You cannot blame them for being concerned lest they offend you. They have their positions to worry about.'

'They should know I would never threaten those without cause. Besides, it's not that. I have not your ease with them, nor your ability to put them at ease.'

'I was a servant once. I understand them.'

Kate nodded. 'Yes, but it's more than that. You have a way of making most people feel understood, regardless of their status. People warm to you. Look at Giles.'

'Look at your Aunt Wilhelmina.'

'That is different. My aunt has never warmed to anyone.'

'And your father, you surely do not think he will warm to me either? If I ever have the pleasure of making his acquaintance, that is.'

'You need not indulge me, Virgil. I was only a very little jealous,' Kate said. 'In truth, I admire you for it. I wish that I had a lighter touch with people. I make them nervous.'

'Perhaps you try too hard.'

'My father would say I do not try hard enough.'

'But why should you set any store by what your father says, when by your own admission he knows you so little?'

'I was not aware that I did,' Kate said stiffly after a short silence.

Virgil raised a sceptical brow. 'I wonder how *he* would be received, were he to choose to take tea in the servants' hall?'

Once again, she was forced to laugh. 'Thank you, I shall now consider my conscience salved.' The corridor was narrow, the only light coming from the wall sconces which were lit at long intervals. She did not know how it was, but suddenly Kate was very much aware of Virgil standing beside her, was conscious, too, of the odd intimacy of the space, a no-man's land between upstairs and downstairs. She fought her own battles, and if challenged would have said unequivocally that she was not just more than capable but quite content to do so. Nothing had changed, but it was pleasant, just this once, to have someone on her side. She smiled up at him. 'Thank you.'

'Kate.'

He was standing close enough for her to feel this breath on her cheek. Her heart was beating too fast again. Her skin felt too tight, straining for his touch. 'Yes?'

Virgil touched the pulse below her ear. He seemed fascinated by the spot. His fingers trailed down her neck to her collarbone. 'Giles told me that there is to be an assembly in Buxton in a couple of weeks. I thought I might take you.'

Kate gave a start. 'Oh, no. I cannot.'

His fingers stilled. 'Why not?'

'I told you, Virgil, I am not acceptable in certain company. Surely Giles told you so?'

'I was not aware that I was expected to ask Giles for permission to take you to a dance. You are four-and-twenty, even in this country that is well beyond the age of consent.'

'Virgil, I can't. You don't understand.'

'Surely you're not afraid, Kate? Or is it that you're worried I can't dance?' Virgil slipped his hand around her waist and pulled her close against him. His cheek brushed hers as he bent to whisper in her ear. 'Wouldn't you like to dance with me?'

She could think of nothing she would like more. Save perhaps a kiss, which she would not think about. 'Yes,' Kate said, 'but, Virgil, you would be my only partner.'

His hand tightened on her waist. 'If that's your way of trying to dissuade me, it's not working. It's been five years, Kate. I think you'll find that it's not nearly as bad as you imagine. Say yes.'

She wished she could believe him. She wished she did not care. But more than anything, what she wished was to dance with him. 'Yes.'

He smiled. He pulled her tight against him. She tilted her head towards him, but his lips had barely grazed hers when the baize door to the kitchen swung back on its hinges. Mrs Stratton, carrying a large tray, all but collided with them.

'Lady Kate, I was coming to fetch Mrs Landes-Fraser's tea things in the hope I'd find you, but I see you have pre-empted me. And, Mr Jackson, I expect you were looking for these.' She produced a pack of cards from her apron pocket. It didn't seem to occur to her that their presence in the kitchen corridor was in any way strange.

Impossible, Virgil had called their attraction, and it seemed he was right, Kate thought, as he took the cards with a polite thank-you and turned towards the main part of the house. Impossible, she reminded herself as she followed in the housekeeper's wake, wondering what that so-staid woman would have said if she had stumbled upon them a few seconds later.

In her bedchamber a few days later, as Polly put away her evening dress and jewels, Kate prowled restlessly. She wore her favourite dressing gown of heavy scarlet silk lined with quilting in the style of a Japanese kimono, the sleeves trailing almost to the ground. Ornately embroidered with wildly improbable flowers and tied with a long sash, it was both exotic and sultry, a garment quite contrary to Kate's practical, prosaic self.

Or so it would have appeared to any who saw her clad in it. But the truth was, Kate had a liking for fripperies and feminine folderols. Since she knew perfectly well that such indulgences ought to be despised, and furthermore, that they were quite at odds with her looks, she kept her gowns plainly cut and, contrary to the current fashion, free from beading, ruching and tucking, confining her love of such things to her undergarments.

In these items of apparel, however, Kate indulged her sybaritic tastes to the full. Her stockings were black, clocked and held up by extravagant garters. Lace and ribbons made frivolous her chemises and even her pantaloons. Thanks to Polly's connections with a specialised milliner, Kate had recently acquired a selection of decadent corsets in poppy red, sapphire blue, vibrant pink and even rich black velvet. Had she wished, Polly had informed her mistress, she could have had stays made of the softest of leather, but here Kate drew the line. It was one thing to wear, under her gowns, the undergarments of the doxy her father believed her to be, but quite another to wear something which she was pretty certain belonged to more specialised, if unimaginable, tastes.

It was late, past midnight. Outside, the night was clear, the moon half full, casting an eerie glow over the grounds. She wondered what Virgil was doing. Still closeted with Giles discussing politics? Perhaps he had retired for the night. Was he sleeping? Lying awake? Was he thinking of her?

Kate gave herself a little shake. They would go to the school tomorrow, no matter that there were still a hundred things to be done at the Dower House. She sat down at the inlaid escritoire which faced the sashed window embrasure to write a note to the schoolmistress. Picking up a quill, she trailed the feather over her lips. He would have kissed her the other day.

She could have cursed poor Mrs Stratton for her untimely arrival. Kate knew she wasn't a *femme fatale*. She was not even a *femme* a-little-bit-intriguing, but for some reason Virgil found her attractive. He had said so. He had shown her so. She was not imagining it.

She tried to remember how it had been with Anthony. She'd been curious, she'd even expected to find it enjoyable, and Anthony, as he had never tired of telling her, was a man with lusty appetites, so she'd been persuaded. It was the threat of those appetites being slaked elsewhere which had won her over. But she hadn't ever been particularly moved by Anthony's kisses, which even at the time had seemed perfunctory, something he felt obliged to do, but which were merely a precursor to the main event, like sitting through the farce be fore the play. Virgil's touch had made her tingle in a way that Anthony's never had. Virgil's kisses were complete in themselves, not a means to an end. If she had not known herself better, she would almost have been able to convince herself that she would have enjoyed whatever Virgil decided to do next. Though she did know herself better.

'If I didn't know you better, I'd say the last thing you were thinking about doing with that feather was writing with it.' Kate jumped. Polly was leaning against the window seat with that look in her eye which preceded something outrageous. 'There's men will pay good money to have a woman stroke them with a feather like that—or stroke themselves, depending. On the lips. Though not them lips,' she added with a smirk.

Usually Kate found such insights embarrassing as well as incomprehensible, a fact which she was certain contributed to Polly's persistence in sharing them with her. Not wishing to seem naive, she was wont to pass them off with a knowing laugh and change the subject, but tonight her curiosity got the better of her. 'Why would they do that?'

'Why? What do you mean, why?'

'Tickle themselves. Why would that be—you know, why would a man pay to see that?'

Her previous pretences of understanding had obviously been too convincing. Her maid was looking at her in disbelief. 'Well, you know.'

'I really don't,' Kate said.

'Lord Almighty!' Polly plonked herself down on the window seat. 'You mean you and that Lord whatshisname—him that you were going to marry— But I thought—I heard— They told me downstairs that he ruined you. Isn't it true? What was his name?'

'Lord Featherstone,' Kate said.

Polly tittered. 'That's a bit of a coincidence,' she said, looking meaningfully at the quill. 'Isn't it true, then? Didn't you and him—*you* know!'

Kate blushed painfully. 'There weren't any feathers involved.'

Polly rolled her eyes. 'Usually there aren't. And it's not tickling so much as— Do you mean to tell me you haven't ever? Not with him? Not even by yourself? Never?'

If Polly was astonished, Kate was now utterly lost. 'By myself? Without a man, you mean?'

'For the Lord's sake, Lady Kate, you don't need a man to bring yourself off. Do you mean to tell me you haven't ever? And that lord of yours, he didn't do it for you either?' Seeing her mistress's blank face, Polly tutted extravagantly, sat down beside her and began to whisper.

By the time her maid had finished her explanation, Kate was fiery red and still not entirely sure what was being described, though she was certain it was something she'd never experienced. 'Do you mean that *every* woman can—can…'

'Well, not all the time,' Polly said, drawing her an odd look. 'If the man doesn't—I mean, some men, they just don't know their way around a woman. Listen…'

But as her maid, now she had recovered from her incredulity, determined to initiate Kate into what she obviously believed was some sort of natural rite, began to explain using even more graphic terminology, Kate stopped her. 'I understand, really,' she protested.

Polly shook her head. 'Do you? Sounds to me as if that lord of yours is the one who didn't understand. That Mr Jackson now,' she said.

'What about him?'

'I bet he knows what's what. Fine figure of a man, he is. And don't say you haven't noticed, because I know you have. I saw you looking at him the other day in the servants' hall and I don't blame you. I'd look myself if I thought it would do any good, but he's not interested in me. Or Daisy—and that flighty piece has done her best to get his attention, thrust that chest of hers practically in his face, and he didn't even notice. I bet if Virgil Jackson stripped down for you, it would, um, tickle you,' Polly said with a leer. 'I know it would tickle me. He's got muscles on his muscles, your American. I'd like to see him work up a sweat. There's something about a man working up a sweat, isn't there?'

Was there? Kate decided not to answer this, but she thought most likely Polly was right. The candles on the mantel started to gutter, and she took the opportunity to cover her high colour by snuffing them out and telling her maid it was much too late to talk any more.

After Polly left, Kate, forgetting all about her note to the schoolmistress, discarded her kimono and pulled back the bed covers. The warming pan was cold. She hauled it out and placed it on the hearth. Jumping into bed, she blew out the last candle. In the all-encompassing dark, she snuggled down under the bedclothes and pressed her hands between her legs, and thought of Virgil, sweat, muscles and tickling.

Kate's opportunity to discover for herself whether there really was, as Polly said, something about a man working up a sweat, came quite unexpectedly the next morning. Though she made a point of being down to breakfast early, Giles informed her that Virgil had already eaten.

'Said he had business of his own he needed to take care of today,' he told her.

'What business?'

Giles shrugged. 'I didn't ask him.'

Kate's hand hovered over the bread basket. The temptation to throw a roll at her brother was almost irresistible, but if Giles was teasing her, then he'd know he'd hit home, and if he was not, he'd wonder why she was so upset. She picked up the roll, but only to put it down on her own plate. 'He didn't give you any idea where he was going, then?' she asked with studied indifference.

'Why should it matter, you're going to be tied up at the Dower House all day. That woman arrives soon—you don't have much longer to get the place shipshape, and you certainly don't want Aunt Wilhelmina saying that you weren't up to the job, now do you?'

She knew he was trying not to smile, which meant he knew perfectly well where Virgil was and was determined to make her beg for the information. Her whole life, she had made a point of never begging for anything from any of her brothers, but she had never been so tempted as now. Though *damn it*, Giles was right. She didn't want Aunt-bloody-Wilhelmina saying that she could have done a better job. Kate swallowed a cup of very hot coffee far too quickly and pushed back her chair. 'You are, as ever, quite right, Giles. I have a lot to attend to,' she said, smiling sweetly, picking up the roll from her plate and aiming it as his head as she quit the dining room.

Storming off, muttering under her breath about infuriating brothers, managing at the same time to mentally review her still horribly long list of tasks while wondering where on earth Virgil could be and wondering if she was ever going to be able to spend time with him before he took himself north, Kate got to the front door of the Dower House in record time.

Since it was not yet eight o'clock, the servants had not arrived from the village. Inside, the house was taking shape, but it was the garden which concerned Kate most. Cornelius Wright, the head gardener at Castonbury Park, was a tyrant who would not tolerate temporary labour in the grounds, and though he had promised three days in a row to send two of his lads round to start cutting back the bushes, as yet he had failed to do so. Not even Giles had been able to persuade the stubborn old man to do as Kate asked. She suspected the gardener resented the implied criticism of having let the place go in the first place.

Cursing the man under her breath as she made her way through the house making notes on her list, Kate wondered if Aunt Wilhelmina was at the root of Wright's claim that the orangery must take precedence. As she opened the French doors to take a closer look at the wilderness outside, it was the smell which she noticed at first. Wood shavings. Then the sound, the regular whack of an axe. Casting a glance to the right, she saw immediately that the best part of the overgrown bushes had been pruned ruthlessly. The side path was now clear. Giles's quiet word with Wright must have done the trick, after all. Smiling broadly, Kate made her way through the stone archway which bordered the rose garden, and over to the small huddle of outbuildings in the far corner.

Virgil had his back to her. A broad back, covered by a white lawn shirt. His coat and waistcoat hung on the door handle of the wash house. His movements were graceful, perfectly synchronised, his whole body caught up in perfect rhythm as he hefted the axe above his head, then swung it down to the branch, cutting through it neatly, sending chips of wood flying, before shifting on the balls of his feet readying for the next blow as his arms swung the axe high again. His movements were precise and ruthless. Each cut was made in one movement. When he was done with one branch, he moved forward to the next in line.

Kate was mesmerised. By the way the soft leather of his buckskins clung lovingly to his form, knees slightly bent, strong thighs, tightly rounded buttocks. By the way sweat made his shirt stick to his back. By the bunching of his powerful shoulders, the flexing ripple of the muscles on his arms. His movements were fluid and lethal. Each blow of axe on wood seemed to emanate not from his shoulders but from much lower, powered from the taut band of his abdomen. She recalled the first time she'd seen him at Maer Hall, the way he'd moved down the long gallery like a predator. Watching him now, she shivered, excitement tinged with fear. He was beautifully lethal.

He stopped suddenly mid-blow, sensing her presence, though she was still some yards away and had not moved. He looked straight at her, but for a moment she felt as if he were looking straight through her. His expression was remote and quite blank, frighteningly so. The mask a man would wear when he would show nothing, behind which he suffered torments.

'You don't need to do this,' Kate said, taking a few tentative steps forward. Despite the fact that he quite clearly wanted to be alone, she was impelled towards him, fascinated.

'You said last night that you were worried the gardener—Wright?—wouldn't turn up.'

A flash of his impossibly white teeth, but it wasn't a smile. Kate took another few steps. His shirt was open, showing an expanse of chest. Smooth, save for a few woodchips which stuck to his skin. He had pushed the sleeves of the shirt up. Sweat gave his forearms a sheen. In the bright sunlight, his skin seemed darker. She wanted to touch him. 'Did you tell Giles what you were planning on doing? Surely he discouraged you?'

Virgil shrugged. 'I knew how much it meant to you, to have the house ready, not to give your aunt the opportunity to criticise your efforts.'

This time his smile, though fleeting, was real enough. Encouraged, Kate covered the last few yards which separated them. Virgil smelled of wood sap and salty sweat. Without his modish coat and waistcoat, he seemed bigger. Not so much less civilised as more powerful. She looked around the small yard at the stack of wood, smaller branches and clippings which Virgil had placed ready to burn. 'You must have started very early.'

'I never sleep past dawn. What are *you* doing here so betimes?'

'I wanted to catch you before you disappeared off with Giles again. I want to show you my school today.'

'Though that task list of yours is still pages long?'

'I know, but I was afraid you would leave before I had the

chance to take you there, and it's what you came here for, after all.'

'Yes. Yes, I suppose it is,' Virgil said, though he had almost forgotten. It was Kate who kept him here when he should have continued on his planned journey north. The thought of Kate's kisses and Kate's touch. Passion, so long dormant, had refused to go back into hibernation. He dreamt of her, and knowing how impossible it was only served to legitimise his wanting.

Eleven years ago, he had surrendered wanting. Eleven years ago, he had ceded all rights to the comfort of affection, to the deeper dangers of love. But since he could never love Kate, he could want her. He could have her because they could never mean anything to each other. It was the kind of logic which made perfect sense when she was standing beside him. He longed to touch her and so he did. Just her hand, that was all. 'I will be leaving before your new relative arrives,' he said, to remind himself of that fact, to remind himself that they could measure the time left to them in hours, if they were so inclined.

She caught his hand between hers. His right hand. The brand was on the inside of his forearm, above the wrist, where the skin was most tender. It was covered, usually, by his sleeve. As her eyes fell on it, he tried to conceal it with his left hand, but she was too quick.

'*B. VA*. What does that mean?'

'Booth. Virginia.' Virgil tried to snatch his hand away, but Kate would not let go.

'Booth. Was that the name of the plantation?'

'And the owner.' It had been his name, too, before he was sold, though he had never claimed it.

Kate's face was ashen. 'I didn't know they branded you.'

'They didn't unless you were inclined to run away.' He

hated the mark. It reminded him of his guilt and filled him with shame. The brand kept the memories of that place, that day, etched fresh. Virgil broke free of Kate's hold, turning away from her to roll down his sleeve. He didn't want her to look at it. He didn't want her to see what it told of him.

He did not want his wounds touched, nor his past discussed, he'd made that quite clear, but this time Kate could not let it be. Horrified by the brand, she took his arm again, pushed up the sleeve and touched it. The letters were indented in his skin, the skin itself puckered, a darker colour than the rest. It would have been a long time healing. She traced the shape of the letters with her fingertip.

Virgil stood stock-still. She sensed him, bunched tight, ready to spring, flee, repulse her, but he didn't. Wanting only to heal, she bent over his arm and kissed him. Her tongue traced the letters. The skin felt tight over them, stretched, as if it was struggling to contain the darkness underneath. She kissed the brand softly, then kissed it again and again, little sucking kisses, as if she could draw out the poison which was embedded in those three vicious letters.

Still Virgil did not move, but she could feel his chest rising and falling more quickly. She ached with tenderness for him. Hot tears dropped from her lashes onto his skin. She licked them away, the salt of her tears mingling with the salt of Virgil's sweat on her tongue. She kissed her way up his forearm to the crease of his elbow. Then she was caught, yanked close, and Virgil's mouth descended on hers in a kiss which stole her breath away.

Polly was right. Sweat. Muscle. Skin. There was something about that combination. Raw man, strength which could snap her but which was instead channelled into holding her, at the same time drinking from her, extracting the passion which she hadn't known was pent-up there, and fanning its flames. Virgil's arms were tight around her. She was pressed hard against his chest, bowed back in his arms, her mouth ravaged. He was kissing her as she had never been kissed before, his tongue first duelling with hers, then thrusting, claiming her mouth for his own.

He tasted feral, his touch was fierce, making her own equally so. She tore at his shirt, her hands feverish on his back, her fingers clawing the linen free from his buckskins so that she could feel the flesh of his stomach, his chest. Skin. Heated skin. His heart beat wildly under her palm. Their kisses were wild. Long and deep, then urgent and quick, then harder, more penetrating. His manhood was hard against her thigh. His hands were like hers, feverish on her back, her bottom, cupping her into him. She rubbed herself against him and he moaned. Her nipples thrust against her chemise, hard and aching, though they were enclosed in silk and satin.

She had no idea how they came to be inside the outbuilding. She did not recall moving, and was only vaguely aware of the door closing behind her before her back slammed against it. It was gloomy inside, for the one window was thick with dust, but Kate could see enough. Virgil's hands on the buttons of her jacket. His eyes, blazing down at her. His face set, focused, concentrated, entirely on her, as if she was all there was.

When he cupped her breasts through her chemise, she thought she would faint from the sensations he aroused. There was nothing soothing or gentle about what his touch did to her. She recognised nothing of the past, none of the mildly pleasant feelings which had faded into mild disappointment with Anthony. Virgil made her wild. His kisses stripped her of everything but a craving for more. When his touch was not enough, she tugged at the ribbons of her chemise herself to give him skin, pulled his head towards her breasts, wanting him to taste her, unable to bear waiting any longer to feel his lips on her. Her corset was dark blue today, edged with black lace. He barely seemed to notice as he freed her breasts, and she forgot to care when he took her nipple in his mouth and sucked.

She cried out. Her knees would have buckled under her if he had not supported her with the weight of his body against the door. He sucked, and his hand grazed her other nipple, tugging sparks of heat, sending lightning shards of pleasure directly to her sex. Her belly clenched. He sucked again. She sank her fingers into the leather of his buckskins, clutching the hard mounds of his buttocks. A trickle of perspiration ran down her back. She felt anxious. Tense. Waiting. She knew it would be worth waiting for.

She moaned when Virgil lifted his mouth from her breast, but then he claimed her lips again, and she sank into his kiss with a hunger that made him jerk against her.

Kate ran her hands up Virgil's back, over his shirt. Bunched muscles, damp with sweat. She wanted to see him. Touch his skin. Feel his muscles. Taste his sweat. Some of the woodchips which had stuck to him were sticking to her now. Together they smelt of resin and sweat and something else tangy, musky. She tugged at his shirt, but he stepped just out of her reach.

'No. Not me. I want to see you,' Virgil muttered, tucking his shirt back into his breeches. Her jacket was hanging open. Her breasts were quite bare. Her nipples were dark. And hard. He dropped his gaze. She wore a white thing, a shift, but it was silk not cotton, and the ribbons which tied the low neckline were satin. Over it she wore stays, but they were stays about as far from ladylike as any he could imagine. Dark blue silk, bordered with black lace. It made him wonder what she wore underneath. Boots? Or stockings?

He covered her breast with his hand. She shuddered, and his shaft tightened in response. He dipped his head to kiss her. Slowly this time, lingeringly. She tasted so sweet. He wanted to taste her. All of her.

Sweet Jesus, how he wanted her. It frightened him. He wanted her too much for it to be explained away by turning points or crossroads or wanting what you could never have. He wanted her with a pureness of need which scared the hell out of him.

He would have stopped, but he did not have to, for Kate pulled herself free quite suddenly. 'I have work to do,' she said.

A few days ago he would have happily accepted this, but perversely, though he had every reason to welcome her calling a halt, though it was what he should have done, Virgil was hurt by her having done so. 'What's wrong?'

'The morning will have run away from me if I do not make haste.' She looked shocked, almost dazed, as she turned her back on him to right her clothing.

'Are you afraid someone will see us?' Virgil asked.

Kate whirled around at this. 'No, though I ought to have been. I am afraid of what you do to me, if you must have it,' she said shakily. 'It frightens me. I don't know what to do with all these feelings. I don't understand them. I've never felt—not like this.... It's too much.'

'Never?' He remembered then, she'd said something similar in the Dower House that day. 'Kate, you cannot possibly have thought that you're incapable, cold?'

'I don't *know* what I think! I don't want to talk about it. I thought it was all in the past. I thought I was over it, I thought I had dealt with it, don't you see?'

'No, I don't see. You're not making sense.'

'I *know*,' Kate exclaimed wretchedly. 'None of this makes sense. For God's sake, Virgil, you are not the only one who is scarred.'

'What do you mean?' Virgil snapped, immediately defensive.

'You think I didn't guess why you tucked your shirt back so hastily? They whipped you, did they not? Do you think I am so shallow as to find such marks repellent? The very first night we met, I guessed you could never have been anything other than a renegade slave. I did not know about the branding, but I am not so naive as to be unaware of the punishments meted out for disobedience. They whipped you and you don't wish me to see your scars.'

She thought him vain. Or ashamed. For a terrible moment, he'd thought she'd somehow guessed at the scars he bore inside him, guessed the truth of what the physical ones represented. She had not, how could she have, but his relief was short-lived. 'What did you mean, I am not the only one? Was it that man…?'

'You can unclench your fists, you are five years too late. Besides, you are well off the mark. Anthony never beat me.'

Kate forced the last button through her jacket and squared her shoulders. She had not answered his question. He could see from that defiant glare that she would not. She was going. It was what he wanted, even though it was not how he wanted it. It hurt. He should have remembered that. Desire and pain went hand in hand, how could he have forgotten?

'I appreciate the effort you've made with the garden,' Kate said in clipped tones, 'but it was not necessary. I'm sure Wright will turn up.' She turned to go, but it was not in her nature to be so ungracious. 'I do appreciate it,' she said, her voice softening. 'It was very kind of you, but there's really no need to do any more.'

'I'll finish.' Virgil summoned what most people would take as a smile. 'It will be one less thing for you to worry about.'

Kate left him to his chopping. She felt defeated and angry. Her body, so strung out with anticipation, throbbed in protest at the anticlimax. She understood now what Polly had been whispering about. She wished she didn't. She'd rather not have known what she was missing.

At least her frustration was understandable. Why was she so angry? For the rest of the morning, Kate worked frantically in an effort to regain her frayed temper, ticking off task after task from her list. The force of her feelings astonished her. It was not just their intensity, she realised as she supervised the village women in the final cleaning and disposition of furniture, it was the fact that they existed in the first place.

All these years she had thought herself cold, had accepted Anthony's judgement of her, and by implication the world's condemnation. She had come to believe herself lacking, and as such responsible, at least in part, for what had happened to her. For the past five years, she'd carried that burden of guilt unnecessarily. It was that, she thought as she discussed the ordering of supplies with the new cook, which rankled most. That, and the fact that her family, and in particular Aunt Wilhelmina, had acted as if she deserved her fate.

Five years. Five whole years! And now it turned out that she was not cold, and that realisation turned everything she thought she knew about herself on its head. She had been foolish, there was no question of that. She wished she had had the confidence to act on her instincts earlier. But that didn't alter the fact that she had also been unfairly judged, and had unfairly judged herself.

Lord, but she was *furious*! Virgil had unlocked a passionate nature she hadn't known she possessed, but he'd also unwittingly let loose a torrent of pent-up emotions. Until today, if anyone had asked her—though they never had—she'd have sworn she was over it. Over Anthony, over the guilt, over the shame. She'd have said that it all meant nothing to her now, save that she was determined not to repeat her mistakes. Virgil had seen that for the lie it was. Right from the start, when she'd told him the bare bones of her history with Anthony, he'd heard the anger in her voice. Why had not she? Why had it tumbled out this morning as it had? Was she scarred? She had thought herself healed.

For the next few hours as she worked and fumed, she was at the same time acutely aware of Virgil out there in the garden. When the women stopped for the lunch which Kate had sent over from the Castonbury kitchens, he lit a bonfire on the lawn. She watched, calmer now, from the window of the bedroom which had been prepared for the house's new mistress, as one by one her helpers joined him. They sat, Virgil and the village women, eating game pie in the autumn sunshine warmed by the blaze of the fire. He seemed just as much at his ease as he had in the servants' hall. She could hear the women's laughter through the half-open window. She recognised in it the hint of admiration. She could see, from the way they looked at him, that they were as fascinated by Virgil as she. She felt excluded. She could not possibly be jealous! Kate turned on her heel and headed for the linen cupboard. There were sheets to count.

But sorting bed linen did not occupy her mind nearly enough. Virgil's scars were certainly real. The whipping he had received must have been vicious indeed to have raised such long-lasting welts on his back. How many years ago? How many times? He was such a confident man, such a powerfully attractive one, she was taken aback by his self-consciousness. Like the brand, she supposed his scars were symbolic of a past he wished to forget.

Kate added another pillowcase to the pile of darning. She had thought she had forgotten her past. No, not forgotten, but come to terms with it. She thumped her fist down on a pile of table linen. She had worked so hard to deny Anthony the power of having hurt her, but it was still there, after all. She *was* scarred. The words, said in an excess of defensiveness, were true. Scarred and scared. And since she was being soul-searingly honest with only the linen for company, she was also perversely wishing she had not called a halt this morning. Virgil had proved Anthony wrong there. She was certainly not incapable of pleasure. Virgil made her body thrum. Her body's thrumming terrified her almost as much as it excited her. If she could somehow reconcile the one over the other…

The doorbell clanged in the hall, breaking into this tangle of thoughts. Kate leaned over the banister and saw that some of her new sister-in-law's staff had arrived. Alicia herself would be at Castonbury a couple of days after the dance at Buxton, and Virgil said he would go before then. She didn't want him to go, though she knew he must. He would go to Robert Owen's model village and then he would return home to America and she was very unlikely to meet him again. As she descended the stairs, Kate decided that that was probably the most melancholy fact of all.

Kate returned to the house hoping for some time alone before dinner, but her plans were scuppered by a summons from her aunt. Word on Cousin Ross had finally reached Castonbury. It was therefore with her mind still in a state of turmoil that she tapped on Aunt Wilhelmina's bedchamber door.

'He is married! He has actually married that—that maid-servant.' The disgust in Mrs Landes-Fraser's voice could not have been exaggerated had her cousin married one of Polly's former associates, Kate thought ruefully.

'I hoped he might,' she said. 'He and Lisette seemed to be deeply attached.'

Aunt Wilhelmina had been lying prone on her bed clutching her sal volatile, but at this she sat up. 'Surely, Katherine, you do not condone this match?'

'It is not for me to condone or condemn. Ross is of age and, luckily for him, of independent means. If Lisette makes him happy, then I am happy for him. Do they intend to make their home in India?'

'Yes, I thank goodness.' Mrs Landes-Fraser gave a shudder. 'At least we will be spared the shame of having him set up home with a servant in England.'

'She is not a servant, Aunt. I am not quite sure why she was forced to play the part of Araminta's maid, but she was clearly gently bred. And whatever were her origins, she is now Ross's wife. If she is good enough for Ross, she should be good enough for all of us.'

'I believe I have had cause in the past to remark upon your unorthodox tendencies. I had not quite appreciated that they encapsulated your own kin.' Mrs Landes-Fraser rose from her bed to loom over her niece, who was seated by the window perusing her cousin's letter. 'I do trust, Katherine, that you have not been similarly unorthodox in your dealings with that American?'

Her aunt's gaze was sharp and Kate had never been adept at lying. 'I have barely seen Mr Jackson,' she said, keeping her eyes on Ross's strong, slanting script. 'He has spent the better part of his stay in Giles's company, as you well know.'

'I know he was not with Giles today.'

Kate said nothing. She knew her brother well enough to guess that he would not willingly have disclosed Virgil's whereabouts to their aunt. Giles never willingly disclosed anything to anyone. It was one of his strong points, and one of his most infuriating ones.

Mrs Landes-Fraser sighed, and sat down beside her. 'You understand, Katherine, that while your acquaintance with this man is tolerated at Castonbury because Giles is here to lend you countenance and because your misguided attempts to educate the villagers make you too well-liked for malice, but were the world at large to discover you had been spending time alone with such a man it would be impossible to protect you.'

Kate bridled. 'Protect me from what, precisely? Thanks in

no small part to you and my father, I have very little reputation left to protect.'

Her aunt's lips tightened. 'Had you listened to my advice, your reputation would be spotless.'

It was too much. She had not planned to give vent to her feelings, but she could not, after such a pointed remark, rein them in. 'Had I listened to your advice,' Kate said grimly, 'I would have married a man who blackmailed me into doing his will.'

'Oh, for heaven's sake, don't exaggerate.' Mrs Landes-Fraser threw herself to her feet and began to pace the room. 'You make it sound as if poor Anthony was some sort of criminal. You were to be his wife, Katherine. He had every right to expect your—your co-operation when it came to doing your matrimonial duty. If you had not been so unaccountably eager to do that same duty in the first place…'

'I may never have discovered that the man I was planning to marry was a bully,' Kate interrupted bitterly.

'It does not occur to you that it was your own actions which caused him to treat you with such a lack of respect? After all, by your own admission, you gave him freely what you should have kept for the wedding night.'

'It was not so freely given in the end, Aunt. I told you that.'

'And I told you that you must bear the consequences of your ill judgement.'

Kate clenched her fists beneath the folds of her gown. Not since the day she had announced she was putting an end to her betrothal had she felt such unbridled anger. 'Indeed,' she said through gritted teeth, 'you ensured I would suffer, you and my father.'

Her aunt froze. 'What do you mean by that?'

'Oh, for heaven's sake, you know perfectly well what I

mean!' Kate jumped up from the window seat, glaring at her aunt across the room. 'You could have stood by me. You could have denied the lies Anthony was spreading. You could have tried, just for once, to see things from my side of the fence.'

'Katherine! What has got into you? Why are you bringing this up now, after all this time? We discussed this five years ago.'

'But we did not resolve it! He all but forced me, Aunt. I know you have chosen to think that I jilted him because I did not enjoy what he did to me, but it wasn't that. I did have expectations that were not fulfilled, I did think that our—relations—should have been more…but it wasn't that. He blackmailed me. Coerced me. Call it what you will, he bent my will to his in order to have me do something I no longer wished to. If he could act in such a way before we were wed, what more would he do to me with the bonds of marriage to back him up?'

'Lord Anthony Featherstone is a gentleman,' Mrs Landes-Fraser said haughtily.

It was a shame, Kate thought, that Anthony had never treated her as a lady, but she held her tongue. Her aunt would never understand. She could not possibly be as cruel as she seemed, though she was certainly utterly misguided. 'I doubt we will ever agree upon the subject,' she said wearily.

But, as ever, Aunt Wilhelmina must have the last word. 'What about the others? There have been several less eligible but, under the circumstances, wholly acceptable offers for your hand, yet you have not even made a pretence of considering them, Katherine. You are surely not going to tell me that you thought each and every one of them a bully! Why, you were hardly acquainted with some of them.'

'I had no wish to be further acquainted with any of them.'

Kate had thought her anger abated, but it flared up abruptly again. 'It *hurt*, can't you see that? You hurt me. Anthony hurt me. Even my father hurt me. It was all so unfair. How do you think I felt, all those whisperings, those turned shoulders, while Anthony was welcomed with open arms? Why was it acceptable for him to have taken me to bed, but not acceptable for me to have allowed it? I did not deserve the half of it, but that does not mean I think myself innocent. I behaved stupidly. I knew, deep down, I knew that I did not want to marry Anthony, but I allowed myself to be persuaded, and when I was still uncertain I thought to persuade myself. You say I deserved to be treated without respect—well, you will be pleased to know, Aunt, that I agree with you. Not because I anticipated my wedding vows, but because I did not trust my own judgement.'

Kate broke off, her chest heaving. Her cheeks were overheated. She could feel the burn of tears at the back of her eyes, and was determined not to let them fall. All this rage, she had not realised she had bottled it up so much. 'I do not know how we came upon this subject,' she said shortly, 'but I think we should let it go before either of us says something we may regret.'

Mrs Landes-Fraser dropped onto the edge of the bed. 'We came upon this subject, as you put it, because I wished to warn you about your acquaintance with that American.'

Aunt Wilhelmina sounded shaken. Was her complexion paler than usual? After all these years, had she actually listened? Kate tried to believe it, but the hurt went too deep for her to be generous enough to do so. More likely she was simply outraged at her niece's insubordination. 'Mr Jackson is leaving soon,' she said wearily. 'Before our new relative arrives, as you well know.'

'That is as well. You will oblige me by keeping out of his company until then. It is ridiculous, of course, for you are a duke's daughter, when all is said and done, and he is a—a...' Mrs Landes-Fraser caught Kate's eye, and obviously thought the better of however she was about to describe Virgil.

'If it is so ridiculous, I wonder why you put yourself to the bother of warning me.'

Kate's aunt smiled thinly. 'We are never likely to see eye to eye. Certainly my sense of duty and yours rarely coincide, but my promise to my sister was not made lightly. I told her I would do my best by her children, and I would not be doing my best if I did not caution you. However, I see it is unnecessary. You have made your sentiments regarding the opposite sex quite clear. You and I are cut from the same cloth in many ways, Katherine. I myself found the physical side of my marriage most...unpleasant. Perhaps if you had been able to disguise your disgust as I did, Lord Anthony would have treated you better.'

This astounding insight would have silenced Kate, were it not for the underlying implication. Upon one thing alone she and her aunt could agree: they would never see eye to eye.

'You may leave me now, the bell has long gone to dress for dinner.' Aunt Wilhelmina got to her feet. 'I am glad we cleared the air. I trust we understand each other a little better.'

Kate studied her aunt's countenance, but she could see no trace of irony there. 'What of Ross's letter?' she asked, at a complete loss. 'Has my father seen it? What does he have to say?'

'Obviously he will have nothing more to do with his nephew. Were it not for the imminent arrival of this putative grandchild, I suspect His Grace would say a lot more, but as it is, your father is somewhat distracted.'

'You will be pleased to know that I am confident the Dower House will be ready in plenty of time for our new relative,' Kate said with satisfaction.

'Save for the gardens, of course. I am afraid Wright cannot be spared at present, the orangery is taking up all his attention,' Mrs Landes-Fraser retorted.

'Oh, I got someone else to take care of that.' Kate headed for the door.

'How so? Wright would not have sanctioned an outsider coming to tend his garden.'

'He didn't. And it wasn't.' Kate smiled sweetly at her aunt. 'Mr Jackson saw to it.'

As a result of Ross's letter, Giles dined with his father, and Aunt Wilhelmina's presence was required in the duke's suite, too, after dinner. Though she was obviously loath to leave her nieces alone with 'the American', Mrs Landes-Fraser could not bring herself to refuse His Grace. In point of fact, it was His Grace's valet, Smithins, who communicated the request, but though the words were framed as an invitation, no one in the drawing room could be in any doubt that Mrs Landes-Fraser had been summoned.

Though she tried, before quitting the room, to persuade her nieces that a quarter before nine was more than past their retiring time, neither paid her any attention. The door had barely closed on Aunt Wilhelmina's trailing fringes when Phaedra leapt to her feet.

'Thank goodness she's gone. Now I can go down to the stables to check on Isolde. My bay mare,' she explained to Virgil. 'She was quite out of temper this morning, and though Tom Anderson says it is nothing to worry about, I just want to make sure.'

'Phaedra, it is dark outside.' But her sister had already whisked herself away. Kate shook her head. 'I swear, if she thought she could get away with it, Phaedra would sleep in the stables.'

Virgil ignored this remark, getting up from the gilded sofa to look out of the window. 'I take it you and your aunt view your cousin's marriage rather differently,' he said. 'Is that why you quarrelled?'

Kate stiffened. 'What makes you say that?'

'The atmosphere at dinner was positively frigid.'

'We did have a disagreement, but it was nothing to do with Ross.'

'It was about me, then.'

'Not directly.' Kate tried to smile, but her mouth refused to co-operate. The contretemps with Aunt Wilhelmina had left her drained, and she had not even begun to work out how she felt about this morning.

As if he read her mind, Virgil left his post at the window to sit beside her on the sofa. 'Kate, this morning— I am not accustomed to explaining myself. It's been so long since I— But if I've upset you…'

'You haven't. No, I mean you did. I was angry with you, but it wasn't really your fault.' Kate rubbed her eyes wearily. 'It doesn't matter.'

'It obviously does, but I guess I'm not the only one who doesn't like to explain himself,' Virgil said, taking her hand.

'I guess,' Kate said with a faint smile. 'You'll be leaving soon,' she added after a moment's silence. Did this make it more or less easy to discuss how she felt? Her hand was lost in his. His clasp was warm, reassuring. 'Do you know, I think this is the first time we've ever been alone together in this house.'

'I reckon if you open the door you'll find Lumsden about two steps away. Your aunt will have asked him to make sure I don't ravish you in her absence.'

'You will be pleased to know that my aunt no longer fears any such thing.' Kate smiled abstractedly, smoothing the sash of her gown with her free hand. 'That's how it started, our quarrel before dinner, if you really want to know. She did set out to warn me against being seen too much in your company, but by the end of our conversation she had decided that it was quite unnecessary, for not only are we worlds apart, you and I, there is the fact of my being frigid to be taken into account.'

'Frigid!' Virgil looked at her searchingly. 'Is this your English idea of a joke?'

'No, I was perfectly serious and so, it seems, was my aunt.'

'So it's a pretty safe bet that we weren't spotted this morning,' Virgil said.

'Is that *your* idea of a joke? Was that what was worrying you? Was that why you stopped?'

'It was you who stopped.'

Kate had been studying their clasped hands, but now she met his look squarely. 'If I had not, you would have. How long has it been, Virgil?'

He released her hand and moved a little further away from her on the sofa. 'It doesn't matter.'

'Ah, but it obviously does,' Kate said, quoting his own words back at him. She began to smooth her sash again, frowning down at her feet as she did so. The urge to confide was strong, for she desperately wanted to make sense of her jumbled feelings. It did not come naturally to her, trusting anyone with her innermost thoughts, but of everyone she knew, Virgil was the least likely to judge her, the most likely to understand her.

She wanted to be understood. She wanted to understand herself. She wanted *him* to understand.

Kate abandoned her sash and resettled herself on the sofa, shuffling round to face Virgil. 'I was frightened this morning, that was why I stopped. Not of you, but of myself. There were things I thought buried and forgotten which our— When we kissed, it brought it all to the surface, somehow. I had no idea what I meant when I told you I was scarred, it just came out. Then later—and talking to my aunt—I was so angry. You were the cause indirectly, I suppose, but it was not your fault.'

She had his attention now. His expression had lost that remote look which he used to intimidate. His eyes were fixed on her. She could almost feel him listening, so intently was he concentrating.

'What frightened you, Kate?'

'It sounds silly now, but I was frightened of what I was feeling. I'm not—I haven't ever felt like that before, you see, and I thought...with Anthony— Oh, heavens, I am making such a mull of this. I'm sorry, but I can't even make sense of it myself, let alone explain it. Forget I spoke. It is too— Let us just forget it.'

She made to get up, but Virgil was too quick for her, pulling her back down onto the sofa. 'Do you want to make sense of it?' he asked gently. She nodded. 'Then tell me,' he said, 'from the beginning.'

Kate stared across the room. She could see their reflections in the window. They were sitting far too close. Tall as she was, she looked so slight compared to Virgil. He was such a very definite shape. Such a very distinctively masculine one. She turned back to him resolutely. 'I've already told you the beginning. I told you I was ruined. I told you I was a social pariah. What I didn't tell you was the full story.'

It was impossible to speak with him so close, so she crossed the room to stare out into the night as he had done earlier. It was easier, not seeing his face. 'The truth is, that we—that Anthony and I—we were lovers.'

There! She had said it. Kate forced herself to turn from the window, but Virgil's expression was quite unreadable. 'I've shocked you,' she said, seeking a reaction, but Virgil was not to be drawn.

'Are you saying that this became public knowledge? That's it?'

'Yes.'

'But how? You would surely not have—do you mean *he* made it public knowledge?'

She could have no doubt of his feelings now. Virgil looked utterly astounded. 'He denied it, but it could only have come from him. When I broke off the betrothal he was furious, you see. Anthony has almost as high an opinion of himself as my father.'

'But what of your father? He is the Duke of Rothermere. Surely if he denied— You're his daughter, for God's sake. Didn't he stand by you?'

Kate laughed, a bitter little sound, and threw herself down on an adjacent sofa. 'My father wanted me to marry Anthony. When the whispers started he could easily have quashed them, but he chose not to, thinking that I would choose marriage over infamy.'

'And your aunt?'

It had taken until today for her to realise just how much hurt her aunt's failure to take her side had inflicted. Kate swallowed hard, and dashed a hand across her eyes. 'Sorry,' she said, lacing her fingers tightly together in an effort to regain control. She hated to cry.

'She took your father's view,' Virgil said flatly.

'Yes.' Her voice was tear-filled, but when Virgil looked as if he would comfort her, she shook her head. If he touched her— She could not risk tears. They had been so long pent-up, she was afraid she would not be able to stop them, and besides the fact that she did not wish Virgil to see her as a watering pot, she was horribly conscious of the fact that they could be interrupted at any moment.

'Kate, why did you break it off? You said you discovered you did not suit, but if things between you had become so intimate—you must at one point have believed you were in love?'

'Not in love, I told you it was an alliance. Compatible, I suppose is what I thought. I don't know what I thought, really. I was nineteen. I was curious. With hindsight, I think I was never sure that Anthony and I would suit, but at the time...' Kate sighed and rubbed her eyes. 'At the time, I believed that anticipating our vows would bring us closer together. I wanted affection from my husband, Virgil. I wanted him to care for me. He said he did. He said that it would be proof that he did, if I allowed him. But he didn't force me, not at first. I was stupid. Misguided. And I *wanted* to please. Anthony. My father. My aunt. I know you will think me weak-willed, I think it so myself now, but at the time...'

'At the time you were nineteen years old! What does anyone know of caution at that age?' Virgil exclaimed.

His angry tone grabbed her attention. 'You sound as if you speak from experience,' Kate said.

'I was nineteen when I spearheaded the rebellion which led to my being sold. I remember what it was like to be so sure of yourself that you can't see past your certainties. If someone had cautioned me...'

His eyes glazed as his voice faded. He was obviously lost in the past. Kate waited nervously. It was the first time he had confided in her without prompting, the first hint he had given her of the darkness which was his past. His expression hardened, then he blinked, and she could almost see him packing up whatever images he had conjured back into the boxes where he stored them. 'You said he did not force you at first,' he said, and she knew the moment was lost. 'What did you mean, Kate?'

She cleared her throat. Better to get it over with. 'He never forced me, not physically, but I did not enjoy our encounters as he seemed to, and when I tried to refuse him he told me I had surrendered the right to do so by consenting and that if I didn't want him to stray before we had even said our vows that I must…'

She resumed the pleating of her sash and spoke hurriedly, determined to get her confession out of the way, though with every word she felt herself diminishing, not just in Virgil's eyes but her own. 'It was that, you see. His threats. I realised then what being married to him would mean. If he could coerce me into this, what else would he wish from me? It is such a one-sided bargain, marriage. I would not have the right to gainsay him and I could not trust him.'

'He blackmailed you.'

The anger in Virgil's voice gave Kate courage. His anger made his skin seem stretched too tight across his face, emphasising the beauty of his bone structure, the strong jaw, the slanting lines of his cheeks. His eyes were dark, fierce. He looked like a warrior, a predator, frighteningly powerful, terrifyingly, fatally attractive. And he understood. At last, someone did understand. 'Yes,' Kate said gratefully.

'And your aunt—did you tell her the truth?' Virgil said grimly.

She dug her nails into her palms. 'I did.' Her voice was reduced to a whisper. 'Aunt Wilhelmina said that duty was not always pleasant.'

'She advised you to marry a man who was forcing himself on you?' Virgil swore viciously under his breath. 'It must have taken a hell of a lot of guts to break it off.'

'All the guts I had,' Kate said with a shaky laugh. 'But I did it, and—well, you know the consequences. Anthony put it about that I was unwomanly. He implied that the decision to call off the wedding was his, but that he had allowed it to appear to be mine because he was a gentleman. Until I met you I believed him. That's what frightened me this morning, and that's what made me angry, Virgil. And somehow, when I got angry it was like a release. I realised I was furious with my aunt, and so when the subject turned back on the whole affair this afternoon, I lost my temper and—and that's what we quarrelled about.'

She slumped back against the embroidered blue silk of the settee. She felt no sense of relief, only as if all the air had been let out of her. Deflated, that was the word. And tired. 'I thought I was done with it, and today made me realise that all I've been doing is burying it. I've been pretending it didn't matter when it does. My aunt is the nearest thing I have to a mother. Knowing I was right doesn't stop it hurting. And I behaved so stupidly. It is all very well to say I was just nineteen, but I can't run away from the fact that I was responsible. I wish I had not—but there is no point in wishing. No matter how hard I try, I can never be the person my family think I ought to be.' She paused. 'I wish you would say something, Virgil.'

He smiled at that. 'I like the person you are, though I doubt that's any consolation,' he said, getting up from his sofa and sitting beside her, putting his arm around her and pulling her against the comforting shelter of his shoulder. 'Before you say it, I don't give a damn if Lumsden walks in.'

His fingers stroked the exposed flesh between the puffed sleeve of her evening gown and the top of her kid gloves. The superfine of his coat was rough against her cheek. Kate let herself relax against him, closing her eyes, relishing his strength, his solidness, the smell of wool and linen and soap and deliciously musky man.

'It's been eleven years.'

He spoke so quietly that she thought at first she had misheard. 'What has?'

'You asked how long it's been since I made love. Eleven years, that's how long.'

Kate sat up. Virgil's eyes were dark, bleak. Her heart contracted. 'What happened?'

'I lost someone.'

'Oh, Virgil, I'm so sorry.'

'No. I don't want your pity. I just wanted you to know. This morning, you weren't the only one to worry about it being too much. I don't mean it was the same. It could never be the same. But I guess we both underestimated the strength of our attraction. I guess that was it.'

It could never be the same. That hurt, but did it also make sense of how she felt? 'Do you mean—is it possible to be so attracted without it meaning anything?'

Virgil's brow cleared. He smiled down at her, his mouth curling sensuously in a way that made her belly clench. He touched the skin below her ear, and she felt the pulse flutter under his fingers. Her breathing quickened. 'I think we've already proved that, don't you?'

'I thought it was different for women. One of the things which has always seemed to me most unfair is the way the world takes it for granted that men indulge their appetites. I assumed it was so because women are different.'

'It's not different. Didn't you ever—with that man?'

'Never.'

As Kate felt the flush creeping over her cheeks, Virgil's smile became positively devilish. 'It would be different with me. You can trust me.'

She was tempted, but it was too much. Kate jerked herself free and got to her feet. 'Can I? I don't think I'm the trusting type. And besides, you're leaving soon. I shan't see you again.'

'Isn't that the point?'

'I don't know what the point is. This morning you were as happy to call a halt as I. Tonight you seem to have changed your mind. I don't know whether I am on my head or heels.'

She made for the door, but Virgil grabbed her before she could open it. 'You're not the only one who's confused. You're not the only one with scars. Remember that.'

He flung open the drawing room door and strode out into the marble hall, startling Lumsden, who had been dozing in a chair. As the butler stumbled to his feet, Virgil made for the staircase which led downstairs, obviously intent on escape. Exhaustion hit Kate. She wanted nothing more than the comfort of her bed.

Despite having walked for over an hour round the grounds, Virgil was wide awake. He paced his room, then tossed restlessly in bed, going over the day's events. He had to admire Kate for her courage in confronting all that had happened head-on. It went against the grain with her to confide, he could see that, but that hadn't stopped her dealing with some very painful facts. She had real guts. And she was loaded down with guilt. That, too, he recognised.

How he'd like to get his hands on Lord Anthony Featherstone. The bastard deserved a hiding for what he'd done to Kate. And as to her family. That father of hers, who spent all his time these days hiding in his room and nursing his wounds instead of facing up to reality. And her aunt—she was the worst. She at least should have understood. The more he thought about it, the more he realised how much strength of will it must have taken for Kate to stick to her guns in the face of such opposition.

He hadn't asked what her brothers had thought of the matter. But five years ago both Giles and the dead heir, James, would have been abroad fighting. And the other one, Ned, the one whose name Kate could not say without crying. Most likely he'd been away, or too young to help. They were a patriotic lot, the Montagues. Shame they did not think to look closer to home for their battles. Though they had a hell of a fight on their hands now. Virgil had not given much thought to the implications of the dowager marchioness's claim to the dukedom on her son's behalf, but he suspended his anger long enough to wish the woman well. It would serve the Montagues right to have an heir foisted upon them.

It was dawn. Virgil sat on the window seat watching the early-morning mist swirl over the lakes. They were both confused, both scarred, he and Kate. Neither of them trusted their feelings. Neither of them wanted to feel, yet together there was such passion between them. What he felt for Kate was nothing like what he'd felt for Millie. Not love, but a desire so strong it had overwhelmed him yesterday. Too exhausted to pretend, he had to admit that he was tempted. He knew she was, too, though she would not trust him enough to admit it. And why should she, when he had given her no cause?

Worse. She had shown him her scars, and he had given her

almost nothing in return. He'd met her courage with a blank wall. His fingers traced the brand on his arm, shadowing how Kate had touched him. He reached behind him, feeling the welts of the whip marks beneath his linen nightshirt. He thought more of her, not less, for what she had revealed. But the mere thought of telling her all made him sick.

Outside, the mist had lifted. A slight figure dressed in white slipped like a wraith from the fishing pavilion and stood on the edge of the upper lake. Virgil opened the casement window, straining his eyes. The figure was poised, slim and female. His body knew, before his brain assimilated it, that he was watching Kate. She stretched her arms to the grey sky, then to his utter astonishment sprang into the air and dived into the water.

He was still fastening his buckskin breeches over his nightshirt as he ran barefoot down the curved corridor, where Kate's ancestors eyed him askance from their gilded frames. Down to the gloomy entrance hall, where the marble pillars were like a regulated forest in the shadowy light. Without caring who heard him, Virgil yanked open the locks and bolts on the heavy front door and sprinted towards the lake.

He couldn't see her. For one heart-stopping moment, he thought that she must have gone under, but then he remembered that graceful dive. She could obviously swim, but where was she? His feet sank into the mud, which oozed between his toes. The water was icy. There was an island about four hundred yards out, but it was a wild tangle of trees and bushes, impenetrable to the naked eye from here. A faint splash caught his attention. He would get a better view from the bridge, but if she needed help, then he'd be further away. He was being irrational; she could swim, she would be perfectly safe, Virgil told himself as he waded through the reeds until he was thigh-deep and dived in after her.

The cold took his breath away. His feet had stirred up mud and leaves, making the water cloudy. He came up for air spluttering, heading half blind towards the island. He had learned to swim in the creek at the plantation, where the water had been a delightfully refreshing relief from the summer humidity. The Castonbury lake was fed from water which originated in the Peaks. The cold gripped him like a vice, making his breathing painfully sharp. The water soaked the leather of his breeches, dragging his body downwards to the murky depths.

Virgil struck out with renewed determination. He was panting heavily as he reached the sandy banks of the little island. Chest heaving, water streaming from the tails of his nightshirt and the cuffs of his breeches, he forced his way through the bushes to the other side, just in time to see her at the far end of the lake, next to the bridge, heading back round. Unlike him, she seemed perfectly at home in the water. She swam with effortless grace, arm over arm, her head under the water, then up for air, sleek as an otter, cleaving through the lake with barely a ripple, clearly in no need of rescue. He watched her, thinking that he would be content to watch her for ever, while at the same time feeling excluded, shut out from whatever place it was her mind had gone to, for she seemed to make her way by some other sense than sight.

As she rounded the corner out of sight again, Virgil made his way back into the centre of the island in two minds. He wanted to call to her, but he didn't want to disturb what was obviously a customary swim and a private moment. He would wait until she circled back again, then he would make his own way back to shore without her seeing him. He felt foolish now at having come rushing out half naked to rescue someone in absolutely no need of help. There was a clearing in the middle of the shrubs and trees, a little hollow of ground quite hidden from view. A circle of blackened stones had obviously been used for a fire. Around it the ground was bare, packed dirt and sand, where the undergrowth had been worn away from use.

'We used to come here as children.' Virgil started. Kate was standing in the clearing behind him. He hadn't heard her approach. 'It's one of the few places at Castonbury out of Aunt Wilhelmina's reach,' she said. 'There's a box down by the beach with wood and kindling—will you help me fetch it?'

Virgil dragged the heavy chest through the undergrowth, and Kate opened the lid. She took out a quilt and handed another to him. 'You look as if you need this. I'm used to it, but I expect you found the water cold. What are you doing here?'

'I saw you dive in from the window of my bedchamber.'

'Did you think I needed rescuing?'

'Not once I saw you swimming. You're very...lovely.'

He'd meant to say *good* or *strong* or even *graceful*, but the truth slipped out before he could stop it. The quilt was draped over her shoulders. She wore what looked like underwear, a short, sleeveless cotton chemise and a pair of knee-length drawers. The sodden material clung to her figure, revealing tantalising glimpses of the pink flesh beneath, hugging every contour, from the swell of her breasts, the flare of her hips, to the dark cluster of curls between her long legs. Her nipples were hard peaks, clearly visible. Long damp tendrils of her hair had escaped the bun on top of her head and stuck to her throat, her neck, her cheeks. Water dripped from her lashes. It dripped from the ends of the ribbons which tied her drawers at her knees and at her neckline. 'Charybdis,' Virgil said with a smile, 'daughter of Poseidon.'

He still held the quilt folded in his hands. If he would wrap it around himself, then she wouldn't have to look at him, Kate thought. Dripping wet. His skin dark, glistening through his shirt. Was it a shirt? It looked more like a nightshirt. She should be cold, but under her skin she felt unaccountably hot. She laughed nervously. 'That's not very flattering. Charybdis makes whirlpools to drown men at sea.'

'I know, but she was once a nymph.'

'So it's a compliment?' It was the swimming which made her sound so breathless. It must be the swimming which was making her shaky too. She'd overdone it. Was it the swimming which was making her mouth dry? It was definitely the cold which was making her nipples ache. Virgil looked—oh, heavens, there was no getting away from it—he looked magnificent.

'I'll light a fire.' Kate hunkered down over the chest, fumbling for the kindling. 'You'll catch cold, else.' It didn't occur to her to suggest that Virgil would be better getting back to a warm bath and dry clothes.

'Let me.'

He tended to the fire efficiently and quickly. Of long habit, Kate sank onto the sandy hollow and pulled her quilt around her as the flames took life. Virgil had abandoned his quilt. The ridges of his whip marks could clearly be seen through his shirt. They were vicious, long welts, some overlapping.

More than one whipping or one particularly fierce event? He looked as if he'd been flayed. She swallowed the lump in her throat, determined not to show him she'd noticed.

Virgil dropped down beside her. Through the cold lake water, his body was already starting to emanate heat. 'Last night, it must have taken a great deal to say what you did,' he said.

Kate turned round to face him, dislodging the quilt from her shoulders. 'You don't despise me?'

'On the contrary. You are very hard on yourself, Kate.' Virgil wiped a drop of lake water from her cheek with his thumb. Her skin was softened by the water, chilly to touch, whereas he felt as if he were burning up. 'Yesterday, it wasn't that I was afraid of your reaction to my scars, I was afraid of my own.' He still was, but he could manage it. He could. He owed her this much. No, it was more than that, he wanted to show her. Virgil lifted up the hem of his nightshirt and pulled it over his head. 'These are not just from one whipping. I don't know how many. I lost count,' he said, swivelling round to show her his back.

Kate gasped. He wasn't surprised; he knew it was a horrific sight. He'd seen it reflected in the mirror, though it was a long, long time since he'd seen it reflected in anyone's face. 'At the slave market, it's what saved me.' The words came out stiff, cold, but at least they came out. 'It shows I lack discipline, you see. My scars, they mark me out as a rebel. A clean back would have brought a much higher price for Master Booth. This back, it's what made Malcolm Jackson buy me.'

'Why?' Kate asked.

Her voice was ragged with horror. She hadn't touched him. Virgil managed a shrug. 'He said it was because he saw a free spirit. A man with dreams, he said I was. A stubborn man.

A man who would fight for his cause. He took a chance on me, and I made sure it paid off.' Another debt. In Glasgow at least he would have the opportunity to pay that one in full.

Kate touched him. Virgil flinched at the unexpectedness of it. 'Did I hurt you?' she whispered.

'No.' These scars no longer ached, though what they stood for would hurt him always.

Kate's fingers traced the fretwork of lines, some threads, some thick like ropes, where his flesh had been opened and healed, opened and healed. The skin was tight in the bigger scars. It still pulled sometimes, tugged at him, wanting him to remember, making sure he could not forget. *You are not healed. You will never heal.* His scars spoke to him.

'Did you run away?' Kate asked.

Her hands smoothed over his back now, as if she would erase the mess, as if she would make him new. As if she could. He wished she could. Virgil nodded. 'Once. Mostly I refused to do as I was bid. Spoke when I wasn't supposed to. Looked them in the eye when they spoke. Once, they wanted me to fight and I wouldn't.'

'You mean box? Young Charlie was right?'

'No! I wouldn't fight. I saw Molineaux once. Prizefighting is how he earned his freedom in the end, but I wouldn't let myself be treated like that, like an animal. I never fought that way, but I fought them every other way. Working too slow. Not working. Working too fast. I learned to read and write and they didn't like that.'

'They whipped you because you could read?'

He would have laughed at the utter shock in her voice, only it hit him like a punch in the stomach that she was right. It *was* beyond belief. He'd survived because he hadn't let himself think about what was happening to him. He was afraid the horror of it would sap his strength. He had no energy to waste on railing against what he could not change. 'They whipped us for any reason, and for none at all, but the last time I guess I gave them cause. I led a rebellion.'

Talking of his plans to force concessions by striking, to add weight to their strike by spreading it through neighbouring plantations, Virgil remembered what he had forgotten all these years, that despite all the evidence to the contrary, he'd believed that reason would triumph. 'I thought if they could just be forced to see our point of view, they'd realise how wrong it all was.' He laughed bitterly. 'I thought that if we could show them we had some power, if they could see that we were strong enough to stand together, they'd realise they would have to change. I was so wrong.'

'What happened?' He could see she already knew. Could tell from the way she gripped her hands together in her lap that she wanted to be wrong.

'Just exactly what you think,' Virgil said with a twisted smile. 'It's one thing to make promises, another to keep them when you know what the consequences are likely to be. Some didn't strike. Some caved early.'

'But not you?'

If only he had. Virgil shook his head. 'Not me.' He told her of that final whipping. He told her about the hellhole. And then he stopped.

Kate swore long and viciously in response, words even Virgil would not have spoken. Then she wrapped her arms around him, and leaned her body against the breadth of his back. 'I would kill them.'

She took it for the end and he was too relieved to do anything but follow her lead. Her voice contained real menace. 'I believe you,' Virgil said. If it came to it, he doubted she would, but he believed she would want to, as he had, and it was a sweet revenge in its way, knowing that a duke's daughter wanted to do what he had chosen not to. His vengeance had been slow in coming, but it was worth every second of hard slog it had taken. He had proved himself better. Now he would make sure others like him could do the same.

He could feel Kate's breasts flattened against him. Her breath was warm on his neck. Her hands were wrapped around his body, her palms resting on his chest. 'We should get back,' he said, telling himself that he meant it.

Her arms tightened around him. 'No.'

She nestled closer. Despite the cold, Virgil's manhood stirred to life. 'Kate…'

'Did you tell me all that to show me I can trust you?'

'And because I wanted to.'

'Do you want *me*, Virgil?'

The evidence of just how much he wanted her was taking solid shape in the chafing leather of his buckskins. 'You know I do.' He twisted around in her embrace. Her mouth was soft, trembling, pink. Her eyes were grey rather than blue. 'Kate, I don't want to hurt you. I would never use you or force you or any of the things you're afraid of, but if you're not sure…'

'I am. I think I am.'

Was he? He was sure he wanted her. He was sure it was different. The power of it came from passion heightened by abstinence, not love. But his abstinence had been one of the sources of his strength. Still, he wanted her and there were ways for both of them to have what they wanted without risk. Without compromise. Without hurt. He did want her. He was so tired of fighting it.

Virgil wrapped his arms around her and pulled her down onto the quilt which had fallen from her shoulders, and kissed her.

Was she sure? Kate locked her arms around Virgil's neck and kissed him back. She was sure of him. Sure she wanted him. Sure she wanted what she had never had, what Anthony had taken from her.

He tasted of lake water. His lips were warm against hers. He rolled her onto her back and covered her body with his own. So large. Kissing, she stroked the breadth of his shoulders, then let her fingers flutter over the tortuous mess of his back. And so powerful. His kisses heated her. His hands on her face, her shoulders, her breasts, made her shiver in anticipation.

He kissed her deeply, his tongue thrusting into her mouth, then tangling with hers, teasing, tasting, then taking again. He kissed her neck, her throat, the valley between her breasts. The damp cotton of her chemise clung stubbornly to her body, but he was patient, untying the ribbons and buttons, feasting on each inch of skin as he opened it. Hot mouth on cold nipples. She arched up in delight, for his actions connected straight to her throbbing sex.

He kissed her lips again, as if he couldn't get enough of her mouth, and that, too, delighted her. She watched him avidly as he kissed his way back down between her breasts, cupping them, his thumbs stroking, as his mouth nipped and licked at her ribs, her belly. Skin. The delicious abrasion of his skin on hers. Was there anything more delightful?

There was. The ribbons on her drawers were knotted. When she would have torn them, he untied them with care, easing them down her legs. His face was taut, his eyes glittering, fierce and focused. The way he looked at her filled her with the most glorious sensation. She knew herself powerful. She knew herself wanted. Truly wanted. She let him look, made shameless with his need, her own need making her wanton. She kept her eyes open, fixed on him, his hands, his face, his mouth, his body.

She fumbled with the fastenings of his buckskins, but the leather was so wet her fingers could make no sense of them. She could have cried out in frustration but Virgil saved her, sitting up, quickly dispensing with buttons and falls, pulling them down his long, muscled legs.

He was utterly naked. Kate looked. She had seen a naked man before. She knew what an erect member looked like. She had been curious enough to look, and Anthony had been determined that she touch, but this was different. She'd thought the male body strange. Ugly, almost. Now, fascinated by the differences between them, she thought Virgil simply beautiful.

He sat down on the quilt opposite her and pulled her to him so that they were facing, her legs over his thighs. They studied each other, touching, tracing their shapes with their fingertips, exploring. They kissed. Virgil cupped her breasts, kissed her nipples. Kate arched back, her heels digging into the sandy floor of the hollow behind his back. He touched her belly. He kissed her again. He stroked her flanks, and then the soft flesh inside her thighs.

But when he began to stroke into the folds of her sex, she tensed, and Virgil stopped. 'What's wrong?' he asked.

'I'm afraid I'll fail you,' Kate whispered.

'Did *he* say that?' Virgil swore. 'Kate, *he* failed *you*.'

He tilted her chin up, forcing her to meet his eyes. 'What do you mean?' she asked.

'Just trust me.' He kissed her. He kissed her breasts. Then he kissed her mouth again. When her breath came shallow against his, he eased her back and stroked her thighs. Then stroked again, and slid easily past the folds of her sex and inside her. She gasped. Her muscles tensed around his finger. He eased into her a little more.

'Do you like this?' he asked. When she nodded, he took her hand and wrapped it around his shaft. They both stared, fascinated by the contrast of her skin on his.

The muscles in Virgil's belly tightened. His erection thickened. He eased his finger higher inside her, seeing from the way her eyes widened that she liked it. 'Stroke me, like this,' he said, showing her, for he had no faith in her previous experience, and was glad, if he was honest, that she seemed so unsure.

She did as he asked; he had to close his eyes to hold himself back. 'Again,' he said, thrusting into her as she stroked, watching her as she touched him and he touched her. He could see his desire reflected in her eyes. It was intoxicating. He could see that she found it so too. He kissed her. Her lips were hard on his now, her tongue thrusting into his mouth.

Kissing. Stroking. Thrusting. 'This,' Virgil said, pushing harder and higher with his fingers, stroking over the smooth moist nub of her with his thumb, 'this is what you're doing to me.' He could feel her swelling. He could feel himself thickening, pulsing. Her face was a mixture of confusion and delight. The knowledge that in this way he would be her first gave him immense satisfaction. He thrust and stroked and stroked and thrust, and then he kissed her, claiming her mouth with his tongue as she tightened around him and cried out, the pulsing heat of her, and the taste of her, and the feel of her hand, her fingers, on the length of him sending him over the edge seconds later, dragging a deep moan from his depths as he spilled his seed onto her hand and she slumped against him.

* * *

Solid. Virgil was so solid. Kate clung to him as if she were drowning. She felt as if she had been broken apart. Her body throbbed, wave after wave of sensation rippling out from the heat between her legs up, down, making her lightheaded, dizzy. She had been so furled tight and now she was—she didn't know what she was. Unsprung? Was that a word? Like a clock which had been overwound. What she felt was red and sparkling and bright, bright, bright. Like a shower of sparks. A cascade. Her heart was pounding against Virgil's chest. Or it was his heart. His hands on her back, his arms circling her so easily. When she wrapped her arms around him like this, her hands struggled to meet. His skin was like velvet, not soft, not rough, just velvet. Except his back. She traced his scars. She smoothed his scars. She nestled her face into the crook of his neck and kissed him. He smelled of lake and sweat and what they had just done. She didn't know a name for it. No, Polly had given her several names, all of them far too vulgar-sounding for what she'd just experienced. It most certainly didn't feel the least like a tickle.

Virgil hadn't shaved; his chin was rough with stubble, though she could barely see it. She didn't want to spoil the moment, but she had to ask the question which had been bothering her most of the night. 'The girl you lost, did you love her?'

He tensed. 'Yes.'

It was terrible of her, horrible, but Kate's first emotion was jealousy. Virgil had loved someone. It was like picking at a scar, but she had to know. 'How did you lose her?'

He put her from him, and got up, pulling his breeches on. His face was hard, his eyes hooded. 'We should get dressed.'

'I thought you trusted me.' It was unfair of her. She could tell from the set of his shoulders, from the way he held himself, tight, the muscles on his abdomen clenched so hard she could count them. Kate scrabbled to her feet and began to drag her sopping swimming attire on. 'Don't answer that. I didn't mean it. I shouldn't have said it.'

'No, you shouldn't.'

She had as well cut the connection between them with a knife, but what had she expected? It was just physical, what they had shared. Pleasure, nothing more. It was not life-changing or any other sort of changing. They were still the same two people, scarred and confused both of them. She had acquired no extra rights over him.

Virgil folded the quilts and tamped down the fire as she struggled with her buttons and ribbons. He picked up the heavy chest and disappeared down to the beach to return it to its hiding place.

'I can fetch the rowing boat, if you don't wish to take another wetting,' she said when he returned.

'Don't be ridiculous.' Virgil ran his hand through his cropped hair. 'She died. Her name was Millie, and she died. It's not a question of trust, Kate. It's none of your business.'

She was shivering as she followed Virgil down to the water's edge and began to wade in to the lake. Virgil dived in and began to swim in a powerful if rather splashy style for the shore. Kate took her time. Swimming always helped her think. Virgil was right, Millie was long dead and none of her business, but she wished all the same that she could ask more. What happened to her? Were they separated when Virgil was sold, or had she died before? Eleven years ago he'd only been nineteen. The same age as she had been when she'd broken her betrothal. Just a boy. No. Nineteen years on a plantation would have made a man of him many years before then.

Whatever had happened had scarred him more deeply than

the savage marks on his back, that much was certain. Perhaps that was why his lovemaking had taken the form it had. They had not been truly joined. She was not Millie. Virgil, thank goodness, was not Anthony. Though those first few times with her betrothed, she hadn't been completely indifferent. She'd forgotten that. Funny, but what she remembered until now had been boredom, indifference morphing into pain and humiliation, but in the early days she'd been interested enough to feel let down afterwards, disappointed. Now she knew what she'd been missing, she could quite see that what she'd experienced back then was a shadow of what it could have been.

Virgil was wading onto the grass at the side of the lake. As she walked towards him, she could almost touch the barricade he seemed to have erected around himself. He wanted to be alone. 'Go back to the house,' she said. 'I have dry things in the changing room below the fishing pavilion—there is no need for you to wait for me.'

He hesitated, then turned away. Kate watched him go. On the horizon, in direct contradiction of her own mood, the sun began to break through.

A few days later, despite the cold which hinted at the winter to come, Kate and Virgil walked through the woods to the village. Finally, the visit to the school had been arranged. Conversation between them was stilted at first, but their shared enthusiasm for Robert Owen's educational experiment soon broke down any awkwardness.

The Castonbury school was a single-storey purpose-built building with an enclosed garden to the rear. The local vicar, the adopted father of Lily, Giles's betrothed, awaited them with Miss Thomson, the schoolmistress, in the bright entranceway. 'Mr Jackson, it is an honour.' Reverend Seagrove was a portly man whose benevolence was writ large on his beaming countenance, and his handshake was as warm as his smile was genuine. 'Lady Kate, always a pleasure. And this is Miss Thomson.'

The schoolmistress dropped a shy curtsey. Allowing the vicar to do the honours, for he was every bit as proud of the school as she was, Kate watched Virgil's reaction on tenterhooks.

The school room itself was spacious, with two rows of desks separated by a central aisle. The children were ranked, with the littlest ones at the front and the eldest at the back. The entire wall at the rear of the room was covered with a depiction of the two central hemispheres, and a large globe stood beside them. Light streamed through the long windows, and every other bit of wall space was taken up with bright pictures of animals and wildlife, both familiar and exotic. The atmosphere was happy and relaxed. The children were smiling, clean and alert. As he followed the vicar and the schoolmistress around the room, watching as Miss Thomson led a spirited history lesson which included a battle re-enactment, Virgil was extremely impressed.

'Mr Owen believes that a happy child will be more receptive to learning,' Reverend Seagrove said, beaming at him, as the children gathered round a table for morning milk. 'We try to mix some play with our lessons. It is not good for the children to be seated at their desks for hours on end.'

'You have quite an age range here,' Virgil said to Miss Thomson, 'how do you manage?'

'We have the older children help the littlest ones with their reading and numbers, and I have a young woman who helps me three days a week,' the schoolteacher replied, blushing.

'Lady Kate is eager to recruit another full-time teacher,'

Reverend Seagrove said, 'but we must first persuade the villagers of the benefits of keeping their children in school past working age. Unfortunately, Mr Jackson, many families depend upon their children's income, and do not have the foresight to understand that the income could be significantly increased in the future were they permitted to learn more.'

'What about educating the parents?' Virgil asked.

Miss Thomson looked shocked, but Reverend Seagrove was much struck with this idea. 'Lady Kate has been telling me all about Mr Owen of New Lanark. I believe he has established some form of institute which purports to offer an education to the adult members of his community.'

'It is that aspect of New Lanark I'm most interested in,' Virgil replied. 'Without learning, you can never be free to choose.'

'Most profound, if I may say so,' the vicar said, nodding vehemently. 'I will use that for a sermon, if I may.' He smiled at Kate. 'Perhaps we shall persuade the good people of Castonbury that there is a place for grown men in the schoolroom, after all.'

'And grown women, too, I hope,' Kate replied drily.

Reverend Seagrove chuckled. 'Quite right, my dear. What do you think, then, of our little school, Mr Jackson?'

'I think it's a lot more than a *little* school. Your ideas are revolutionary.'

'Lady Kate's ideas, for the most part,' Reverend Seagrove said. 'It was she who insisted on our modern heating system. Most of our patrons felt it quite unnecessary to heat a school room. And the lessons, too, the participative elements you have seen...'

'Come, Reverend Seagrove, you are making me blush. I merely followed Mr Owen's tenets. I could never have raised the funds without your help, and while I am happy to take some credit for the principles upon which we teach, it is Miss Thomson here who has put them into practice.'

'Then you are a remarkable team,' Virgil said seriously. 'You should all be proud of Castonbury school. You've given me much food for thought.'

Kate's family were by degrees mildly interested, dismissive and scathing of the hard work she had invested in this enterprise. Many of the children's parents had taken a great deal of persuading to allow their offspring to attend. While Reverend Seagrove and Miss Thomson had been unfailingly supportive and the school's board of governors were slowly coming round to the ethos upon which it had been established, she was quite unused to praise. She had never doubted the worth of what she was doing, but having someone else perceive it and credit her with some of its success almost overset her. She had tried to pretend it didn't matter what anyone thought. She had mostly succeeded. But it did matter, and Virgil's opinion, whether she wanted to admit it or not, meant more than anyone's.

'Lady Kate does not know what to do with compliments,' Virgil said to Reverend Seagrove, seeing her blush, 'but nonetheless, I must tell you all, I think this is a remarkable place.'

Replete and revived by their morning victuals, the first awe which had overwhelmed them upon meeting their American visitor dissipated, the children gathered around Virgil, clamouring for stories, besieging him with questions, not all of which had any grounding in reality, having arisen from the various stories they had heard at home. Receiving Miss Thomson's assent, he sat down on the floor with them in a circle around him and told them stories of the New World.

It was as if he wove a spell, Kate thought, watching. He held them captive, enthralled and yet totally at ease, just exactly as he had done with the servants at Castonbury. His tales of Anansi the spider were not what the school's board of governors would call nice. They were subtly subversive, exactly the kind of story to make the children laugh gleefully, at the triumph not of good over bad, but of small over large.

'I meant it, Kate,' Virgil said as they made their way back through the woods at Castonbury afterwards. 'You should be proud of what you have achieved there. I gather from the reverend that it was no easy task to persuade some of the villagers to send their children to school rather than into employment.'

'There is so much more I'd like to do.'

'There is always more. You cannot do it all.'

'Yet that is exactly what you aim to do, judging by the plans you were discussing with Reverend Seagrove. I hadn't realised they were so far-reaching. It sounds as if you wish to take on the burden of educating every freed slave in America.'

'It's the least I can do.'

She was startled by the sudden weariness in his tone. 'You sound as if you carry the burden of slavery upon your own shoulders. *You*, of all people, have nothing to feel guilty about.'

'Kate, you don't know what you're talking about.'

The atmosphere which had come between them since the morning at the lake returned. 'Virgil, I…'

'Kate, we need to talk.'

She almost panicked. The past two nights had been spent assuring herself that what had happened between them had been purely physical. It had been intensely pleasurable, but it meant nothing more. By day, she could maintain a calm front, assuring herself that nothing had changed save she knew herself capable of pleasure. By day, she had the strength of her conviction. By night, she was as weak as a kitten. And it frightened her.

She had not loved Anthony, but she had cared for him and hoped to learn to love him. What she had discovered was that her feelings could be easily abused, she herself easily manipulated as a result. It had taken her five years to regain control of that life. She was *damn* sure she wasn't going to do an about-turn and hand her heart over to a man who not only swore he could never care for her, but in a few weeks hence would be on the other side of the world. She almost panicked, because for a terrible moment she thought Virgil was about to declare himself, and for an even more terrible moment she thought herself about to accept him. Then she saw his face. Tight. Controlled. Fierce. And she knew she'd got it quite wrong.

'You are leaving?' she said with a sinking heart, because it was the only other thing she could think of.

'You know I am, sometime before that claimant to the Castonbury throne arrives, but that's not what I wanted to discuss.'

'What, then?'

'Is there somewhere we can be private near here?'

'There is the orangery, but I think Wright is still working there. Or the fishing pavilion.'

They walked quickly and in silence. The pavilion sat over the lake with a view out to the island, a small square building which smelled of damp wood. Not the most romantic of places, Kate thought, then told herself that was exactly as it should be. An odd assortment of chairs and stools were huddled together by the window.

She sat in a wooden ladderback chair, but Virgil remained standing. He paced the room like a restless tiger, abstractedly inspecting fishing tackle, picking up a piece of rope and working a knot in it free. Casting it aside, he pulled a three-legged stool over to sit opposite her. 'Millie,' he said resolutely, 'I need to tell you about Millie. You need to understand, Kate, how impossible it is that there could ever be anything between us.'

'Virgil, I already understand that.'

Did she? The problem was, the difficulty was that he wasn't sure *he* did, not after—no, don't think about that. Virgil felt like a knight who had voluntarily laid down his armour thinking the battle won, only to discover that another was starting and his armour no longer fit. He could not allow Kate to penetrate his defences. What he needed to do was to remind himself of that. And if that meant the brutal truth, peeling back his scars to the raw flesh to remind himself, then that is what he would do.

He loosened his neck cloth. This was the only way. He had to close it down, this thing between them. He had to find a way to stop himself thinking of her, dreaming of her, *wanting* her. He had to get her out of his mind. This was for his sake, but even to say so would give her the wrong idea.

'Kate.' Virgil caught himself. Don't say her name, not like that! He tried again. 'Kate.' Better. She looked…anxious. Couldn't be helped. He could do it. The pain would cauterise whatever it was he was feeling, stop it in its tracks. *Damn it*, he had to do it. Virgil breathed deep, as if to dredge it all up from his guts. He felt sick. Good. That was good.

He closed his eyes. Another deep breath and he was back in the South. Harvest time. He opened his eyes and forced himself to look at Kate. Her face had that fierce look, her brows drawn together, her fine features pinched with concentration. Good. Good.

'There's a heaviness to the air in Virginia in the summer that saps your energy,' he began. 'Everything smells ripe, rotten. There's an art to getting the tobacco leaves in at just the right time, to having them dried in the sheds and packed in the hogsheads ready for the ships arriving so you can get the best price. If you leave them on the plants too long, you lose them.'

'That was why you chose to strike then. I remember you saying so.'

'Yes. As the time passed, the end was inevitable. I saw the men's resolve crumbling, Kate. I could almost taste their fear, but I hung on.'

'And you were punished.' She reached for his hand, but he brushed her away. He couldn't touch her. He would not have her comfort; he did not deserve her admiration. He would put an end to that. 'I was so damned certain I was right. They stuck by me, the men at the Booth place. God forgive me for that. They stuck by me long past the time when I thought we'd have been sure to win, but I hadn't counted on Master Booth's sheer determination, and I hadn't counted on his being smart enough to know that if he conceded just one thing it would be the end. I thought we had the most to lose, but I was wrong. When they sent men from the neighbouring plantations to do our jobs, I knew we'd lost. Yes, they whipped us. They flayed me so badly I thought I would die, but you'd be amazed just how much punishment a body can take.'

There was a sheen of tears in Kate's eyes. He could see her struggling valiantly not to let them fall. How she hated to cry. 'You mustn't feel guilty,' she said. 'Those other men, I'm sure they didn't blame you.'

'That's not it.' Tension enhanced the drawl in his voice, brought out the distinctive accent of the South. He held himself rigid on the stool.

'What else?' Kate asked.

There was doubt in her voice. She didn't want to hear. That was good. He didn't want to tell, but it was too late now to call a halt. 'Millie,' Virgil said. 'We weren't married. Some of the plantation owners encouraged it—they figured a family man was less likely to run away and they could always sell the children for profit, though it didn't stop them splitting those same families up if it suited them—but Master Booth wasn't one who went along with that view. He thought family ties made us more rebellious. We weren't married, but we planned to be.'

Kate flinched. Her eyes were dark, her skin not so much creamy as pale. She hadn't expected that, obviously. She didn't like it. Because she cared? He couldn't let himself think that way. Hell, that was the whole point.

Virgil tugged at his neck cloth and it came away in his hand. He began to wrap the length of linen round his knuckles, pulling it tight. 'Millie, she was mightily against our uprising. She begged me not to do it, but I was so sure I knew best. It was for our future, I told her.' He cleared his throat. 'What I did, it made sure we didn't have a future.'

He told her, and in the telling it was like it was happening again, fresh and stark, every detail etched on his memory, waiting all these years to be released for the first time. The sting of the sun blinding him as he emerged from the hellhole. The way fear tasted, sharp like sweat. Apprehension morphing into disbelief, then horror, as he saw his fellow slaves lined up. The look on Master Booth's face. On Harlow, the overseer's. And Millie. Millie's face. Millie calling his name. Millie, suffering for his crimes. Millie paying for his insubordination. 'They knocked me out. I heard her screaming, I tried to get to her, but they knocked me out. I couldn't get to her. I tried, but I couldn't get to her. I couldn't save her.'

His voice cracked, be he made himself finish. 'When I came back to consciousness, I thought it was over. I knew I would be sold. I thought most likely they'd send me north, because my reputation was too bad to make me anything but worthless in the South. I planned to come back for her. I wanted to tell her but they wouldn't let me see her. I never got to tell her. I thought she would know, but by the next morning—by the morning—it was too late. She killed herself.'

The agony of it all, which he had locked away, which he had kept so firmly tamped down, weighting it with the sheer slog which had been his determination to succeed, binding it tight with the penance which was at the root of his philanthropy, overwhelmed him. Virgil dropped his head in his hands.

Eight

Dry, hacking sobs echoed around the small room. Virgil's shoulders heaved. Kate had never before seen a man in such agony. That it was this man, so powerful, so seemingly invincible, made it all the more unbearable to watch. She ached for him, but she knew better than to offer him comfort. She wiped her own tears away frantically. What he had told her was beyond anything she had imagined. *Why* he had put himself through the trauma of reliving it, she could not quite understand.

Her own feelings strained at the leash she had put around them, like hunting dogs fresh on a scent. It was an enormous effort to control them, but she knew she could not afford to fail. That Virgil may be struggling, too, she had not for a moment imagined. Was he afraid, as she was?

Looking at his hunched, distraught figure, the horror of his story fresh in her mind, Kate could not believe that. Such a trauma would surely sever all emotions for ever. No wonder he had chosen celibacy. No wonder he had been so reserved since the island. He obviously felt he had been unfaithful to

Millie's memory. *It could never be the same*, he'd said. She understood that fully now. It hurt. It was good that it hurt. He'd put himself through this for her sake, Kate realised. He knew she was not indifferent. He'd seen what she would not admit to herself. His seeing made her realise how far from indifferent she had allowed herself to become. But it was not too late.

Virgil got to his feet and stared out of the window. Kate joined him, close but not touching. There was a heron on the lake shore, its wings spread to dry. When he began to speak again, his voice was flat, drained, exhausted. 'So now you know it all. I killed her. My stubbornness, my ambition, my certainty, killed the woman I loved. If I had listened to her, if I'd thought for one moment about the consequences of what I was doing, I wouldn't have done it. Surely to God, I wouldn't have done it.'

Kate stared at him, stunned. He couldn't possibly blame himself, but he quite obviously did. 'You can't have guessed what they would do to her!'

'I should have. It wasn't the first time I'd been whipped for insurrection, and this was one hell of an insurrection. We must have scared them. A whipping was never going to be enough, and I knew when they put me in the hellhole that they weren't going to hang me. I should have known.'

'No!' Kate exclaimed, the single word rebounding violently round the wooden walls of the pavilion. 'How can you say that? Virgil, for goodness' sake, if anyone is to blame it is that man, Booth.'

'I put myself first. I didn't think about her. The woman I wanted to marry, and I didn't think about her. It's not a lesson I ever want to repeat. When they told me she was dead—then I felt flayed. I don't ever want to go through that again, Kate. Do you understand that?'

There could be no mistaking the warning note in his voice. Though it hurt her, Kate told herself the pain was welcome. It was a warning she would be a fool to ignore. 'You could not be clearer, Virgil. I assure you, I understand completely. How could I not? What you have suffered…'

'I don't want your pity,' he exclaimed sharply. 'What I've suffered is nothing. I wanted to kill them at first, when I was in the hellhole, before it—before Millie—but I knew there was a better way. When Malcolm Jackson brought me to Boston, I felt like providence had finally given me a card I could play. I would show them I was better than them, and I have. Better. Stronger. More powerful. And I did it on my terms.'

'That's what's driven you all these years?'

'That's part of it. I've had my revenge. Now I can make good for what I did to Millie.'

There was so much, too much, for her to assimilate. Kate smiled weakly. 'With schools?'

'And homes. And work. A library. I don't know what else.'

Emotional isolation, Kate thought. Physical deprivation. 'So I was right,' she said instead. 'You do want to take on the burden of providing a future for every freed slave in America. How will you know when you've done enough, Virgil? When will you have paid?'

'I took a life. How can I ever repay that?'

'Millie took her own life,' Kate said gently.

'Because of me.'

She would not have given up, Kate thought, but bit her tongue. How could she possibly tell what she would have done? She could not even begin to put herself in Millie's position. 'You were nineteen, Virgil. "What does anyone know of caution at that age?" That's what you said to me, remember? Don't you think it's time to forgive yourself?'

Virgil had been leaning against the wooden wall. Now he stood up, rolling his shoulders. 'Don't you think you should be asking yourself that question?'

He sounded utterly drained. Kate, too, felt quite empty save for a gnawing sense of loss. She caught his hand and rubbed it against her cheek. 'I can't begin to tell you—to imagine...' She blinked furiously. No tears. 'It wasn't your fault, Virgil. I wish you could see that, but I can see there is no point in my trying to persuade you. What I'm trying to say is, I understand. Why you told me, I mean. You have no cause to worry, I understand completely.'

They agreed that it would be for the best that he leave Castonbury and continue north with his planned visit to New Lanark sooner rather than later. Paradoxically, the certainty that he was leaving and the knowledge that his truly shocking history made the very notion that he could care for her impossible allowed Kate to admit to herself that she *had* begun to care for him. Virgil's tortured confession had torn at her heart, but the warning behind it had been entirely effective. She had no option now but to pull herself back from the precarious brink upon which she had, quite obliviously, been teetering.

'Yes,' she agreed as they walked back to the great house from the fishing pavilion, 'it is for the best that you leave.' But saying what she ought and accepting its consequences were two different things. She had never been inclined to melancholy, but she could sense its grey mantle hovering over her as she pictured a Virgil-less Castonbury. 'Though now we are in accord, perhaps there is no need for you to go straight away,' she said cautiously.

Beside her, she sensed Virgil hesitating. 'I do have some business I haven't had the chance to tie up for Giles. And there is the Buxton assembly the day after tomorrow, if you still wish to go?'

They could dance together. Since no one else was like to ask her, they would be obliged to dance together, Kate thought. 'There can be no harm in us dancing, surely.'

'Surely,' Virgil agreed with a semblance of a smile. 'I shall make arrangements to leave the following morning. In fact, I think I'll walk back to the village and book a place on the mail right now.'

It was not that he was eager to be rid of her, Kate told herself as she watched him striding off. Were he so, he would not have agreed to stay a moment longer at Castonbury than necessary. This business with Giles could be quickly concluded. And as to the dance…

She had mentioned it to no one. Not even Aunt Wilhelmina knew she was considering attending with only Virgil as a chaperon. She had assumed that Virgil would invite Giles and Lily, but he had not. Under other circumstances, of course, she would have suggested it herself, but with Virgil leaving Castonbury so soon, this would be their last chance to be alone together. Alone together in a crowded ballroom, that is, but at least they would be free of the oppressive atmosphere which prevailed whenever Aunt Wilhelmina and Virgil were in the same room.

Kate's mood lightened a fraction. She would not ask permission. She was four-and-twenty; there was no need for her to ask permission of anyone. She would order the carriage for after dinner, and she would wear her best dress, and she would hold her head high in front of all who snubbed her, and she would dance with Virgil for the first and last time.

'What will you wear tonight, my lady?' Polly's head poked over the screen behind which Kate was bathing in a large copper tub in front of the fire. 'The claret velvet? Or what about the green silk with the French trim? Only I heard His Grace was joining you, so you'll want something a bit grander than usual.'

Kate dropped the lavender-scented soap into the water. 'My father is coming to dinner?'

'So I heard downstairs. Didn't Mrs Landes-Fraser tell you?'

Kate made a wry face. 'I've been avoiding my aunt today. The truth is, Polly, that I'm going to the assembly at Buxton tonight, and I haven't told her.'

'You're going dancing?' Polly edged around the screen, her eyes narrowed. 'You never go to public assemblies. *Why* haven't you told that aunt of yours? Who is escorting you?'

Kate picked up a large sponge and set about soaping it industriously. 'Mr Jackson.'

Polly swore colourfully. 'You've got some brass. They'll never let you go, especially not now that His Grace will be at dinner.'

'I don't see how it makes the slightest bit of difference. Virgil—Mr Jackson—has been a guest in this house for some time, and my father has shown absolutely no inclination to meet him. Yet on the eve of his departure…'

'So that's it,' Polly exclaimed.

'What do you mean?'

'Come on, my lady, you don't fool me. He's leaving tomorrow. It's a last fling, isn't it?'

'I don't know what you mean by *fling*…'

Polly pursed her lips. 'I think you do—leastways, I think you know more about it now than you did before your Mr Jackson came to visit.'

'He is not my Mr Jackson.'

'No, nor likely ever to be. His Grace would have you banished.'

'It has nothing to do with my father, Polly. Mr Jackson is not—we are not— There is no question of such a thing. We are friends, merely. And he's leaving tomorrow.'

'And you want one last night with him, and I don't blame you. If he was mine—'

'He is *not* mine,' Kate interrupted, trying not to notice the wistful note in her own voice.

Polly ignored her. 'Right, then. The blue crepe, I think—you've never worn it. Have you ordered the carriage? Good. Now, let's get your hair washed. We need to make sure you look your best.'

Two hours later, Kate stood in front of the looking glass. Her gown of celestial blue crepe was worn over a white satin slip and trimmed with a deep border of tulle embroidered with silks and chenille in a variety of contrasting shades. The sleeves were puffed, the décolleté low, trimmed with net lace and tulle, which frothed seductively over her tightly laced bosom. Polly had dressed her hair high on her head, teasing several wispy curls out from the severe chignon, which suited her far better than the fashionable Grecian styles. She wore only pearls—a tight choker with a diamond clasp around her throat, several bracelets over her French kid gloves and a pair of pearl and diamond drops in her ears. Her silk slippers were the same celestial blue as her gown. Her chemise was white silk, as were her stockings, though they were white tied with dark blue garters, the same colour as her corset.

Kate smiled with satisfaction. 'I look very well. Thank you, Polly.'

'You look lovely.' Polly handed Kate her reticule. 'Don't you dare lose courage, my lady. No matter what His Grace says.'

'No,' Kate said with far more conviction than she felt. She took a last look in the mirror. Her heart was fluttering with excitement. Anyone would think she was a girl making her debut, not a grown woman, for goodness' sake. 'Wish me luck, Polly.'

'Knock 'em dead, my lady. And if you don't,' Polly said grimly, 'I will.'

Though she knew that Virgil's valet would have been as well-informed as Polly regarding the duke's presence, Kate made sure to be the first in the drawing room. They saw so little of her father since Jamie and Ned had died, that at times she quite forgot all about him. Smithins, His Grace's proprietorial valet, kept him abreast of household matters, but as her father's health deteriorated so, too, had his interest in these affairs. Giles, she knew, kept the duke in ignorance of a great deal of his worries for fear of the effect it would have on him. She suspected that Smithins, too, filtered out much of the household gossip. Though the impending arrival of the child he already claimed for his grandson had revived the duke somewhat, Kate was rather astonished at his decision to take dinner *en famille* tonight. Virgil's last night. Could it be that her father actually felt guilty at not having met the man who had been his guest? No, she thought with a curl of her lip, more likely her father wished to flaunt his heritage at an American who, she had no doubt Aunt Wilhelmina would have informed him, had not a drop of aristocratic blood in his body.

'Have you heard?' Giles stormed into the room, looking harassed. 'Our father has deigned to join us for dinner tonight.

I tried to stop him, but he was insistent. Said he wanted to meet the American, something about showing him how the Old World did things.'

'Oh, Lord, are we to dine in state, then?'

'Heaven knows how many courses. At least it will give that Frenchman who rules the kitchens something to do. Didn't you know? I thought you must, when I saw you in your finery.'

Kate took the glass of Madeira gratefully. 'This, brother dear, is a ball gown,' she said. 'I thought you were a connoisseur of women's clothing too.'

Giles grinned. 'Those days are well in the past now. I'm a happily— What do you mean, a ball gown?'

'I'm going to the Buxton assembly. It was all arranged before I discovered our revered sire was joining us.'

'*I* never heard anything. Who is escorting you?'

'Virgil.'

It was not often that her brother was at a loss for words. Kate raised an eyebrow at him, and sipped her Madeira.

'You can't!'

'Why ever not?'

'Kate, I know you have no time for the proprieties...'

'Why should I? I am a ruined woman, as my aunt never fails to point out. For heaven's sake, Giles, it is a public ball. No one would bat an eye were you to go unescorted.'

'You wouldn't catch me dead there, unless I was dragged kicking and screaming.'

'Which is quite beside the point. You cannot have it both ways, you know. Either I am ruined and it matters not what I do, or what I did with Anthony Featherstone did not ruin me and therefore does not matter.'

'Sophistry, sister dear!' Giles drummed his fingers on the

high mantel, where he had taken up his accustomed position, standing with his back to the fire. 'You are set on this?'

Kate nodded.

'May I ask why?'

'I am tired of allowing the opinions of others to decide my actions. Anthony is happily married and, as ever, the darling of society. I did nothing more than he did. Less, for I did not talk. Why should I continue to pay when he does not? It's not fair.'

'Kate, it's how things are,' Giles said with a sigh. 'If you wish to return to society, why did you not discuss it with me? With my sponsorship—'

'Had Papa and Aunt Wilhelmina *sponsored* me five years ago, you would not have to offer now.'

'You feel they let you down?' Giles nodded slowly. 'Yes, I can see that you do, and I admit you have cause. Had I been here—'

'But you were not, and I doubt you'd have persuaded Papa to listen back then, in any case.'

'You do see, Kate, that turning up without any female to lend you countenance, in the company of an unmarried man, and one who moreover is not even related to you—'

'And an *American* into the bargain,' Kate interjected sarcastically.

'It has nothing to do with his heritage,' Giles said. 'Virgil Jackson is the kind of man who will be treated with respect wherever he goes. What do you think we've been doing while you've been setting the Dower House to rights? There's barely a house in the county Virgil hasn't visited with me, and in every single one he's been well received, not to say downright toad-eaten. I'll wager he's plagued with invitations, though he's chosen to accept none of them. You'd best make sure he marks your dance card before you go, or you'll find yourself without a partner.'

'He has said nothing of all this to me.'

'Why would he, save to rub your nose in it? Most of these people won't open their doors to you. Virgil's not so insensitive.'

'No.' Kate finished her Madeira. 'Does this mean you won't object to my going to the ball, then?'

Giles gave a bark of laughter. 'Was there ever any chance I could stop you?'

The drawing room door opened and Virgil entered. 'What is the joke?'

'You and my sister,' Giles said. 'Lord, I'm looking forward to seeing the old man's face when you tell him you're taking her to the Buxton assembly.'

'Yes, I heard His Grace was joining us at dinner. Do you wish to change your mind about the dance, my lady?' Virgil turned towards Kate as he spoke. She rose from the gilded settee, and had the satisfaction of seeing her appearance reflected in his expression. 'That is a very beautiful ball gown,' he said. 'And you look quite breathtaking,' he added softly, taking her hand between his.

She blushed. 'You look very smart too,' which was an understatement. In silk knee breeches and a tightly fitting black coat, with a white shirt, white waistcoat and white stockings, Virgil looked starkly magnificent. She could not quite believe that after tomorrow morning she would never see him again. Though she knew this for a fact, it was one thing, she was discovering, for her to know, and another for her to accept. She didn't want him to go, though she knew there was no reason at all for him to stay, nor ever could be.

He really was magnificent. She watched him, standing beside Giles. The two men were of very similar build. Funny, she'd never thought her brother either attractive or handsome, but he was both. She wondered now if Lily felt, when she looked at Giles, as Kate felt when she looked at Virgil.

Not that the cases were the same, for Giles and Lily were in love, whereas she and Virgil were…in lust? No, it wasn't that. Though her heart was beating quite erratically. And her corsets felt too tight. And she couldn't help thinking of the skin and muscle under those tight-fitting breeches. The curve of his buttocks. The span of his chest. The seductive potency of his manhood.

'Katherine?'

Kate jumped. 'Aunt Wilhelmina.'

'Why are you wearing a ball gown?'

'His Grace, the Duke of Rothermere,' Lumsden intoned, as if he were announcing war.

Giles rolled his eyes as the door was flung open. Phaedra stopped short, a comical look of dismay on her face. Kate smothered a smile. Obviously her sister had not benefited from any sort of warning.

'Your Grace.' Mrs Landes-Fraser, more than usually draped and bedecked in shawls and turbans and feathers, abandoned her interrogation of her niece to drop into a curtsey so low Kate feared she may require help in recovering. It was an absurd gesture, in her opinion, but her father seemed to appreciate it, for he held out his hand and allowed it to be kissed, for all the world as if he were a prince.

He was looking much frailer than when she had last seen him. He had been a tall man, but he was stooped now, bent over like a question mark, his evening clothes loose on his wasted frame, the last remnants of his white hair wispy on his mottled pate. His once hawk-like features were blunted by saggy skin and watery eyes. Crispin Torquil Fitzmerrion Montague had the appearance of a man headed shortly for the grave.

'Father.' Giles made a curt bow. 'May I present our guest, Mr Virgil Jackson.'

'Your Grace.'

Kate was pleased to note that Virgil's bow was neither deferential nor particularly low. His tone was not cold, but nor did it contain any warmth. He did not say it was an honour. Her father, too, noted all this. His brows snapped together. His expression, which had been benignly supercilious, now hardened, giving his audience a fleeting glimpse of the ruthless despot he had once been. 'I believe my daughter invited you, Mr Jackson,' he said. 'Under the mistaken belief that she will warm me to this abolition nonsense, no doubt. Katherine's propensity for supporting lost causes knows no bounds.'

'Papa! How—'

'Mr Jackson is as much my guest as Kate's,' Giles intervened hastily, 'as you are perfectly well aware, Your Grace, for I have informed you myself. Mr Jackson is an extremely astute businessman and has, amongst other things, been so kind as to give me some very sound advice regarding your investments.'

'Giles!' Mrs Landes-Fraser exclaimed. 'There are ladies present. I am shocked that you should raise such matters in mixed company. Girls, where are your manners? You have not yet greeted His Grace.'

'Papa.'

'Phaedra. You smell of horse.'

'I am just back from the stables, Papa. There was no time to bathe. No one told me you were joining us,' Phaedra muttered, glaring at her aunt.

'And, Katherine.'

'Papa.' Kate made a very small curtsey.

'I believe I have you to blame for oversetting my arrangements for my grandson. The boy is my heir. It is not at all fitting that he stay in the Dower House.'

Giles sighed heavily. 'We have been over that, Father. We agreed—'

'I did nothing of the sort. I may be sick in body, but I am quite in control of my own mind. I want that boy here, under my roof in the Castonbury nursery. This will all be his one day.'

'*If* he proves to be Jamie's child,' Giles said.

'Of course he is Jamie's child,' the duke snapped. 'He must be.'

Giles, abandoning any pretence of keeping the peace, opened his mouth to argue, but was interrupted by the clash of the dinner gong and Lumsden's stately announcement that His Grace was served. When Mrs Landes-Fraser would have taken the duke's arm to support him in the short journey across the marble hall to the dining room, Smithins appeared like a ghost, leaving her to be escorted by a most reluctant Giles.

'I'm sorry,' Kate whispered as Virgil took her arm, motioning to Phaedra to take the other, 'my father is unforgivably rude.'

Virgil shrugged, and squeezed her fingers. 'You think I care about him looking down his patrician nose at me? What's unforgivable is the way he treats you.'

'Oh, that was nothing,' Phaedra said chirpily. 'Before Jamie and Ned died, Papa and Kate used to argue hammer and tongs. Why are you wearing a ball gown, Kate?'

'Because she's going to a ball,' Virgil replied. 'With me.'

'Just you?' Phaedra eyed Kate with respect as they entered the dining room. 'Goodness, dinner is going to be interesting.'

Interesting, Kate thought grimly as course followed course, was one way of putting it. Tedious, fraught, embarrassing and interminable were others. His Grace had Virgil sit on his left-hand side in what should have been a position of honour. It was, however, patently obvious that the duke wished merely to have the convenience of alternately interrogating his guest and snubbing him without the inconvenience of having to turn his head too far or raise his voice. Several times Giles tried to intervene, but when it became obvious that Virgil was neither intimidated nor insulted, merely blandly indifferent, Giles grinned at Kate and devoted himself to his dinner.

It was a most magnificent repast. Monsieur André, Castonbury's haughty French chef, had obviously relished the challenge of putting a meal worthy of the duke on the table. It groaned under the weight of carp Chambord studded with truffles and braised in red wine; lobster Parisienne; cold scallops glazed in aspic and decorated with artichokes; veal Périgourdine, cooked in butter and stuffed with fois gras; noisettes of lamb; pigeons *bonne-femme*; a whole pickled tongue; soup julienne à la Russe; stuffed cucumbers; eggs Polonaise; and any number of vegetable dishes in aspic jelly moulded into extraordinary shapes.

The duke ate sparingly. 'I believe you visited that school my daughter has established,' he said, graciously allowing Lumsden to help him to a sliver of lobster.

'I was impressed,' Virgil replied. 'Castonbury now has as fine a place to educate its young as any other in the country. I think even Robert Owen would be pleased.'

'That man is a subversive!' the duke exclaimed. 'Servants and farmers and mill workers have no use for reading and writing.'

'Perhaps not, if they are to remain mere servants and farmers and mill workers,' Virgil said mildly. 'But what if they wish something more?'

'More?' His Grace looked incredulous. 'What more could they possibly want?'

'Lady Kate wishes to offer the villagers the chance to attend classes at night.'

'It is time that my daughter learned that her wishes are of absolutely no consequence. Her place is with her family. When my grandson arrives, Katherine will have no time for these misguided attempts at charity. Since she has signally failed to do her duty by marrying, the least she can do is devote herself to the service of her nephew. I fear my ill health has of late allowed her too much latitude. *That*,' the duke said with an air of finality, 'will come to an end now that I am a little recovered.'

For a moment, it looked as if Virgil would rise to the bait. Instead he pushed his chair back abruptly. 'You will excuse us, Your Grace, but I am afraid we have a prior engagement.'

An expectant hush made Kate's heart bump hard against her chest. She put her napkin on her plate of untouched food, acutely aware of the eyes of every one of her relatives, fixed fascinated, astounded and disbelieving, upon her. Not since she had jilted Anthony had she openly defied her father. This time, she was no frightened child but a grown woman. She smiled up at Virgil as he pulled her chair back, and then smiled benignly over at the duke. Their confrontations, as Phaedra had so inelegantly put it, had always been hammer and tongs. Tonight, watching him become increasingly querulous as his barbs failed to wound and his most pointed insults were greeted by Virgil with bland indifference, she saw that her tactics had been quite wrong. It had been a struggle not to rise to the baited remarks about her future, but she had gritted her teeth and held her peace, and it had paid off.

'How dare you, sir!' The duke, turning an alarming shade of puce, broke the silence. 'Katherine! Where the devil do you think you're going?'

Aunt Wilhelmina cast her a furious look. 'Katherine! We have not finished dinner.'

'*I* have. Mr Jackson and I, as he has already informed you, have a prior engagement. We are going to the Assembly Rooms at Buxton.'

The duke gasped. Phaedra muffled her nervous laugh with her napkin. Mrs Landes-Fraser looked as if she would swoon. 'Katherine Mary Cecily Montague,' she hissed, 'you cannot be serious. Have you any idea what people will say?'

Kate laced her fingers tightly together behind her back. 'How can I not, Aunt Wilhelmina, when you remind me on a daily basis.'

'Sit down at once!'

'Get her out of my sight,' the duke cried, clutching his chest. 'That any daughter of mine should— You will go to your room, Katherine, and you will remain there until you see the error of your ways.'

'Oh, for heaven's sake, she's not a child. This is turning into a farce.' Giles pushed back his chair so violently it fell over. 'Get out, Kate, go to Buxton before he has an apoplexy. Lumsden, call Smithins. Phaedra, stop smirking.'

As Polly, waiting in the marble hall, helped Kate into her evening cloak, and the dining room door burst open again, her sister came bounding out with Giles in her wake. 'That was marvellous. I haven't enjoyed dinner so much in an age. Have a lovely time,' she said, surprising Kate with a hug before disappearing down the back stairs, obviously headed for the stables.

'I hope you know what you're doing,' Giles said to Kate. With a curt nod at Virgil, he, too, disappeared.

Virgil took Kate's arm. 'Well, I think you've certainly made your point. Are you sure you want to go?'

She smiled up at him. Tomorrow she would face the consequences of her insubordination, but tonight she did not give a fig. 'Just try and stop me,' she said.

Nine

The Buxton Assembly Rooms were brightly lit, with a crowd of carriages jostling for position in the cobbled street outside. Flambeaux lit the way as Kate and Virgil mounted the shallow flight of steps to the main entranceway, where they discarded their outerwear before ascending to the ballroom on the second floor. Two rows of marble columns supported the high ceiling of the long room, which was lit by three glittering chandeliers. A card room and withdrawing room served those who wished to play and those who sought relief from heat and the crush of dancers.

As Kate entered on Virgil's arm, a country dance was under way. She recognised the young woman at the head of the set in a gown of primrose jaconet as the daughter of a neighbour, and her partner as one of Giles's boyhood friends. Around the rooms, seated on gilded chairs, were the cream of the county, almost every one an acquaintance of her father, her aunt and formerly of herself. With a sinking heart, she realised that the eyes and lorgnettes of most of them were turned upon her and Virgil. She stiffened.

'Don't show them you care,' Virgil said softly. 'You have no reason at all to be intimidated by them. I doubt very much if any of them could lay claim to the kind of spotless reputation they pretend to. Think of it as a game, Kate. Don't be the first to back down.'

She tried to do as he bid her, meeting disapproving gazes with a bland smile, and holding her head high. To her surprise, several women nodded—not the friendliest of nods, but they did not shun her. Virgil led her determinedly from one group of people to another, and she recalled the reaction he had generated the first time they'd met, several weeks ago now, though it felt like months, at Maer Hall. All eyes turned towards him. Whispers turned into murmurs of appreciation. Ladies vied surreptitiously to greet him. Gentlemen edged closer, as if he exerted some sort of invisible attraction. It was just as Giles had predicted. Virgil was received with effusion and bombarded with suggestions that he partner this daughter, this niece, this granddaughter, in the next country dance or cotillion or quadrille.

He agreed to some, but only those for which Kate was also solicited, and he insisted that the first dance and the waltz—which the master of ceremonies had daringly introduced some months before—were saved for her. 'You see,' he said to her as they joined their cotillion set, 'if you lead, they will follow.'

Kate laughed. 'It's true, only a very few people actually snubbed me, but I think it was rather the case that if *you* lead they will follow.'

'Stop undermining yourself. You are the one who looked them all in the eye and held your nerve. And while we are on the subject, I must congratulate you for the way you handled that tyrannical old goat who is your father tonight. He couldn't believe it when there was not a rise to be got from you.'

'I took my lead from you.'

'Well, now you know what to do, you can take the lead from yourself. You don't need me, Kate. Have a little faith in your own ability.'

Their set was now formed, with six other couples. For the first time since they had arrived, Virgil looked doubtful. 'I have not danced the cotillion very often.'

'I have not danced one in years.' Kate looked towards the orchestra, where the master of ceremonies was consulting a card. 'It looks like he will call the changes, at least. I shan't mention it if you stand on my toes provided you return the favour,' she said with a teasing smile.

'Kate.'

It was the way he said her name that made her heart flutter. No one ever said her name like that. And the way he looked at her, really looked at her, his tawny eyes focused only on her, that made the muscles in her belly clench. She forgot about the disastrous dinner and the strain of facing the world and even the six other couples in their cotillion set. She forgot all about the need to restrain her feelings, to keep a leash on her thoughts, and gave herself up to the raw strength of the attraction between them. It was still there, fiercer than ever. He felt it too. She saw it reflected in his eyes.

The orchestra struck up and the dance began. Each touch of their hands ran like a shock up her arm, making her skin tingle. When they separated, their eyes retained the contact. Glove on glove felt like skin on skin. Every glance was a caress. She was barely aware of the other dancers, barely aware of the changes, tuned in not to the orchestra, but to some internal rhythm known only to the two of them.

When it was over, the polite applause startled them both. They blinked as if waking from a reverie. For the next two hours they danced with other partners, but the connection between them grew as they exchanged glances across the throng, as Virgil's hand sought hers under cover of the folds of her gown when he stood beside her talking at tea, as his arm brushed against hers, or hers against his thigh. By the time the last dance, their first and only waltz, was called, Kate felt strung tight as a bow.

'I see you are not so unaccustomed to the waltz as the cotillion,' she said, striving to retain a little control of herself as they made their first circuit of the floor. Having his hand on her waist was conjuring up all sorts of memories. Of his skin against hers. Of his lips on hers. Of the way he felt against her, hard and muscled and yet velvet-smooth. Her voice sounded breathless. He would think it was the dance.

'I've danced it several times back home. If a man is to be a success, he cannot be completely antisocial.'

'So you charm the ladies of Boston with your dancing and your polite conversation so that they will persuade their husbands to do business with you?'

Virgil's smile faded. 'I succeed on my own terms, Kate. I don't need anyone to oil the wheels for me, and I never cross the line of what is proper. I mean that I'm part of that society, so I can't live outside it.'

'I know what you meant, I was only teasing.'

His hand tightened on her waist. 'I'm sorry. I guess I've had enough of socialising for tonight. I was beginning to think it would never end. No, don't look like that. I didn't mean I was bored. I meant—damn it, I just meant I wanted to dance with *you*.'

'Oh.'

'Just "oh"? You're supposed to say that you only wanted to dance with me.'

'I would, if I could be certain you wouldn't remind me of how impossible it is.'

'Do I have to?'

'No,' she said sadly. 'You're leaving tomorrow and I shan't see you again. I know that.'

Virgil pulled her closer as they turned. 'Let's not talk about tomorrow,' he said harshly. 'Let's just enjoy what is left of tonight.'

She was happy to do so. As the dance progressed, she began to see why it was deemed so shocking. Above the waist they held themselves rigid, but below, their legs, thighs, knees brushed and touched, a constant teasing, tantalising contact. They did not talk, but their eyes spoke. Yearning and loss. A flare of passion quickly repressed. Desire flickered, was tamped down, then flickered back to life. By the time the waltz ended it had taken hold. They did not wait to bid anyone goodnight, but made their way quickly down the central staircase, among the first to collect their coats.

John Coachman was waiting with the landau. The hood was up. They sat together, facing forward in the dim of the interior as the coach rumbled over the cobblestones of Buxton.

'Kate.' Even in the dark, he could find the pulse below her ear. He had taken off his gloves as soon as they had left the ballroom. His lips were warm on her skin. His fingers stroked the nape of her neck. His thigh was solid against hers. 'You are so beautiful,' he whispered.

'In the way that a greyhound is,' she said, remembering that first night.

'In the way only you can be. You are Kate. Perfectly Kate. Don't let them change you. Don't ever change.'

She swallowed hard. She would not have his last memories of her be marred by tears. 'I shall try not to.'

'What he said, your father, about the future. You will not allow him to force you into the role of an old aunt?'

Had he any idea what he was asking of her, to live at Castonbury and to defy its lord and master? To be herself, as he asked, would mean she could never please. 'I shall try,' Kate said hesitantly, for she would not lie to him.

Virgil sighed. 'There is no alternative, but to remain there?'

'If I made an effort to become truly eccentric, I suppose there is a chance they would exile me to the Dower House. Always assuming that Jamie's wife chooses not to live there. Always assuming that she *is* Jamie's wife.'

'Your father seems to have decided.'

'The lawyers will require more concrete proof than a ring and a child,' Kate said.

'Giles cannot accept that his brother would have married without informing him, I know.'

'Giles has confided in you?'

Virgil shook his head. 'He had no need. It's obvious.'

'To you, perhaps. You are very perceptive.'

The crump of the landau's wheels on the gravel of Castonbury's driveway took them both by surprise. The journey had been too short. As they proceeded towards the house, Kate began to panic. She was not ready to say goodbye.

'Virgil, I...'

'Come for a walk with me. It's cold, but it's a clear night. Let's go look at the stars by the lake,' he said, handing her out.

Kate looked towards the door, where Lumsden stood waiting. 'I can't. My aunt—'

'Wait here.'

She had no idea what he said to the butler, but as John Coachman headed for the stables, the front door closed and Virgil rejoined her. 'He won't wait up, and he won't tell.'

They walked in silence towards the lake. Above them the stars glittered in the midnight blue of an unusually clear night. It was cold. Winter was not long away. At the head of the north lake they stood looking out at the island. The water lapped gently on the pebbles and Virgil pulled her into his arms, crushing her to his chest so tightly she could hardly breathe. 'I won't forget you, Kate.'

She swallowed hard. She clenched her fists, digging her nails into her palms in an effort to control the sudden spasm of tears which threatened to overwhelm her. She hadn't thought about this moment, she wasn't ready for it, but she would not spoil it. 'I won't forget you either.'

He tilted her chin up. His face was set, fierce, but she knew him better now. He was not angry. 'Will you kiss me good-bye?'

He did not wait for her answer. His lips were gentle, but she was having none of that. Kate pressed herself against him, twining her arms around his neck, and kissed him hard, pouring all her regrets and all the passion they could not share into that one moment. When he would have pulled away, she pulled him back.

With a groan which seemed to come from the depths of his being, Virgil surrendered to the kiss and the moment. This wasn't what he'd planned, but then since he'd met Kate nothing had gone as he'd planned. He couldn't pretend he didn't want her. It didn't change a damn thing, but he couldn't lie to himself. Not tonight.

He kissed her. Then he told himself to stop, and kissed her again. When he kissed her again, he was still sure it was not too late. But then he kissed her again, and she made that little growling noise deep in her throat, and he knew that it was. 'Kate,' he said, meaning *stop*, but it came out sounding the opposite. How could he not want her, with her breath on his cheek, the scent of her perfume and her skin and her Kateness going straight to his head and his groin, her body pressed, melting, pliant into his?

He wanted her. He couldn't imagine a time when he would not want her, though he knew this would be the only time he could ever have her. 'Kate, we can't.'

'Don't you want to?'

'You know I do.'

'Then show me,' she whispered, 'but not here.'

She led him to the Dower House, retrieving the key from its hiding place in the portico, lighting the lamp which sat on the marble hall table. Of one accord they climbed the stairs to the room with the fantastically carved mythological bed. Kate placed the lamp on the chest of drawers and turned to him, suddenly nervous.

'Are you sure?' Virgil asked her.

'Are you?'

'Right now, I am.'

Kate smiled. 'That's all that matters.'

They both knew differently. In the morning he would be gone. In the morning they would face their different futures alone. But right now, at this moment, his imminent departure was an urge to completion.

Virgil's kiss was deeply sensual. It seemed to reach right down inside her and extract the sweetest, most delicious ache. Kate twined her arms around his neck and kissed him back fervently, spilling all the pent-up emotion of the night into him. She felt drugged, heavy, weighted, weightless, by what he was doing to her. His tongue stroked and licked, his mouth shaped hers and heated hers. His lips were like velvet.

He dropped his greatcoat onto the floor, then undid the clasp of her cloak. The velvet pooled at her feet. The tiny buttons on her gloves were next. He undid them slowly, licking the exposed skin of her wrist before pulling them down over her arms, trailing kisses in the wake of the soft French kid, on the crook of her elbow, her forearm, her wrist again, each one of her fingers. And then the other hand. She shivered violently.

He shrugged out of his coat. Her fingers plucked at his clothing but he slowed her, muttering her name like an incantation, smoothing his hands over her, taking his time, as if they had all the time in the world.

He ran his fingers through her hair, casting pearl-tipped pins onto the floor. His hands were like magic. Could hair feel? It was tingling at the roots. He kissed her mouth, her eyes, her throat.

His hands traced the shape of her body through her evening gown, skimming over her breasts, her belly, her hips. Heating her from the inside. His mouth drove her wild. His kisses grew more focused. He turned her around and kissed her neck. His fingers on the laces and hooks of her robe were less certain, but still he wouldn't hurry, slipping it down, kissing the crook of her elbow as he freed her from each sleeve, cupping the flesh of her bottom, her thighs, as he helped her step out of it.

Moonlight slanted through the windows, casting a ghostly light over the carved bed. Nymphs, goddesses and fantastical sea creatures peered out at them, watching. Virgil said her name again as he looked at her. She could melt from the way he said it. He undid her stays slowly, his smile taking on a new sensuality as he enjoyed the look of her in dark blue satin and pristine white lace. She had always thought the purpose of wearing such exotic undergarments was for her pleasure alone. Until now. The way he looked at her made her bones liquid.

She tugged at his waistcoat. He quickly unbuttoned it, casting it off with his neck cloth and shirt. Her breath caught in her throat at the sight of him. Smooth skin, barely a mark on his chest in contrast to his back. Muscles that strained at his skin. Gleaming ebony. She ran her fingers over him, marvelling at the way he shivered under her touch, counting down his ribs.

He sat her on the edge of the bed and pulled off her slippers. They were damp with dew, quite ruined. He rolled down her stockings and kissed her knees, her feet, each one of her toes. He kicked off his own shoes, his silk knee breeches, his hose. She had forgotten how beautiful he was. Her imagination had failed her. His body was hard-packed, the muscles rounded, the whole infinitely male. She reached for him, and his touch became more urgent, tearing at the last of her undergarments, oblivious of the silk and lace and ribbons, interested only in that most intimate of covering, her skin.

Finally, he lay her down on the bed. She relished the weight of him on top of her, the breadth of him, the solidness of him as he held her, breast to breast, thigh to thigh, the hard length of his erection nestling between her legs. Kate moaned, low and guttural.

He kissed her mouth again. Then he kissed her breasts. Hands and mouth on her nipples, on her flank, kissing, teasing, tugging, much more urgent. She was not prepared for how fast it built, her climax. She was sky-high, taut, unbearably tense as he cupped her sex, just cupped her, the heel of his hand pressing against her, nothing more, and she thought she might explode.

Kate clenched tight. Not yet. She bucked under him. Not

yet. She mimicked the way he cupped her, and felt him tighten in her palm. Not yet. Virgil moaned. His fingers slipped inside her and she gasped with pleasure. He slid in so easily, she was so wet. Not yet. Not yet, please, not yet. She was tight, tight, tight. His fingers slid over her, over the tightest, hottest bit of her, and she felt herself unravelling.

She slid her hand up the length of his shaft. Thick. Hard. Silky. She wanted him inside her. 'Please,' she breathed desperately. He kissed her. He thrust his tongue into her mouth. He stroked inside the folds of her sex, over the hot, tight, hard part of her. She couldn't hold back. She felt herself toppling, shattering, crying out, and then he thrust, one long hard thrust deep inside her and she shattered.

She came, pulsing, throbbing, crying out, but he didn't let up. He tilted her up, he wrapped his arm around her back to brace her, and thrust again. She hadn't ever felt anything like it. Virgil inside her, thick and hard and pushing higher, her own muscles pulsing around her, her climax ebbing and then building, like an echo, as he pushed into her. She held him tight there, clinging to him, watching the effect of what she did to him dancing across his face as he withdrew and she clung and then opened for his next thrust. And his next. It was like a race now. He was pushing her hard and though she wanted to give in to him she didn't want him to stop, not yet. Higher and harder, she clung and she gasped and then it happened so suddenly, not an echo but something more, as he touched a spot she hadn't known existed high up and she let go, truly let go, had no choice but to let herself fall, and with a harsh cry Virgil pulled himself free, spilling onto her belly.

He wiped her clean with his kerchief. Such a little thing, but it brought a lump to her throat, for Anthony had never shown such care. Grabbing her cloak from the floor, Virgil threw it over them, and then pulled her back into his arms, spooning her against him, nestling her bottom into his thighs, one hand over each breast, nuzzling the back of her neck. It brought a whole new meaning to the word *bliss*. Kate closed her eyes and floated.

Later, not much later, Virgil stirred. He kissed her mouth again. Then her breasts. Then lower. Her thighs. And then her sex. He didn't just taste her, he savoured her, licking into her, around her, thrusting his tongue inside her. Kate was too aroused to be shocked. His tongue teased and stroked and circled. He seemed to know exactly how to bring her close to the edge, and then to leave her there teetering, hovering, wanting to fall, wanting to cling on. She arched shamelessly against his mouth. It felt different this time. More intense. A brighter colour. A wrenching of her guts. When she came he stayed with her, and when she thought she was done, he licked her into another of those rippling echoes.

Afterwards, she rolled over on top of him, taking him by surprise, wanting to taste him and to taste what he did to her. She could feel him, hard and hot between her legs. She wriggled down his body, enjoying the way his skin rubbed on her breasts, relishing the contrast of her skin on his. She slid down, until she had the tip of his shaft against her lips. His eyes were glittering when she looked up. She licked him and felt him jerk under her. She licked him again. He moaned. She liked making him moan. She flicked her tongue down the length of his shaft. She licked back up. She drew him into her mouth. A tiny bit. A bit more. She could feel him swelling. That's how he knew to tease, she thought with satisfaction, to bring her to the brink. So she stopped.

She looked at his face, and saw exactly what she'd felt when he'd done it to her. She took him in her mouth again. Stopped again. But when she went to do it again, he caught her by surprise, his arms on her waist, pulling her up his body, positioning her, and instead of her mouth, the pulsing tip of him was inside her and she forgot all about teasing and slid down on him and set about riding them both hard to a climax that felt as if it turned her inside out.

She forgot to be careful but he did not. He lifted her clear of him as he came. Wrapping her hand around him to capture the last pulsing of his seed, Kate felt a deep sense of loss.

Time marched relentlessly on. They touched but did not speak. Words were pointless. They had said everything. Kate resented every moment that passed, hated every minute which brought them closer to the hour of his departure.

They made their way, still silent, back to the big house. One last kiss at the door. Bittersweet. More bitter than sweet. She would not cry in front of him. In the morning she must say a composed goodbye. Covering her mouth with her hand, Kate fled up the stairs to her bedchamber.

She did not sleep. Heavy-eyed but determined to say farewell with the dignity Virgil expected of her, Kate was dressed and downstairs for breakfast by seven the next morning, but he was already gone.

'The mail leaves the Rothermere Arms at seven,' Giles told her.

'He told me nine. Did he leave a message?'

'Said all that was proper.' Her brother drew her one of his sharp looks. 'Was there something in particular you were expecting him to say?'

'No.' Kate poured herself a cup of coffee. Her hands shook. She sat down at the table and began to pick at a bread roll.

'I liked him, Kate. He's a sensible man. An impressive one. But…' Giles broke off frowning, and took a long draught from his tankard. 'I hate to agree with our aunt, but in this she was right. It would never do.'

'I know that.' Giles pressed her hand. It was this small token of affection, so very unlike him, which was Kate's undoing. 'I know!' she said, dashing her hand over her eyes, for to cry in front of him would be to admit that there was something to cry about and how could there be?

Kate pushed her cup aside. Coffee splattered over the polished surface of the table. 'I must get on. I have a hundred things to do today,' she said, and fled from the room.

There was no sanctuary in her bedchamber, where Daisy was making up the bed. 'Mrs Landes-Fraser was looking for you, my lady,' the chambermaid told her. 'Said to tell you that she was going over to inspect the Dower House to make sure all is well for the lady's arrival tomorrow, and that she'd expect you there at your convenience. I told her I was sure you'd got everything under control, but you know what she's like, Lady Kate. Thinks no one can do anything properly but herself.'

Kate liked Daisy, and encouraged the girl, who was in her opinion far too bright to earn her living as a servant, to work at her lessons with a view to helping Miss Thomson out at the school. This morning, however, she managed only a perfunctory smile. She couldn't face her aunt yet. She couldn't face anyone at the moment. Alone in her bed last night, she'd worked so hard at persuading herself that Virgil's leaving was not the momentous event it felt. Finding him gone had made her face up to the fact that she'd retained a tiny sliver of hope that he would stay. With that hope extinguished, she was forced to admit that she had wished for more. A lot more.

'If my aunt asks, you haven't seen me,' she told Daisy. 'I'm going for a swim.'

It didn't do much good. Her thoughts circled as she made her laps of the lake, but the usual calm which the physical effort of swimming invariably gave her failed to descend. She understood that he had left without seeing her again to spare them both pain, but she couldn't help wondering if he was running away.

As she abraded her icy skin with a towel in the little changing room under the fishing pavilion, shivering, her numbed fingers struggling with the ties of her garters, she told herself she was being irrational. She pulled her gown over her head and began to wrestle with the fastenings.

'To be sure,' she muttered to herself, 'Virgil Jackson is a fascinating person but there are surely lots of equally fascinating people in the world.' Though not another who had understood her the way he had. 'That is simply because I've never confided in anyone else,' she told her shoes firmly, slipping her cold feet into them. 'Virgil is gone and will not be coming back. I should be grateful to have met him, and I won't forget him, and absolutely will never forget last night, but I must put all these other silly thoughts out of my head else I will end up a weeping willow with absolutely no cause.' She nodded decisively. 'It is a mistake to waste energy on things one cannot control. Far better that I focus on what I can. Like making sure that this poor woman is given the welcome she deserves. Always assuming she deserves it. Which I must do, until it is proved otherwise. So that is what I shall do,' she told the changing room door staunchly.

Closing it behind her, quite convinced, for the moment, that she meant every word she said, Kate strode off towards the Dower House to see what havoc her aunt had wreaked in her absence.

It would have been some consolation to Kate to know that Virgil was having a similarly difficult time in rationalising his feelings. Thinking him by now well on the way to Manchester, she would have been extremely surprised to learn that he had in fact been forced to delay his departure by at least one and likely two days. Snow had come suddenly and unseasonably early in the north and the mail coach had fallen victim the day before, breaking an axle, delaying its journey south and thus its return journey north, so the landlord of the Rothermere Arms explained to him.

It had been a wrench to leave Castonbury without saying goodbye to Kate, though he had no doubt it was for the best. It would be a mistake to return, no matter how much he longed to do so. For Kate's sake, he told himself. He would like to reassure himself that she was coping. But that putative relative of hers arrived tomorrow, and they had, after all, said their goodbyes.

Sitting in the private parlour he had bespoken at the inn, Virgil tried to distract himself with business, but images of Kate smiling, laughing, frowning, Kate kissing and Kate swimming and Kate lying in his arms, and Kate crying out as she climaxed, crowded his head. He put aside his notes on the new venture with Josiah Wedgwood and turned to a collection of recent essays by Robert Owen on the formation of the human character.

It was not easy, but Virgil was a very determined man, and by the time dinner was served, he was quite caught up on Owen's *New View of Society.*

The Dowager Marchioness of Hatherton arrived in the ducal landau the next morning, having been collected by John Coachman from the Rothermere Arms, where the London mail had deposited her. It being another pleasant day, the hood of the carriage was down. As John Coachman brought the horses to a halt, and Joe Coyle opened the door with a flourish, Kate thought for a moment that the woman inside looked terrified. But when she looked again, her countenance was smooth and shyly smiling.

Giles was making a stiff bow. 'Welcome to Castonbury.'

Ross had not underplayed the lady's charms, was Kate's first thought. Jamie's wife was very pretty indeed. Petite, slender and angelically fair, she had a pair of blue eyes which Kate had no difficulty at all in believing Jamie had fallen victim to. Her travelling dress was neat but shabby, several seasons out of date, but she carried herself with dignity, and her smile was just the correct mix of confidence and deference.

'This is Lady Katherine, my sister, who has been making all the arrangements for you and your boy, ma'am.'

Giles's introduction was cool. Despite the fact that her brother was dead set against inheriting the title, he seemed also dead set on proving this woman a sham. It made Kate all the more determined to welcome her. She beamed, and instead of dropping a curtsey, enfolded her new relative in a warm hug. 'You must call me Kate, since we are to be sisters,' she said, unable to resist casting a defiant look at Giles over her shoulder.

'Then you must call me Alicia, if you please. I don't feel

entitled to call myself a dowager marchioness, for Jamie and I were married such a brief time.'

'Long enough,' Giles said shortly. 'Is this the boy?'

The child, whom John Coachman had lifted down, shrank against his mother's skirts. 'Yes, this is Crispin James. He is a little tired from the journey, my lord.'

Giles eyed the child with obvious scepticism. Fair-haired like his mother, he had also inherited her blue eyes, but his features had still too much of a chubby infant about them to be definitive in any way. 'They all look the same to me at that age, he could be anyone's.'

'Giles! For heaven's sake…'

'Please, my lady—I mean, Kate—it's perfectly natural that your brother should question…. I am sure this has been a shock to you, as indeed Jamie's death was a shock to me. I did not expect to be coming here to Castonbury under such circumstances. It is such a—a— I find it difficult to believe that one day all this will belong to my son.'

'*If* he is proved also to be my brother's son,' Giles said, unmoved by the flutter of a lace handkerchief over a pair of big blue eyes drowned in tears.

'You must forgive my brother, he is a little overwrought,' Kate said, putting a protective arm around the widow. 'Now, come into the house and meet the rest of the family.' She held out her hand to the little boy, giving him a warm smile. 'Monsieur André, our chef, has made a special treat just for you. A sugar castle, what do you think of that?'

The child's eyes widened in astonishment. Waiting only for a nod from his mama, he took Kate's hand and tripped happily up the sweep of stairs into the magnificence of the marble hall, which had been opened up in preference to the usual entranceway downstairs for the occasion.

The Duke of Rothermere himself it was who had insisted on the formal line-up of Castonbury servants to greet the new heir. Kate stopped short in the doorway at the sight of the military line of menservants on one side, women on the other, and her father seated in state at the top with Aunt Wilhelmina in regal purple, not one but three nodding ostrich feathers in her turban, standing behind him like a queen consort. No wonder Giles was in a mood. Papa was making it very clear where his alliances were. Poor Giles, Kate thought. And come to that, poor Alicia, who was like to lose her precious child if her father had anything to do with it.

With Alicia settled in the Dower House and her most pressing duties over, Kate wanted to escape, and decided to go for a drive. It was John Coachman who told her. 'Snow in the north,' he said as he got the gig ready for her. 'That Mr Jackson's been kicking his heels at the inn for two days now.'

'Mr Jackson?'

'Aye, my lady. Though it looks like he'll be off tomorrow right enough. Weather's turned again. You know what it's like at this time of year.'

'Mr Jackson is still here?'

'Didn't you know, my lady?'

'No,' Kate replied, 'I did not. I wonder why he—oh, Alicia, of course.'

'My lady?'

'John, I'm sorry, I was talking to myself. I shan't need the gig, I've changed my mind.'

She hurried off in the direction of the village. Virgil was still here at Castonbury. It was because of Alicia. He knew Alicia was arriving today, that was why he had not been in touch.

As she made her way along the path through the woods, it occurred to her that perhaps he had stayed away for another reason. He had not said goodbye for fear of upsetting her. He would be worried that another goodbye would be more upsetting, no doubt, but truly, he was quite wrong. Since he had left, she had been perfectly fine.

Apart from the lack of sleep, but that was nothing, completely irrelevant. Everyone had sleepless nights. Besides, Virgil would be wondering how Alicia had been received. She could reassure him and bring him up to date and say goodbye in a civilised manner all in one visit. It would be wrong of her to forego the opportunity to do so. Very wrong indeed.

Albert Moffat, the landlord of the Rothermere Arms, raked a hand through his wiry thatch of salt-and-pepper hair. 'Mr Jackson, yes, he's here all right. He's in the best parlour, my lady. If you'll wait here, I'll go and fetch him.'

Now that she had arrived, Kate's confidence was beginning to falter. Virgil had made his feelings quite clear, and he was not a man who liked to have his hand forced. But it was too late, she was here now, and he was so tantalisingly close she could not go away without one last chance to see him.

'I shall announce myself,' she told Albert, 'I know the way.' Without giving herself the chance to change her mind—or indeed Virgil the opportunity to refuse her—Kate ran quickly up the stairs, tapped lightly on the door and pushed it open.

'Kate! What are you doing here?'

'Good afternoon, Virgil. I heard you were delayed. The snow. And I thought you would wish for news of how Alicia's arrival went. And I thought that— You did not say goodbye.'

Virgil had been trying to work. He had been only partially successful. He had never before found it difficult to concentrate; his utter focus had been one of the keys to his success. He blamed the noise of the inn. He blamed the inconvenience of the delay. It was frustrating, to be frittering his time away here. He blamed himself for having taken so much time away from business while staying at Castonbury. He was out of the habit of work, but it would come back to him if he persisted. So he had persisted. He just needed to persist a bit more. What he didn't need was Kate, her skin flushed from the cold, looking at him with her chin tilted in that defiant way of hers, looking at him as if she was half afraid he might show her straight out the door, half wishing he would kiss her.

She was dressed more elegantly than usual. Not her customary riding habit but a dress of dark claret trimmed with black beadwork. Instead of her usual jacket she wore a full-length fitted pelisse with very tight sleeves. The simple lines suited her svelte figure. He wished he didn't remember every lean line of her. The elegant curve of her neck. The long, supple length of her legs. Virgil got to his feet slowly. 'You shouldn't have come.' Which was true, but he couldn't find it in him to regret that she had. 'But you're here now. Come in and tell me the news.'

She remained leaning against the door. 'You need not worry. I'm perfectly fine. I have not come here to—to cause a scene.'

He had to laugh at that. 'I can think of nothing more unlikely.'

Still she did not move. 'I am quite resigned to your going, Virgil. In fact, that is one of the reasons I'm here. To—to reassure you.'

He held out his hand. 'I'd be more reassured if you came over here to the fire. It's freezing out.'

Kate took a couple of steps into the room. 'I went for a swim the other morning.'

'And you didn't turn into an icicle?' She was nervous, Virgil realised. The last time they'd been together—best not to think about that. He smiled at her, more warmly this time. 'Come over to the fire, Kate. You should have stayed away, but there's no harm done. We're in a public inn, we're hardly likely to— I mean, I won't—we won't…' What he had to do was stop thinking about it. 'Tell me about Alicia. And your aunt. Is she still talking to you?'

Kate finally left the door, unbuttoned her pelisse and cast it carelessly over a chair, before sitting opposite Virgil at the fire. 'No. She addresses everything through whoever else happens to be in the room. "Lumsden, you will inform Lady Katherine," she says, or "Giles, you will instruct your sister not to," and once, when there was no one else, it was, "Margaret, you will let Lady Katherine know,"' she said with a chuckle.

'Who is Margaret?'

'Daisy, but my aunt will not lower herself to remembering the names of the housemaids, so she calls them all Margaret. She always has. Oh, Virgil, the day after the ball she gave me such a lecture—it was so absurd, I wish you could have heard it. According to her I am ungrateful, immoral and undutiful. I'm not exactly sure where it is I can expect to end my days in exile, but according to Aunt Wilhelmina, it is some sort of frozen wasteland full of old maids with only cats for company and gruel to eat.'

'The Dower House, does she mean?'

'Oh, no, that is far too close.'

Virgil cursed under his breath as an awkward silence fell. Why had he mentioned the Dower House? Now they were both thinking of that night. That bed. 'And your father?'

he asked, grasping at the subject most likely to quench any thoughts of passion. 'How did he receive his grandson?'

Kate rolled her eyes. 'With all the pomp and ceremony you'd expect. He had the entire household lined up to welcome them, though he did not, incidentally, deign to speak to me. Unless I apologise on bended knee, I doubt he ever will, which is absolutely fine by me.'

'And what do you think of her, your brother's wife-apparent?'

Kate pursed her lips. 'I'm not sure. She is very pretty, but she is no mere cipher. I would say she is holding her own. She was quite happy to have little Crispin—that is the child, named for my father, which needless to say has confirmed him in his belief that the boy cannot be anything other than his legitimate flesh and blood, though she could have easily picked the name by looking up the title in *Debrett's Peerage*. Anyway, she allowed the boy to be dandled on my father's knee, and tomorrow, I believe, the pair of them are to be given a tour of the house, but she was quite adamant that she have sole care of the child in the Dower House. The ducal cradle in the Castonbury nursery remains empty. Not but what the child is far too old for a cradle.'

Virgil began to relax. He had missed Kate's acerbic tongue and caustic wit. He had missed her conversation, and the way she told a story. She always viewed things from a different angle, usually a wholly unexpected one. There could be no harm in talking, after all. They were only talking. He sat back in his chair and stretched his legs out towards the fire. Kate had on short boots today of black leather. He could see them peeping out from under her skirts. Her feet were narrow, high-arched. Her stockings would be black, too, he reckoned. She'd told him once they were her favourite. He caught himself just in time as he began to speculate about what colour her corsets were. 'And was your father right? Does the child look anything like your brother?'

'Lord, what do I know? I think one blond-haired moppet looks very much like another at that age, though naturally my aunt disagrees, and as you know, my father had already made up his mind before they arrived anyway. Alicia is having her lawyer review the trust deed, incidentally, and the guardianship too.'

Virgil raised his eyebrows. 'Another female in the Castonbury household who will not fall into line. Your father will not be amused. Either the widow has an astute business head on her shoulders, or she doesn't trust your family.'

'Would you? If my father had his way—but Giles will make sure he does not. He believes that the child needs his mother, which I have to confess rather surprised me.'

'Do *you* think she's a fraud?' Virgil asked.

Kate shrugged. 'Like Giles, I find it very difficult to believe that Jamie would have married without telling us. He is—he was—the heir to a dukedom, and no matter how pretty and astute she may be, Alicia is, in my father's terms, a nobody.'

'Perhaps your brother was in love?'

'And knowing that my father would forbid the match, he simply decided not to ask for permission? It's possible, I suppose, only from what I gather they had not known each other very long.' Kate pursed her lips. 'Alicia does not talk like a woman in love—at least, she most certainly does not go starry-eyed when she mentions Jamie, and she does not actually mention him very often. *Can* you fall in love upon such short acquaintance?'

The question hung in the air between them for a few seconds, before Kate rushed on. 'It is different in wartime, I expect. Under normal circumstances—but there is no point in speculating about it for it is quite beside the point and— Oh, the funniest thing, when I was discussing the matter with Giles and I asked him if he had sought Papa's permission to marry Lily, he said, "Of course not! Who I marry is my own business" in that snappy way of his.'

'Why *has* Giles not married Lily yet? I had the impression he was very eager to tie the knot. What is he waiting for?'

'The resolution of Jamie's affairs. At present Giles is still nominally the heir, and so tied to Castonbury. Neither he nor Lily wish to make their home there, and so until matters become clearer they have chosen to wait. It is one of the many things which makes my brother ill-tempered, but I cannot blame him. He must feel as if his life is suspended, and not his own.'

Her voice trailed away. She was nervous again, looking not at him, but into the fire. Her hands smoothed her gown. She always did that when she was thinking. What *was* she thinking? Virgil wondered. 'So, Giles is still determined not to allow this child to step into your brother's shoes, then? Even though the last thing he wishes is to inherit himself?'

'He certainly doesn't want to live there after he is married. Jamie loved the place, he was raised knowing it would all be his one day. It's different for Giles,' Kate said, still staring into the flames.

'He told me once that Castonbury stifles him.'

'Did he?' Kate looked up. Her smile was crooked. 'I can certainly understand that. I know it's fanciful, but there are times when I feel that every one of our ancestors in those portraits which line the guest corridor are looking at me disapprovingly.'

'I don't think you fanciful at all—they do the same to me. Kate, you won't let them turn you into…'

'Aunt Wilhelmina? Can you see me in a turban?'

'Don't joke, you know what I mean.'

She nodded slowly. 'You asked me before, remember? That night at the Dower House, you asked me, and I said I would try. And I will, Virgil, but I cannot pretend it will be anything other than a battle. I think—I can see now, mostly thanks to you, that there are different ways of fighting. I can never be what they want me to be, but I don't have to be so confrontational about it, and I certainly don't have to feel guilty about it. You were right about that—despite what I thought, I do still wish to please my father, and it's an impossible task.'

'What of your aunt?'

'*That* is not so clear-cut. She is neither malicious nor a despot. I do believe that she means well, but she will never really understand me. Perhaps we can reach a détente, I don't know.'

'You will be happy, Kate?' It was only as he said it that Virgil realised how much it mattered to him. If he could know she was happy, it would make it easier to go. He had no doubt he was doing the right thing—it had not crossed his mind that there was any other way—but if he could be sure that Kate felt it too…

'Kate?'

'You ask a lot of me. I have never been one to lament what I cannot change. I mean my situation,' she added hurriedly, 'not you. I shall keep on with my own projects, but I cannot ignore the fact that I owe my father my bread and butter and, while Castonbury is my home, I still have a duty to perform at least some *auntly* tasks. I shall be content enough. What about you, Virgil?'

Now she did look at him directly. Her eyes were more blue

than grey today. When she looked at him like that, he always felt she saw too much. 'I shall be content enough,' he said, choosing to echo her own words. 'When I return to Boston, I'm planning to make a fresh start on my plans. Once I've seen New Lanark for myself, I'll have a better idea of what I want to do. And there is the new business with Josiah too. I will have plenty to keep me occupied.'

He sounded bleak. Why did he sound so bleak? He needed to get on, that's what it was. All his plans, he was anxious to put them into motion. He didn't like the way Kate was looking at him. As if she didn't believe him. As if she felt sorry for him. Why should she feel sorry for him? Perhaps if he told her about his business in Glasgow, then she'd understand that he really was making a new beginning. Then she would see, as he did, that he was putting the past behind him and building a whole new future. She needed to be reassured, that was all. He could do that quite easily.

'I haven't explained,' Virgil said, getting to his feet, 'what it is that takes me to Glasgow.'

'You said it was business.'

'There is always business,' he said with a grin, 'but it's more than that. Wait here.' He returned a moment later with the locket from his portmanteau, and handed it to her.

It was a simple piece of jewellery. A hinged oval of chased gold decorated with sapphires. Kate had gone quite pale as she held it in her hand. 'Is it Millie's?'

'No!' It hadn't even occurred to him that she would think that. The denial came out far too harshly. Kate flinched. 'Of course it's not Millie's,' Virgil said in a quieter voice. 'What would a slave have been doing with something so valuable?'

'I'm sorry, I just assumed…'

'It belonged to Malcolm Jackson. To be completely accurate, it belonged to Malcolm Jackson's betrothed. That's her inside. Here, let me show you.' He took the locket from her and opened it, then returned it to her. On one side was a miniature executed in watercolours, somewhat faded. On the other side was a lock of hair. 'Louisa Gordon, that was her name,' Virgil said, squatting down beside Kate's chair. 'She wanted to marry him before he left Scotland for America, but he was set upon making a home for her first, and left her behind. She was killed in a carriage accident about a year later. The letter telling him of her death crossed his asking her to come to him, he told me.'

'That's tragic.' Kate touched the lock of hair. It was brown, slightly lighter than her own. Louisa's eyes were brown too. 'And your Mr Jackson, he never married. He must have loved her very much.'

'I guess,' Virgil said uncomfortably. 'The point is, he asked me to bring this back, to bury it beside her.'

'So that he could feel he was with her, you mean? Your Mr Jackson sounds as if he was quite the romantic. How he must have repented leaving her behind. I feel sure she would have preferred to be with him in the New World, no matter how difficult or dangerous. I feel sure he underestimated her. Look at her, she has a very determined set to her mouth.'

'Kate, you can't know that. It's just a picture, and poorly executed at that. She died almost forty years ago.'

'And he never forgot her.'

'More likely he discovered that he was perfectly content without her. He could easily have married if he wanted to.'

Kate shut the locket with a snap. 'Why did you show me this?'

Virgil took it from her and slipped it into his coat pocket as he got to his feet. She was angry. What had he said to make her angry? He tugged at his neck cloth. He'd sent Watson back to London, but somehow he'd got into the valet's habit of tying it too tight. 'I thought you'd understand. When he asked me to bury the locket, I didn't plan to come all this way across the Atlantic just for that obviously, but the opportunity to do business with Josiah came up, and I read about New Lanark, and it was as though—I felt it was the chance to make a fresh start.'

'To bury the past, you mean?'

'Yes.'

'But it's not your past, it's Malcolm Jackson's,' Kate said with a frown. 'When you talked about your future a few moments ago, it was all about schools and libraries and houses. How many must you build before you forgive yourself, Virgil?'

'You asked me that before, and I told you. I can never forgive myself.'

'Then burying a locket won't make you free,' Kate said sadly as she got to her feet and picked up her pelisse.

'What about you, Kate?' Virgil grabbed her by the arm and spun her towards him. 'You wouldn't have to worry about dwindling into an aunt if you married. You could leave Castonbury, have your own home, your own family, but you won't, will you? Because you can't forgive yourself either, can you? Admit it, there's a bit of you that thinks you deserve your fate, isn't there? And there's a bit of you that thinks every man you meet is like Lord Anthony Featherstone. And there's another bit of you that's afraid, is there not? Between that cold-blooded family of yours and that ambitious bastard you were betrothed to, they've got you thinking that no one could love you. Well, isn't there?'

'Why are you shouting at me? Why are you so angry? You

have no right to tell me what I should or shouldn't do with my life.'

'Any more than you have to tell me, but that didn't stop you.'

'You have it all wrong. I'm not at all afraid of—of love,' Kate said furiously. 'I could marry if I chose to, I have not lacked offers. I simply don't choose to, that is all. You sound as if you want me to throw myself at the first man who comes my way.'

'I don't.' He didn't want to think of her with any other man, but he knew that was wrong. 'Kate, don't cry. I didn't mean to make you cry.'

'I'm not crying,' she said, scrubbing at her eyes with the backs of her hands.

Virgil pulled out his kerchief and dabbed at her cheeks. 'I just want you to be happy.'

'I don't need a man to make me happy, any more than you need a woman.' Kate sniffed. 'You are right, I should not have come here today.'

'Don't say that. Kate, I just— I want— Oh, hell, Kate don't cry. Don't go. Not like this.' He didn't mean to but he couldn't not. His arms went around her. He dragged her hard, tight up against him, and he kissed her.

If she had not kissed him back. If she had not been so upset. If she had not thrown all those things at him that he didn't want to hear, he wouldn't have had to block them out. If she hadn't looked so tragic and so brave at the same time. If he hadn't been thinking of her day and night since he left her. Then…then he would have been able to stop.

But she did kiss him back. And she made that little noise that sent the blood rushing to his groin. And her kisses were so angry and so hungry, just exactly like his own. She savaged him with her mouth and he thrust his tongue into hers. She arched against him; he pushed her up against the door, the better to mould her to him. She said his name, the way no one else said his name, and he said hers, the name which could only be hers. Passion consumed them. He hadn't thought it was possible to burn so hot and so high so quickly. There was no gentle build, no slow burn, but a white-hot searing which made him achingly hard and had her panting, her fingers clutching at him, tugging at his clothes without any sort of finesse.

'We can't, not here,' he said, at the same time as he pulled her clear of the door only to ram a wooden chair under the handle.

'Albert could walk in at any time,' Kate agreed, as she unbuttoned his waistcoat and yanked it with his coat down over his arms.

They staggered, entwined and kissing frantically, towards the table. Virgil lifted her onto it. Her dress buttoned up the front. Tiny buttons. He tried to undo them, but they defeated him and so he pulled at the fabric, scattering jet buttons across the floor. Her corsets underneath were black silk. 'Sweet heaven, Kate. If anyone knew how you look underneath. Have you any idea what it does to me?' He breathed in the sweet scent of her, kissing her throat, and down, to the mound of her breasts. Her skin was flushed. He could feel her heart hammering. Same as his own.

Kate moaned. She yanked at Virgil's shirt. 'Take this off. I want to see you. Take it *off*.'

He pulled it quickly over his head and tossed it over his shoulder. The action drew in his abdomen, making his chest expand. She could count the muscles. He was like velvet. Every time she saw his skin that's what she thought of. Dark, luscious velvet that cried out to be touched. His muscles weren't sinewy but round and hard. She hadn't ever seen muscles like that. She was so tense she thought she might break. Hot and shivery. Throbbing and fluttering.

He pulled her back to him, to the edge of the table, and kissed her again. Her hands stroked and plucked at his skin, his shoulders, his chest, his nipples, the shadow of his rib cage. She didn't have enough hands. His lips were hot on hers, and hard. He rucked up her dress. 'Black,' he said, looking at her stockings with satisfaction. 'I knew they would be black.'

His hands stroked up to the flesh at the top of her stockings, then hovered over her sex. 'I don't want you, Virgil,' Kate said, digging her nails into his shoulders. Still he hovered. 'I don't need you,' she said.

With his other hand, he pushed her skirts higher. 'You don't need any man,' he agreed, stroking her.

'No.' It was a struggle to keep her eyes open, but she managed it, holding his gaze, tawny rimmed with gold. He had hardly touched her, but she was struggling to contain her release. 'I don't.'

'You don't,' Virgil agreed.

He kissed her mouth hard. Then he tipped her, suddenly, back onto the table, and dropped down to his knees before her, and licked into her. She cried out as his tongue flicked over her sensitive flesh. She could have sworn he made sparks shoot out. It felt like all her blood rushed to that single spot as he licked and sucked, and she tumbled, headlong and out of control, shoving her fist into her mouth to stop herself from screaming.

Virgil pulled her towards him, sliding his finger inside her, feeling the clenching of her climax around him. She pulled at his wrist, put his finger in her mouth, then kissed him, mingling the taste of them, the essence of her. He thought he would explode, the way she did it. Deliberate. Challenging.

'I don't need you,' she said, her voice husky with sex.

He needed to be inside her. Urgently. 'No more than I need you,' Virgil said, unfastening his buckskins, pulling her to the very edge of the table, wrapping her legs around his thighs, and entering her, pushing right into her, into the sleek, slick heat of her, in one thrust.

Her eyes darkened. She said his name. Urgent, just as he felt. She wrapped her arms around his neck. She tightened her ankles around his waist and tilted so that he pushed higher inside her.

Her eyes were fixed on his. She clenched around him, holding him completely still. He let her, for a moment. Then he moved and her eyes widened. He slipped his hands under her bottom to lift her, and thrust. Her hands were icy on his neck. He thrust again, and felt the delicious eddy of her climax. Another thrust, and she gave a muffled groan, and it was like being caught in a maelstrom inside her. He was whipped up, tossed high, pounded, helpless. He lost control, thrusting into her again and again until it took him, too, and at that moment he would have given anything to be able to spill himself into her. But he pulled himself free just in time, and afterwards, as he held her, clutched tight around him, he had never felt emptier.

Kate sat on the edge of the table, stunned by what had happened. Virgil was pulling on his clothes. She tried to fasten her gown, but half the buttons seemed to be missing. It didn't matter, she could button her pelisse over it. She couldn't believe what they'd just done, in Albert Moffat's best parlour. If she was a different kind of woman she would be ashamed of herself. If Virgil was a different kind of man…

If he was a different man, he wouldn't be Virgil. She retied one of her garters and made a vague attempt to pat her hair into order. She most likely looked as if she'd been dragged through a hedge backwards, but she couldn't bring herself to care. She dragged her pelisse over her dress and fastened it.

This time, she had no doubt it was goodbye. At the Dower House, she realised, she'd still had some hope. She had none now, but still she felt a sadistic urge just to make sure. 'It is impossible, isn't it?'

Virgil had been looking out of the window while she dressed, but he turned now, and came to stand beside her, taking her hands. He held them against his chest, bracing her. She didn't want him to brace her; it meant he thought she was going to be hurt. 'Don't answer that,' Kate said hurriedly. 'I know the answer.'

'You will take care of yourself, won't you, Kate?'

She nodded. 'And you.' She pinned a smile to her face. 'I will see myself out. Don't watch me go. I won't look back.'

She thought he would kiss her again. She thought it was something akin to pain she saw in his eyes, but it was gone before she could be sure. 'Goodbye, Kate.'

'Goodbye, Virgil.'

He pulled the chair away from the door and opened it for her. Kate made her way down the stairs of the inn, feeling as though she were descending into Hades. She didn't look back.

She did not remember the walk back to Castonbury. In her bedchamber, she rang the bell for Polly and a bath, then sank down on the window seat as the tub was filled. She was aware of Polly casting her anxious looks, and thankful that she said nothing until the bath was ready, the screens draped with towels set up by the fire.

For once, she allowed Polly to help her undress. 'What happened to your gown? You look as if you've been in a fight.'

Kate shook her head, biting her lip. Tears again. What was the point in tears? She had nothing at all to cry about. 'Nothing. I don't want to talk about it.' She sank gratefully into the depths of the lavender-scented water.

'I heard Mr Jackson was still at the inn. Snow, I heard, though it's to clear by the morning.'

Kate said nothing.

'John Coachman said you didn't take the gig. He said you went walking instead. Did you see him? Mr Jackson, I mean.'

'Yes,' Kate said with a sigh. 'I did. I wanted to say goodbye.'

'You didn't— I hope you were careful, my lady. There's ways and means if you weren't, but they're not pleasant and they don't always work.'

She considered pretending ignorance, but Polly was too perceptive and Kate was a terrible liar. 'There's no need to worry. Virgil was—was careful.'

Polly nodded. 'He's a good man, but it wouldn't have done, my lady. They would never have tolerated it.'

'There was never any question of that, Polly. It was just—we were just— I am not in love with him, and he's certainly not in love with me. It was just—what did you call it? A fling. And now it's over, and I'm fine. I'm absolutely fine.'

'Of course you are, my lady. You don't need him. You don't need any man.'

'No, I don't,' Kate said. Her lip quivered. It was ironic that the only person in the world—in her world—who knew her well enough to see beyond her words was a woman who had spent the better part of her life selling her body on the streets of London. She burst into tears.

Kate spent the following days keeping extremely busy, ensuring that Alicia was comfortable in the Dower House, taking her and the child on short drives around the countryside when the weather permitted, keeping out of Aunt Wilhelmina's way and reviewing her plans for extending the Castonbury school. She did not think, would not let herself think, about Virgil, in the daylight hours. She was bright and cheerful and useful, and that was enough, she told herself. At night it was a different matter. She did not cry, but she ached. Under cover of darkness she could admit that she missed him, but that was as far as she would go. She would not hope or even dream. There was no point and no need. She was lonely here at Castonbury, but she had always been lonely. It was just she hadn't noticed before.

In Scotland, Virgil emerged from the noise of the mill house at New Lanark in much the same frame of mind. Three waterwheels and thousands of spindles worked by over five hundred people made it a noisy place, no matter how light and clean it was in comparison to other mills. Walking down the main thoroughfare of the model village, he passed the other two mill buildings and headed towards the school which formed the kernel of Owen's Institute for the Formation of Character. There were aspects of his host's philosophy with which Virgil disagreed, but he was awed by the man's vision and utterly convinced by his arguments that education was fundamental to social reform. This visit had given him ideas enough to last him decades.

Through the windows of the school, he could see the little ones at their desks, their faces rapt with attention as James

Buchanan, weaver turned teacher, told them a story. He had intended going in to take more notes, but a restlessness kept him going down the cobbled road towards the majestic Falls of Clyde, thinking for the thousandth time how much Kate would have enjoyed this visit. It wasn't that he missed her so much as that he regretted the missed opportunity. He would have liked to have seen her reaction to it all, heard her opinions of it—which would be bound *not* to be anything like he imagined. Without her, the experience was somehow less than he expected.

Autumn was almost over this far north. The trees which bordered the falls were bereft of leaves. There was a decided nip to the air. The cascade which frothed and thundered over the river on its way down to propel the water wheels which powered the mills was mesmerising. The spray was icy. It made him think of the lake at Castonbury. The lake made him think of Kate, though not even she would consider swimming in water this cold. Kate, nymph-like and naked, her wet skin gleaming. Kate kissing him. Kate, hot and damp for him. Kate's climax, the look of shocked delight on her face. The jolting pleasure of his own release.

Virgil swore, and began the by now tried and tested process of forgetting about Kate by thinking of other things. He had plans now, thanks to Robert Owen, not for just one village but for a whole string of institutes and schools.

How much would ever be enough? Kate's question haunted him. This was what he'd worked for so tirelessly these past eleven years. This was what would start to make good some of his guilt for what he had done to Millie. So why was he feeling so down? Not just down, but tired, worn out, his energy sapped. The future he had worked so hard for, the castle he had built in the air which was now within his reach, they had lost their appeal. It wasn't that he didn't want it all, the schools and all the rest of it, but he did keep wondering, damn it, if he could ever do enough.

He was tired of carrying the burden of guilt around with him, but he couldn't see it ever easing. Why was he so tired? Was he being punished for having broken faith with his celibacy? Until he met Kate, it was a pact he had never thought of breaking. Well, Kate was in the past now, and so he would have no trouble keeping to it again. He wouldn't ever hold her again. Or kiss her. Or hear her laugh. Or...

Virgil jumped to his feet with an exclamation of disgust. What he had to do was get on with his life. He would go to Glasgow tomorrow. He would put his past to rest. And today, he would write to Kate and tell her all about New Lanark. He owed her that much.

Eleven

The grey December sky reflected Kate's mood. It was not raining but the air was damp and it was cold. It looked like it might rain, it looked as if it might clear up, it couldn't make up its mind. Ambivalent. Could weather be ambivalent? More like confused, she thought, that's what she was. She was sitting in the dining room drinking a cup of cold coffee when Lumsden informed her that Giles wished to see her as soon as conveniently possible.

Thinking that her aunt must have lodged another complaint, Kate made her way to her brother's private study with a heavy heart.

'You look tired,' Giles said.

'Can't sleep,' Kate replied, in quite his own terse style.

Giles grinned. 'Mind my own business, you mean. Well, I will, since I've a hundred other things to think about, provided you can assure me you've done nothing new to set our aunt off.'

'She seems quite taken up with little Crispin,' Kate said, dodging the question.

Her brother gave her one of his searching looks, but Kate returned it blandly, and he shrugged. 'We've had a letter from Harry,' he said. 'He sent it from Madrid. It's—well, interesting. Here, read it for yourself.'

Kate unfolded the missive. Harry's scrawl, unusually for a man who most often considered three or four lines sufficient, covered the entire sheet of paper, leaving barely enough room for his signature. The contents were, as Giles had said, interesting. 'So there's hope, then, that he might get the evidence he needs to prove Jamie's death?'

'Looks like it. If he does, at least it means we'll be able to access the funds.'

'And you may be a step closer to marrying Lily.'

'I wish it were more than a step. This waiting is the very devil,' Giles said grimly. 'Let us not talk about my affairs, it is frankly too painful. I haven't told Father about the letter. His health is still so frail. If Harry can't track down this chap in Seville, if it proves another false lead, then we're back to where we started. I haven't said anything to our aunt either.'

'Quite right. Aunt Wilhelmina wouldn't be able to resist telling Papa. It's best to keep this to ourselves until we have more certain news.'

'Good. I'm glad you agree with me, I was pretty sure you would.' Giles folded the letter up and tucked it into a drawer in his desk under a pile of other papers. 'What about the widow though? I don't feel right keeping it from her. Apart from anything else, if Harry can talk to this chap, the one who was with Jamie at the end, it may well be that it helps her cause. He'd have been bound to mention his marriage, wouldn't he?'

'I don't know. What do you think, are you still sceptical of her claim?'

'Honestly?' Giles locked the drawer. 'She seems genuine. She's not a money-grabber, though she's protective of the boy's rights, and that's natural enough. I could wish she did not allow him so often in the company of our father, but I can't deny it gives him pleasure. But honestly, Kate? I just can't get rid of the feeling that there's something—I don't know, something not right about Jamie's death. If we could just get the full story—but I won't count on it, not until we hear from Harry again.'

'Nor I.' Kate touched his hand briefly in sympathy. They were not a demonstrative family; this was the nearest she could imagine to hugging Giles. She hadn't noticed, not until she met Virgil, how little physical contact she had with anyone. 'We'll just have to bide our time and hope that Harry comes through, one way or another. In the meantime, do you wish me to tell Alicia the news?'

'If you would. It will be better coming from a woman.'

'Which means it will save you the bother of coping with her tears,' Kate said, laughing. 'Tell me, Giles, do you run the other way when Lily cries?'

'No, I try to make damn sure she has no cause to,' her brother retorted.

She almost ran into Aunt Wilhelmina on the staircase. 'I am going to Buxton with your sister-in-law,' Mrs Landes-Fraser, who had thawed enough since Alicia's arrival to address Kate directly once more, informed her. 'His Grace has commented several times now on the dowdiness of her wardrobe, and whether she proves to be an imposter or not, we cannot have it said that we dressed the woman in rags. I shall stop at Ripley and Hall in the village to select some silks, then we shall go on to Buxton to have them made up. We shall take the landau and shall be gone the better part of the day. I would ask you to accompany us, but she won't go without the boy, and you would be quite cramped. If you are in need of occupation I suggest that you turn your hand to the pile of sheets which you removed from the Dower House. Such common work should not be beyond your rather meagre skills. Your sister-in-law sets a surprisingly beautiful stitch.'

Suppressing the urge to set a beautiful stitch to hold her aunt's mouth shut, Kate continued up the stairs to her chamber. Was this what she was to be reduced to—darning sheets! Alicia did not even trust her to play nursemaid. Giles, who was off to inspect a horse somewhere, had asked Phaedra to accompany him. Giles had always favoured Phaedra. In a family of six siblings—eight if you counted Ross and Araminta—there were bound to be alliances and differences, but while she was undoubtedly well down the chain of popularity, Kate couldn't count herself as the favourite of a single one. Even dearest Ned had preferred Giles.

She threw herself onto the window seat and drew a frowning moon face in the condensation caused by her breath on the window pane. Drawing was another accomplishment she had not mastered. Her attempt at a horse had reduced Phaedra to tears of laughter once. She wiped the face away with her hand. It wasn't like her to be moody. She wondered how Virgil was getting on at New Lanark. She envied Virgil this trip. She envied Robert Owen Virgil's company.

Heavens, but she missed Virgil. There, she could admit that. No one could see inside her head the way he did. No one seemed particularly interested in her, the way he was. No one had ever made her feel the way he did.

Goodness, but she wanted him too. His body. His touch. His kisses. Their passion. Remembering what it had been like to have Virgil inside her made her muscles clench into a shiver. Alone in bed, she touched herself as Virgil had done, but it wasn't the same. She wanted *his* fingers. *His* mouth. His body.

Giles hadn't asked after Virgil once since he had gone, despite the fact that he'd been more than happy to monopolise him when he was here. It could be tact, of course, but Kate wasn't in the frame of mind conducive to giving anyone any credit. A man of ideas, Giles had called Virgil, but he had never considered him as anything other than a mild distraction from the burdens of trying to pull the estate out of the financial crisis in which their father's unfortunate investments had left them. Aunt Wilhelmina had practically danced in the wake of Virgil's departure. And Phaedra was so caught up in her horses that she barely noticed anything or anyone else. Whereas Kate…

Outside in the driveway, her aunt was being helped into the landau by John Coachman. She and Aunt Wilhelmina would never be close, but the stand-off they had reached, if not outright peace, was at least better than open warfare. Though her aunt remained almost as sceptical as Giles about Alicia's claims, contradictorily, she seemed to accept without question the child's parentage. She remarked pointedly and repeatedly that Crispin's arrival gave Kate the perfect opportunity to practice her role as aunt.

But the fact was, Kate thought, watching Alicia lifting the boy into the carriage, now that the hiatus of Alicia's arrival was over, and Alicia herself was patently able to take care of her own interests and equally wary of the friendship Kate offered, there was very little for Kate to do. Alicia's lawyer was negotiating a settlement for her. He was insisting on joint guardianship. His Grace would be obliged to consult her on all matters pertinent to Crispin's well-being. She would take care, too, she told Kate, that His Grace understood that nothing short of death would separate her from her child. She would see that Crispin had what was entitled to him.

Alicia was evidently not so fragile as her appearance gave everyone to believe. Kate was relieved. She looked forward to the day, which must surely come, when Alicia did pitched battle with the duke. She would not lay odds against her.

'Devil take it, I will not spend the day mending sheets!' Kate threw herself from the window seat, then stopped short. There were plenty of things she could be doing. Much more important things. If only she could think of them.

'Lady Kate, I'm so sorry, but this letter was overlooked in the mailbag this morning.'

Daisy's head poked round the bedchamber door. Kate's mouth went quite dry as she took the epistle. She had never seen the neat script before. There was no cause at all to imagine that it would be from him, and even if it was, it did not necessarily mean anything. 'Thank you.'

Kate locked the door behind Daisy and with trembling hands sat down again on the window seat to break the wafer.

It was from Virgil, and it was everything and nothing. Scanning it quickly, aware that her heart was beating fast, that she was shaking, Kate lurched from anticipation to extreme disappointment in the space of a few seconds. She read it again, forcing herself to go more slowly now, but there was nothing personal in it at all. Virgil had written her an account of New Lanark '*in order that you may better understand Owen's methods as well as his theory*,' he wrote. There was no return address. Only a postscript, informing her that he would not be returning to Stoke to see Josiah, but would conclude their business in London. She would never see him again.

She had thought she had understood that. She had thought she had accepted it. She had not. Staring at the letter, reading it for a third time, and for a third time failing to find anything remotely personal, the dreadful truth which she had hidden away, ignored, denied, buried deep down inside her, peeped out.

'Oh, no, not that.' Oh, heavens, let her contrariness not

have led her to that. Surely she couldn't possibly have been so stupid as to fall in love with him?

But it was too late, and it had nothing to do with contrariness, her love for Virgil. 'Well done, Kate,' she said bitterly. 'Trust you to give your heart to the one man in the world determined not to have it.'

She loved him. She had thought herself incapable of love, but it seemed she was wrong. When had she stopped being afraid? She didn't know, but sometime between the day at the Rothermere Arms and now, she seemed to have crossed the border and left the past behind. She had paid for her mistakes with Anthony in full. What's more, she had, she realised with surprise, accepted that trying to become the person her aunt and her father wished her to be was wrong. Worse than wrong, it would make her unhappy. Virgil said she had to forgive herself. She hadn't really understood what he'd meant, but it seemed she'd done it all the same.

If only Virgil could forgive himself too—but that, Kate knew, looking down at her letter, really was asking the impossible. She loved him, but he would never, ever love her back. No one understood her as Virgil did. No one would ever touch her, mind or body, as he did. She could not imagine that anyone ever would.

Tears clogged her throat, but she would not let them fall. She had promised him that she would try to be happy. In this letter he had written, there was no love, but there was much which could help her to follow some of her dreams. Sniffing resolutely, Kate took it over to her desk and began to read it again.

Robert Owen, Virgil told her, employed one of his former mill workers and a young village girl to teach the infants without books. Mr Owen boasted that his mill workers were the happiest, healthiest and most productive of any in the country, though Virgil was not convinced they were all equally so. In the evenings, they attended classes and dancing lessons. There followed a host of facts and figures which Virgil hoped would give Kate the real evidence, practical proof, to make her patrons pay attention.

Kate smiled as she read Virgil's views on some of Mr Owen's more controversial methods, then she drew a clean sheet of paper onto the blotter, dipped her pen in the inkwell and began to make notes.

Virgil reached Glasgow in the early afternoon. The crowd of ships on the river Clyde marked his progress towards the bustling city, long lines of them anchored in the channel with their heavy sails furled; the exposed rigging looked like complex trails of cobwebs slung between the masts. There was a constant to-ing and fro-ing of small boats ploughing the waters from the ships to the wharfs like worker ants.

As the Edinburgh mail approached the town itself along roads thick with mud it slowed, weaving through the clutter and throng of carts and drays, of carriages and sedan chairs, avoiding stray dogs and clucking hens and a herd of lowing cattle being brought back from the common grazing grounds in the west to their byres in the east.

The mighty cathedral rose high on the hill above the city. In amongst the cluster of smallholdings and cottages which dotted the land nearest the river, merchants made rich by tobacco, sugar and slaves had built huge mansions. The foundations of a large house stood oddly in the midst of a field planted with cabbages. Further east, just before the Trongate, inns and taverns of the lower sort contested the traditional space of houses and food markets.

Virgil stopped at the posting house only to eat the half crown ordinary of mutton and barley stew. Ramshorn Kirk, where Louisa Gordon was buried, was known locally as the Merchant's Graveyard. Armed with directions, the gold locket tucked safe in an inside pocket of his coat, he set out on foot. Glasgow owed much of its wealth to the crop he had spent a large part of his life growing and harvesting and he was eager to see what his servitude had created. Though the trade was no longer what it had been, there was a time when almost every hogshead of tobacco grown in Virginia had come through this city.

He walked up to the cathedral past the cheese and meat markets, whose business was done for the day. Descending the hill via the university and skirting the large expanse of the green where lines of washing flapped in the breeze, he came to the tower of the tollbooth prison. In the paved square outside, he stopped to watch the merchants hold court while those wishing to do business with them vied for attention.

By the warehouses and offices which lined the docks, the air was thick with the scent of spices, sugar and, above all, tobacco. That sweet, almost rotten smell made Virgil stop in his tracks, oblivious of the bustle around him, of clerks with their tied documents, of ships' crews in search of their next voyage, of the warehousemen who lurked in the alleyways taking a sly break, and through it all the merchants who strutted and preened. Eleven years ago, the tobacco which had been packed by the strike breakers would have come here. Twelve years ago, thirteen, fourteen, more, the hogsheads he had packed himself would have been sold on at this exchange, too, more than likely. Now he was probably richer than any of these merchants. If he wanted to, he could outbid them all for tobacco, sugar, molasses, silks. The knowledge gave him no pleasure. *How many schools and libraries and houses would be enough?* Kate's question haunted him. It would never be enough. Never. Because his crime was so great? Or because he was looking at it all the wrong way?

He stopped abruptly in front of the Trade's House. It looked uncannily familiar. He could not imagine why at first, and then he saw it. The carved pediment above the pillared entrance, the pleasing symmetry of the building. It reminded him of Castonbury.

Kate.

Kate had said he had to forgive himself. Kate had said that this locket he carried was someone else's past. Kate had said he would never be free. He missed her. God, he missed her. That last day, when he'd told her to be happy, he hadn't meant it. He *did* want her to be happy, but not with another man. Not with any man. Except him.

But that was impossible.

Wasn't it?

The graveyard was north of the river, just a few hundred yards from the Trade's House. It was raining as he entered it, a long narrow space enclosed by warehouses on three sides. Gloomy. Ominous. It did not feel particularly peaceful. He would not like this to be his last resting place.

Reading the stones, he could see how the place got its name. Tobacco, sugar, cloth—the remains of any number of merchants lay here with their families, touting their wealth in the huge slabs of stone which covered their crypts. Several of the tombs were large enough to be enclosed by wrought iron fencing. The Gordon tomb was one such. Virgil turned the heavy latch, relieved to find it was not locked.

Tragic, Kate had called Malcolm Jackson's story. If Louisa Gordon had married her lover and gone to the New World, she would not now be lying beneath this cold, damp sod. A month's happiness, a year's, or many more, she would have had with her husband. Had Kate been Louisa, she would not have stayed behind alone. If Kate had been Millie, she would not have killed herself.

Virgil sank down onto the gravestone and opened the locket. Kate would not have given up as Millie had. Kate would have known without him having to tell her that he would come back for her, because Kate understood him. No one had ever understood him as Kate had. Could he forgive himself?

If he did not, one thing was for sure; he would never be free of his chains. The past kept him bound and manacled. He could not undo it, he could repent it and he could try and make good, but how much good was enough? He could build schools and libraries and model villages even. He could give others the opportunity to free themselves, but still deny himself that chance. Kate was right. He was still in shackles.

Millie would not have wanted that. Would Millie have forgiven him? Freedom was about having choices. He'd made some poor choices, and he'd paid for them, but Millie had chosen too. She'd chosen death over hope. Kate said that Millie would have forgiven him. That hadn't ever sat right with Virgil. Millie had made it impossible for Virgil to be forgiven. Wasn't the point that *he* had to forgive *her*?

He tried to remember what it felt like to be with Millie—to laugh with her, to walk with her, to make love to her—but it was like someone else's memories. Even the images from that fateful last day which had been so painfully fresh when he'd painted them for Kate seemed to be fading. Perhaps his confession had been cathartic, after all.

He'd been a boy when he'd fallen in love with Millie. Their passion had been joyful, but nowhere near as intense as what he'd felt making love to Kate. When Kate climaxed she looked right at him. When he was inside her, inside the intoxicating heat of her, he felt as if she was inside his head, as if she was communing with him. He hadn't ever felt that with Millie.

Could he really forgive himself? And even if he could, and come to terms with what Millie had done, too, where did that leave him?

It left him without Kate.

Virgil took out his pocket knife and began to dig a hole. He dropped the locket into it, and said a last prayer for Malcolm Jackson and Louisa Gordon. Maybe in the next world he and his Louisa were together.

Virgil was in this world, and he had no desire to quit it yet. If he could forgive himself, he had a future, and he was damn sure he didn't want to live it alone. Closing the gate of the crypt behind him, he made his way quickly back to the posting house. Eleven years of celibacy. It seemed so obvious now that it had been easy because he hadn't met Kate. He did love her. He had no idea what she felt for him, but he did love her. He had done everything possible to kill any feelings for him she may have had, but that last day at the inn…

Could he hope? Dare he hope? He had been afraid to love her because he was terrified of losing her, but if he didn't ask her, if he didn't try, then he'd have lost her anyway. He missed her so much. Now that he had allowed himself to consider the possibility, he couldn't bear to think of how empty his future would be without her. It was all very well to insulate yourself against hurt by denying yourself affection, but it was too late for that now. He had to see her. He could not wait to see her.

He ran the last half-mile to the posting house. 'Change of plan,' he said to the landlord. 'I need to hire a post chaise and six. Now.'

Kate rose each morning with a list of tasks constructed overnight and went about them methodically, focusing on achieving something new every day. She made the days long. She worked hard. She did not cry, or lament, or allow herself to dwell on her hopeless love. Virgil was gone. There was nothing she could do about it, and all she could do to keep her heart intact was to be true to what she had promised him. It was not her way to try to change what she could not. She was a survivor, one who coped and continued regardless, and this was how she found the reserves to face each day. She loved him and would always love him, but there was nowhere for her love to live, and so she kept it hidden, tucked up inside her like a wingless bird. Helping others had always been her consolation. She would simply have to help them a lot more now.

This morning, the first task on her list was to see Alicia, and finally bring her up to date with the contents of Harry's letter.

'I have some news.'

They were sitting in the drawing room of the Dower House. The child, Crispin, played contentedly in the corner with a set of wooden blocks. Jamie's wife looked well, dressed in a morning gown the same colour of blue as her eyes. Her fair hair was prettily dressed, tied in a top knot which fell in a cluster of curls around her neck. She did not wear a widow's cap. Aunt Wilhelmina had been vocal upon this subject at dinner. Alicia looked much too young to be a widow. She was much too beautiful to hide her charms under a cap. Not that there was anyone in Castonbury to appreciate Alicia's charms that Kate could think of.

Had Alicia loved Jamie? Loving Virgil as she did made Kate look at everyone differently. Now she knew the signs, it was obvious to her that Giles was deeply in love with Lily. Of Alicia's feelings she was not at all certain. There were times when she seemed quite cold, indifferent almost, in the way she said Jamie's name, as if he was not her husband but a stranger. Of course, she had Crispin to remind her of Jamie and so no real need to talk about him, Kate supposed. Polly said she'd never been in love and thank the Lord for having been spared. Despite everything, Kate was glad *she* had not been spared.

'What news, Lady Kate?'

Alicia was looking at her expectantly, and Kate realised she had been daydreaming again. A new habit. 'We have had a letter from my brother Harry. As you know, he's in Spain.'

'Trying to discover what happened to my husband.'

'Jamie. Yes. Harry writes from Madrid, but he is on his way to Seville. There is a man there, Pablo Garrido, who was apparently in command of the unit to which Jamie was assigned. Harry's letter says—Harry believes that this man Garrido may be able to put him in touch with the man who was actually with Jamie when he died.'

Alicia's hands fluttered to her breast. 'You mean Xavier Sanchez?'

'I believe that was the name. You know this man?'

'No, no. Only—I have heard his name. I— Jamie must have talked of him.'

'Jamie discussed his mission with you?'

'No, that's not what I meant.' Alicia leapt to her feet and picked her child up, folding him in a tight embrace, ignoring his protests. 'I meant—I merely meant that when Jamie died, it was no secret that man Sanchez was with him.'

'Of course, it's only a slim chance, but if Harry can speak with Sanchez, perhaps then we can find out the details of how Jamie lost his life. And then there will be the proof of death that we need in order to sort out the estate.' Kate smiled encouragingly. 'It could even be that Jamie talked to Sanchez about you.'

'About me?' Alicia repeated, the colour draining from her face. 'Why should he?'

'Mama, Mama, you're hurting.'

The child set up a wail. Alicia got to her feet, kissing the boy's golden head. 'It is time for his nap,' she said to Kate.

There was no mistaking the dismissal in her voice. 'I'm sorry to throw this at you so suddenly, only Giles and I felt that you should know. We have not told anyone else. You understand, Alicia, my father knows nothing of it.'

'You need not worry, I won't say anything to the duke. Jamie is dead. What do the details matter?' Alicia said flatly. 'Excuse me, Lady Kate. I must see to my son.'

Walking back to the big house, Kate felt rebuffed. Recounting the meeting to Giles, who had been waiting for her by the bridge, her natural sense of justice restored her. 'It was a shock,' she told her brother, 'that much was obvious. She must have cared a great deal for him. It's just too painful for her to hear the details.'

'Well, you told her. She can't accuse us of not keeping her informed,' Giles said. 'Kate…'

'What is it?'

'Kate, Virgil Jackson is here.'

'What?'

'He arrived half an hour ago.'

'Is there something wrong? Has he been hurt? Why didn't you tell me? Where is he?'

'Why the devil should you think he was hurt? He looked perfectly healthy to me. He's in my study. I thought it best—no one knows save Lumsden that he's here. Kate…'

'What is it, Giles?' Kate was almost dancing in exasperation. Virgil was here. *'What?'*

'Devil take you, Kate, you know damn well what! I can't stop you. If you love him—Lily says you do, and she's—well, God help you.'

Under any other circumstances, Kate would have found this disjointed speech utterly fascinating. She didn't think she'd ever seen her brother beyond words, but right now she didn't give a damn. Picking up her skirts, she ran across the lawn at full tilt and did not stop until she burst into Giles's study, when the sight of Virgil standing there made her heart flip.

'Kate!'

'Virgil!'

'You look tired.'

'It's been a long journey.'

Kate closed the door and leaned against it. She was out of breath. Her hair was falling down. She was shaking. 'How did you get here?'

'Post chaise. I hired a carriage. Four horses. I asked for six but they said not even royalty could harness six horses to a hired chaise.'

He looked quite dishevelled. His neck cloth looked as if it had been tied without the aid of a mirror. His boots were splashed with mud. He looked anxious. Nervous. Worried. She had missed him so much. Giles seemed to think—but she would not let herself hope. 'What are you doing here?'

'I had a speech,' Virgil said. Kate hadn't moved from the door. She looked wary. He didn't like that look. 'I had a speech,' he said again. He couldn't remember a word of it. He crossed the room to stand beside her. There was only one bit of what he wanted to say that mattered right now. 'I love you, Kate.'

'How do you know?'

That made him laugh. He should have known her reaction wouldn't be what he expected. 'What you said, about never being free. When I was burying the locket, I realised you were right. Millie had a choice too. I made it difficult for her to live, but I didn't make it impossible. Once I saw that, I saw lots of other things too.'

'Such as?'

'I was afraid to care. I thought that love and loss went hand in hand. I didn't want to love you because I couldn't bear the idea of losing you, but then I realised that never having tried, regretting not trying, would be so much worse.'

'Like Louisa Gordon and Malcolm Jackson,' Kate said.

Virgil took her hands in his. 'Exactly. And more. I couldn't understand why you were so impossible to resist. I see now that it was you. It could only ever have been you. I love you, Kate. I don't know what you feel, but I'm asking you to give me a chance. It won't be easy. Your father will disown you. Even in Boston, a marriage like ours would be—there will be many people who will never accept us into their world. But if you love me, we could make our own world, Kate.'

A single tear escaped her and rolled down her cheek. He still hadn't touched her. He was afraid to touch her. He was terrified he had left it too late. 'Don't cry, Kate.'

She sniffed. 'I'm not.' She rubbed her eyes with the heel of her hand. 'If that was your speech, it was the most beautiful one I've ever heard.'

It took a moment for her words to sink in. 'I'm not too late?'

Kate shook her head.

'You love me?'

'How could you doubt it?'

'And you'll marry me?'

'Oh, Virgil, I thought you'd never ask!'

He kissed her so hard then that if she had not been leaning against the door she would have fallen. He kissed her desperately, clinging to her, murmuring her name, his hands feverish on her. He really had thought he'd lost her.

'You would never have been too late,' she whispered, kissing him back, pressing herself as close as she could against the delightfully hard, solid bulk of his body. 'Never, never, never. I love you more.'

'No, me more.'

'No, me. More.'

They were laughing and kissing at the same time. A wild euphoria ripped through them, turning their laughter into passion. Kate reached behind her to turn the key in the lock, saying a quick apology to her brother for the use they were about to make of his private room.

'We can't,' Virgil said as she rubbed herself quite blatantly against the length of his erection. 'It would be wrong.'

'All the more reason,' Kate said, stroking him through the leather of his buckskins. 'Think how outraged my aunt would be,' she said, slipping down onto her knees before him and undoing the buttons of his falls.

'We should wait. Until we are married. That's what I planned. Oh, Kate…'

With a sigh of satisfaction, she freed him and wrapped her fingers around him. Silky and potent and hers. She tasted the tip of him, relishing the way it made him shudder, drawing a groan from deep inside him. She was hot. Wet. 'I don't want to wait,' she said, slanting a mischievous look up at him before tasting him again. 'I don't think you *can* wait, my love. Doesn't it add a certain something, knowing what my family would think? This isn't wrong. It couldn't be more right, could it?'

Virgil dropped down onto his knees beside her. 'Nothing could be more right,' he said, cupping her face. His kiss left her utterly certain. 'Nothing could be more right than this,' he said, tilting her back onto the floor and kissing her again.

'And this.' He pushed her skirts high, parting the legs of her lacy drawers. 'Do you know, there is something about the curve of your knee which fascinates me. And here, the crease right here, where your bottom curves into your thigh. And here.' He cupped her sex, gazing deep into her eyes as the pressure of his palm on the swollen core of her brought her to a frenzy.

'And this.' The tip of his shaft stroked over her, throwing her over the edge as he entered her. She pulsed around him, panting and clutching at him, urging him on, harder.

'I love you, Kate,' Virgil said, and he exploded, staying inside her, holding her, shuddering against her.

Kate wrapped her arms tight around him. Her hair streamed out across the ancient rug. The leg of a chair was sticking into her shoulder. There was a large cobweb suspended from the cornicing above her. 'I love you, Virgil.' She had never been happier.

Epilogue

His Grace the Duke of Rothermere was predictably outraged by his eldest daughter's choice of husband. Having met Virgil just once, His Grace was completely unprepared for the astounding news that his wayward daughter had fallen in love and accepted a proposal from a man who, as far as he was concerned, barely existed. That the man was an American, albeit one of that country's richest inhabitants, was bad enough. That he was a commoner, and ex-slave with a lineage which could be traced back precisely one generation and only on one side, made the marriage, as far as the duke was concerned, simply impossible.

He was incandescent. When it became clear that Virgil was not actually *asking* him for his daughter's hand but telling him that he had already been accepted, consent was refused. When it was pointed out to His Grace by his outspoken daughter that his consent was not required, the duke informed her that she would be cut off without a penny.

'My dowry was settled on me by my mother. You cannot

actually deprive me of it,' Kate said with satisfaction, having made a point of checking the matter with Giles.

'As a matter of fact, we have no need of Kate's dowry,' her future husband said.

'But it's mine. I'm entitled to it. I can't come to you with nothing.'

'You are all I need.'

At this point, the duke's daughter committed the ultimate sin of expressing her emotions in public by throwing her arms around her betrothed and kissing him. His Grace, realising nothing could be done to prevent the match, decided that nothing could make him accept it. Informing his daughter that he never wanted to lay eyes on her again, he sank onto his couch, closed his eyes and opened them only when his valet presented him with a glass of cognac and informed him that Lady Katherine and the American had gone.

Thus relieved of the duty of trying what she had always known would be a vain attempt to bring her father round, Kate set about happily making plans. Virgil, who had at first been inclined to consider using monetary measures to bring the duke on to their side, was persuaded by her complete and utter happiness not to do so. That her brother, sister and even her aunt seemed, respectively, reconciled, happy and inured to Kate's choice was more than Virgil had bargained for.

Though he missed her desperately, he was persuaded that he could leave her to make arrangements for their wedding while he made his arrangements for their departure to America and finished his business in London with Josiah Wedgwood. The potter was so delighted with the news that such a unique couple had been introduced at his own dinner party that he promised to design them their very own dinner service.

Lady Katherine Mary Cecily Montague became Mrs Virgil Jackson on Christmas Eve. It was a private ceremony in the family chapel at Castonbury. The Reverend Seagrove officiated. The groom was represented, most irregularly as Aunt Wilhelmina pointed out, by the bride's brother. This left the bride herself with no one to walk her up the aisle until she hit upon the idea of asking her aunt to give her away.

Mrs Landes-Fraser was torn. Never before had she heard of such a thing. But since it was a private ceremony, her niece pointed out, no one would ever know. And if they did, Aunt Wilhelmina should remember that this was the wedding of the Duke of Rothermere's daughter. Where a Montague led, others would follow. Would not Aunt Wilhelmina wish to set a precedent all by herself?

Mrs Landes-Fraser was flattered.

Kate, existing in a bubble of happiness, pressed home her advantage. It was what her mother would have wanted, she said, disregarding without a qualm the fact that she barely knew her mother, and was fairly certain that she would have spent her eldest daughter's wedding day in protest alongside her husband rather than in the church. But Aunt Wilhelmina was swayed. In honour of the occasion, she purchased a new turban in a particularly regal shade of puce and proudly walked her niece the short journey up the aisle, thus finally proving to Kate that her affection, though well-buried, was sincere.

All the more sincere, Phaedra, the only other person present, whispered later to her sister, since Aunt Wilhelmina had chosen to support Kate against the express wishes of their father, who was notable by his absence.

The church, which had been built and rebuilt by the Montague family on the same site since the thirteenth century, provided any number of Kate's ancestors in the form of effigies and tombs, to make up for the absent duke. Kate, dressed in a vermillion gown cut quite inappropriately low across the bosom, didn't care. There was only one person whose attendance was vital, and he was right there at her side, placing a gold wedding band on her finger. Reverend Seagrove said later that he had never heard a couple make their responses so firmly. Aunt Wilhelmina declared that the church must be in need of airing, for the dust had made her eyes positively stream.

Though the bridal couple wanted no formal party to celebrate their nuptials, Giles insisted that there was one tradition which could not be dispensed with. The Yule log had been hauled in that day, and sat in the fireplace in the huge marble hall. Monsieur André, the French chef, had produced a sugar cake which was an exact replica of Castonbury Park itself, in honour of the occasion. The entire Castonbury staff save His Grace's faithful valet were there to greet Lady Kate and her husband. Most of them were very happy for her. Polly, who was joining her mistress in the New World, was nothing short of ecstatic.

To Kate fell the honour of lighting the fire with kindling formed from last year's Yule log. To Virgil fell the task of proposing a toast to his new bride. Looking around at the sea of faces standing under the gilded domed ceiling in the cavernous and astoundingly beautiful hall, he caught her hand. 'Are you sure you really want to leave all this behind?'

'This is the old world, Virgil. I will miss it, but I can live without it. I can't live without you.'

Every time he looked at her, he thought it wasn't possible to love her more, and every time he looked at her again he realised it was. Virgil kissed his wife's hand and raised his glass. 'To Kate,' he said, 'who is all the world to me.'

* * * * *

Lady of Shame

ANN LETHBRIDGE

When Claire was a child, the house at Castonbury Park had seemed as cold as the stones in its walls. Today, as she paused halfway down the combed gravel drive, the stairs sweeping around each side of the columned portico welcomed her like open arms. The facade, with its swagged decorations and artistically placed statues, gleamed pale yellow in the weak January sunlight and promised sanctuary within its solemn splendour.

Home.

It looked so solid. So impregnable. So safe. Shivering against the north wind gusting down from the Peaks, Claire allowed herself to believe she had made the right choice. If not, she didn't know what she would do. Where she would go next.

At her side, gripping her hand, her daughter, Jane, stared at the house. Seven years old and already her grey eyes were wise and world-weary. 'This is where you grew up? It is huge.'

'Yes,' Claire said, resuming the long trudge to the front door. 'This is where I lived when I was your age. Do not wander off, while you are here. It is a large place and it is easy to get lost.'

'I won't, Mama.'

Gravel crunched under their feet and the clean sharp smell of incipient snow filled Claire's nostrils. She trod firmly. Confidently. Or at least she hoped her inner fears did not show.

It would have been so much better if they could have driven up to the door in a post chaise. More appropriate to her station. But they had no coin for such luxuries and, as Claire had learned these past eight years, what could not be cured must be endured. Instead they had taken the stage from London to Buxton and then accepted a ride in a farmer's cart to Castonbury village. They had walked the rest of the way. To her surprise, the gatekeeper had let them pass on foot without question.

Were they always so lax about visitors? Did they let just anyone pass? She glanced over her shoulder. No one following. Nor would there be. Ernie Pratt knew only the assumed name George had invented after his brush with the law. She hoped.

Footsteps rustled behind them. Her heart leapt to her throat. She spun around, pushing Jane behind her.

No one. There was no one there. Just leaves blowing across the park, tumbling across the gravel.

'What is it?' Jane asked.

'Nothing,' Claire said, relief filling her. 'Nothing at all.'

Yet still she picked up her pace. Hurrying towards the front door and safety.

A quick swallow did nothing to ease the dryness in her throat as she looked up at stone Corinthian columns towering three stories above. A declaration of the Duke of Rothermere's wealth and status. And his power.

Once she had resented that power, now it felt like a lifeline.

They passed beneath the arches hiding the ground floor rustic stonework and marched up to the black painted front door gleaming with brass fittings. The everyday door. Only for very special events did visitors climb the stairs to the grand entrance above.

The lion's head door knocker glared at her in disapproval. Her heart thundered. No. She was not fearful. Definitely not. Just filled with the anticipation of seeing her brother after so many years. She lifted the ring in the great jaws and let the knocker fall with a bang that echoed in the entrance hall beyond.

No going back now. She was committed. For Jane's sake. She smiled down at her daughter, who pressed tight up against her hip.

The door opened. A young footman in red-and-gold livery looked down his nose at them. ''Tis at the wrong door, you are. Don't you people know nothing? Servants' entrance is round the back of the west pavilion.' He pointed to the left. 'That there large block at the end.'

He slammed the door in their faces.

Shocked speechless, she recoiled. Her heart gave a horrid little dip. The footman thought her a servant. She glanced down at herself and Jane. They were respectably, if shabbily, dressed; her widow's weeds had seen better days, and her skirts were dusty, wrinkled from their travels.

The doubts about their welcome attacked her anew. The seed of hope nurtured in her chest all the way from London shrivelled, sapping the strength that had sustained her once she had made up her mind to bury her pride and ask for help.

Should she knock again and risk a more violent rejection? What if none of the family were home? No one to endorse her claim?

'Why did he close the door?' Jane asked, her voice weary.

Why indeed. Might Crispin have left word she wasn't to be admitted? She shivered. 'I think he thought we were someone else.'

Jane tugged at her skirt. 'What shall we do?'

She forced a confident smile. 'Why, we will go around the back just as the nice man suggested.' Perhaps there she would find a servant she knew. She retraced her steps back to the drive.

'He wasn't nice,' Jane grumbled as they trudged along the walkway leading to the servants' wing. 'The farmer with the cart was nice. Why couldn't we stay with him?'

'Because he isn't family.'

Jane looked up at the house, her face full of doubt. 'I want to go home.'

'This is our home.' Claire hoped the anxiety fluttering in her stomach wasn't apparent in her voice. She quickened her pace, heading away from the block for family and guests, feeling very much like a stranger who didn't belong.

Another set of arches hid the kitchens and cellars and quarters for the staff. They stopped at a plain brown door. She squared her shoulders and rapped hard. This time she would not be turned away.

It opened. A waft of warmth hit her face along with a delicious scent of cooking. She swayed as it washed over her and she heard Jane sniff with appreciation.

A tall man in his mid-thirties wearing a chef's white toque and a pristine white apron gazed at them down an aristocratic nose. At some point that haughty nose had been broken and badly set, resulting in a bump that only slightly ruined the elegant male beauty of hard angles and planes. Not English, she thought, taking in the olive cast to his complexion and jet hair.

Onyx eyes fringed with black lashes too thick and long for a man swiftly roved her person. They took in her undecorated bonnet, her black bombazine skirts and her scuffed half-boots. She had the feeling he could see all the way to her plain worn shift with that piercing dark glance.

Sympathy softened his harsh features. 'Step inside, *madame*.' His voice was deep and obviously foreign.

Giddy with relief, she almost fell over the threshold.

'Careful, *madame*.' A muscular arm, hard beneath the fabric of his coat, caught her up.

A thrill rippled through her body. A recognition of his male physical strength. Shocked, she pulled away.

He released her and stepped back as if he, too, had felt something at the contact. He gestured her forward into what must be the scullery with its dingy whitewashed walls and a large lead-lined sink.

'Sit,' he said. 'At the table.' He pulled back a bench.

Claire sank down, glad of the respite, while she gathered her wits. Jane hopped up beside her.

'Mademoiselle Agnes,' he called out. '*Vite, allez*.'

A young woman in a mob cap ran in from the larger room beyond. The kitchen proper, no doubt.

'Bring soup and bread,' he ordered.

The girl ducked her head and disappeared.

'No, really,' Claire managed, gathering her scattered wits. 'I need to—'

'It is fine, *madame*. No need to be anxious,' he said. 'You are hungry, *non*?' he said, smiling at Jane.

'Starving,' the child replied with the honesty of youth.

'You don't understand,' Claire said. 'I need to speak to Mrs Stratton.' She held her breath, hoping beyond hope that the housekeeper she'd known as a girl was still employed here.

'She has no work. I am sorry, *madame*, all I am permitted is to offer you soup and send you on your way.'

Permitted? On whose orders? Heat rushed through her. So much heat, after coming in from outside. Her head spun. She tugged at the button of her coat, tried to undo the scarf around her neck. It tangled with her anxious fingers.

'Are you ill?' He crouched down and with strong competent hands worked at the knot. She could not help but stare at the handsome face so close to hers, so serious as he focused on the task at hand. Such a face might have modelled for an artist's rendition of a Roman god of war. His fingers brushed the underside of her chin. Liquid fire ran through her veins. He glanced up, his eyes showing shock and awareness. His lips parted in a breathless sigh.

For one long moment it was as if nothing else existed in the world but the two of them.

Her skin tingled. Her body lit up from within.

He jerked back, his hands falling away. He swallowed. 'It is free now.' He rose to his feet and backed up a few steps, gesturing to the table. 'You will feel better after you eat.'

Still shocked, she could only stare at him. How could she have responded to him in such a wanton way? Because he was handsome? Or because it was a long time since a man had shown her and Jane such kindness? In either case, it was not appropriate.

'Soup sounds awfully good,' Jane said wistfully.

'No,' Claire said, fighting to catch her breath. 'I did not come here for food. Or work. I must speak with Mrs Stratton. Please tell her Lady Claire wishes to speak with her.'

Confusion entered his dark eyes. Followed swiftly by comprehension.

'Mademoiselle Agnes,' he called out. 'At once.'

The girl popped her head back through the door. 'I'm pouring the soup,' she said. 'Give a girl a minute.'

'Never mind that. Fetch Mrs Stratton. *Immédiatement*.'

'What? To see some vagabond?' the girl said.

Claire stiffened.

The chef glowered. 'Now.'

The maid tossed her head. 'First you want soup. Now you

want the housekeeper. Make up your mind, can't you?' She scampered off.

'Can't we have soup?' Jane asked.

'Later,' Claire said. She wasn't going to let anyone see them begging for food as if they really were vagabonds. They would eat in the dining room, like Montagues.

'I apologise for the mistake.' He grimaced. 'We were not expecting you, I think?'

The apology gave her renewed hope. She offered him a smile. 'It is my fault for coming to the scullery door.'

As he gazed at her face, his eyes darkened, his lips formed a straight line. '*Madame* is generous.' He had transformed from a man who seemed warm and caring to one whose back was rigid and whose attitude was formal and distant. A huge gap opened up between them and they were now in their proper places. Or perhaps he would not think so, once he knew her story.

'Madame Stratton will be with you shortly,' he murmured. 'You will excuse me, I think?'

Claire smiled her gratitude. 'Thank you so much for your help.'

'*De rien.* My pleasure.' He bowed and left.

Pro forma, of course, but her thanks had been heartfelt even if her responses to his touch had been distinctly strange.

He had disappeared into the kitchen.

A strategic retreat.

Jane pressed a hand to her tummy. 'I'm so hungry. Why did you say no to the soup? I can smell it.'

So could Claire. The scent was aromatic and utterly tempting. She was hungry too. It had been a permanent state of affairs these past few months. Recalling the very formal arrangements for family dining at Castonbury Park, she anticipated it would be hours before dinner was served. 'We will ask for some tea and biscuits,' she said. 'As soon as we are invited in.' If they were invited in.

Jane heaved a sigh, but folded her mittened hands in her lap and swung her legs back and forth.

Claire reached out and squeezed the small hands in hers. 'It won't be long.' She prayed she was right.

At the sound of the tap of quick footsteps on the flags and the rustle of stiff skirts, Claire came to her feet, half fearful, half hopeful. Now she would know if she was welcome here or not.

Despite the grey now mingled with the blonde hair neatly confined within her cap and the new wrinkles raying out from the corners of her friendly blue eyes, Claire recognised the housekeeper at once.

The footman who had closed the front door in their faces only moments before peered over the housekeeper's shoulder. 'Saints, another one crawling out of the woodwork claiming to be a relative.'

'Be quiet, Joe,' Mrs Stratton said sharply. 'Go back to your post at once.'

The footman glowered, but stomped off.

The housekeeper turned back to Claire, her kindly face showing surprise mingled with shock. No doubt she saw changes in Claire, too, but it was the shock of recognition and Claire felt a rush of relief.

'Lady Claire. It *is* you.' Genuine pleasure warmed the housekeeper's voice as she dipped a curtsey. 'And sent to the servants' door too. I am so sorry about Joe. It is almost impossible to get good staff these days.' This welcome was far warmer than she had ever dared hope.

'It is Mrs Holte now,' she said with a smile that felt stiff and awkward as her voice scraped against the hot hard lump that had formed in her throat. 'I wasn't sure you would remember my married name after all these years.' If Mrs Stratton had heard it at all. The Montagues had cast her off the moment she had married. 'It is good to see you again.'

Jane tugged on her arm.

She indicated the child. 'Jane, this is Mrs Stratton.' She smiled at the woman. 'Jane is my daughter.'

Mrs Stratton dipped her head. 'Welcome, Miss Jane. Are you hungry after your journey?'

'Yes, if you please,' Jane said. She glowered at Claire. 'We almost had soup.'

Claire took her hand. 'I would like to speak with my brother.'

'I don't believe His Grace is receiving today, but I will check. In the meantime, I will ask that tea be sent up to the small parlour.' Her voice sounded a little strained. 'I am sorry, but none of the other family members are in residence at the moment.'

Not receiving? Would this visit of hers be for nothing, after all? 'Is His Grace unwell?'

'He has been not been himself for a while. Worse since Lord Edward's death, I'm afraid. He rarely sees anyone.' She pressed her lips together as if she wanted to say more, but thought it unwise. Claire knew the feeling. How often had she stifled her words in George's presence for fear of saying the wrong thing?

'I read of Lord Edward's demise in the papers after Waterloo. It must have been a dreadful blow after poor Lord Jamie such a short time before.' She shook her head knowing how she would feel if anything happened to Jane. 'Perhaps I should not have come unannounced.' How could she have thought to impose when he was suffering such sorrow? 'I will go.'

In that moment, she felt like a traveller who had walked miles only to be faced with a cliff she couldn't possibly climb and had to retrace her steps and start all over again. Yet there had been no other path to take that she had been able to see. If she left now, she would never find the courage to come back. And she had so hoped she and Jane could stay, that they could finally have somewhere they could really call home after so many years of moving from place to place.

Mrs Stratton glanced down at the small valise and back at Claire.

What must the housekeeper think of her turning up here after all these years without any notice? Pride forced her spine straight. 'I thought to seek my brother's advice on a matter of importance while I was visiting in the district. I would have written requesting an audience had I realised he was indisposed.'

'I know His Grace will wish to be informed of your arrival,' Mrs Stratton said gently. 'Later. I will ask Smithins to let him know you are here. In the meantime, may I show you to the parlour?'

Confused, Claire could do no more than smile and nod. She followed the housekeeper through the kitchen, with its gleaming pots and huge open fire. The chef looked up from a pot over the stove, his dark gaze meeting hers with an intensity that sent trickles of heat through her blood.

Unnerved by her strange reaction, she looked away and hurried after the housekeeper, along the servants' corridor to the columned entrance hall and up the stairs into the family wing.

As they walked, Claire's heartbeat returned to a more moderate rate and she was able to take in the familiar sights of her old home. Hope once more began to build. She ruthlessly tamped it down. The duke might yet toss her out of his house.

And if he did, somehow she would manage.

The small parlour was light and airy and faced south to get the afternoon sun. The blue paint on the walls contrasted delightfully with the heavy white and gilt ceiling mouldings.

Landscapes and the occasional portrait decorated the walls, and tables were littered with Greek and Roman artefacts collected by her father as a young man on his grand tour.

She sat down on the gold-and-blue-striped sofa beside the hearth and Jane wriggled up beside her. 'Do you think they will bring us something to eat soon?'

'We can hope.' She cupped her daughter's face in her palm and gave her cheek a pat. The child was worth any amount of humiliation, if humiliation was what she had in store. For all she knew, Rothermere might still hold a grudge for her disobedience. Their ages were too far apart for closeness and he had always seemed more like an uncle than a brother.

The door opened. The butler, old Mr Lumsden Claire was pleased to see, ushered in Joe the footman carrying a silver tray. Lumsden proceeded to set a small table in front of her and the footman placed the tray on it.

The tray held the ducal silver service and crested china plates displaying the daintiest sandwiches and most artistically prepared sweetmeats Claire could ever remember seeing.

Her stomach clenched with visceral pleasure at the sight of the food. Jane eyed the plates like a starving wolf, or rather a starving child. Which she was.

'Will that be all, madam?' Lumsden asked. His voice was carefully blank. In that blankness was a wealth of disapproval.

Her appetite fled. The butler would remember her fall from favour, of course, as no doubt Mrs Stratton had. He would know she was returning cap in hand and that left a bitter taste in her mouth that did not go with dainty sandwiches and spun sugar arrayed in a fountain of colour.

'Thank you, that is quite sufficient,' she said calmly.

The butler bowed and left.

A coiled spring could not have been tenser than her daughter as she stared at the food on the tray. 'Are we really allowed to eat those?' She pointed at the sweetmeats. 'They look too pretty.'

Claire wanted to cry. 'Yes. They are for us. Take what you want.' She handed her one of the small frilly edged plates. 'Would you like tea or milk?'

'Milk, please.' Jane's hand hovered over the sweetmeats.

'Try some sandwiches first.'

Disappointment filled the child's face. Claire couldn't bear it. 'Take whatever you want.'

The little girl filled her plate with sugarplums and sugared almonds and comfits. She popped something dusted with sugar in her mouth. She closed her eyes. 'Oh, good,' she said after a couple of chews and a swallow.

Claire poured tea for herself and milk for her daughter.

Her teacup rattled in its saucer as she picked it up. Nerves. Weariness. She sipped at the scalding brew. It was perfect. Brewed only once too. What was she thinking? Dukes didn't need to reuse their tea leaves.

'Aren't you going to try them?' Jane asked, pointing at the tray.

The thought of putting food in her mouth made Claire feel ill. How could she eat when their fate hung in the balance?

Hopefully the duke would see her today and she could have their interview over and done and know where she stood.

A moment later the door opened. Her heart seemed to still in her chest as she steeled herself to meet the duke. But it was only the kindly Mrs Stratton, her blue eyes a bit misty, the smile on her face still tense.

'His Grace cannot see you today, Mrs Holte.'

'Cannot?' Her heart felt as heavy as lead. 'Or will not?'

'Smithins says his melancholy is bad today. He rarely sees anyone at all. The vicar sometimes. Lord Giles when he must.'

Numbness enveloped her. That was that, then. No help

here. She looked at the plate of food and wondered if she could somehow slip some of the sandwiches into her reticule for later. She had enough money for one night at an inn, but not for supper.

She'd have to find work again. Somewhere else. Not nearby. The duke's pride would never allow that. Nor would her own. She would never let her family see the depths to which she had fallen. 'Please present my good wishes to the duke.' Claire rose to her feet.

'Smithins said he is sure the duke would be pleased to see you on a better day.'

Smithins, the duke's valet, had been with her brother since before Claire was born and it was kind of him to offer hope, but there would be no coming back.

'I will have your old room prepared for you,' Mrs Stratton said. 'And the adjoining one for Miss Jane.'

Her heart stilled. Her spine stiffened. 'Is this on the duke's instruction?'

Mrs Stratton's cheekbones stained pink. 'I can only guess at what His Grace might instruct us, Mrs Holte, but I know Lord Giles would insist.' The woman tilted her head. 'That is unless you have other plans?'

They could stay. She felt suddenly weak. 'No. No other plans. Not today.'

'Dinner is at five,' Mrs Stratton said. 'His Grace keeps country hours.'

A roof over her head for the night and a dinner promised. It seemed too good to be true. She just wished she could be certain of Crispin's eventual forgiveness. That he would agree to give them a home. Only then could she feel easy in her mind. Or at least as easy as she could be until she had settled matters with Ernie Pratt.

Two

Two more finicky appetites to tempt. André's hands fisted at his sides as he looked at the tray returned from the drawing room. The sandwiches were untouched and only one plate had been used even though the gaunt woman and child he'd seen in the kitchen had looked half starved. Madame Holte had eaten nothing and the child had eaten sweetmeats. The more he knew of them, the more he thought the English aristocracy were completely mad.

Ire rose in his chest. He was tired of preparing meals for people who cared little about what appeared on their plates. Food he'd prepared with his heart and soul.

Becoming the personal chef to a duke had not been the hoped-for triumph. No grand entertainments for members of the *ton*. No culinary feasts.

But there had been something else. A realisation of the subtle role food played in a life. The duke preferred the comfort of familiar dishes. Almost as if they offered a haven from the devastating changes in his life. André had sought out those dishes and prepared them in the manner of the duke's youth.

And the duke had regained his appetite, somewhat, and Lord Giles had been pleased.

Based on that success, he would return to London at the end of the month with the promised letter of endorsement.

In the meantime, he had a dinner to prepare and he needed to think of something to tempt a woman who looked like a small brown mouse and had turned out to be the sister of a duke. And a child. A little girl with the same sad grey eyes as her mother. What did he know of what children liked? Thoughts of his own boyhood only made him angry, so he'd locked those memories away. Still, he would like to see the child eat something to put a bit of flesh on her bones, and her mother too.

He did remember starving on the streets of Paris for months until he was taken up in the army. He knew what it was to be hungry. It was the reason he'd convinced His Grace to permit a pot of soup on the stove for those wandering the dales in search of work.

He strode to the larder and looked at his plentiful supplies. The pantry always made him feel good. Nothing but the best for the duke and no expense spared. And still the old man preferred a haunch of venison and suet puddings to the delicate sauces and fricassées André longed to prepare. Puddings. Pah. If the great Carême could see him now, he would be horrified.

He brought an armful of ingredients into the kitchen and laid them on the long plank table. As usual, he gave a swift glance around his domain. What he saw made his gut clench. Fear grabbed him by the throat. The swaying skirts of the scullery maid were inches from the flames leaping hungrily at the fat dripping from the meat.

'Mademoiselle Becca,' he barked. 'Step back from the fire, *s'il vous plaît*.'

The scullery maid squeaked and leapt back, her lank hair slipping loose from her cap.

'How many times must I tell you, *mademoiselle*?' André uttered fiercely, visions of other accidents raw and fresh. 'Stand to one side of the spit or you will roast along with the pig.' This kitchen needed modernising. He would speak to the steward again about installing a winding clock beside the hearth, then no one would risk themselves so close to the fire. It just wasn't safe.

'Sorry,' the girl mumbled, wringing her hands. She positioned herself properly and once more turned the handle.

He frowned. 'Where is Charles? I assigned him this duty.'

'Mr Smithins sent Charlie on an errand, chef,' the girl said.

Smithins, the duke's valet, was a blasted nuisance. He seemed to think he ran the household, and had even tried throwing his weight around in André's kitchen. Once. But young Charlie, the boot black, hated turning the spit.

Knowing he was watching, Becca turned the spit slowly, just the way he liked and he gave her a nod of approval. She returned a shy smile. *Pauvre Becca*, she thirsted for approval. He gave it as often as she deserved.

The kitchen maid, Agnes, stuck her head through the scullery door. 'Shall I throw out this soup, then, monsewer?'

He hated the way these English servants said *monsieur.* It sounded as if he had crawled from the privy. But it did no good to correct them.

'How much soup is left?'

'A quarter of the pot. Not so many came today.'

'Then the remainder will go to the servants' hall for dinner.'

'I don't see why we should eat the leftovers from a bunch of dirty Gypsies,' she muttered.

André swallowed a surge of anger at the scorn in her voice. This girl had never known what it was to go without. He kept his voice calm, but instructive. 'The only difference between you and the Gypsies, as you call them, is you have work and they do not. *N'est-ce pas?*'

'Nesper?'

Becca giggled behind her hand.

André frowned. Agnes scuttled back into the scullery and André returned to shucking the oysters.

'I thought we'd prepared everything for dinner,' Becca said, watching him, her arm turning the spit by rote.

'The duke has a guest.'

'His sister,' Becca said, nodding. 'Eloped she did. Years ago.'

That might account for the fear he'd seen in her eyes. A prodigal sister unsure of her welcome. Fear would account for the lack of appetite too. It did not, however, account for the lifeless pallid skin or the eyes huge in her face. She clearly had not eaten well for a long time.

If she had no appetite, she needed something to seduce her into putting food in her mouth. Not that he cared about Mrs Holte. Spoiled noblewomen didn't interest him in the least, except as they could advance his prospects. If this one refused to eat his food, his reputation would suffer. He bit back his irritation. He would use it as a chance to put his theories about food to yet another test. No woman, noble or otherwise, would resist his food. He left the oysters to simmer and set to work braising fresh vegetables. This time the plates would not return untouched.

Normally, once dinner preparation was finished and the food taken up to the drawing room, André would have retired to the parlour set aside for the use of the upper servants—the butler and the housekeeper and any ladies' maids present. Or he'd go to his own room and work on his menus for the hotel he planned to open in London. Tonight he found himself inspecting cuts of meat, counting jars of marmalade and generally annoying Becca, who was up to her elbows in hot soapy water washing the pots and pans in the scullery.

And while he counted and checked, he had one eye on the door.

He barely noticed when Joe returned with the duke's tray. 'Smithins said to tell you that His Grace said the beef could have used a bit more cooking,' Joe announced with a cheeky grin, keeping well out of André's reach.

'M'sieur Smithins can go to hell,' André replied, as he always did.

'Bloody Frenchman,' Joe muttered under his breath, and ran off.

The next set of dishes brought back to the kitchen were from the dining room where the mouse had sat in splendid isolation with her child.

The tureen of soup had been broached, the soup tasted. A spoonful or two from one bowl, more from the other. But neither was drained.

His jaw clenched hard when he saw nothing else had been touched, not the poached chicken or the pheasant pie or even the vegetables. There was something wrong with the woman. There had to be.

Joe leaned close and inhaled. 'Smells lovely,' he muttered. 'We'll be done right proud in the servants' hall tonight.'

André bared his teeth. 'You will touch none of it without my permission.' He glanced at the dishes set ready to go up. 'Take the last course.'

'No point,' Joe said cheerily. 'The little one is sick. They went up to their rooms.'

'Sick?'

'Too many sweetmeats, my lady said.'

Not the food. Of course not the food. His food was delicious. He stared at the untouched meal and remembered the thin face and the grey eyes filled with worry. He recalled the child whose bones looked ready to burst from her skin and wanted to hit something. The child had eaten only sugarplums and made herself ill.

Faced with such a treat a hungry child would fill its belly to bursting. He should have sent only the plainest of food. The most easily digested morsels this afternoon. He should have known. He was an idiot.

'Leave the pie,' he instructed. 'Take the rest to the hall with my compliments.'

Joe glowered. 'Too high and mighty to share that pie with the rest of us, are you?'

André gave him a hard smile.

The lad picked up the tray and scurried off. 'Be back with the rest of the dishes in a minute or two, Becca,' he called over his shoulder.

Becca kept her gaze firmly fixed on her dirty pots in the sink.

The pie was a work of art. Pastry so flaky it melted in the mouth. The contents were cooked to perfection. His fists clenched and unclenched as he stared at it. Not because he was insulted. He knew his cooking was exceptional, but because the woman still had an empty belly after he'd sent up food fit for a queen.

It was nothing to do with the tingle of sparks he'd felt when he'd touched the delicate skin of her throat, or the pang of disappointment when he'd learned who she was. A woman above his touch. Not at all. It was simply a desire to see his patron's family satisfied.

Mentally he shrugged. He'd provided the meal, what they ate was none of his business.

Automatically, he set a tray. The knife and fork just so. A

napkin. A slice of pie on a plate and a selection of vegetables. Beautiful.

He glanced over at Becca. 'Take the rest of the pie to Madame Stratton and M'sieur Lumsden.'

La pauvre, as he thought of her, bobbed a curtsey. For some reason the sad little creature treated him like royalty no matter how often he explained that kitchen maids didn't curtsey to chefs. There was a time when maids and footmen had curtseyed and bowed before running to do his bidding. Before the revolution that had ripped France apart and put it back together differently. He never looked back to that time. The looking back no longer hurt, but those times had become foggy, like a dream. Or a nightmare.

So why was he thinking about it now? Because of her. Mrs Holte. Curiosity and desire mingled with a longing he did not understand. Should not try to understand.

He picked up the tray. No one would remark on his absence. It wouldn't be the first time he'd taken his food to his own rooms to eat.

He strode up the servants' staircase.

Claire left Jane finally sleeping and returned to her own room, leaving the door between their chambers ajar. She sat in the chair by the window and stared out into the darkness. What if Rothermere refused to see her? Nausea rolled in her stomach. To have come so close to rescue would be too cruel.

Would remaining here when the man was so ill be similar to her husband preying on young green youths new to gambling? Except Crispin was family. And while he hadn't despised her mother, who had been the old duke's nurse, as some of his younger siblings had, he had not held her mother in any great affection either. The birth of yet another daughter so late in the duke's life had come as a shock to all, but

Crispin had always been kind to Claire. Until she had rejected his ducal decision and had more or less forced him to wash his hands of her.

While she had admitted her mistake to herself a long time ago, it would crush what little remained of her pride to beg his indulgence.

Perhaps if the Montagues had treated her more like family and less like an interloper in the years after her father died, she might not have been so vulnerable to the practiced seduction mounted by a fortune hunter like George Holte. Which ultimately left her forced to beg for her brother's help.

And she would not be here, she reminded herself fiercely, if not for her daughter. Jane was the real victim of Claire's mistake.

A light tap on the door brought her head up. Was this the summons to meet with her brother?

'Come,' she said, gripping her hands tightly in her lap.

The door opened to reveal a tall man in a dark coat. The chef from the kitchen, minus his white hat. The handsome man for whom she had warmed from the inside out at the slightest touch. Unless that was all in her imagination. Everything about him was dark. His eyes brooded. Lips finely moulded for kissing looked as if they rarely smiled.

He pushed the door wider, revealing the tray balanced on one large hand. She recognised the pie as part of the meal she'd been forced to leave behind. The delicious smell made her stomach growl so loudly she was sure he must hear.

'You did not eat your supper, *madame*,' he murmured.

His voice was deep and the trace of his French accent as attractive as the man himself. Her insides clenched with the pleasure of just looking at him. Madness.

An intense dark gaze riveted on her face. She had the feeling he could see right into her mind. As if he could see her lustful reactions. An answering spark flared in his eyes. Her cheeks warmed. This was not behaviour befitting a duke's daughter.

'My daughter felt unwell.'

'Too much rich food before dinner.' His face remained impassive, but she was sure she heard condemnation in his voice. He thought her an unfit mother.

'It has been a long time since Jane had such delicious treats.' Oh, why was she offering up an excuse? Servants always gossiped and they had enough to scorn without her giving them more ammunition.

Why should she care what a chef thought? Was it the delicious smell of the food on the tray undermining her reserve?

'Now the child is settled,' he said briskly, 'there is time for you to eat.' He set the tray on the small table at her elbow, then lifted the table and set it before her.

Her mouth watered. 'This is very kind of you, Mr…?'

'André. Monsieur André.'

She smiled. 'My thanks, Monsieur André.'

He acknowledged her gratitude with an incline of his head and folded his arms over his wide chest. 'Eat.'

'Yes, thank you.' She looked at him, expecting him to leave. He didn't move. 'Is there something more?'

His eyes widened a fraction. Chagrin flickered across his face. Or was it anger? His expression was now so impassive, so carefully blank, she couldn't be sure. 'I wish your opinion on the pie, *madame*,' he finally said. 'Is it good enough to send up to the duke?'

'Oh.' Her chest tightened at the idea that he would think she had such authority. 'It is not my place to say, I am sure.' She looked down at the plate, at the pastry, golden and flaking at the edges, the thick creamy sauce coating the vegetables and meat. 'It looks and smells delicious. I am not sure—'

'You will taste it, *madame*.'

That was an order if ever she'd heard one. French chefs. She'd heard they were difficult. She had no wish to upset him. No wish to anger her brother. Not before they had a chance to talk. She picked up the cutlery.

Monsieur André leaned forward and shook out the napkin and spread it over her skirts. He moved so close, she could see the individual black lashes so thick and long around his dark eyes, and the way his hair grazed the pristine white collar showing above the black of his coat. Her breath seemed to lodge in her throat at the beauty of his angular face so close to hers and the warmth of him washing up against her skin. The scent of him, lemon and some darker spice, filled her nostrils. Her head swam a little.

Only when he stepped back could she take in a deep enough breath to dispel the dizziness. It must be hunger.

What else could it be?

A flush lit her face and neck. She lowered her gaze to her plate and cut into the pastry. She stabbed a fragment of partridge coated with sauce with her fork and put the whole in her mouth. The flavours were sensational. Creamy. Seasoned to perfection. Tender. She closed her eyes. Never had she tasted food this good. She finished the mouthful and glanced up at the chef who was watching her closely.

Once more she had the feeling he could read her thoughts. The man's intensity was positively unnerving.

'It is delicious. Thank you. I am quite sure His Grace will be pleased.'

She set down the knife and fork, expecting him to depart. Would he take the tray with him? She hoped not.

'You need to eat more to be certain,' he said.

She blinked. 'I really don't think—'

'It might be too rich,' he said. 'You cannot tell from one mouthful. Did you not find the oyster soup too rich?'

'Oh, no, it was delicious. Really.'

He raised a brow. 'You ate so little, how could you tell?'

Goodness, the man was as autocratic as he looked and that bump on his nose reinforced the fierceness in his eyes. A warrior chef? 'Very well.' She picked up her knife and fork and ate two more mouthfuls and found herself wanting to shovel the rest into her mouth. The more she ate, the more she wanted. Before she knew it, the plate was empty and she felt full to the brim. She sighed.

When she looked up, the chef's full sensual lips had the faintest curve. A smile?

Her stomach flipped over in the most decadent way.

What was wrong with her? Hadn't she learned her lesson with regard to attractive men? They didn't want her at all; they wanted her family connections. Mortifying it might be, but it was the truth.

She straightened her spine, picked up the napkin and flung it over the empty plate as if it would hide just how hungry she'd been. Too hungry to leave a morsel. No doubt they would be talking about that in the kitchen tomorrow while they dredged up the old scandal. 'That was delicious, Monsieur André.' She waved permission for him to take away the tray.

His posture stiffened. '*Madame* would like some dessert? There is a vanilla blancmange in the kitchen.'

It sounded heavenly. And he offered it in such velvety tones she could almost taste the vanilla on her tongue as his voice wrapped around her body. Charm. She fell for it so easily. She clenched her hands in her lap. 'No. Thank you.'

A muscle in his axe blade of a jaw flickered as if he would argue. A mere twitch, but it broke the spell. What was she doing, letting this man order her about? Never again would she be any man's doormat. Her spine stiffened in outrage, at him, at herself. 'That will be all, Monsieur André.'

He recoiled, his eyes widening. 'I simply saw that you did not eat and thought—'

'What I eat, when I eat, is my concern alone, *monsieur*.'

'I beg your pardon, *madame*,' he said stiffly. There was anger in his tone, but something else gleamed in his dark gaze. Hurt? Gone too quickly to be sure, he was once more all arrogant male as he bowed. 'I will relieve you of my unwelcome presence.' He swept up the tray and strode from the room.

Blast. Now she'd upset Crispin's chef. Montague pride, when she had nothing to be proud about. Hopefully the man would not vent to her brother, or take his anger out on the kitchen staff. She would probably have to apologise, even though the chef was in the wrong.

The breakfast room overlooked the lawn at the side of the house. If one stood close to the window, one could just get a glimpse of the lake, with its decorative bridge and the island in the middle. Now it was frozen and dusted with a fresh fall of snow. She would take Jane outside later to look at it. Tell her about rowing over to the island in summer. Right now the child was tucking into coddled eggs and ham and had ceased to chatter for once.

'Don't eat too quickly, dearest, or you will be ill again,' she cautioned.

She glanced at a sideboard weighed down with platters of food—eggs scrambled and coddled, bacon with curly brown edges and a hint of a sear, assorted breads and pastries and a juicy steak. The footman had delivered the food under Lumsden's eagle eye from the moment she arrived.

'Will His Grace be coming to breakfast soon?' she asked Lumsden as she added cream to her coffee.

'His Grace breaks his fast in his chambers, madam.'

She stared at the array of food on the sideboard and down

at her plate of ham and poached egg and the bowl which had contained deliciously stewed plums and prunes. She and Jane had scarcely made a dint in the feast. At most she might manage a piece of toast and marmalade when she was finished with this.

'Then who else is coming for breakfast?'

Jane looked up with interest.

'No one else, madam,' the butler said.

Claire frowned. Such extravagance. All this food would be wasted.

Lumsden must have guessed the direction of her thoughts because a fleeting smile crossed his face. 'The food will end up in the servants' hall, madam. The staff had a small piece first thing this morning, bread and cheese, before the fires were alight, but they will have breakfast proper when early-morning chores are done.'

Heat travelled up her cheeks. She had forgotten how it went in a house full of servants; she had never had more than a couple of live-out maids during all of her marriage and sometimes none at all. These past months she'd been her own cook and housemaid. How would she ever fit back into this world of privilege and idleness if she kept thinking like a poverty-stricken widow?

'Will there be anything else, madam?' the butler asked.

Claire looked at her plate and at the piles of food on the sideboard and couldn't eat another bite. No matter that she'd felt hungry when she first walked into the room, it was all just too much.

'No, thank you. Jane, are you finished?'

Her daughter, who now had nothing but a few smears of egg on her plate and crumbs on the tablecloth, nodded.

'Then that will be all, thank you, Lumsden. You may clear away.'

Lumsden frowned, looked as if he was about to speak, then pressed his lips together. No doubt he wanted to tell her the chef would not be pleased she'd eaten so little. Next the man would be bringing her another plate of food. Surely not after her unfriendly dismissal the previous evening. He wouldn't dare to visit her room again. And a good thing too, even if she did admire his dedication to his work.

As she'd come to admire the hard-working shopkeepers, merchants and other businessmen with whom she'd come into contact while living on her own. Unlike George, who had dedicated his life to doing as little as possible, they were dedicated to the improvement of their families.

Perhaps that was what made the chef seem so attractive. He cared about his work.

Lumsden took her plate back to the sideboard and clicked his fingers, signalling the waiting footman to clear the platters.

'I would like to see His Grace at the earliest opportunity, preferably this morning,' Claire said, rising from her seat.

'Indeed, madam. Smithins will collect you from the blue drawing room.'

'Very well. Come, Jane.' She swept from the room with Jane's hand in hers. At least she hadn't made a complete cake of herself, playing the duke's daughter. As she and Jane wandered along the corridor lined with pictures of her ancestors, she regretted not finishing her breakfast. It seemed that standing up for herself had restored her appetite.

Then she remembered a thought that had occurred in the deep reaches of the night. It hadn't woken her. No, her rest had been disturbed by a low seductive voice in her dreams and images of an arrogant chef running long tanned fingers down her arm, then moving on to the rise of her breast.

Panting and hot she'd sat up in bed, not terrified but full of longing. For passion.

She squeezed her eyes closed against the memory of the heat and the flutters low in her belly. She would not think of that. But as she had lain there in the dark regaining her composure with the ticking of the clock and the howl of the wind among the chimneys for company, she had remembered the words spoken yesterday. *Another one crawling out of the woodwork claiming to be a relative.*

What had the cheeky Irish footman meant by 'another one'? It was a question she intended to ask Mrs Stratton.

Jane skipped into the drawing room with its heavy gilded and scrolled furniture adorned by, Claire blinked, half-naked females. Mermaids. She had better not linger in this room for too long or Jane would be asking her about them.

'Can we go outside now, Mama?' the child asked, looking around her with obvious disappointment. 'To see the lake?'

'Perhaps. After we see the duke.'

Jane slumped back against the chair cushions and folded her hands in her lap. Her daughter was much too obedient, Claire thought with a pang. Too still. Too careful. George's fault. He'd had a temper in his cups. They'd both learned to walk quietly around him.

The child needed laughter and joy.

And she would find it at Castonbury if they were permitted to stay. There would be no more moving. No more running from debtors.

A scratch at the door before it swung back brought her upright. An elegantly garbed gentleman of some sixty years entered the room. He was no more than five feet tall and his person was slim. He had thick white hair carefully coifed *à la brutus.*

He held out both hands in a gesture that seemed almost feminine. 'Lady Claire. How wonderful to see you home after all these years. And your daughter.' He executed a flourishing bow.

'Smithins,' she said, smiling at his effusive greeting and obvious warmth. 'It has been a long time.'

'Seven years at least, Mrs Holte.'

'Are you here to escort me to His Grace?'

'Madam, I am. His Grace is quite chipper this morning.' He beamed at her, then his smile dimmed. 'Of a surety you will find him much changed. It is the doctor's opinion that too much excitement is bad for him, but knowing you are here, he has made a great effort to be up and about this morning.' He smiled triumphantly as if bestowing a gift.

The nerves in Claire's stomach leapt around like butterflies in boots. 'So he has agreed to see me.'

'He looks forward to it.' He glanced at Jane. 'And to meeting the little lady.' He spun around and headed out of the door.

She took Jane's hand and followed.

'His Grace uses the old state apartments these days,' Smithins said as he directed her along the corridor to the central block. 'Fewer stairs to climb. I am sure you remember the way.'

'Smithins?' she asked as they travelled through the antechamber towards the great double doors, 'who else has come to claim relationship to the duke?'

Smithins stopped and pivoted a hand to his lips. 'You have heard already?'

'I heard a chance remark. It is not one of his…his…'

The duke had been a bit of a rake before his marriage. And after, if some of the tales were true.

'No, no.' The man waved an elegant hand like a lady batting away a fly. 'It is Lord Jamie's wife.'

'I hadn't heard that Lord James had married.' She'd always watched the newspapers for news of her family. Births, deaths and the occasional mention in court reports.

'Nor had anyone else,' Smithins said with a sly smile. 'Married her on the continent. She arrived just a few months ago with her son, Lord Jamie's heir.' He lowered his voice. 'And very little proof, I'm told. But His Grace is happy to be convinced.'

'She's here at Castonbury?' It was strange she hadn't taken dinner with Claire or that Mrs Stratton hadn't mentioned her.

'She lives in the Dower House.' He flung back the door and ushered her and Jane into a vast room where the curtains covered the windows and only one branch of candles shed any light apart from that given off by the hearth.

A smell of illness pervaded the room. Sickly smells. And the smell of elderly man. Someone should open a window and let the fresh air in. It reminded her of visits to her aged father, the previous duke.

It took a moment for her eyes to adjust to the gloom. When they did, she made out a male figure sitting close to the flames in a scarlet banyan and slippers with a matching embroidered cap perched on a balding pate.

He looked like a man of eighty instead of the sixty summers she knew he owned. The gaze fixed on her seemed bright enough though. She approached his chair. 'Your Grace.' She dipped a curtsey. 'It is Claire. Your sister. I am come home. This is my daughter, Jane.' She drew the child closer.

Jane bent her knees and wobbled only a little. Claire felt very proud. Jane might carry the name Holte, but she was also a Montague through and through.

'Claire,' His Grace said with a vague wave of a trembling hand. 'Welcome. Forgive me for not rising. Knees aren't what they used to be. Pull up that stool and sit in the light where I can see you. I don't see as well these days.' He shook his head.

Claire did as she was bid and once seated she gazed long at her half-brother, looking for the man he had been, proud, tall, full of authority. She found only a face etched in lines of grief and a body bowed over with sorrow.

'What brings you home, Claire?' A shade of his old smile kicked up one corner of his mouth. 'I thought you'd brushed off all signs of Castonbury dust. How can I be of help?'

Her angry words coming back to haunt her. It saddened her that he realised she had not simply come to visit. He must be used to receiving petitioners, people who came because of his power, not for the man himself. She regretted it could not be otherwise with her.

'My husband is dead.'

'I am sorry, my dear.' The regret sounded genuine.

'I am not. You were right. He was not a kind man. Or a good one. But I made the best of it until he left us destitute.'

Worse than that, in truth. But she would hold that information until she had a sense of his reaction.

Rothermere sat silent for a moment staring at the fire and Claire wondered if he had slipped away into his own melancholy and forgotten her. She glanced at Jane, who was staring at her uncle intently.

'Why is he wearing his night clothes?' the child whispered. Jane's whispers were piercing.

'Hush,' Claire said, thinking she would have to leave and try another day. 'Your uncle is not well.'

The duke raised his head and looked at her. 'I followed, you know. I almost had you just before the border. Hit a rut and broke a wheel.'

'You came after me?'

He nodded.

So a wheel had altered the path of her life. 'I had no idea.'

Jane slipped off her stool and wandered across the room to look at a portrait of a man in a full Elizabethan ruff, then moved on to peer into a glass cabinet full of snuff boxes.

'When he came later, for his money,' Crispin said, drawing Claire's attention back to his face which looked quite sad, 'he said you never wanted anything to do with us, but he wanted the dowry I owed.'

Claire gasped. 'You didn't pay it?'

The bushy brows drew down. 'I did. Not that he was all that grateful. I think he thought it would be more.'

She gasped. The money was gone? Her heart twisted, her mind reeled. She'd been relying on her dowry to resolve her troubles. 'George said you refused to part with a penny.' George had cursed the name of Montague. Blamed his failures on not receiving his proper due. This was worse than anything she could have imagined. 'He told me you threatened to horsewhip him for his audacity.'

The gnarled hand tightened on his stick. 'I should have.'

Jane moved on to look at a suite of armour. 'Don't touch it, please, darling,' Claire said.

'I'm glad you came home, Claire.' Crispin's eyes glistened. Tears? For her? 'I made a mess of things, Claire. Cocked it up.' He shook his head. 'No. Wrong words in front of a female. I sold when I should have bought.' He lowered his head as if to hide his anguish.

'I don't understand, Crispin,' she said softly.

'The funds. I sold them. Jamie would have known better. And now, finally when you come to me for help, I'm of no use to you or anyone. Not any more. Not any more.' His lifted his head, his eyes focusing sharply. 'I was right about Holte though. You wouldn't listen to me. But I was right. I told you he was a dashed loosed screw.'

'Yes.' She swallowed. 'You were right.'

He glanced over at Jane, who was now inspecting a statue of a Roman soldier. 'Your daughter looks like you.'

He meant Jane was not pretty. Was not a true Montague.

All the Montague women were lovely. And the men handsome as sin. It hadn't carried through to the child of the duke's second marriage or to her daughter. But to Claire, Jane was the most beautiful child ever born. 'She has some of me and some of her father.'

'Hmmph. Well, why did you come back?' His mind seemed to dart hither and yon and there would be no point in beating about the bush if she was to get an answer.

'Holte left debts. I thought to ask for my dowry to pay them off, but it seems he was before me.'

'Money,' he said gloomily. 'You'll need to speak to Giles about financial matters. There's little to be had.'

She knew a refusal when she heard one. She'd humbled her pride for nothing, but in truth she was glad to know her brother didn't hate her. Glad to know he was happy to see her again, even if he couldn't be of assistance. 'I am so sorry to have troubled you,' she said. 'You clearly have more important things on your mind. Jane and I will leave in the morning.'

'You need a husband.'

She gasped. The beautiful face of the chef flashed into her mind, leaving her aghast at the wayward turn of her thoughts. 'It is the last thing I need.'

He shook his head. 'Every gel needs a husband. You are young. You are still in your child-bearing years. A duke's sister is quite a catch, you should do very nicely on the marriage mart.'

She didn't want another husband. She did not want to be at another man's beck and call, subject to his temper and foibles. She'd wanted to come home to Castonbury and hide. 'Who would want to marry me, after all the scandal I caused?'

'There are still plenty willing to ally themselves with this family, aye and pay for the privilege. If you want my help with these debts, you will be guided by me.'

The snare pulled tighter around her. 'Crispin, please, I have my daughter to think of.'

'Then think of her, not yourself. There are a few good men in this county who would see marrying my sister as a step up, and who are deep in the pockets too.'

She hesitated, panicked, not sure how to answer. She had not expected this.

'I can't force you to marry anyone, Claire.' He cracked a laugh and put a hand to his chest as if it hurt. 'I learned that lesson, but perhaps you would trust my judgement this time? You would be helping the family.'

The anxiety in his voice made her nervous. 'How?'

'As I said, there are some who would pay handsomely to claim kinship to a duke. And for the influence they'd gain. The estate could use an infusion of money.'

Money for the dukedom. He wanted to sell her to the highest bidder in return for welcoming her back into the family. Heart pounding, her gaze sought her child, now seated on the floor with the statue, making him march along the patterned edge of the carpet. Jane needed security and safety. This would provide it.

And this time Crispin would choose. Wisely. A choice made of reason and logic. 'Do you have someone in mind?'

He looked pleased. 'I'll make up a list of possibilities. Then I advise you talk to Seagrove. Get a sense of the men. He knows people's hearts.'

'Seagrove?'

'Bloody parson. You remember him. Plays chess.'

So she was to consult with the vicar about a suitable husband. It seemed a little embarrassing to say the least. 'How is Lily Seagrove? Does she still live at home?'

The duke raised his head. 'Aye. For the nonce. She's to marry Giles in the summer.'

Now that was a surprise. 'I didn't think they liked each other.'

The duke's eyes began to glaze as if the topic wearied him. Dash it, she had one more thing to ask. 'I was wondering if Jane and I could stay here at Castonbury.'

'Stay? Yes, stay. What else did you think? No females here at the moment, I'm afraid. No one to act as chaperone. Phaedra is off somewhere with her aunt Wilhelmina. Ask Smithins where they went. He'll know.' He lowered his voice. 'Kate married, you know.' He leaned closer. 'An American.'

He made it sound as if she'd married a criminal. She'd seen the notice in the papers and had dithered about sending congratulations. She wasn't even sure Kate would remember her. And Phaedra had been so young when she left.

The lost years saddened her. 'I'm a widow. I don't need a chaperone, but if I am to meet these men, I will need to entertain a little.'

'That's the ticket. Catch yourself a husband.' He nodded as if they hadn't just discussed the matter in detail. 'I'll have that steward of mine give you some pin money. We can't have you looking like a crow. You are a Montague.'

Tears scalded the back of her throat. 'You really are too kind, Crispin.'

'Should have run the bugger through. That would have been kind. I was as hotheaded as you, I suppose. I wanted you to learn your lesson.'

She bowed her head. 'I did. You don't know how often I regretted what I did.'

He glared at Jane, who had wandered back to stand at Claire's side. 'Learn from your mother, girl. Do what your family expects.'

Jane visibly wilted.

Crispin turned his head to stare into the fire. 'We need Jamie. That's who we need. He would have known what to do.'

Smithins appeared as silent as a wraith at Claire's elbow. 'Best leave now, Mrs Holte. I will issue his instructions.' He gestured to the door.

Claire rose and took Jane's hand.

'Why, he has fallen asleep,' Jane said, looking at her uncle, bending over to peer right up into his face. 'Uncle Duke?'

Smithins smothered a giggle. 'He'll rest now until lunch. It's the laudanum, you know. It keeps the pain at bay.'

'Come, Jane,' Claire said. 'Let us leave your uncle Rothermere to his nap.' She led the child outside.

The smell of illness lingered in her nostrils.

'Why don't we go for a walk?' she said to Jane.

The little girl gave a skip. 'Can we make a snowman?'

'I don't see why not.' Fresh air would help her come to grips with this new development. Find a husband? She almost laughed hysterically. Seemingly she had stepped from the frying pan into the fire.

Her stomach gave a sickening lurch.

Four

'No eggs?' André growled.

Becca shrugged.

'*Sacrebleu*. How am I supposed to provide dinner without eggs?'

The girl looked at him with a considering gaze. André half expected her to tell him. The girl was as nervous as a cat most of the time, but when they were alone in the kitchen, she sometimes displayed a hidden courage. He tried to encourage it.

'What flea's biting you this morning, *monsieur*?' she asked instead.

'I beg your pardon? I do not have fleas.'

'You've been as bad tempered as a dog with fleas since you got in here this morning. Which one bit you?'

Ah, the English vernacular. It always caught him out.

Yes, he had been out of temper. Not screaming and yelling as some chefs did when angry, but edgy and perhaps a little too sharp. It was his unexpected response to the Englishwoman that had unsettled him. His urge to help, when she had been quite clear she needed nothing from him. Such concern for a highborn woman wasn't like him. And it certainly wasn't Becca's fault that there were no eggs in the pantry. 'I beg your pardon, *mademoiselle*.'

She stifled a giggle behind a red work-roughened hand. She always did that when he called her *mademoiselle*. It made him smile back.

'The boy didn't bring no eggs yesterday afternoon,' she said, bending to grab another potato. 'I wondered why you didn't ask him.'

She could have said something. He was lucky they'd had enough for breakfast. *Merde*, he'd been so incensed about Mrs Holte eating none of his sandwiches, so keen on making something to tempt her at dinner, he hadn't noticed.

She'd made him forget what he was about, with her pale face and the crescents of lavender beneath sad grey eyes. And led him to go where he was not welcome. Her dismissal still irked.

He let go a sigh. There was no one to blame but himself and therefore he must solve the problem. He would go to the Dower House and see if the cook there had any eggs to spare. If not he would be walking to the village. In either case a walk would do him good. Clear his head of visions of the mousy Englishwoman who intruded upon his thoughts when he least expected.

He didn't like skinny women. He liked them plump and curvaceous, with hearty appetites at the table and in bed. Women who did not cling or need cosseting. Women who enjoyed and moved on as he did. It was better that way.

Mrs Holte looked as if she needed a strong arm at her waist, or she would blow away in one of the infernal winds that swept down from the foothills they called Peaks. No, Mrs Holte was not his style at all.

So why could he not get her out of his mind?

He tossed his hat on the desk in his tiny office where he kept his papers and accounts and hung up his apron. He grabbed his coat from the hook behind the door. 'I will not be more than an hour or two. Finish the potatoes and the root vegetables. They should keep you employed until I return. Agnes can help you when Madame Stratton has finished with them. Tell Charlie to bring in more wood, and coal too.'

Tonight there would be no untried dishes.

He stepped out into a grey day. Clouds obscured the hills he scorned and had left a fresh layer of white over the ground. Barely enough to cover the toes of his boots. He turned up his coat collar and headed for the path that wandered across the grounds to the small house set aside for the widow of the heir.

As he left the courtyard the wind hit him full force, tugging at his coat and making him grab for his hat. But it wasn't the wind that took his breath away; it was the sight of the woman and the child in the middle of the lawn scooping snow into a pile.

Building *un bonhomme de neige*. How many years was it since he had entered into such a childish game? A long time. If ever. He shook his head. Once, he recalled, the soldiers in his company had flung snowballs around. Then they'd created a man of snow and topped it with a shako, calling it their captain's name and telling him what they thought of him. They'd all been very drunk, but they had laughed until they fell down. They were lucky not to have been flogged for such foolishness.

He'd been fifteen.

He stood watching them, mother and daughter. He heard their laughter carried on the wind. It made him want to smile. He liked children. He liked their innocence. Their lack of guile. He especially liked that Madame Claire would spend time with her child, instead of leaving her to a nursemaid. She was a woman to be admired.

He narrowed his eyes. They were making a very poor job of the man of snow.

He found himself walking closer. The child saw him first. 'Have you come to help?' she asked in a high piping voice. Her cheeks were rosy from the wind, her eyes bright, her smile welcoming.

'Good morning, *madame, mademoiselle.*' André looked at her mother, who regarded him warily. Her grey eyes reminded him of clouds full of rain. Her smiles for her child hid fear and sadness. He had a terrible urge to offer his help, not with the snowman, but with the deeper troubles reflected in her gaze. It wasn't his place to offer anything.

He glanced down at the heap of snow at his feet and back at the child. 'I do not wish to intrude, but if you take a handful of snow like this—' he bent, picked up a handful of snow and formed a ball in his gloved palms, squeezing it until it was round '—and then you roll it like so…' He rolled the ball and it gathered all the snow in its path until it grew three times its size. He looked up at the child. 'Then you will soon have his body.'

He stood up.

'Mama, look, isn't he clever?'

'Very,' the woman said, but she did not smile. She no doubt found him impertinent. And he was. It was in his nature. Dictated by his heritage, he presumed. It had got him into all sorts of trouble in his youth. But he did not need trouble now, not when he was so close to achieving his dream.

He bowed. 'I wish you both a good day.' He headed for the path.

'Don't go,' the child called. 'Stay and help.'

He hesitated, then turned back.

'I am sure Monsieur André has better things to do than play at making snowmen with us,' her mother said. She had a nice voice. Light yet musical. She spoke his name beautifully, like a Frenchwoman.

'I have time to build *un bonhomme*.' The words were out of his mouth before he thought about them and the little girl was looking at her mother for agreement.

The woman raised her hands from her sides in defeat. 'Then I am sure Jane and I will appreciate the help.'

In short order the three of them were pushing a very large and very heavy ball of snow around the lawn. Twice his hand touched that of the English *madame*. He felt the shock of it all the way from his fingers to his chest. And then lower down. Deep in the pit of his belly. The rise of desire.

She moved her hand away so quickly he had the sense she had felt the tingles too. After the second time it happened, she was careful to keep the child between them.

Finally they could barely push the uneven-shaped ball it was so heavy.

'I think it is quite big enough,' Mrs Holte said, laughing and panting.

'I want him to be the biggest snowman ever,' Jane said.

'He is,' André said. 'Now we need a head. Make a ball the way I did and we will start again.'

Jane pressed snow together in her hands, then raced around in larger and larger circles gathering snow on her ball, the green grass being revealed in an increasingly wide track behind her.

Breathing hard, Madame Holte watched her daughter with a smile on her lips. She was really pretty when she smiled. Not pretty. Striking. Because it was so unexpected, and so full of joy.

A joy he'd made possible.

Insanity. He'd simply stopped to help the child. He'd wanted to see the little girl happy, that was all. Children deserved to be happy.

Did they not? His childhood, the parts he allowed himself to remember, must have had some happy moments. He tried to recapture the feeling he saw in Jane's bright eyes and flushed cheeks. The delight and the innocence ringing in her laughter. He couldn't do it. Yet he had the sense of memories buried deep inside.

What would it be like, having his own child? A family. During the war, he had always avoided thoughts of family, children, ties. Life was too dangerous. And since then he had been working too hard to establish himself.

Watching this child at play today had created a longing that had nothing to do with lust for the mother. It was far too much like a need of the soul. It cut the ground from under his feet in a way he did not like, yet could not seem to resist.

For some reason he felt as if he stood at the brink of an abyss.

He turned away from the sight, turned to speak to the mother. 'She is having a good time, *non*?' He was shocked at how husky his voice sounded. How unsure.

Her face tipped up to meet his gaze. The love in her smile held him entranced. 'She is. Thank you for your help.'

The smile was not for him. It was for the child. And still it burned a path through his chest. Not all smiles were honest. Bitter experience had taught him not to believe them. He waved a dismissive hand. '*De rien.* We will build the head and then I must go.'

'Of course. Thank you.' She gazed at him, at his face, as if seeing the man, him, André, not the servant. His breath caught as warmth changed her eyes to silver, sparkling with female interest, disguised, but there nonetheless. It fired his blood and stirred his body to life.

Breaking contact with that considering gaze and the promise it held cost him a good deal of effort.

Bad idea, André, *mon ami. Très mal.*

He strode to the child, helped her finish the head and carried it back to the body all the while refusing to think about the watching woman. Refusing to think about his body's urges.

He was a man, not a beast, after all. He'd become used to denying those urges when the only women available were those who wanted more than he had to offer, more than mere dalliance with no strings attached.

Because he'd learned early, there were no guarantees. Women were as frail in their promises as men. It was far better to trust only in oneself.

So why did this woman stir his blood to the point he could not keep these important lessons at the forefront of his mind? Was it her vulnerability feeding an urge to protect those weaker than himself? After all, he'd been fed a diet of chivalry as a very small child. Until he'd learned better. Had learned if he didn't take care of himself, no one else would. Bitter experience had made it second nature.

And yet here he was playing in the snow with a child, to please this woman.

Whatever it was that drew him to her, it was not something he could or would do anything about.

Tomorrow was his day off. He would go to town and be rid of his excess energy in the boxing ring. And afterwards, if he still felt the need, he would find a willing woman. Then this little brown mouse would have no more effect on him after that. None at all. He wished he believed it.

'There,' he said to Jane, forming the shoulders. 'Scoop some grooves to make his arms and then go to the kitchen and tell Mademoiselle Becca you are to have some coal for eyes and a carrot for a nose.' He glanced at her mother, who was smiling admiringly. 'Perhaps one of the other servants has an old hat he would be willing to donate.'

Mrs Holte nodded. 'I expect we can find something.'

'Then I bid you good day, *madame*, *mademoiselle*.' His bow was jerky, as if his body wanted to refuse the instruction from his mind.

He strode away, angry at himself for wanting more than life permitted.

A man's prick could land him in all sorts of trouble. He'd seen it time and again. He had no intention of losing everything he'd worked for in the hope of making a quiet woman smile.

He groaned out loud as he felt a surge of warmth in his veins at the memory of her smile. A soft tender warmth that made no sense. The woman was of the nobility. Not for him, a servant, even if he could ever be interested. Which he could not. He knew that kind of woman and did not like them at all.

He smiled ruefully. He had his life. His passion. He didn't need a woman to complete him. He didn't need anyone.

What he needed was eggs.

Buxton was the same thriving market town Claire remembered from her youth. It had not taken her long, after descending from the duke's carriage, to remember her way around. Now Joe had an armful of parcels and she had depleted most of the money Mr Everett, the Castonbury steward, had given her from the duke's strongbox.

She'd done well with her money. A couple of ready-made gowns for her and Jane to be going on with until the seamstress came by to measure her for gowns in the lovely material she'd picked up from Ripley and Hall in Castonbury village. She'd bargained well for her items as she'd learned to do over the past years and now she was exhausted. And cold. Her toes were numb in her worn boots where the slush on the pavement had seeped in, dampening her stockings.

Opposite her was the Bricklayer's Arms. A coaching house boasting a coffee room, a taproom and private parlours for gentry, but it would not do for her to be seen there. Hard up against the inn was a gymnasium through whose portals men were to be seen coming and going singly and in groups.

But there was one place she could go to warm up without embarrassment. She turned back to Joe. 'Take those to the carriage and wait for me there. I am going into the lending library.'

She pointed to the building opposite the market cross. She couldn't remember the last time she had borrowed a book. Goodness, she couldn't remember the last time she had read one.

A bell jingled as she walked through the library door and a clerk at the counter looked up with a smile. She nodded as only the daughter of a duke could do.

'Can I help you, madam?' the clerk asked.

'What do you have that is new?'

The clerk handed her a sheet. She could have asked for every one of the titles listed. 'Waverly, please. Oh, and these two, if you have them.' She pointed to a couple of names she thought she knew.

'Yes, madam. Right away. If you would care to wait in the reading room, there are newspapers and magazines. The girl will bring you a pot of tea while we find your items.'

Claire had left Jane with one of the parlour maids, who Mrs Stratton had said was to be trusted. The girl had younger siblings and the family was known to the housekeeper. While Claire didn't like leaving Jane for too long, a hot cup of tea would warm her inside and out before the cold journey home.

Claire sat down and picked up a copy of *La Belle Assemblée* on the side table.

'Tea or coffee, madam?' a young woman asked.

'Tea please.'

'And a cream cake?'

Claire raised her eyebrows.

'Many of our customers come from far afield,' the girl explained. 'So we provide refreshments.'

What a good idea. 'Yes,' she said in a rush. 'I will have one of your cream cakes, if you please.'

The clerk nodded and moved away.

It must be the Castonbury chef's cooking making her feel hungry all the time. There had been an excuse for her devouring her dinner last night; first it was delicious and secondly she'd spent a good deal of the day outside with Jane. And the exercise seemed to have helped with her appetite at breakfast this morning too. Along with the pleasurable thought of shopping, no doubt. But cream cakes? Wasn't she being just a little greedy?

She looked around to call the girl back, but she was nowhere to be seen and a gentleman sitting on a sofa on the other side of the room caught her eye.

Blushing, she quickly turned away, staring out of the window to collect her composure, barely noticing the people passing by. Perhaps coming in here hadn't been such a good idea, after all. She certainly didn't want to cause any kind of a scandal, not now when there was every chance that she was to be accepted back into the family.

Perhaps she should leave.

A man walking along the street outside glanced in. He stopped and raised his hat.

Monsieur André. Oh, bother, what was he doing in Buxton, and looking positively elegant in his dark overcoat and beaver hat?

She nodded slightly and he moved on, but the bell tinkling above the doorway and a quick glance confirmed her worst fears. The chef had entered and was making straight for her table.

She gripped her hands together. It would be stupid to flee without her tea. And terribly rude. But surely the man understood they could not be friends. He had been charming with Jane yesterday out in the snow. The child had obviously adored the attention, but it just couldn't be something they allowed beyond that very casual meeting.

Oh. He wasn't trying to join her. He had taken a table near the window and had opened a newspaper he must have picked up on his way in. He didn't even try to catch her eye.

Disappointment made her feel hollow. She ought to be disappointed. In herself. Apparently she still had the impulsive streak that had sent her galloping off into the night with George. She must quell it or everything she'd sought by coming here would be ruined.

She stared blindly out into the street, trying to pretend she hadn't even noticed he was there, despite her racing heart and dry mouth. What was it about the man that made her so nervous?

She knew. Of course she did. It was the little thrills that raced through her body when his hand accidentally touched her skin. Like in the kitchen, and again making the snowman. Just thinking about it made her insides flutter and clench. Could she be more wanton?

It was the loneliness these past few years, the lack of any warmth in her marriage, making her want things she had once glimpsed with her husband, until he discovered she was not the path to gold and fortune.

The waitress arrived with a tray of tea and a cake on a small plate. It was a flaky confection decorated with white icing. It looked delicious, but there was no way Claire could eat a bit of it, not now.

She poured the tea and took a sip. It was hot. Too hot. She risked scalding her tongue if she tried drinking it too quickly. Oh, how she wished they'd hurry with her books so she could go. She opened *La Belle Assemblée* to a fashion plate and carefully read the description. It seemed heavy swags of fabric around hems were all the fashion. And skirts were fuller. She must remember that when the seamstress came.

It wasn't very many minutes before the clerk arrived with the books she'd requested neatly tied with string. 'There you go, madam. I will have your bill waiting at the desk.'

'Thank you.' She put the magazine down and riffled in her reticule for a sixpence for the waitress. As she did so, she glanced at the table window and Monsieur André. He had his back to her and seemed engrossed in his reading. She should not have looked at all. What if he had seen? Flustered, she stood up, followed the young man to the counter and paid her bill, leaving so quickly that when she got out into the street she became disoriented, turning north instead of walking south to where they had left the carriage. The moment she realised her mistake, she turned around and marched the other way, back past the library window with her head held high and her cheeks burning.

She hadn't gone but a few steps when a large figure came up beside her and matched his steps to hers.

'May I escort you back to your carriage, Madame Holte?'

'Oh,' she gasped. 'Monsieur André. You startled me.'

'My apologies,' he said. 'Did you find some books to your liking in the library?'

She winced. 'I did.'

They walked in silence for a moment or two. Then finally she stopped and turned to face him. Shoppers passed around them like a swiftly flowing river around an island. 'Why did you follow me?'

Then she gasped in shock as she saw his face full on. There was a cut on his lip and a red mark on his cheek that would surely be a bruise in the not too distant future.

'Did someone attack you?'

He touched a gloved finger to his cheek and smiled. 'In a manner of speaking, I suppose. I came from the gymnasium.'

'Pugilism,' she said.

'You sound as if you don't approve. I get very little in the way of exercise in the kitchen, so I come here once a week on my day off.'

'The result seems more like torture than exercise,' she said. 'You could be badly hurt.'

An eyebrow went up. His dark eyes reflected surprise, but his voice was calm and practical when he answered. 'Not really. Not when sparring. Not if one pays attention.'

'Then you need to pay better attention,' she said, starting to walk again.

He chuckled, a deep sound that seemed to curl low in her belly. When she glanced up he looked grave, but his eyes twinkled.

'You are right,' he said seriously. 'I had something else on my mind, I must admit. I promise I will take more care in future.' There was a seductive note in his voice. A shiver shook her frame. A shudder of pleasure. Horrified, she quickened her pace.

'It is of no concern to me what you do,' she said sharply and far too defensively. She drew in a quick steadying breath and stopped, for they had reached the livery where John Coachman had drawn up the carriage and was now chatting with

Joe. 'I thank you for your escort, Monsieur André. Did you need a ride back to Castonbury?'

His face was inscrutable as he gazed down at her and she was reminded of how impossibly tall he was and broad shouldered. And she fleetingly wondered if he showed well in the boxing ring. Canting talk she'd learned from her husband. She repressed the thought instantly.

'I thank you, *madame*, but no. I have another engagement.' He bowed and left.

There had been something significant in the way he had said the word *engagement*. She didn't want to think why that was because he was a servant and she was a duke's sister. It was nothing to her what he did. It must not be. Even if he was the most attractive man she had ever met in her life.

Her course was set. She was to marry a man of Crispin's choosing this time. Her stomach dipped.

'Same flea or a different one?' Becca asked André the next day.

He frowned, then laughed. At himself. 'No fleas.'

Just frustration. After meeting Madame Holte, he had been unable to so much as look at the saucy barmaid in the Bricklayer's Arms, let alone give her a tumble.

For some reason, no other woman held the attraction he felt towards Madame Holte. And, he thought, she wasn't as oblivious to him as she tried to make out which wasn't helping matters.

But what was it about her in particular, when usually any woman would do? Her delicacy? Or the inner strength he sensed. Whatever it was she was out of bounds to him. The kind of woman he'd spent a lifetime avoiding.

He didn't believe in titles. Not his own or anyone else's.

What he accomplished, he achieved by his own efforts. And he had every reason to be proud of the result.

At the end of the month he would be on his way back to London, and Madame Holte would no longer trouble his mind. Or any other part.

He brought the cleaver down on the joint and separated the thigh from the drumstick.

The door to the kitchen creaked.

André looked up. The door inched open a fraction more.

He narrowed his eyes. If it was the cursed cat from the barn looking to steal…

A small head poked through the opening, grey eyes darting around the room. The child. Mademoiselle Jane, with her eyes too large for her small face. She had the same hungry look about her that haunted her mother.

Which scarcely made sense for people in their position. 'Come in, *mademoiselle*,' André said.

The child jumped, then stared at the knife in his hand.

He put it down. 'How can we be of service?'

Becca looked at him and back to the child. 'You shouldn't be in here, miss.'

The child backed away.

André put up a staying hand and smiled. 'It is all right, *ma petite*, tell us why you came.'

'I wanted to help you cook. I used to help Mama after my lessons were done.'

Becca made a sound of shock. He should let it go, but the child had roused his curiosity. 'What sort of things did you help your mother cook?'

'Everything. She makes jam tarts on Sunday, when she didn't have any mending to return to the customers in the afternoon.'

Becca's jaw dropped. 'Your mother took in mending?'

Damn. That was not the sort of thing Madame Holte would want bandied about by the servants. Noblewomen did not work for money. At least not openly. If they were poor, they simply faded into genteel obscurity. But the fact that she had done something to support her and her child was admirable.

Mrs Holte was clearly different from his own mother. A bitter taste flooded his mouth as a glittering image of a dark haired beauty filled his vision. Bitterness followed by anger. Only anger kept the pain at bay.

He looked at the hopeful expression on the little girl's face, a reflection of his own face in the glass of a window a long time ago, and knew he could not turn her away.

With a sigh at his own foolishness, he put the chicken parts in a bowl, covered them with a cloth and washed his hands in the sink. He glanced over at Becca, who was swiping the table aimlessly with her rag. 'Onions next, Mademoiselle Becca. In the scullery, please, or we will all have sore eyes.'

She muttered something under her breath, but retreated to the small room.

'Mama hates peeling onions,' the child announced. 'They make her cry.'

So she really did cook. 'They make everyone cry.'

The child nodded gravely. 'But they make the food taste good, so it is worth a few tears. What are you making today, *monsieur*?'

Such impeccable manners and her accent was almost perfect.

'Does your mama know you are here, little one?'

She drew herself up straight. 'I'm seven and I am tall for my age.'

André kept his face straight. 'So you are. I thought you were much older than seven. Still, your mother might not like to find you here.'

'She's busy with the seamstress and doesn't have time for lessons. I was fitted already.' She sounded disconsolate. Lonely.

'Surely you are happy to have pretty new dresses.'

She made a face. 'I'd sooner have a hat like that.' She pointed to his head.

'A chef's toque? Would you indeed?' He reached into the drawer where he kept several clean and freshly starched hats. He pulled one out and opened it with a snap. He popped it on her head.

It immediately fell down over her eyes and nose.

'It's too big,' she said sadly, taking it off and offering it back to him, her face full of disappointment.

'So it is.' It was a small disappointment in the grand scheme of things, yet the sad face pulled at a cord in his chest. Painfully. He stilled in shock. What was happening here? Why did he care? The child wasn't his. She was well fed, beloved by her mother, yet still he hated to see her unhappy. He lifted the hat high and gazed at it from all angles. 'You know, the same thing happened to me once.'

'What did you do?'

He went to another drawer and pulled out one of the large needles he used for stitching fowl. 'I used a hat pin.'

'That's not a hat pin,' the child said disdainfully. 'My mother has a hat pin. It has a pearl on top.'

'I suppose we could go and ask to borrow it,' he said with a smile, and raised a brow.

'Oh, no. She's busy.'

And besides, she would probably tell the child to go back to the school room, or wherever it was she was supposed to be. André wasn't fooled for a moment. 'Or we can see if this will work.'

The little girl nodded.

André folded the hat along its length and then pinned it. This time it fitted her small head perfectly.

'Better, *non*?' He pulled up a stool to the table and stood her on it. 'I am going to make a chicken pie for your uncle. Would you like to help?'

She nodded. 'What can I do?'

'You can make the decorations for the top of the pastry.'

It didn't take him long to prepare the dough, and soon she was rolling and cutting and generally making oddly shaped little bits covered in flour. She had flour on her hands, on her cheek and some on the tip of her nose. But she seemed perfectly happy.

Becca popped her head around the door, her eyes streaming. 'Onions are done, monsewer.'

André nodded. 'Go outside and get some air. It will help with the tears, then there are carrots to scrub.'

The girl scampered off and he heard the scullery door bang shut behind her. He wished there was some way to stop the misery caused by peeling onions, but he'd peeled his share in the past and it was part of her job.

The door into the hallway opened to reveal Madame Holte, who looked terribly anxious, and she had Mrs Stratton right behind her.

'There you are, Jane,' the mother said. 'I've been searching everywhere.'

Guilt hit André hard when he saw the panic fading from her eyes.

'I'm making leaves for Uncle's pie,' Jane said without looking up.

Her mother's expression shifted from worried to nonplussed in a heartbeat. Her gaze rose to meet André's. 'I am sorry if she has been troubling you, Monsieur André.'

'Not at all, *madame*. Mademoiselle Jane has been most helpful. *Regardez*.'

Madame Holte took in the pile of mangle and grubby bits of pastry and the flour on the table, the floor and her child, and she smiled.

The kitchen became a bright and cheery place.

His heart lifted and he recognised an awful truth. It was the mother's smile he wanted every bit as much as the child's. Clearly, he was on a very slippery slope and heading downhill at a rapid rate.

'Monsieur André,' Mrs Stratton said. 'You might have let me know Miss Jane was here. We have been searching the house from top to bottom.'

The housekeeper looked frazzled, which was very unusual.

Still there was an understanding twinkle in her eyes, so it seemed now the child was found, everything was fine. 'I beg your pardon. Next time I will indeed send word.'

The *madame*'s smile faded. 'I really don't think—' She bit off her words. 'Jane, are you finished? You know, I did ask you not to wander off.' She gave André a quick smile. 'Jane is rather adventurous.'

Jane looked at her mother and down at the pile of bits of pastry and then up at him. Something clenched in his stomach. A desire to give the child a hug.

'I think I have all the decorations I need for today, Mademoiselle Jane.' He bowed. 'I hope you will visit me again.'

She took off her hat and handed it to him. 'Will you keep this for me for next time?'

There likely wouldn't be a next time. And probably for the best. He didn't want to become fond of either of them. He would be leaving soon. Yet he nodded. 'It will be here waiting.' He tucked it back into the drawer.

Madame Holte helped her daughter down from the stool, brushed the flour off the front of her dress, then walked her to the door.

The little girl tugged her hand free and turned back to him. 'Next time I should have an apron too.'

Her mother shook her head and led the child away, with Mrs Stratton bringing up the rear.

Becca ran in flustered, then stopped short. 'She's gone?'

'Her mother collected her.'

'Joe said as how they was tearing the house apart looking for her in a proper panic.'

It was odd, that panic. The child could not have gone far. And the look of utter relief on Madame Holte's face had been completely out of all proportion to the discovery of the child in his kitchen.

He sighed. Now he was seeing mysteries where there were none. What the family of the house did was none of his concern. He simply had to fulfil his contract and at the end of the month return to London.

He went back to his pie, but somehow the joy had gone out of it.

Two days later, André was working at his accounts when Mrs Stratton popped her head around his door. 'Mrs Holte requests you attend her in the small drawing room.'

For a moment his heart lifted, then he got a grip on reality. No doubt this was a reprimand for keeping her child in his kitchen. He should have given her a sweetmeat and shooed the child away as most chefs would. If the child hadn't seemed so lonely…

He rose to his feet with a sigh. *'Immédiatement, madame.'*

The housekeeper's eyes glinted with something that looked like amusement. Perhaps even excitement. He could ask her if she knew what was wanted, but that would taste of lack of confidence.

They parted company where the corridor divided east and west, family and staff, high and low, and he squared his shoulders as he strode along a rug that had seen better days. Castonbury looked well enough from the outside, he thought morosely, but inside, in the family quarters and those of the servants, it had seen better days. He couldn't wait to leave Derbyshire and get back to London. Going sooner than he'd expected would not be so bad. As long as they didn't renege on his contract. Getting this position had required he call in several favours. It would set him back years if things fell apart.

He knocked on the door and entered the cheerful room.

Madame Holte looked up from her book, one of those she had borrowed from the library.

How tiny she looked in the overstuffed armchair. A shaft of wintery sunlight caressed her caramel-coloured hair and made it glint gold. She had shed her widow's weeds for a gown of pale blue. A modest gown, but it showed her womanly curves to perfection and gave her grey eyes a bluish tinge. Her neck was long, he realised, elegant as a swan's. And the thought of touching his lips to the pale skin below her ear gave his body a jolt.

Arousal. Because she had a beautiful neck? He took a deep breath and ignored the inappropriate desire. Aristocratic women were out of his league. And not just because of their status. Like his mother, they were idle creatures, with no thought for any but themselves. They served little purpose except for decoration as far as he had ever seen. Or at least most of them. Madame Holte was not like that. He wished she was. She would be easier to resist.

'Madame Stratton said you wished to see me,' he said stiffly, holding himself erect much as he would have for a superior officer when he was a soldier.

'Yes.' Pink stained her cheeks.

Here it came, then. The lecture. The putting him in his place. He kept his face impassive.

'I am planning several dinner parties for the duke over the next few weeks. I thought we might discuss menus.'

If she had stripped off naked and run round the room he would not have been more surprised. Or any better pleased, though that would have pleased him a great deal.

He forced his mind out of the gutter and his body to calm. 'I should be pleased to give you any assistance required.' He frowned. 'Is Lord Giles aware of this?'

It really was not his place to ask, but Lord Giles kept a firm hand on the purse strings for his father, according to the duke's steward.

Her colour heightened. 'I do this at His Grace's request.'

Something in her voice did not quite ring true, but it was not his place to question the duke's sister. He might, however, enquire of Madame Stratton. Or Smithins.

'How many events are you planning?' he asked. 'And who are the guests? Are the same people to be invited more than once?'

She picked up a piece of paper from the table where she had placed her book. 'There are to be three dinners in all, the first next week. I am hoping His Grace will attend, but it will depend on his health.'

Elation began a slow build inside him. This was the chance he'd been waiting for. It would be better if the duke attended, and he could quite see why she would want to hold out his presence as an inducement. Very few people would turn down an invitation from a duke.

'The Reverend Seagrove will be present for all of the dinners as well as myself, and perhaps his daughter. And if Lord Giles should return, the duke would expect him to attend also.' She consulted her paper. 'The first dinner will include Mr Dyer and his mother. At the second I expect Sir Nathan Samuelson. And at the third, Mr Carstairs and Miss Carstairs.'

Small intimate dinners. He could do them with one hand tied behind his back.

'Oh,' she said, 'and the dowager marchioness is to be invited too.'

Interesting. For the most part, Lady Hatherton had been kept at arm's length. Servants' gossip said there was doubt about the validity of her claim. It seemed those doubts were past.

The other guests Madame Holte named were from prominent families in the neighbourhood. Gentlemen and ladies who travelled to Town for the Season. People who would speak of his skill, if he pleased them. Yes, this was just what he had hoped for when he'd accepted this contract. A chance to grow his reputation as a chef among members of the *ton*. To move his own plans forward. The fact that he would do so for Madame Holte made it doubly rewarding. Saints save him, he was grinning from ear to ear. He pulled himself together. 'How many courses do you wish to serve?'

'Enough to appear generous, but not so many as to seem ostentatious. I would be grateful for your suggestions.' She cast him a brief smile. It held shyness and hope and a shred of wariness. It was that last that caught at something in his chest.

Women often smiled upon him. Women from all walks of life, high and low. He'd learned to ignore the glances from the highborn. They carried nothing but danger. But this one was different. There was no arrogance in her glance, no speculation, just a plea for his help.

Her problems should hold no interest for such as him. The opportunity of cooking these dinners was all that concerned him. With such small numbers, it was hardly a challenge, but it was an important step on the ladder of his ambition.

Yet he did care. He just didn't know how to get to the source of her concern. 'Do you have specific dishes in mind or would you prefer I draft some menus for your approval?'

'I do have some ideas, if you would be so kind as to take a seat.'

Only years of practice at never showing emotion prevented his mouth from falling open. A servant never sat in the presence of his betters. Not that he thought any man, or woman for that matter, above anyone by right of birth. If he ever had, it had been beaten out of him. But they did, these aristos. It was ingrained into them from birth. It took a great deal to change such deeply held beliefs. A crucible of fire.

He'd been through the flames.

The thought that this small woman might have similarly suffered made his gut clench. It wasn't possible. England had never endured the ordeal that had changed France for ever.

She was a widow. Perhaps his earlier instincts were correct. Perhaps she was looking for a lover. His body hardened at the thought. And he sneered at the reaction. He was not a man to risk all for a tumble. Nevertheless, as he sat beside her, he was aware of her skirts not quite touching his thigh, aware of the curve of her cheek and the way little wisps of hair touched the nape of her lovely neck.

She handed him the piece of paper. Not only were the guests listed out in detail, but there were notes of the dishes favoured by the men.

He glanced at her sharply. She returned his gaze with a steady stare. 'Reverend Seagrove dines with these gentlemen from time to time and has been able to draw an opinion as to their favourite foods. I thought we might use them as our starting place.'

'These are purely social functions?' he asked, staring at the names and at the handwritten notes. 'Or the duke wishes to—' he hesitated '—make a case for something? Some investment, some plan?'

She lifted her grey eyes. A pink wash stained her cheeks.

André couldn't think why she should look embarrassed. There was some subtlety here he wasn't grasping. To do with her.

'The duke? Not that I am aware,' she said breathlessly.

A prevarication. An aristocrat lying to an underling. But why should it matter? It didn't. He would do his job and do it well.

'I would suggest, then, *madame*, eight courses, with two removes.'

She looked a little shocked. 'So many?'

Why would she be surprised? Surely she was accustomed to the groaning boards set by the wealthy here in England? Or perhaps not, given how pale and thin she had looked the day she arrived. He kept his face impassive, his voice gentle. 'It is expected, *madame*.'

She lowered her head in acceptance. 'Then that is what we will do.'

'When are the dinners to take place?'

'The first next Saturday, and likely two more the following week. I will know better when I have received replies to the invitations.'

Three major dinners in two weeks? Life was looking up.

She must have seen something in his face because she frowned. 'Is it not possible?'

'*Madame*, of course it is possible. I was just a little surprised. I beg your pardon.'

She looked relieved. Clearly, these dinners were important to her as well as the duke. And he was beginning to suspect why. All of these men were bachelors. Men worthy of marriage to the daughter of a duke.

Something inside him did not like what he was thinking. Indeed, the idea made him feel tense, angry.

With force of will, he kept his hands loose. This was not his concern. If the duke wanted to find her a new husband, that was his prerogative. And if she was willing, then so be it.

His opinion of these self-satisfied country squires counted for nothing. Even so, the slow burn of anger that she would sell herself to any one of them refused to be extinguished. He needed to escape before he said something he would regret. And it had been a long time since his tongue had led him into that kind of soup.

'May I bring you my ideas tomorrow? I need to look at my supplies. See what is available from the butcher and so on.'

'Tomorrow will be fine.'

André rose to his feet and stood looking down at her. She looked lovely. Glowing. And it warmed him to know that his artistry with food had restored some of that beauty. Yet there were still shadows in her eyes. Still a tightness to her mouth as if the path on which she had set her feet caused her anxiety. It was as if she was haunted. Or hunted.

'Is there anything else I can do for you, *madame*?' Was he out of his senses? What could he do that her family with all their power could not do? If indeed what troubled her was more than what to serve for these dinners.

For all that, he waited while she pondered his question.

'Wine,' she said suddenly. 'And port. The wine provided at dinner is not always the best. Do you…' She blushed.

His question had not been about food or wine, but he was a chef and their common ground was these dinners. And if she had occasionally looked at him as a woman looked at a man, it was simply in passing. And he would do well not to think of her as a woman, but as his employer. 'I know wine, *madame*, and I have seen the duke's cellars. I will instruct Lumsden regarding what to serve with each course.'

She stood up. 'Monsieur André, thank you for all of your help.'

He bowed, acknowledging his dismissal. 'Tomorrow morning at nine, if that is convenient, I will bring my suggestions for the rest of the menus.'

'That will do very well. Thank you.'

It didn't matter why she was holding these dinners. It was his job to make the food a memory never to be forgotten. Much as he would never forget the picture of her standing there, the golden gleams of sunlight in her hair. A small delicate woman with grey eyes full of shadows.

* * *

Seated at the escritoire in the library, Claire sealed the second batch of invitations she had issued this week and rang the bell. Lumsden arrived within moments.

'Please have these delivered, Lumsden.'

'Yes, madam.' He bowed and took all but one of the invitations. 'I wonder if I might speak out of turn?'

Claire couldn't hide her surprise. Since her return, Lumsden had barely unbent enough to indicate he remembered her at all. He reeked of disapproval. And she didn't blame him. She had behaved very badly and an old retainer like Lumsden would see her insult to the family name as an insult to him too.

The duke was lucky to enjoy such loyalty.

'Please, feel free to speak your mind.'

'It is about the young lady, Miss Jane.'

Claire stiffened. Perhaps she wasn't so sanguine about allowing the servant to speak his mind, after all.

Lumsden either did not notice, or ignored her reaction. 'She's in the kitchen again, madam. Disrupting the work of the servants.'

Oh, dear. She had left Jane in the school room studying India on an atlas while she wrote the invitations, but it must have failed to hold her interest, and if she was wandering she must be feeling more at home at Castonbury Park than Claire had thought. Hopefully, she wouldn't mind one final move, once Claire had a new husband.

A shiver rippled down her back. Not a helpful reaction. 'Thank you, Lumsden. I will go and collect her. I will let her know that she should remain on the family side of the house.'

Lumsden bowed. 'Thank you, madam.' His back was ramrod stiff as he left.

The life they were leading now was different from how they had lived in their small cottage in Rochester this past year.

There were rules and boundaries that must not be crossed. Claire winced inwardly. She was reluctant to force too many changes on the child. The past year had been difficult enough. Time enough to do so when she married.

If she married. None of these men might be interested in coming up to scratch, despite Crispin's confidence. The thought of failure was terrifying.

Her husband's debts once more loomed large, along with the man to whom they were owed. She could not risk him finding her and Jane before she was ready with the money. She would run and hide again sooner than face him. One of these men had to make her an offer. And soon.

The man she had invited first was a confirmed bachelor according to Reverend Seagrove. Devoted to his mother, who kept his house and ordered his life. On the other hand, the prospect of wedding the sister of a duke might be enough to change the habits of a lifetime. The thought of competing with another female living in the same house made her stomach churn. Yet she could not afford to pass up any opportunity. For Jane's sake.

And for the sake of the Montagues. It was a heavy responsibility Crispin had asked her to bear on behalf of the family. But it was only fair.

Outside the kitchen, her heart began to beat a little faster. Monsieur André did that to her each and every time they met, and they had been meeting more often because of these dinner parties.

A chef? Surely not? It was simply a feminine appreciation of a handsome face and a strong manly form. Nothing more. Any woman with blood in her veins would notice. She certainly knew better than to believe that what was on the outside in any way reflected a man's worth.

She straightened her spine, let a mask of cool reserve fall

over her features and stepped into the large warm room. Flames from the huge fire danced in the surfaces of pots and pans stacked neatly on shelves. Windows in the walls provided fresh air and daylight to augment the candles in wall sconces. The scent of baking bread filled her nostrils.

There was something completely entrancing about the smell of warm yeast. Heart-warming. Earthily seductive. And here was Jane with her chef's cap listing over one eye, crumbs and jam around her mouth, sipping a cup of tea with two young women. Becca the scullery maid and one of the kitchen maids, Agnes.

Becca leapt to her feet, wringing her hands and bobbing sporadically, while the other kitchen maid rose slowly, staring at her with interest. Of Monsieur André there was no sign.

Disappointment dipped her stomach. Followed swiftly by anger. At herself. This was how she'd ruined her life before. Falling under the spell of an unsuitable man. This time she would keep her impulses firmly under control.

'Good afternoon, Becca,' she said coolly. 'I am sorry to interrupt your tea, but Miss Jane is required to accompany me.'

'Did you know Monsieur André fought with Napoleon?' Jane said, setting down her cup.

Becca flushed scarlet. She gestured weakly at the other girl. 'Agnes was telling her.'

Gossiping servants. This was why she should keep Jane away. She shot the other girl a severe look and held out her hand. 'Come along. We are going for a walk.'

Jane popped up from her stool. 'They murdered the king and all the arist...arist...people with titles in France. Like Uncle. I'm glad I don't have a title.'

'England is not France,' Claire said, holding out her hand. 'And the King of France is back on the throne.'

'Without his head?'

Becca fled for her scullery. Agnes picked up a broom and began sweeping the flagstones. Gruesome creatures, filling the child's head with lurid tales. Or was it the chef who had done so?

'A new king,' Claire said. 'Come, let us get you cleaned up and we can talk about what happened in France on our way to the Dower House.'

'Are we going to see the baby?'

She had told Jane about her cousin earlier in the week. 'Perhaps. That will depend upon his mother.' They walked along the corridor side by side. 'Where is Monsieur André this morning?'

Oh, no, had she really asked that? She felt herself warm. Well, she needed to know if he had left Jane alone with those girls after he had agreed Jane would not spend time in his kitchen.

'He went out.' She shrugged.

It was a very small shrug, like the one Monsieur André often employed. On the man, it was a slight lift of very broad shoulders, and heart-stoppingly attractive. On the little girl, it made Claire laugh.

'You, young lady, are a minx. You were supposed to await me in the school room. Now we will have to wash your face before we can set out.'

'I finished my book.'

'You could have started another.'

'I wanted to see what Monsieur André was cooking for supper.'

'You wanted sweetmeats.'

'That too.' Jane grinned up at her.

Claire pulled her close and gave her a quick squeeze. 'I just wish you would let me know where you are going.'

'But then you wouldn't let me go.'

The child was right. In fact, if it was possible, Claire wouldn't let her out of her sight for a minute. But everyone would guess something was wrong if she behaved in such an extraordinary way.

'Promise me this, then. That you will not leave the house without letting me know.'

Jane nodded solemnly. 'I promise.'

'Then I shall say no more. But if Monsieur André is busy and asks you to leave, you will do as he asks.'

Again a nod. 'He won't though. Monsieur André is my friend. He is teaching me French and I am helping him with his English.'

Claire didn't know if she wanted to laugh or cry. Of all the people her daughter had to latch on to, it was the man who presented the most danger to her peace of mind. The horrors of French learned in the gutters popped into her mind. 'What do you mean, he is teaching you French?'

'Comment allez-vous, Maman?' Jane said. 'It means "How are you today?" You must say, *Très bien.* It means "I am well." A cow is *la vache.* Milk is *le lait.* He names all the things in the kitchen and teaches me how to speak the words. Like a Frenchwoman.'

A sigh of relief left Claire's lips, but there was a warm feeling too. Monsieur André was extraordinarily kind to a little girl who haunted his kitchen. She would make sure she thanked him next time they met. Which would be tomorrow in the morning, before her first dinner party.

Her stomach tightened. If only she could look forward to it with a little less dread.

Lady Hatherton was one of the prettiest young ladies Claire had ever encountered. Her blonde hair shone like spun gold and framed a round angelic face. Her eyes were blue as forget-me-nots and she used them to effect, glancing up from beneath her lashes with a smile on her full rosebud lips. But she seemed nervous.

It was not unexpected that she was a little on edge. Or that she was a little cool, Claire thought. Smithins's comment about the lack of proof of her marriage was probably the reason for the wary look in her eyes.

'How old is little Crispin?' she asked, hoping to put the younger woman at ease. What mother did not want to talk about her child?

Lady Hatherton was obviously no exception because her smile became radiant. 'He is approaching eighteen months and growing so fast.'

'Can I play with him?' Jane asked.

'He is sleeping,' Lady Hatherton said. 'But you can peek in on him before you leave.'

Jane did not look impressed by the offer and wandered off to look out of the window.

'What will you do with the child tomorrow night?' Claire asked.

'Why, bring him, of course,' the girl replied. The light in her eyes became rather hard.

Much as she loved children, entertaining one at dinner wasn't quite what she had in mind. 'Don't you have a nanny who could look after him?'

Lady Hatherton's smile didn't falter. 'Oh, yes, his nurse will take care of him in the nursery. The children can eat together. Come let us take a peek at him before you go.'

Clearly, her audience was at an end. It was impossible for a mere Mrs Holte to argue with a dowager marchioness, even if it was only a courtesy title awarded to her nephew. And the child was the next heir, if Alicia's claims were true. Claire had no reason to believe otherwise. She had decided it was just the family refusing to admit Jamie had died.

And she didn't blame them. But eventually they would have to embrace the hard truth, just as she had been forced to acknowledge the mistake she had made in her marriage. Only Jane's arrival had made her existence bearable.

She rose to her feet and followed the young widow up the stairs. She had thought they would have more in common, being widows and having children, but the younger woman seemed inclined to keep her at a distance.

Claire also had the sinking feeling she'd made a mistake in agreeing to the request that the woman be invited to these dinners. What man would look at her, when the beautiful Lady Hatherton was in the room?

But since the duke was footing the bill and had surprised her by sending word that he had every intention of attending tonight, there was nothing for it but to accede with good grace.

The child's room was on the second floor, and when they entered a young woman leapt to her feet from her chair beside the cradle. She bobbed a curtsey and slid unobtrusively from the room.

Lady Hatherton tiptoed to the cot against the wall and gently drew down the covers to reveal the sleeping child.

The boy looked like her. Blond curls damp against the pink skin of his cherubically round face.

'He's lovely,' Claire whispered. And nothing like Jamie. The Montagues tended to darkness. Their Norman heritage, everyone said.

Jane pushed closer. 'He's so little,' she whispered.

Lady Hatherton froze as the baby, disturbed by the loudness of Jane's whisper, stirred. She pressed a finger to her lips and signalled for them to leave.

Claire took Jane's hand and led her out of the room.

'He's just a baby,' Jane said, clearly disappointed.

'That he is,' Claire agreed. 'And he needs his sleep so he can grow big and strong.'

Lady Hatherton caught them up at the top of the stairs. 'I do thank you for calling,' she said to Claire.

'And I look forward to dinner tomorrow night,' Claire offered.

'As do I.' She smiled vaguely and turned back for the nursery, while Claire and Jane continued down the stairs.

The footman in Rothermere scarlet who had let them in stood waiting with their outer raiment and in a short space of time they were out in the cold north wind heading home. As they reached the path that would take them back to Castonbury main house, they noticed a tall figure striding ahead.

'It's Monsieur André,' Jane said.

Claire's stomach gave a funny little lurch.

'Monsieur,' Jane yelled.

'Jane, no,' Claire said. But too late. The chef stopped and turned.

'Now I remember.' Jane gave a little skip. 'He said he was going to the Dower House to talk to the cook.'

Claire frowned at her daughter. 'Your memory seems very convenient?'

Jane looked blank.

As she should. What seven-year-old child would plot a meeting?

Unfortunately there was no ignoring the man, now the child had called out to him. She pinned a smile on her face as they drew close.

His bow emphasised his masculinity, the size and strength of him and his innate confidence. 'Madame Holte. *Mademoiselle.* What a coincidence.' His dark eyes twinkled at Jane. 'I thought I left you in charge of my kitchen, Mademoiselle Jane. Now Mademoiselle Becca will have drunk all the tea and eaten all the biscuits.'

So he had known Jane was in his kitchen.

He must have sensed her thoughts for he glanced at her swiftly. 'I left word with Madame Stratton as to her whereabouts.'

Jane giggled. 'We had tarts. Becca only had one. And so did Agnes. I made sure.'

It seemed no matter the age of the female, he managed to charm. And Mr Lumsden had delivered the information in his own way. Downstairs politics, no doubt.

'Lumsden informed me,' Claire said. 'I was hoping to see you today, Monsieur André.'

A brow winged up, making him look dashing and, if possible, more handsome. 'A happy coincidence, then, *madame.*'

Was he flirting? Or was she seeing what she wanted to see? His face was perfectly serious, but there was a gleam of something in his eyes. Interest? Her stomach gave an irresponsible little flutter. She ignored it. 'Lady Hatherton plans to bring her child with her tomorrow night. I wonder if you could arrange for an appropriate meal for the two children and the nurse to be taken in the school room. I will let Mrs Stratton know of these new arrangements, of course.'

'With pleasure, *madame*.'

The silky soft way he said *pleasure* made her toes curl inside her boots. It was his accent that made even the most pro forma of words sound sensual.

He fell in beside her as they began walking again. Somehow the wind seemed less sharp. And it wasn't just the bloom of her own warmth at his nearness. His body sheltered her from the worst of the wind. A coincidence, surely? Or a kindness.

It had been a long time since a man had strolled beside her. George had never taken her out after their marriage. And she'd been glad. The company he kept was not of the best. Now it felt oddly comforting, even though she really ought to repress his presumption. He really should know to let her go on ahead and then follow discreetly. The man was a foreigner, she told herself, and from a country that had done away with its nobility. Perhaps on those grounds he could be excused for not knowing English customs between employer and servant. He just never seemed like a servant.

There was something he wanted to say, she could hear it in the silence, feel it in the dark glance he sent her way from time to time. How strange that she should be so attune to his thoughts.

Perhaps he had something to say about the dinners? 'Feel free to tell me what is on your mind, Monsieur André.'

This time his glance was direct and full of surprise. 'Very well, *madame*. There is talk among the servants that the aim of these dinner parties is to find you a husband.'

She could not contain her gasp. Smithins. It could be no one else. The man abused his privilege and so she would tell her brother. Ire made her want to tell the chef it was none of his business and walk ahead, but something inside her resisted. Pride.

And besides, the cat was out of the bag. Servants always knew what went on in a house like Castonbury, even if they pretended they didn't.

'The dinners are a means of introducing me back into society, and a way of showing the duke's support. The rest is pure conjecture, although any one of these gentlemen is eligible.'

'You sell yourself short, *madame*. These gentlemen are by all accounts worthy, but they are far too old, too set in their ways, for a woman in her prime. One is bullied, another a bully, the third, well, he is known for his wit.'

Aghast at his frankness, she stared up at him. 'You can't know this.'

A muscle in his jaw flickered. His eyes were as hard as onyx. 'Gossip is rife in inns where tongues are loose. If I was your brother, I would not let you entertain any of these men as a match.'

She laughed then, albeit a little hysterically. 'You are far removed from being my brother, sir. Or from being a person to offer me advice.' The moment she said it, she regretted the words.

He didn't flinch, though she sensed him stiffen. 'But I offer it, nonetheless,' he said. 'There are many suitable men to be found in London, *madame*. Young men of good heart as well as fortune and title.'

'Your concern is heart-warming, *monsieur*. However, I will follow my brother's wishes in this matter. I went against him once. I will not do it again. For Jane's sake.'

Why did she feel the need to explain, to make him understand, as if his good opinion mattered? But it did. In him she sensed more interest that she had felt in a very long time. And Jane liked him.

That intriguing muscle flickered again. 'If it is your wish to woo one of these men to the altar, then we need to think further about our menu.'

Was that the reason for his enquiry? A professional interest? Her heart squeezed a little. A small pang in her chest, as if she had wanted him to talk her out of this decision.

Now she really was being ridiculous. 'What sort of changes?'

'It is true that the path to a man's heart is often by way of his stomach,' he said. 'And you have been wise in choosing their favourite dishes. However, I doubt that this is a matter of the heart.'

'No.' She inwardly shuddered. She had tried that once and been sorely disappointed. 'I am the daughter of one duke and the sister of another, Monsieur André. Marriages are a matter of connections and alliances.'

'And I gather the most recent alliances leading to marriage have not been particularly advantageous to the duke and so you are to be the sacrificial lamb.'

His matter-of-fact tone was rather insulting. 'You go too far, sir.'

His firm lips pressed together in acknowledgement of her words.

If she was honest, she would admit her anger stemmed not from insult, but from the way his words echoed her own doubts.

Not to mention the longings she had for more than mere conversation with this man. Those longings had led her astray once. From here on she was determined they would be ignored.

'I do not say this out of impertinence, *madame*. I say it as a well-wisher. I fear the duke might not be the best man to offer you advice.'

'You would criticise His Grace?'

He gazed at her for a moment, then shrugged. 'I see you are determined on this course. Then may I offer a suggestion?' His deep voice seemed to sooth her ire.

'I have the feeling you will, whatever I say.'

He gave a short laugh. 'As you say, *madame*. It is a fault I have found difficult to break.'

It was a strong man who could admit to having faults. George never had and his had been egregious. 'Let me hear your idea.'

'In addition to the favourite dish, provide something more sensual to the palate.'

The words stirred her blood in the wickedest of ways. A trickle of heat ran through her veins. Her chest had trouble rising and falling to accommodate a breath. 'What do you mean?'

'Leave it to me.'

He sounded sincere. Just as sincere in this as he had sounded in his criticism. And besides, it was only food. The key was the duke's support and all that would mean for a suitor. Power drew men the way nectar drew the bees.

Monsieur André must know his business. Why not leave such matters in his capable hands? Strong hands with long fingers, she had noted when he was working in the kitchen. Hands scarred by hard work. Like her own.

They had reached the path where it divided, one direction heading to the stables and the servants' pavilion, the other to the family's quarters.

A cat stalked across the courtyard and stopped to groom its fur. Jane was on it before she could say anything.

Monsieur André watched the child for a moment, then looked down at Claire, his eyes once more intense and dark, yet there was warmth there too, the kind of warmth a man might have for a woman, along with speculation.

He was no doubt wondering what had brought her home to wed a man of her family's choosing when she had chosen for herself before. Or perhaps he thought he knew. After all, the servants knew the scandal, knew she'd been ostracised for her choice. Perhaps he was wondering how she could humble herself to obey with such meekness. But as she had learned these past few years, pride came at a heavy price.

And as he stood there looking down at her, something shifted between them. A shimmering thing that warmed her through. Breathing became a chore, as if the air had become liquid. Her weighted limbs refused to move as she stared back at him and saw the seductive heat in his eyes. Their hot darkness drew her in and her body leaned towards him as if it would partake of more of that heat.

Desire. She knew its name and she knew its dangers. Yet the impulse remained. The pressing urge to rise on her toes and press her mouth to those beautifully moulded lips and feel his strong arms go about her. There was something about his strength, his acknowledged ability to fight, that drew her weaker self.

She dragged her gaze from his face, let it skitter away over the distant fields, the bare trees, the grey sky. A breath of sense filled her lungs and she managed a smile. 'I bid you good day, Monsieur André. Come, Jane.'

Jane reached out to pet the cat and it darted away. She skipped back to Claire. 'I will see you tomorrow, Monsieur André,' she called out.

'You will be busy tomorrow,' Claire said as they entered the house. She had been neglecting her daughter's lessons. Giving her too much free time to wander. 'Tomorrow you can resume pianoforte lessons.'

'I hate the pianoforte.'

Everyone had to do things they hated. Pianoforte was the least of them.

The past few years had been no more generous to Mr Frederick Dyer than they had been to Claire. Nine years had added silver to what was left of his rapidly receding hairline and deep grooves to his thin cheeks. *Dour* was the word that popped into her mind. Perhaps even *grim*.

'We had heard the duke had a French chef,' Mrs Dyer, his mother, said, her hair also silver beneath her cap. She had been a widow for many years. 'This soup is certainly most delicious.' She dipped her spoon again.

Pleased, Claire smiled at her.

'Monsieur André has excelled himself,' Reverend Seagrove said, smiling and nodding at the widow.

'I will pass along your compliments,' Claire said.

'I am only sorry the duke is not here,' Mr Dyer said. 'He's a difficult man to see.'

'I agree with you there, Mr Dyer,' Lady Hatherton said in her soft voice.

Mr Dyer shot her a glance. There was admiration in that glance and Claire wondered again if inviting the young widow had been a terrible miscalculation. Not that she'd had a choice. Crispin had insisted. And then cried off at the very last moment.

'The duke had every intention of joining us this evening, but found himself indisposed,' Claire said.

'Nothing serious, I hope?' Miss Seagrove asked in her kind manner.

'I don't believe so,' Claire said.

'I am sorry,' Mrs Dyer said. 'It is an age since I had conversation with His Grace.'

'Not half as sorry as me,' Dyer said. 'I wanted to talk to him about the mill.'

So that was why he was so grumpy about the missing duke. 'Surely Mr Everett would be a better person for such discussions. Or Lord Giles upon his return.'

'I have found Mr Everett most accommodating and helpful,' Lady Hatherton said gently.

Another one of those glances from Mr Dyer. 'Aye, mayhap. But 'tis the duke who put that man in the mill, and the duke who should take responsibility for getting him out.'

Reverend Seagrove pursed his lips. 'I assume old Blekin has been causing trouble again. I will have words with him if you wish.'

'Gentlemen, surely we are not going to discuss business at the dinner table?' Mrs Dyer cried with a rather critical glance at Claire for not keeping order.

Her son straightened in his chair as if the admonishment stung. 'It is business such as this that keeps food on our table, Mother.' Then he smiled and his face changed, became softer, less grim, even handsome in a severe way. 'But you are right, matters such as this can await the passing of the port.'

Claire breathed a sigh of relief. For a moment she had begun to think the man would insist on bursting in on the duke to discuss the matter of the drunken miller.

Lumsden gestured to the footmen to clear the first courses. Monsieur André had indeed excelled himself. Even Mr Dyer's disgruntlement at the duke's non-appearance had mellowed since tasting the food and fine wine.

'How is the little marquess?' Miss Seagrove asked Lady Hatherton.

'He is well, Miss Seagrove, thank you for asking.'

The footmen returned with silver trays full of food for the next course. Two roasts—woodcock and fowl—held pride of place, the *entremets* included a lobster salad *à l'Italienne* and whole truffles with champagne. There was also the cream of cods' heads specially prepared for Mr Dyer, which the chef had made look and smell thoroughly appetising. The sweet dishes consisted of a charlotte of apples with apricots and a dish of dried fruits.

A heavenly scent filled the room. Claire's mouth watered, despite having just eaten well of three previous courses. The handsome chef had indeed turned this meal into a seduction. To her shame, warmth trickled up from her belly. Seduced by food. Whoever heard of such a thing?

With the servants in the room, the conversation had slipped easily into the neutral topic of the weather when Miss Seagrove said, 'And do you think the winter will be harsh this year, Mr Dyer?'

'I hope not, Miss Seagrove. After the winter of '14 and followed by a very bad harvest, we have suffered enough, I believe. Fortunately corn prices remain high.'

Not fortunate for those who had no money to buy bread, as Claire had seen firsthand. Hers was not a view that would find much sympathy with the landowners at this table. After all, it was they who had passed the corn laws restricting the import of grain to keep prices high.

'It seems to me that this winter is much milder than those I remember as a girl,' she said. 'We have had hardly any snow.'

Lady Hatherton shivered. 'After living in Spain, this winter seems brutal.'

'But there was snow in the mountains, surely?' Miss Seagrove asked. 'Giles tell me that the winters in the mountains are far more severe than anything we experience in England.'

'I didn't go up in the mountains,' the marchioness said, looking dismal.

Claire could see that the gentle Miss Seagrove wished she had bitten her tongue.

'What did you think of other parts of Spain, Lady Hatherton?' Claire asked. 'I understand there are some fascinating cathedrals and architecture?'

'And a great many hovels too, I shouldn't wonder,' Mr Dyer put in.

The servants finished their work and disappeared like wraiths.

Lady Hatherton smiled at Mr Dyer. 'You are right, sir. It is not an experience I would care to repeat.'

Well, that put paid to that line of conversation. But Claire couldn't blame the young widow. She had experienced the worst of war.

'Will you carve the chicken, Mr Dyer, while Mr Seagrove divides the woodcocks?' she asked calmly.

Meat was carved and platters passed between the guests with much anticipation on their faces.

'When will Lord Giles and Lady Phaedra return?' Mrs Dyer asked the room generally, but with her eyes on the young bride-to-be.

'Next week, I believe,' Miss Seagrove said.

'And your wedding plans move on apace?' the widow asked.

'Yes indeed.' Miss Seagrove's face glowed.

'I look forward to it,' Mrs Dyer said, clearly anticipating her invitation.

Miss Seagrove took a mouthful from her fork, making it impossible for her to reply. A very smart young lady, Miss Seagrove. She would make Giles a good wife.

Mr Dyer piled his fork with cod covered in a cream of mushroom sauce. Claire watched him from the corner of her eye, looking forward to the same reaction of pleasure and delight that had accompanied the first course. As hostess of the dinner, the credit would fall to her as well as the duke's famous French chef.

Dyer masticated with evident pleasure, then his face turned red, he gazed wildly around and then lifted the tablecloth and spat the contents of his mouth into its folds.

Everyone at the table stared at him in astonishment, too polite to say anything, but clearly revolted by the sight.

Mr Dyer's face turned purple. He grabbed up his wine glass and gulped its contents, while fanning his hand in front of his face.

'Mr Dyer,' Claire said. 'Are you all right? Did you swallow a fish bone?' There should not have been any in this dish. This she had agreed with André.

He coughed and spluttered and drank some more wine. 'All right?' he choked out. 'No, I am not all right.'

His mother patted his back. Miss Seagrove did the same thing from the other side.

The vicar poured him a goblet of water from the pitcher on the sideboard. The man seemed ready to expire.

Slowly the gasping and coughing subsided, though the man's high forehead remained a deep red and beaded with sweat as he drew in one rasping breath after another.

Could he be suffering an apoplexy?

The Reverend Seagrove pulled the fish platter towards him. It was the only dish no one else had sampled. He spooned a small amount onto his plate and tasted it warily.

'Horseradish?' he said with a wince. 'Or too much pepper?'

Mr Dyer, with his bulging eyes and opening and closing mouth, looking a bit like the cod that was causing him such distress, shook his head.

Claire blinked. 'Are you saying there is something wrong with the food, Reverend?' It wasn't possible.

He pushed the dish towards her and she dipped her dessertspoon into the sauce. She tasted it carefully just on the tip of her tongue and recoiled. It was like eating fire.

What a disaster. She looked at her guest, at his red and sweating face, and her stomach lurched sideways. 'Oh, Mr Dyer, I am so sorry. I don't know what could have happened.'

Liar. She might not know, but she had a horrible feeling she could guess. Anger reddened her vision.

Mr Dyer shrugged off his mother's hand and waved away Miss Seagrove's flapping fan. He took another drink of water, then rose to his feet. 'That is what comes of employing a damned Frenchman. He can't cook plain food fit for an Englishman. Always got to be messing around with it. Making it better. Hotter. Or sour.' He bowed. 'Please give my regards to the duke, Mrs Holte, and tell him it is no wonder he is unwell if that is the kind of food he is served on a daily basis.'

He stomped from the room, his mother making little cries of dismay as she bobbed a curtsey before fluttering after him.

'Oh, dear,' the reverend said. He tasted the rest of the food on his plate cautiously. As did the other guests. Claire tried the buttered parsnips. And the truffles. It was all perfect, all delicious. Exactly the way she had planned with the chef. All except Mr Dyer's favourite dish.

The heat in Claire's cheeks scalded. No doubt she was as scarlet as her guest had been moments before. 'Please,' she said to the Seagroves. 'Finish your meal. There must have been some misunderstanding. I sampled this dish yesterday and there was no trace of heat.'

But there could be no misunderstanding, she realised miserably. Monsieur André had sabotaged the meal. After his harsh words yesterday, there could be no other explanation.

She got up and rang the bell for Lumsden. When he arrived, she pointed to the offending dish. 'Please return that to the kitchen and inform Monsieur André that I hope he enjoys it as much as we did.'

The butler's right eyebrow twitched. The most expression of shock she had ever seen on his face. Ever. Shock was nothing to the painful sensations of betrayal writhing in her breast. If Monsieur André had been standing in the room at that moment, she might have stabbed him with one of the carving knives.

Humiliation. That was her predominant emotion. She knew it well. George had taken great delight in letting her know her shortcomings. Punishment, she'd always thought, for the Montagues cutting the connection. She hadn't expected Monsieur André to treat her so shabbily.

While the Seagroves and Lady Hatherton kept the conversation going, talking of local matters and people, Claire could only breathe around the hard hot lump in her throat. Anger and tears. They made a bitter combination.

At long last the meal was done and the final plate cleared away. Claire pulled the threads of herself together. Having survived all the misery George could dish up on her plate, she could swallow this and move on. Mr Dyer was only one of her prospects and, after reacquainting herself with the man, she wasn't entirely sorry to cross him off her list.

But she would have liked to have made that decision for herself, not had it thrust upon her by an interfering chef.

'Shall I call for tea in the drawing room?' she asked the ladies.

'I'm sorry,' Lady Hatherton said, 'but I think it is time I took little Crispin home.'

'Oh, is he here?' Miss Seagrove asked.

'He is in the nursery with Jane,' Claire said. 'The two of them are becoming acquainted.'

'I haven't yet met your daughter,' Miss Seagrove said.

Claire had no wish to prolong the evening. 'I expect she will be in bed by now.'

'Then will you bring her for a visit to the vicarage? I would love to meet her, and the little marquess too. Perhaps you could both come one afternoon?'

'Perhaps,' Lady Hatherton said, not very encouragingly.

'It is very kind of you, Miss Seagrove,' Claire said, glad of this kindness after all that had gone before.

The young woman blushed. 'I should like it if you would both call me Lily. After all, we will be family very soon.'

'Only if you would call me Claire.'

Lady Hatherton did not offer her first name, though they all knew it was Alicia.

Claire accompanied the Seagroves to the front door and saw them out. Lily kissed her cheek and patted her shoulder. 'Don't worry, Claire. There are still two more dinners to come. I am sure nothing will go wrong next time.'

The heavy weight in Claire's chest did not ease. She was sure of it too, but what on earth would she say to Monsieur André. And the duke. If he learned of this, he would surely insist the chef be let go at once.

It might be for the best, a little voice whispered selfishly in her head. It would be cowardly. But it might remove temptation.

She turned to follow Lady Hatherton up to the nursery.

Slumped on a stool, the kitchen empty except for him and the cat who wandered in every night to sleep by the hearth, André glared at the congealing cods' heads. They looked back at him, mouths open, grinning.

How the hell did a perfect sauce with a dash of cayenne acquire the heat of hell between his kitchen and the dining room? He'd tasted every dish before it had gone on the platters. He must have tasted this one. He would never make such a beginner's mistake.

It had been perfect. He was sure of it. Then what could have happened? Who wished him harm? Joe Coyle, never his friend, had carried the platter up, but the lad had no access to his spices. No one did. Except him.

The servants hadn't liked him much when he first came. The French Devil, they had called him, a play on Deval, his chosen last name, but that had been over a long time ago. The war was over too, and if people still fought it in their minds and in the taverns, they did not fight it here at Castonbury Park. Or not openly. The butler and the housekeeper saw to that. Of all the servants, though, only Joe would have the temerity. And the lingering hatred. He'd lost brothers in the war with Napoleon.

André got up and threw the contents of the dish into a slop bucket. It was so bad, not even pigs would eat it. It would have to go into the privy.

It wasn't so much the problem with the food that had him fuming inside; it was the message from Claire. Not Claire. Not even in his mind. He'd given up that right willingly. Yet now he felt torn by the difference in their station. He found himself speaking to her as an equal instead of obeying orders with a shrug as he had for so many years. It was because she looked at him as a man. The attraction that danced between them. But always she withdrew, as she should. But that distancing made him sometimes wish he had not given up all claims to his birth.

No. He would not go down that path. Not for anyone. Especially a woman. That part of his life was over.

She was Madame Holte. And must always be so. Otherwise he would probably let her name slip from his tongue in some unguarded moment when they were alone, tasting food, talking, feeling the sparks that exploded between them.

How could she believe he would ruin a dish deliberately?

He had said things he had no right to say, it was true, but that she would believe him capable of such cruelty was gut-wrenching.

It was quite obvious from her message, delivered in such a colourless tone by the butler, that she indeed thought he had deliberately ruined her attempt to woo this Mr Dyer.

His fists clenched. He would not let her go to bed thinking he had deliberately ruined her chances with this man. He might have wanted to do so. He might even secretly feel a little glad, but he would never have given in to such a temptation. Not with his reputation on the line. And especially knowing how much she would be hurt.

On his way through the grand hall to the family wing, one of the servants told him that she was to be found in the nursery with the dowager marchioness.

So not all of the guests had left. Perhaps he should leave this until the morning. He would, if he was wise. But he was too angry, too disappointed in himself, to wait.

He took the stairs two at a time to the third floor. A dreadful thought occurred to him on the way along the corridor. What if the children's meal had been similarly spoiled? What if she was up there, comforting a child with a stomach ache or a throat burning with fire?

Would she know what to do? He quickened his pace.

But as he approached the nursery and adjoining school room, the voices were calm and there was laughter. Children's laughter.

He let go a sigh of relief. Why had he been worried? He had delivered the food to Miss Jane personally because the footmen were too busy looking after the dining room and the duke.

The door was open and he cautiously looked inside.

His jaw dropped.

Not only were Madame Holte and Lady Hatherton seated on the floor with their children, but so was the duke, in banyan, cap and slippers. He had the baby bouncing on his knee and was listening to Mademoiselle Jane recite. The little girl stood in front of him twisting her body from side to side, but her smile said she was happy.

Lady Hatherton was a very pretty woman, but tonight Claire, Madame Holte, had never looked more radiant. The gown of shimmering bronze looked stunning. The artfully arranged curls at her temples drew attention to her fine widely spaced grey eyes. She was smiling at her daughter. But the smile was tight and her eyes seemed a little sad.

His gut gave a lurch. Had she been so set on this man, then? This politician? He was a man chosen by her brother, but she might also have loved him. Stranger things had happened, he supposed. The oddest people fell in love in books. Why not in real life?

It was not something he had ever experienced. Love of a woman. Nor did he want to. Once he'd believed in the love of his family. Discovering it was all a lie had ripped out his heart. Left him confused and weak. He never wanted to feel that way again.

And it seemed that the more he saw of Claire, the more in danger he became of forgetting that.

The duke bounced the little boy on his knee harder. The child giggled wildly. Mademoiselle Jane chucked him under the chin and the duke pulled her close for a hug. 'A niece and a grandson,' he said, his voice husky. 'How lucky can an old man get?'

André crept away. It was not his place to be here watching this private moment. This family. He had no family. And nor did he want one. The odd feeling in his chest was merely his frustration with the occurrences of the evening. The knowledge that his words with Madame Holte would have to wait.

Thinking of her as *madame* cooled the storm of emotion, but left him feeling cold inside.

Seven

Claire trudged along the corridor to her chamber door. What a calamity of an evening. From the dinner party to the duke entertaining Alicia in the nursery. Giles would be furious. Smithins had said so when he collected his charge. How had His Grace learned of his grandson's presence in the house? When Claire had asked him, he'd looked at her blankly.

She sighed and turned the handle on her chamber door.

A shadow loomed out of the darkness. Silent yet forceful.

On a gasp she swung around.

Monsieur André stood a few feet away, barely discernable in the shadows cast by her candle. But she knew him by his height and build.

André. She lifted her candle, casting him in light and flickering shadows. It seemed to make him all the more menacing. 'What on earth are you doing here? You gave me a start.'

He leaned against the wall and folded his arms over his formidable chest. His eyes dark above the stark lines of his cheekbones and jaw bored into her. 'There is a little matter of a message, Madame Holte. We need to talk.'

She swallowed, her throat dry, as she recalled her angry words. She was too tired for this now. Too weary to fight. 'Not now, *monsieur*.'

'Yes, now.'

How dare he speak to her this way? She'd resolved that never again would she suffer this kind of abuse. The heat of her earlier anger rose up in a red mist.

'It is past midnight. It will wait until tomorrow.'

A clenched fist struck the wall behind him. A silent blow. A physical manifestation of anger held under control. 'Now, if you please, *madame*.' His voice was low and harsh.

With any other man she might have been fearful, certainly with George, who had not the least control on his temper. She did not fear this man because beneath the anger she sensed a need she could not in all fairness deny. A driving need to present his side of the story.

She sighed. 'Very well.'

She opened the door a crack and from inside her chamber she heard the sound of the maid, Daisy, tidying up her chamber, preparing to help her to bed. If she should catch her and Monsieur André having a conversation outside her bedroom door, it would be the icing on the worst evening of her life.

She closed the door quietly. 'Not here. Meet me in the library in five minutes.' She turned and swept back the way she had come, surprised to discover her weariness had fled and her footsteps were swift and sure.

He did not follow her, naturally. He could not. He turned for the servants' stairs.

He was already waiting when she stepped into the library, standing by the open curtains and looking out into the night, his shoulders stiff and uncompromising. Much like her brother's shoulders had been the night she had told him of the man she had fallen in love with.

Why did that memory have to come back to haunt her now? That part of her life was over and done with. She had learned her lesson. She was not the same girl who had fallen madly in love and run off to get married.

She was a sensible widow and a mother.

He swung around to face her when she stepped over the threshold.

She lit a table candelabra and set her night candle down. She rubbed at her arms in their thin silk, feeling the chill of a room with no fire, as she stared at this handsome arrogant Frenchman. He wanted to explain and therefore only one word came to her mind. 'Why?'

His expression was grim, his jaw hard. He looked like some avenging dark angel. Still angry, then. She was the one who should be angry.

'Why what, Madame Holte?'

Oh, why did that voice of his have to strum every nerve in her body. Why did the intensity in his eyes give her the sense that he could see right through to her very essence? And why was he pretending he didn't know what she meant?

'You did it deliberately,' she said. 'You spoiled that one particular dish on purpose. When I tell my brother what you did—'

'I did nothing of the sort.'

Her own anger rose. 'Who else would have done such a thing?'

He pressed his lips together. Gave a sharp shake of his head. 'I swear that dish was perfect when it left my kitchen. As good if not better than the dish you tasted when we agreed on the menus. If I had wanted to do that, I would have been far more subtle about it. Mr Dyer would have enjoyed every bite and only the following day would he have felt the effects of something bad in his diet.'

'Good God, you have thought about this.' The laugh she gave was hard. 'Do you suspect one of the footman, perhaps?'

He winced. 'Much as I would like to say one of them did it, they could not. None of them have access to the pantry.'

'Are you saying it was an accident? Come now, Monsieur André, surely you do not expect me to believe it was a mistake? Not after our conversation yesterday when you presumed to give me advice.'

He breathed in through his nose, his chest rising and then finally falling as if he was doing all in his power to restrain his temper.

Claire retreated a step or two, memories of George, his stinging slap to her face one day when she had argued, making her put up a hand to keep him at bay.

His eyes widened. *'Madame,'* he said softly. *'Milles pardons.'* He backed up, giving her the space she needed for comfort. He took a deep breath and his rage seemed to subside in an instant. 'Forgive me. My anger is not directed at you, but at whoever ruined that dish.' His gaze remained on her face, unflinching and level, and she believed him.

'It would afford me nothing to serve inedible food,' he said with a lift of his shoulders. 'All I have is my reputation. These dinners are as vital to me as they are to you. Mr Dyer is an important man, known in society. One word from him and my future would be ruined. Please believe me, the dish was fine when it left my kitchen.'

The passion in his voice, the way he looked directly into her eyes, convinced her. 'Then who? And why?'

He frowned, not at her but at the carpet. 'I don't know.' He raised his gaze, shaking his head. 'I don't know if it is someone who meant to do you harm, or me. Some of the servants here do not like a Frenchman in their midst.'

Could that be the explanation? 'The war is over.'

'But the consequences linger on.'

'You have been here for months, have you not? Did something like this happen before?'

He huffed out a breath. 'No. And yet I honestly do not believe any of the servants would dare. Not even Lumsden, though he is a pretty cold fish.'

'Not all fish are cold,' she said, remembering fiery cod's heads.

He flashed a faint smile. 'Not a matter for laughing.'

'Not at the time, the poor man.' The image flashed into her mind and she felt a chuckle grow in her chest. 'I wish you had seem him. His face looked just like one of those awful fish he favours, only red.' She pressed a hand to her mouth to stifle a giggle.

He grinned, shaking his head. 'The sauce was as hot as Hades, *madame*. He will suffer for days.'

They smiled at each other, the anger so fraught only moments before dissipated by the laughter they'd shared.

'Perhaps it was some dreadful mistake that will not happen again,' she said.

'*Non.* It was deliberate. Could it have occurred in the dining room?'

'Well, I can assure you that neither Reverend Seagrove nor his daughter would tamper with one of the dishes.'

'Nor Mr Dyer's mother,' Monsieur André said in musing tones.

They looked at each other. 'Lady Hatherton,' they said together.

'Why?' Claire asked.

'Mayhap she sees you as a rival. Mayhap she had designs on Mr Dyer before you arrived. She is a widow.'

'And quite lovely.' Claire sighed. 'If she wanted Mr Dyer, she could no doubt have him with a snap of her fingers.'

Monsieur André stared at her for a very long moment. He took another step forward. 'You mean that, don't you?'

She shrugged. 'I have no illusions about myself, Monsieur André. I am far beyond the age most men think eligible for marriage. I never was a diamond of the first water like Lady Hatherton. My only advantage is my connection to the duke. But she is the mother of his heir. That is a powerful situation for any woman.'

He reached out, his hand steady as a rock, and placed one finger under her chin, turning her face with the gentlest of pressure towards the light. 'You are wrong about not being beautiful, Claire,' he murmured. 'Your beauty goes deeper than mere features, lovely as they are. It is in the depths of your eyes, and the glow of your skin and in your spirit.'

His voice was like a drug on her ears. She could listen to the sound of it for ever. Her skin absorbed it like gentle summer rain on the parched earth. And the words were a balm to her feminine soul.

She couldn't move for the pull of his body on hers. The magnetism that seemed to hold her in thrall. Slowly she raised her gaze to his harsh dark features, to his gaze that scorched her skin as he searched her expression.

Looking for what?

'It is something else too.' A crease formed between his brows. 'You have…calmness. It soothes me.'

As he spoke, he lowered his head, his eyelids drooping, his gentle touch angling her face to receive the touch of his mouth. A brush of warm lips on hers. Velvet soft. A whisper of a kiss.

A small cry issued from her throat. A protest. Not that he should stop, but that he not leave it at only a kiss.

She cradled his face in her hands and returned the kiss, with fervour, with passion, with the heat raging out of control.

And then he was kissing her. Really kissing her. His mouth

open on hers, their tongues tangling silkenly as they tasted each other.

He tasted of wine and mint. He smelled of dark spices, some hot, some subtle. Like the most tempting of the dishes he had prepared for this evening.

But the appetite and hunger driving her on had nothing to do with food and everything to do with the beauty and maleness of this man.

And she tasted and she took.

He pulled her close, up against the hard length of his body. A body hardened by exercise, muscled and lean. And heaven help her, young and strong.

And she gave herself up to the kiss. Sank into it. Disappeared into its darkness, hearing only their hearts beating in unison. Feeling only the brush of his hair on her hands, the warmth of his skin above his collar, the breadth of his shoulders and the muscles beneath his coat. And then the pressure of his hard wall of chest against her breasts and his hands wandering up her back and pulling her tight against him. A large palm followed the contours of her back, the dip of her waist and the rise of her buttocks.

He pulled her firmly against his hips and she arched into him, feeling his burgeoning arousal.

A bolt of what felt like lightning shot through her body, leaving in its wake the flames of desire.

A need so powerful she gave voice to it in a long heartfelt moan.

He broke the kiss and raised his head, looking down at her. The raw sensuality in his expression was as seductive as hell.

Overwhelming.

And completely inappropriate.

She pushed him away. He looked surprised, then puzzled and finally chagrined.

He stepped back. Spun away. *'Milles pardons, madame,'* he said, his voice husky, his breathing as laboured as hers.

'No apology is required, Monsieur André.' She picked up her candle. 'Under different circumstances…' She shrugged. 'However, things are as they are and this must not happen again.'

'It will not,' he said softly, regretfully, and she saw determination in the set of his jaw.

She strode out of the library on legs that felt too weak to carry her, and headed for her chamber. It will not. The words ran through her head over and over. He was much stronger than she was, clearly. And tears welled in her eyes.

Trembling inside, but outwardly calm, she hoped, Claire waited for the chef's arrival. If she thought of him as the chef, it would keep her distanced.

Initially she had thought she would not meet with him this morning, but then she had issued a very public request. She could hardly go back on it.

He knocked and entered. He didn't scratch the way most servants did—oh, no, he knocked, brisk and businesslike.

That was why he was different. He did not act like a servant, not even an upper servant. He acted as if he was equal to anyone or anything.

It ought to be a mark against him, in her world, but it was not. Instead he instilled in her a trust which had been so often lacking in her marriage. He made her feel like a person whose thoughts and ideas mattered.

George on the other hand had scorned her opinions.

She forced herself not to clench her hands when he closed the door behind him and stood before her, waiting.

His expression was carefully blank. No hint of what had passed between them the previous evening reflected in his dark eyes. He looked at her as if she was a stranger. His employer. Nothing more.

Damn her, why did that hurt?

She allowed herself a brief smile. 'Thank you for coming, Monsieur André.'

He waited silently.

The frankness with which she had spoken the previous evening seemed illusive. She struggled to put her thoughts into some sort of order. 'What happened yesterday was regretful, but we shall speak no more about it.' Oh, that did not sound right. He would think she meant the kiss. Not that she planned to talk about that either.

Heat flushed her cheeks. 'I mean, what happened with the meal. I shall expect our next dinner to go off without a hitch. I assume you can manage that?'

'Yes, *madame*. Thank you, *madame*.'

Even uttering the servile words, he sounded arrogant, but was there some relief in his gaze?

'I sent word to Mr Dyer apologising for what happened and indicating that it was the duke who requested the extra heat with his cod fish. That he finds it helps to clear his head. You were not aware, of course, that the duke had decided not to join us, or that a separate dish was required.'

A dark eyebrow flickered upwards. '*Madame* is very kind.'

Yes, she was, wasn't she? Weak, George had always said. She lifted her chin. 'I do think it would help if you could determine how the dish was spoiled, Monsieur André. Because if something similar happens again next time, there will be no way to keep it from the duke. It seems that Smithins is not a particular friend of yours.'

André grimaced. 'We have had our differences of opinion.'

'About politics, I understand.'

He opened his mouth to speak but she waved him off. 'No

matter. He and Lumsden have agreed to say nothing of what occurred as a personal favour to me. However, I can probably only ask for one such favour.'

He nodded stiffly. 'I am obliged, then, *madame*, and if I can return the favour at any time, please do not hesitate to ask.'

The man was apparently a revolutionary yet steeped in courtly charm. The dichotomy of it was highly confusing.

'I do not need anything, Monsieur André, apart from a successful dinner party.' She glanced down at her hands in case she was tempted to apologise for her stern words and icy demeanour.

She stifled a sigh. 'That will be all.'

He bowed. She knew he did, because she could sense every movement without even looking his way. She did not lift her gaze until he left the room and closed the door.

'Dash it all.' No doubt he thought she was punishing him for what happened in the library. But truly she was punishing herself. Making sure it could not happen again.

Making sure there would be no gossip.

She pushed to her feet feeling decidedly raw, as if she'd been flayed. And deservedly so.

Montague women did not kiss servants in the library in the middle of the night, no matter how attractive...even if Montague men did.

She had to make sure it could not happen again and the best way to do that was to remove temptation.

Now it was time for Jane's lessons. And she also needed to visit the duke. She needed to know more about Lady Hatherton than what she had heard from the servants and the Seagroves. Because she was the only person who seemed likely to have doctored last night's meal.

Claire shook her head. As a theory, it didn't make any

sense. Perhaps His Grace might have some ideas. In his prime, Crispin's mind had been sharp and political. But that was before he lost his sons.

'Mr Anderson said I could have one of the kittens.'

The words penetrated Claire's fog as she scanned the *Times*. Anderson was the head groom and Jane had recently taken to visiting his domain too.

'Oh, dear, Jane, I don't think we can bring a kitten inside the house.'

'Why not?'

'It just isn't done. The duke wouldn't like it.'

'Can I ask him?'

'We cannot trouble him. He is not well.' She had been refused admittance this morning. Smithins had been most obdurate.

'But Mr Anderson said I could have one.'

The old groom, dear though he was, and kindly, should not make promises without asking permission. She was here on sufferance. And without Giles's approval too, though Lily had been quite sure her fiancé would welcome her arrival.

But then Miss Seagrove was remarkably optimistic about all sorts of things. A product of her father's calling, no doubt.

'Not until we have your uncle's approval. Or that of your cousin Giles.'

'Does my cousin have any little girls?'

'He isn't married yet.'

Jane looked at her with narrowed eyes. 'Do you have to be married to have children?'

Saints preserve her. 'Yes. Or at least that is what everyone expects.'

Jane returned to the picture book she was looking at. 'That

black-and-white cat is the daddy of the kittens. He lives in the barn too.'

'Cats help keep the vermin down.'

'They catch the mice. Tiny will be a top-notch hunter, Mr Anderson said.'

Claire was going to wring his neck. Tom's, that was, not the cat's. 'Jane, a barn cat is not easily turned into a house cat. He will be happier if left in the barn, but I will talk to Mr Anderson and make sure he understands this is your cat and though it must live in the barn it will be yours to care for.'

Jane's eyes widened. 'He can be my cat even if he lives in the barn?'

Claire nodded. 'You can feed him and give him water, night and morning. But if you forget about him, then he goes back to being a barn cat, the same as all the other barn cats. Is that fair?'

Jane frowned, then smiled. 'Yes, it is fair. Can we go and tell Mr Anderson right now?'

Claire put aside her paper and glanced outside. It was grey and lowering but as yet no rain or snow.

'Yes, we can go and tell him.'

Jane hopped down from her chair. 'I'll go and ask Mr Lumsden for my coat and hat.'

'While we are there we shall see if John Coachman can take us to the village in the carriage. I need some embroidery thread.'

Jane hopped from foot to foot. 'Can I drive?'

'The coach? I think not.'

The child's face fell.

'But perhaps we could take the gig. You could drive it, I think.'

'Oh, yes, please, Mama.' She dashed out of the room.

Claire followed. It seemed she could deny her child nothing. But then she'd denied her a great deal for far too long. These small concessions would do her no harm.

They would need to dress warmly; the wind had been howling around the house all morning, but she needed fresh air and an errand was a good way to get it. Something to take her away from the house and its stifling effect on her senses.

It had been years since she'd driven the gig and Claire was surprised how quickly the skill came back. She'd never been particularly dashing with the ribbons, but definitely more than competent. The freedom of driving with the wind in her face and the wild Derbyshire country all around her lifted her spirits.

She could do this. She could make a good marriage and salvage the shreds of her life. For Jane. For herself too. No more running and hiding and fearing every knock on the door. No more living a lie.

Life would be comfortable and safe. Once George's debts were paid and Ernie Pratt was no longer a threat.

'Can I help drive now?' Jane asked. Her cheeks were glowing from the wind and her eyes sparkling at the thought of doing something so grown up. Her eyes had been sparkling a lot just lately. She seemed younger, more her age.

There was no reason why she shouldn't try her hand at the ribbons. Claire had learned from her brothers at around the same age. She lifted her onto her lap. 'Look at the way I am holding the reins.'

Jane looked.

'Sit up straight and hold out your hands, palms up,' Claire instructed, and handed over the reins.

Terror filled the child's face as she felt the movement of the horse and realised she was in control of the large beast in front of the gig. Claire kept her hands ready to help.

When nothing happened, Jane relaxed. 'How do I make him go faster?'

'You don't. Always respect your animal. The road is rutted and full of holes. Let him go at his own speed.'

Jane frowned. 'Can't I make him trot?'

'No. It is your job to watch between his ears. Keep a careful look out for muddy places where the wheels might become stuck and guide him around them. A small amount of pressure on the reins left or right is all he needs. His mouth is sensitive and if you pull too hard you will hurt him.'

A crease formed between the child's brows, her eyes fixed on the road ahead. So intent. So very careful. Almost too careful. She'd learned to be careful around her father. Perhaps she shouldn't have sounded so strict.

The child was quick-witted as well as sensitive and it wasn't long before she had the hang of it, guiding the horse around potholes and through the occasional puddle. She dared a quick smile of delight over her shoulder and Claire grinned back, relishing her daughter's joy. The child deserved the same happy carefree existence she had enjoyed as a child.

She would not let the past destroy the future.

Pratt would not ruin their lives. She shuddered and looked around her, half expecting danger to leap over the walls. Not possible. No one knew where she was or her real name.

'What do I do now?' Jane's voice held panic. Claire focused on the road. Ahead, a puddle stretched from one side of the lane to the other. No way around it.

'I wonder how deep it is,' Claire said. 'Pull back gently and evenly on both reins and bring him to a halt so I can get down and take a look.' When they were fully stopped, Claire tied off the reins so Jane could not inadvertently set the horse moving and, umbrella in hand, climbed down.

The water reflected the clouds scudding across the sky

above, but Claire could see pebbles and mud an inch or two below the surface. Reaching out as far as she could, she poked at the mud with the tip of her umbrella. It disappeared into the mud, but no more than an inch or so. It really didn't look very dangerous. Traffic travelled from the Park to the village constantly; indeed, the post had arrived earlier in the day without any problem. Surely, if there was danger, one of the grooms would have mentioned it before she set out.

She headed back for the trap and a very proud-looking Jane in charge of the horse.

Claire clambered up beside her. 'I think it will be fine, but it would be good if we gained some momentum so we do not get stuck in the middle.'

Jane looked at her, clearly expecting instruction.

Every instinct inside Claire strained to take the reins from the child. To ensure nothing went wrong. To protect the child from harm. Or failure.

But wasn't that what they'd done to her? Set her about with cotton wool, sheltered her from the dangers of the world, until she broke free and brought disaster down upon her head?

'Shake the reins and make a clicking sound with your tongue,' Claire said. 'The horse will know you want him to go and go fast.'

The child did as she was bid and the horse pulled forward, then broke into a brisk trot. In seconds they were splashing through the puddle. The wheels dragged a little when they got to the middle of the water, but the horse was already on dry ground and Jane flicked the reins again and the little horse picked up speed and pulled them clear.

'Well done,' Claire said with a grin at her child. 'Slow him down now—there is a sharp bend coming up.'

Jane pulled back gently on the reins until they were once more travelling at little more than walking speed.

'That was fun,' Jane said.

'So it was. And here we are in Castonbury village already. You must drive very slowly to avoid pedestrians. Pull into the inn courtyard. We will leave the gig there and go the rest of the way on foot.'

The manoeuvre into the inn courtyard proved beyond Jane's newly learned skill and she handed over the reins without demur. Claire soon had the gig safely in the hands of one of the ostlers, leaving them free to walk to the the haberdasher's. Claire had decided to trim one of her gowns with a smidgeon of lace, to make it more fashionable. She also needed more hairpins and a ribbon or two for Jane.

Their errands did not take very long and indeed a servant could have easily been despatched to undertake these small purchases, but the trip had helped dim the events of the previous evening. The later events. The meeting with André that had kept her awake half the night. Not to mention how much Jane was enjoying their jaunt.

It kept the child from visiting the kitchen and meant Claire was relieved the task of fetching her and facing Monsieur André in his own domain.

Such a coward. In her own home too.

She would have to face him sooner or later. Later would be better, when she stopped feeling heat flood her veins each time she remembered his touch on her body and the feel of his lips on her mouth. Those delicious wicked feelings that left her feeling boneless.

So wanton. So dangerous.

When they emerged from the haberdasher's after making their purchases, the sky lowered with dark grey clouds. The temperature of the air had plummeted too. The weather was about to take a rapid turn for the worse as it so often did in this part of the country. It might even snow. It was a good thing they didn't have far to travel, since the gig did not offer much in the way of shelter.

A man ran to fetch her vehicle from the barn while she and Jane waited in the courtyard.

A well-dressed man, military by his bearing, came out of the taproom and loosed his horse tied to a post. Upon seeing Claire and Jane he gave them a sharp look, then raised his hat and bowed.

He had the reddest hair. Something about him felt odd. Not the courtesy, but the glance that took her in as if he was seeking someone. A shiver slid down her back. Could he have come from London?

Eight

The ostler brought the gig over and touched his forelock. 'Rubbed her down well, I did, Mrs Holte.'

'Thank you. The man, who just left, do you know who he is?'

The ostler scratched his unshaven chin. 'Aaar, you mean Sir Nathan's new man. Likes a pint, he do.'

The back of her neck prickled. 'Has he worked for him long?'

The ostler looked a little startled. He rubbed the back of his neck. 'A week, mebbe more, I reckon. Come from down south.'

'From London?'

'Aye. Likely enough.'

Could Pratt have sent him? Unlikely if he was working for Sir Nathan. A cold sensation licked down her spine. Fear. She wouldn't be free of it until she had paid the man off. She handed the ostler a coin and turned to help Jane into the gig, but the child scrambled up like a monkey and Claire had nothing to do but follow. She shook out the travelling blanket and put it over their knees.

'I'll drive,' Jane said importantly.

'When we get on the road and out of the village.' Claire guided the gig out of the courtyard and the full force of the wind hit them.

Jane snuggled deeper into the blanket. 'Is it always so cold here?'

'No. In summer it is warm. And very beautiful. We will go for a picnic out in the dales and you will see what I mean.'

'I would like to be here in the summer.'

A pang struck her heart. The child was used to moving on. George had always been sure the gold at the end of the rainbow was around the next corner, when in reality they went further and further downhill. Each set of lodgings more dreary than the last. Only this past year had they stayed in one place for any length of time, only to move again. 'I hope we will still be here.' She would make sure of it.

'If we have more snow, can we make another *bonhomme* with Monsieur André?'

Just the mention of his name made her heart beat faster and a blush glow on her cheeks. 'We mustn't bother Monsieur André. He has duties. And besides, we do not want snow until after we get home.'

She should not have said that, about not wanting snow. She wasn't superstitious, but George had always warned her about tempting fate. He had believed in lucky tokens and favourable signs. Or he had said he did. She had begun to think they were just excuses for doing what he knew he should not.

When they were clear of the cottages, Claire handed the reins over to Jane as she had promised and looked out over the countryside. The sky was growing darker by the minute. The clouds looked quite ominous.

Jane urged the horse into a trot. Claire stopped daydreaming and focused ahead. Ah, the water on the road. The child had remembered to pick up their pace. Ice had formed in a thin skin at the edges. It crackled under the horse's hooves. Then the creature was splashing through the middle. A tree to one side of them gave a resounding crack and a branch fell into the road.

The little horse threw up its head. It jolted into a canter, the gig bouncing along behind. Jane let go of the reins to cling onto the side of the seat. Claire made a snatch for them. They slipped through her grasping fingers and disappeared. A swift glance over the side showed them trailing on the ground. The horse stretched into a gallop.

'Hold on,' she said to Jane, clasping her tight around the shoulders with one arm while gripping the side with the other. 'He will stop in a minute.' Either because he ran out of breath, or because the gig had tipped over and acted as a brake.

The brake. She leaned over the side and pulled on the handle. It broke off in her hand. 'Oh, no.'

The wheel hit a rut and the carriage bounced. Jane blanched to the colour of snow and Claire's spine jarred. She clung tighter to her child.

Then something launched from the verge at the horse. A man. He grabbed the horse's bridle and turned the animal's head, hard. A hat went flying off, revealing a dark head of hair, but she didn't need to see his face to know who it was. Monsieur André.

Be careful, she wanted to yell, but her voice seemed stuck in her throat. All she could do was hang on tightly to Jane.

The wild careening slowed to a walk and then a halt. The horse stood trembling.

Monsieur André walked back, picking up the reins as he

came. His dark eyes flashed anger. 'Madame Holte, what are you doing out in this weather alone?'

'The weather was fine when we left,' she said, the thanks on the tip of her tongue driven off by the accusation in his tone.

'Mademoiselle Jane,' he said gently. 'Everything is fine.'

Claire looked down at her daughter, still clenched beneath her arm, and became aware of tears streaming down the child's face. 'Monsieur André is right. We are safe now, Jane. No need to cry.'

'I couldn't stop him,' she said between sobs. 'I pulled, but he wouldn't stop.'

Monsieur André's brows went up. 'You were driving?'

'She was learning to drive,' Claire said. 'She is old enough. I learned at the same age.'

His dark eyes came to her face, inscrutable, despite the rapid rise and fall of his chest from his exertions on their behalf. 'As did I, *madame*,' he said.

'I can't do it,' Jane said.

'You can,' Claire replied. 'Really you can. I promise. You know, horses are the stupidest creatures. They run when they are scared. I would have been in exactly the same boat if I had been holding the reins. Now dry your tears or Monsieur André will think you are a watering pot.'

Jane took the handkerchief and dried her eyes and blew her nose.

'Feeling better, *ma petite*?' Monsieur André said, his face gentle. He looked like a different man when his gaze fell on Jane, she realised. He looked younger, even a touch out of his depth, as if he found her fascinating.

'Oui, monsieur,' Jane said. 'But I don't want to drive any more.'

If the philosophy Claire had learned in her own childhood was right, she should make the child drive right away, but Jane had suffered a terrible fright and Claire couldn't see torturing her. 'You can try again another day.' She looked down at the chef. Goodness, he looked magnificent with his skin brightened by the wind and his dark eyes watching her child with concern.

'We are most grateful for your timely appearance, Monsieur André. Were you leaving Castonbury Park or returning?' she asked.

'Returning, *madame*.' He bowed and stepped back.

The action of a servant. Of course, she had made it very clear last night that their worlds were far apart.

'May I offer you a ride, then?' she said, knowing she should not. It was not done. If they were seen… Dash it all, she was a widow, not a debutante. If she wanted to offer a man who had saved her life a ride, she would. And to the devil with the gossips.

He shook his head. 'I enjoy the exercise.' There was pride in that dark face. In the set of his shoulders. Even in the slightly broken nose that ruined the chiselled perfection of his features.

'It is going to snow, Monsieur André,' she said. 'I will not have it said that I caused dinner to be late because I let you get lost in a blizzard.'

He looked up at the sky and back at her. A rueful smile twisted his lips. 'I suppose it is my duty, then.'

'Indeed,' she said.

'I'll squeeze up next to Mama and make room,' Jane said.

'I am much obliged, *mademoiselle*.' His long legs took the step up in one easy stride and he settled in beside Jane. He still held the reins. He shot Claire a sideways glance and a small smile curled his full lips. 'I will drive. It is better if my hands are busy, no?' He urged the horse into a walk.

Claire's face flushed hot. She prayed it looked like a burn from the wind.

'I really must thank you, Monsieur André. I do not know what might have happened if you had not been there.' She was glad to hear her voice did not echo the trembles inside her.

He stared straight ahead, but even in profile she could see the twinkle in his eye. 'The horse would have slowed and you would have continued on your way.'

About to object, she noticed the way his gaze flickered down to her daughter. A warning. Do not scare her more than she is already scared, it said. She blinked. How on earth could she read all of that into a mere flicker of an eyelash? The very idea.

Yet she knew in her heart, in the depth of her being, that was what he had meant.

'You are right,' she said. 'Poor little beast. A branch broken by the wind scared him.'

'I think you are right about a coming storm,' he said, glancing across the valleys and hills. 'It is a wild place, this Derbyshire.'

'Where in France did you come from?' she asked.

'Bordeaux,' Jane announced. 'In the south. Monsieur André showed me on the map.'

Claire raised her brow. 'I didn't know we had maps in the kitchen?'

Monsieur André gave Jane a pointed look.

'I took a book of maps from the library. I wanted to see France.'

'Blaeu's *Le grand atlas*.' Monsieur André's voice was dry.

'Oh, goodness. That book is worth a king's ransom.'

'I put it right back,' Jane said.

'Without the addition of any flour,' Monsieur André added. He was smiling down at the child and Jane was looking back at him with worship in her eyes. He'd charmed the daughter as much as he'd charmed the mother. Was this his intention?

Was he deliberately trying to worm his way into her affections? Thinking to move up in the world? As George had.

Somehow she couldn't picture him doing anything so underhanded. He'd been nothing but honest with her. Straightforward to the point of rude, on occasion. And she admired him for that. A great deal. He might be a servant but he was unquestionably honourable.

It was part of what made him so dashed attractive. Warmth flowed through her veins and her heart seemed to open in welcome.

So unwise. She forced her mind back to the conversation. 'Did you find Bordeaux on the map?'

'Yes.' Jane nodded hard. 'You can't see it from England. It is in the south. You can see Calais from England though. From Dover on a clear day, Monsieur André says. And you can see Dover from Calais too. There are white cliffs across the…the *manche*.'

'In Britain we call it the English Channel,' Claire said, smiling.

'In France it is the "sleeve,"' Monsieur André put in.

'Does the sea belong to England?' Jane asked.

'Yes,' Claire said.

'No,' Monsieur André said at the same moment. Then he laughed. 'It depends on your perspective, I suppose. But really, how can water belong to anyone? You cannot hold it. It never stays in one place for long, and if you heat it up, it disappears.'

'Like magic?' Jane asked.

'In steam,' Claire said, enjoying the back and forth of conversation. Monsieur André was a surprisingly well-educated man and very patient with her daughter's interminable questions. The more she knew him the more there was to admire.

She ought not to admire him. They really ought not to be

talking about things the way they did. She just couldn't seem to help herself.

'Are fog and steam the same?' Jane asked.

'No,' Monsieur André said. 'Steam is hot. Fog is cold. But they are very similar. Snow is also water that is very cold.'

'And so is ice,' Jane said.

'And clouds,' Claire added.

Jane frowned. 'How?'

'I think your daughter is going to be a scientist when she grows up,' Monsieur André said. 'She is so curious.'

'Women do not study science.' Or law. Or medicine. Not in any meaningful way.

'In France they did. For a while,' Monsieur André said.

'Did you believe that philosophy about all men being equal?' Claire asked. 'The Jacobin stuff.'

He looked at her askance, his eyes unfathomable. 'A great many men died for their beliefs in that "stuff," as you call it.'

'And others died because they did not.'

He inclined his head in acknowledgement. A sad looked crossed his face. 'Too many in my own country, I am afraid.'

'So you do not believe in it. My family does not.'

His brow lowered. 'I believe that men should have the opportunity to make the best of their lives by their own efforts. If they are skilled, if they work hard, then they should be recompensed accordingly. I do not believe that any man is better than another because of his birth.'

'Positively revolutionary. Yet you work for a man who believes he is better for that very reason.'

He turned the gig through the gates of the Park and raised a hand to the gatekeeper as they passed by.

Claire noticed that Jane had fallen asleep against Monsieur André's shoulder. She glanced up at his face in surprise. He smiled sweetly at the child and her heart tumbled over. This man would be a wonderful father. But not to her children, she reminded herself. It would not be permitted. She reached for Jane.

'Leave her, she is fine,' he said gently.

She tried to stave off the soft feelings melting her heart and focus on what she should not admire in him. 'I am surprised you came to England, feeling as you do.'

He grimaced. 'That is because you do not know France. I love my country. I fought for her. But England had the Magna Carta. This country too, is changing—the changes began long ago, and continue steadily if slowly. In France it happened quickly. And with many losses.'

She wanted to ask him if he had suffered losses, but wondered if he might resent her probing too deeply.

'There are still many here who would like to follow France's example. The workers in the mills are in a terrible turmoil. Look at the riots at Spa Field only a few months ago.'

His mouth flattened. 'There have been some mistakes, it is true. And there are many who cling to outmoded beliefs. The world passes them by. Eventually they will become obsolete.'

'Many like my brother, for example?'

'His sons already understand the new world. Or at least Lord Giles does, I think. And Lady Kate. I see England as a land of opportunity for a man such as me. And if it is not, then I will go elsewhere.'

Another man always on the move. A pang of regret touched her heart. Still, what business was it of hers? She had her own plans. 'Where would you go? America?'

'Possibly. Or Canada.'

It sounded terribly far away. And there was absolutely no reason for her to feel a sense of disappointment, but she found she did not want to talk about him leaving. 'I don't suppose you found out who doctored the fish?'

His lips pressed together. He shook his head. 'Not yet.'

No doubt when he did that person would be very sorry indeed.

He drew the gig up at the front door, jumped down and held up his arms for Jane. Claire shook her awake. 'We are home, child.'

Jane blinked sleepily at the house. 'This isn't home. Our home is in Rochester.'

'Not any more, sweet,' Claire said, reaching up to lift her down. Soon they would have a house, a place where they could settle permanently. A place Jane could call home for the rest of her life.

'Allow me,' Monsieur André said. He lifted the child down with impressive ease, carried her to the front door and handed her off to a footman. 'Mademoiselle Jane suffered quite a shock on her way home—carry her up to her chamber,' he commanded. The footman shot him a dark look, but did as requested.

The footman was wise. The man exuded danger and not only because he held Jacobin views about the rights of men. There was an indefinable quality about him that made others bow to his will that would have seemed quite ordinary for a nobleman, but seemed quite at odds with his situation as a chef.

And now she owed him a debt of gratitude for his help today. The question was how to repay it. Somehow she did not think he would be pleased by an offer of money. Not that she had any.

She didn't look back, but she did hear the front door close and felt a strange sense of loss.

The footmen milled around the kitchen, dropping off dirty dishes and reloading their silver trays with steaming tureens and platters. They lined up ready to ascend the stairs. As he had for the first course, André went ahead of them and stood at the dining room door with his spoons at the ready.

Before he allowed any of them to pass, he tasted each dish again. He would not allow anything to go wrong this time.

Everything was fine until the beef stew. At first, he could not believe his palate. He had to be imagining it. He took a fresh spoon and tasted again.

The unmistakable flavour of peppermint filled his mouth. Overpowering. Dreadful.

He glared at the footman in livery, Joe Coyle, the one who muttered against him because he was French. 'You.' His voice was more growl than words. He threw down the spoon.

'Bastard. What's the matter with you?' Joe tried to push past into the dining room.

André snatched the tray out of his hand and pressed it onto one of the men on his way out, lifting the tureen off the tray as he did so.

Joe stared at him. 'What the hell are you doing, poltroon?'

'Cochon. Fils d'une salope.'

'I don't know what you said, mate, but whatever it was, you got no right talking to me like that.'

Bravado. The boy had it by the bushel full. Ire coloured André's vision red. He grabbed the boy by his stock and pulled him out of the way of the men waiting to go in. 'You think I am stupid? Mint. You ruin my food with mint?'

'What are you blethering about?'

André could scarcely contain himself. 'You like mint in your *boeuf bourguignon*? Then you shall have it.'

He thrust the bowl at him. 'Eat.'

The dining room door opened and Claire slipped out with Lumsden hard on her heels. Her glance took in the scene and her face filled with horror. 'What is going on?' she whispered. 'We can hear you from inside.'

'I beg your pardon, Madame Holte. Try the beef stew. This *cochon* ruined it with mint.'

'I d-didn't,' Joe stuttered, looking to Mr Lumsden. 'I carried it up. I never touched it.'

Claire leaned forward and delicately sniffed the dish and then raised her gaze to meet André's. 'It definitely smells like peppermint.'

André handed the dish to one of the footmen who was lingering watching the show. 'Hold this.'

He turned to Joe, grabbed his lapels and shook him. 'It was perfect before you got your hands on it.' He could scarcely contain his rage, not so much for himself but because this cretin, this fool who liked to play tricks on his fellows, had almost ruined Claire's dinner. Again. 'How dare you? How dare you ruin my food? How dare you shame Castonbury with your prejudiced antics?'

The boy cringed. 'I never.'

A touch to his shoulder had him swinging around, fists clenched, expecting one of the others to try to help his friend.

He drew up short when he realised it was Claire. She looked anxious. 'This is neither the time nor the place.' She glanced at the butler. 'Please find somewhere for Joe to remain under lock and key until we get to the bottom of this.'

She was protecting the lad. From him. From his temper. Sickness flooded his mouth. He stepped back. 'I think that would be wise. We do not wish to give him another chance to tamper with the food.' He glanced over at the dish. 'I will bring more. Or I will, if what is left in the pot is not also ruined. Once more it is the dish you particularly requested.'

'I see that.' She sounded so calm, so collected, while he wanted to murder someone. Her coolness quieted his anger. Melted his rage.

It was the second time her calm voice and quiet manner

had taken the edge off his temper. Reason swiftly returned as she smiled at him. He stared at her in awe.

'I think it would be a good idea if Mr Lumsden brought up the replacement,' she said. 'Please go with him, Monsieur André. Now I must return to my guests.'

He watched her walk away, shoulders straight, the erotic sway of her hips in the silken gown a siren's call. No longer angry, she inflamed him in a different way.

'Lock him in the cellar,' Lumsden said to one of the other men.

'The wine cellar?' Joe said with a shadow of his normally cocky manner. He was afraid. André could see the fear in his eyes. Because he was guilty and he knew it.

'The root cellar,' Lumsden said.

'I never done nothing, Mr Lumsden,' Joe said, pleading.

'Anything,' Lumsden said. 'I do not have time to deal with this, Joe.' He cast a look of dislike at André. 'I have a dinner to serve. I will speak with you both later.'

'The duke's chef has excelled himself,' Samuelson said, leaning back in his chair and folding his hands across his stomach.

'I am glad you approve, Sir Nathan,' Claire said softly, thankful that there had been more beef stew and that all of the other of the dishes had remained unadulterated, which did not bode well for Joe.

'Mrs Holte chose the menus,' Reverend Seagrove said. 'And a wonderful array of dishes it was.'

Claire doubted Mr Seagrove had eaten so well in years. 'I let myself be guided by Monsieur André.'

'A wise women lets herself be guided by a knowledgeable man,' Sir Nathan said with a smile that seemed almost a leer.

Claire wished she could like this man better. He was the sort of man who would protect what he had. If only he did not see women as chattels, not quite the equal of his property or his horses. But it might not be such a bad thing, having a man who would not quail before a fight.

He was one man she felt confident could stand up to Ernie Pratt and his henchmen. André was another, she realised. He wouldn't be the slightest bit intimidated.

Surely it would not come to that? The only man who might attempt a challenge had no idea of her real identity. He would never find her here. The moment she was married, she and Jane would be safe, because she would have paid off her late husband's debts.

'I hear your stud has gone from strength to strength, Sir Nathan,' Claire said, having done her homework. 'Do you plan to enter the Derby, this year?'

'Always do, Mrs Holte. I anticipate doing very well. Very well indeed.'

'I had heard your Green Dragon had come down lame,' Reverend Seagrove said.

'Aye. That fool horse master of mine ran him too hard last time out.' His face took on a grim expression. 'He won't make that mistake again.'

That sounded terribly like a threat.

'Will you come to the races, Mrs Holte?' Samuelson asked. 'I would be happy to have you as my guest.'

There it was, the kind of invitation she had been hoping for. Only it did not lift her spirits at all. Two hours in Samuelson's company and she felt battered. By his opinions. And by his personality. There was no doubting his power.

She might not have minded him so much if the glances he sent her way were for her as a woman, but it was incontrovertibly clear that it was her name that held his interest.

She smiled sweetly. 'I would love to be your guest.'

Samuelson turned to the dowager marchioness. 'And what about you, my lady. Would you like to join us?'

Two widows to choose from. Claire gritted her teeth and kept smiling.

'I don't know,' Lady Hatherton was saying in her light little voice, but her lips were smiling and Sir Nathan licked his. The man clearly intended to keep all his options open.

'You'll have a grand time, won't she, Seagrove?'

'I have to admit,' the Reverend Seagrove said, 'there is no more magnificent sight than the Derby.'

'Especially if you've a guinea or two on the outcome, eh, Seagrove?'

'I think it is Lady Phaedra you should be asking about the Derby,' Lily said with a smile.

Samuelson reared back. 'Ask a woman?'

'I believe it is Lady Phaedra's fondest wish to win the Derby. She is an excellent judge of horseflesh, according to my fiancé.'

'A woman's place is beside her husband's hearth,' Samuelson said harshly. The repressive way he said it felt like a rock in the middle of Claire's chest. She couldn't breathe for the weight of it for a moment.

It was her duty to endure it. For the sake of Jane's future.

'Shall we leave the gentlemen to their port?' she asked brightly, and rose to her feet lest her face display her worry.

The gentlemen rose with the ladies and bowed as they left for the drawing room and tea.

It had been a successful dinner. Everything had gone swimmingly well as far as her guests were concerned, but the heaviness in her chest remained.

Nine

Later could not come soon enough for André as he paced the length of his kitchen and back. Claire had cooled his temper outside the dining room, but now André was filled with cold rage. The boy had to be punished. His crime had not only harmed André, but it had also harmed Claire.

And that was what had aroused his temper to such an extent earlier.

When Mr Lumsden arrived he ceased his pacing. 'A bad business this, *monsieur*,' the older man said, shaking his grizzled head.

'Indeed. Shall we speak with the boy now?'

'Better to strike while the iron is hot.'

A doleful sniff came from the scullery maid, Becca.

'What is the matter with her?' Lumsden asked.

'I gather she is concerned for Joe.'

Mr Lumsden harrumphed. 'Well, come along. Let us get this over with.' Silently they made their way down to the cellars. Coal was stored here and the duke's wines, as well as potatoes and other supplies that preferred the cold and the dark.

Mr Lumsden withdrew a key from his pocket rather like a child withdrawing the crown from the king cakes of André's childhood.

No sound came from the other side of the door.

Mr Lumsden unlocked it and pushed it open.

Joe charged out, knocking the old man off his feet and barrelling past André. Instinct acted quicker than thought and André caught the lad by the collar, swung him around, then, catching his shoulders, pressed him back against the wall.

'Monsieur André,' a female voice cried. 'What on earth are you doing?'

Claire.

André kept Joe pinned to the wall with one arm across his chest and turned his head to watch her stride down the dim passageway.

'Unhand him,' she said.

Stern. Assuming the worst, of course. '*Non, madame*, he stays where he is. Monsieur Lumsden, are you all right?'

Lumsden emerged from the cellar, brushing himself down and muttering under his breath. He glared at Joe. 'You'll pay for that, my lad.'

Claire's gaze went to each face. 'Will someone tell me what is going on?'

'He tried to escape,' Lumsden said. 'Knocking me down in the process.' His brows lowered. 'What do you have to say for yourself, boy?'

The lad glared back, his face sullen and full of defiance. 'I ain't going to prison. Not for something I never did.'

'Oh, Joe, no one said anything about prison,' Claire said softly. 'But I would like to understand why you did it before I decide what should be done.'

'I never did anything. The Frenchie did it and is trying to blame me. He's got it in for me, he does.' He swung a punch at André, who caught the fist in his hand and twisted the lad's arm behind his back, pushing him face-first against the wall.

'Liar,' André said, his anger red behind his eyes. 'The stew was fine when it left my kitchen. Did you meet someone on the way?'

Pressed with his face against the wall, Joe grunted out a muffled no.

'Perhaps you should let him go,' Claire suggested. 'So we can talk.' She glanced at André, clearly asking him to follow her lead.

Soothed by her voice and her calm cool logic, he eased the pressure on the boy's back. She was right. The boy could not escape. Nor did André want to hurt him. He just wanted him to pay for his crime.

The boy leaned his back against the wall, rubbing his wrist.

'You won't run away, will you, Joe?' Claire continued in a serious tone. 'You see, Monsieur André will catch you very quickly if you do and it will be proof of your guilt.'

Joe eyed André warily. 'You're stronger than you look.'

'Monsieur André is a pugilist,' Claire said. Was that a note of admiration in her voice?

Joe's eyes widened and something filled his expression, something that looked a bit like respect.

'I spar,' André said.

'Is that how your beak got broke?'

'My beak?'

'He means your nose,' Claire said. She looked as if she was trying not to laugh.

'Let us return to the matter at hand,' Lumsden said testily. 'Why did you put mint in the stew?'

'I didn't.'

'It would be better if you told the truth, Joe,' Claire said gently. 'Really it would.'

'I'm not admitting to something I never did.'

'Then you can pack your bags and be gone in the morning, and without a reference,' Lumsden said. 'You've been troublesome since the day you arrived.'

Joe hunched a shoulder. 'Fine with me.'

André winced at the fear behind the bravado. It was a hard time for a lad to be out of work. He didn't want him dismissed, just punished.

He looked at Claire, for he could not step into Lumsden's bailiwick. He was surprised to find her looking at him.

She turned to Lumsden. 'I do realise this is your domain, Mr Lumsden, and far be it for me to interfere, but perhaps we could give Joe another chance.'

Saints above, had she read his mind?

'Not unless he admits his guilt,' Lumsden said, crossing his arms over his narrow chest.

'I didn't do it.' The boy's chin thrust forward.

'There is no proof that he did,' Claire said.

She didn't want the lad dismissed. It was obvious in her eyes and in the droop of her soft lower lip.

'There might be a way to tell if he is guilty, though it will not prove his innocence,' André said, and felt a rush of gladness that there was a way he could make Claire feel better about this whole thing.

Joe regarded him warily. 'How?'

'Hold out your hands.'

The boy jerked his hands behind his back.

'Hold them out, Joe,' Claire said.

'I'm not letting him touch me,' Joe said.

'Tell me what to look for,' Claire said, coming to stand between André and the young footman.

'If he handled mint, he would smell of it. It would be on his skin, or in the fabric of his coat.'

'Hold out your hands, Joe,' Claire said crisply.

The lad thrust his fists at her face, then turned them over flat. Claire inhaled and shook her head.

'Please take off your coat,' she instructed gently.

He did so and, with Lumsden's help, they established that there was not a whiff of mint on the lad.

'Could it have dissipated already?' Claire asked.

'Dissi-whated?' Joe asked.

'Faded,' Claire said.

André shook his head.

'Then you know I didn't do it.' He glowered at André. 'You did it. You were trying to get me into trouble. You Frenchies are all the same. Killed my brothers, your lot did.'

'Joe,' Claire rapped out. 'Enough. As Monsieur André said, this does not prove you innocent, though it certainly helps. And it was Monsieur André's idea, so you should be grateful. While we cannot punish you for a crime we cannot prove, we can punish you for your rudeness and for knocking Mr Lumsden down.'

Joe's mouth dropped open.

André's jaw wanted to drop too. The little brown mouse had the roar of a lion when roused, it seemed. But then he already knew she had hidden passion.

His blood warmed.

Good Gracious, how did she do it to him, when he had already decided not to let it happen again? Was her allure growing too strong for his well-honed control? If so, he should start thinking about leaving sooner than he had planned.

Claire looked at him and at Mr Lumsden. 'I think one of the problems with Joe is too much unspent energy. Too much time standing around with nothing to do but look smart in his livery.'

There was a wicked twinkle in her eye and it seemed to

be directed his way. André felt his stomach tighten with anticipation and a bit of dread as he waited to find out what she would say next.

'Monsieur André is extremely busy in kitchen. If Mr Lumsden will agree, you can be assigned to assist him. It will do you good to learn how much work is required of a chef and how disheartening it is when someone spoils that work.'

A woman with a brain and a dollop of kindness. A rare breed indeed, in his experience. It would give André a chance to keep an eye on the lad, find out if he truly was guilty.

Lumsden hesitated, then gave a hard nod. 'I agree.'

'What, you'll turn me into a kitchen maid? Or a nancy boy finickin' around with food. Not me.'

Claire's eyebrows went up and then lowered. Her mouth lost all vestiges of softness. 'It is that or dismissal, Joe.'

Now that was a firmness he really had not expected.

André bared his teeth in a hard non-amused smile. 'Expect to work hard, *mon ami*, for I will show you no quarter.'

Joe sneered. 'How hard can peeling a few tatties be?'

Goodness, the boy was incorrigible. And Claire. She was extraordinary. If the boy really was guilty, then this was a fitting punishment.

But if Joe was speaking the truth and did not spoil the dinner, who did? And would they try again?

The following morning brought a nosegay of snowdrops from Sir Nathan along with a note hoping he would meet her at the assembly to be held in Buxton at the end of the week.

He was hooked. It didn't mean she could land him as a bridegroom, but it did mean he was interested.

She should feel elated.

She didn't. Quite the opposite. She felt like a woman with her head in a noose. It was the same feeling she'd experienced when she'd seen the list of suitable gentlemen her brother had suggested she marry years ago. So she'd run off with George instead. What a bad judge of character she had been. He'd been charming right up to the moment he discovered he wasn't getting any money, then he'd despised her, made it clear he found her of no value. Over time she'd come to believe him.

This time she would be guided by her brother.

And besides, this marriage wasn't for her sake. It was for Jane. To give her the future she deserved. A settled, safe home. She would have to find a way for Jane to meet Sir Nathan. Introduce the child to the idea gently. If only she could imagine Jane taking to Sir Nathan the way she had taken to André.

And if he didn't come up to scratch, she still had one more string to her bow.

Mr Carstairs was coming for dinner next week, a little bit later than originally planned but he'd been in London on business. Crispin would approve of any one of these three men. Perhaps she would like the next one better. Perhaps she should wait and see before coming to a decision.

She picked up the paper and scanned the headlines. Another brutal murder in the rookeries in the east end of London. She shivered and could not help wonder if the same person responsible for her husband's death was responsible for this one too.

Thankfully, his weakness for gambling and subsequent debts had led him to change his name from time to time. She was sure Pratt didn't know their real last name. Or anything about her origins. George had kept that one promise, she was sure. She bit her lip. Almost sure.

The door flew open and one of the maids rushed in. The ungainly one from the kitchen. Becca. 'You've got to come quick, mum. He's going to kill him.'

Claire shot to her feet. 'Who is killing who?'

'*Monsewer.* He's killing Joe. It is not Joe's fault. It isn't. It isn't.'

Oh, dear, perhaps her idea of having the boy work in the kitchen was not such a good one, after all. She hadn't intended for André to hurt the boy.

Then she remembered the chef's bruises and his cut lip. Perhaps the man took pleasure in taking out his anger on others with his fists. Some men did. Her husband, for example. But only when in his cups. She'd learned to remain silent when he'd imbibed more than usual.

'Where are they?'

'In the carriage house. Thought he could hide what he was doing out there,' the girl said, 'but Agnes heard the row when she went out to empty the slops. She came to get me to watch the show. Half the footmen are out there watching too. And none of them doing a thing to help poor Joe.'

Claire grabbed her shawl and followed the girl down the servants' steps and out to the stables. The wind was freezing and her thin slippers offered little protection from the hard-packed snow.

Entering the stable, they bypassed the stalls and went right to the back of the block where the carriages were kept. The large open space was to allow them to be turned around, but today the girl was correct; half the men from the house and all of the grooms were gathered around in a loose circle, watching something in the middle.

Claire pushed her way through. And stopped. Simultaneously aghast and fascinated.

André was naked to the waist. Her mouth dried at the beauty of the man. A statue of a god brought to life. His chest was broad and muscular, its hardness softened only by a triangle of dark crisp curls. Large well-defined muscles in his arms flexed and bunched as he circled his opponent. There were gloves on his hands. The kind pugilists wore for practice. Now his back turned towards her, a smooth expanse of olive-skinned perfection.

Droplets of sweat sheened his skin and here and there ran down the silken skin of his back. Fascinated she watched them trail all the way down to his waistband and disappear.

This man was nothing like her husband, who had been pasty white and rather soft. He looked almost brutal as he towered over the terribly scrawny Joe, who had a chest like a rabbit and boyish muscles.

'Keep your hands up,' André was saying to the lad.

The boy brought his gloved hands up to cover his face. André jabbed at him, so swiftly it was not much more than a blur of movement. The lad fell on his rump with a thump and the men roared with laughter.

He was hurting the boy.

'Monsieur André,' she said, striding into the circle. 'Enough of this.'

Joe looked at her sheepishly, but sprang to his feet.

André swung around, his face full of shock. 'Madame Holte?'

'I did not intend for you to brutalise the boy, sir.'

Joe took advantage of the chef's distraction and swung a punch at his temple.

Monsieur André staggered sideways. Some of the men sniggered. Most shouted foul.

André shot Joe a glare. 'Remember what I told you about fighting fair. This is not a street brawl. It is a science.'

He looked back at Claire. '*Madame*, I suggest you return to the house.'

'Not until we have had words.'

He closed his eyes in that typical gesture of male irritation.

'Very well.' He looked at Joe. 'The lesson is finished for today. Wash off and return to your duties.'

To Claire's surprise, Joe looked thoroughly disappointed. 'We was hardly getting started.'

'Go,' André said. 'And the rest of you. Everyone, back to work.' He spoke as if he had only just realised how many of the male servants were present.

The servants slunk away. Soon, all that was left was the sound of her own breathing and the blood rushing in her ears.

'Who told you we were out here?' he asked, his back to her as he removed his gloves.

To her disappointment his lovely back disappeared beneath the billowing white of his shirt. It didn't matter. Never would she forget the sight of him bare to the waist, like some primitive warrior about to do battle.

'Becca came and found me.'

'I see.'

'Now what did that mean?'

He shrugged into his coat and turned to face her. 'It means that I think there is something going on between those two. She was distraught when she discovered he'd been accused of tampering with the food.'

'Oh.'

'It may be nothing. She's a very strange girl.'

'I'll speak to Mrs Stratton about her.' She took a deep breath. 'André, I asked you to put the boy to work, not beat him to death.'

His dark eyes narrowed, his head tilted in that arrogant manner. His shoulders tensed. Then he shrugged as if her question barely deserved an answer, but that he would grace her with one. 'I thought it would do him good. He harbours a great deal of bitterness about his brothers. He pines for them.

I know what it is to feel helpless in the face of injustice. It makes a man angry.'

It was hard to imagine this large powerful man feeling helpless. Awkward under his intense scrutiny, she glanced down at her feet, shoving the straw around with her toe. 'I thought you were going to murder him.'

'We were sparring. In gloves.'

'Sparring didn't save you from cuts and bruises the other day.' Her voice sounded defiant rather than calmly logical. The man was putting her in the wrong when she knew very well she was in the right. Or she had thought she was. She sighed. 'I'm sorry. Clearly I panicked. I saw how angry you were last night—I thought the worst.'

He turned away from her, gripping a post that supported the roof. 'I was angry last night.' He gave a hard laugh as if he didn't quite believe he was saying the words. 'For you. I knew the importance you placed on that dinner after the previous debacle.'

The way he said *debacle* was like the brush of velvet against her skin, soft, seductive. She shivered.

The man was made for seduction, his voice, his body. Oh, dear heavens, she had seen far too much of his body. But the sensations were caused by more than that. It was his passion for life she admired. 'It meant a great deal to you too.'

'Yes.'

His voice sounded dispassionate, but she sensed a far deeper emotion. Something dark and savage kept on a firm leash. Something that had nothing to do with anger at all and everything to do with her. Something that awakened longings she must repress. They had betrayed her in the past. Only before, with George, she'd been a girl. Innocent. Those feelings had been negligible compared to the deep stirrings this man aroused. She swallowed.

She should walk away. Now. While she still had her mind intact. While she still had the strength.

Her feet refused to move. She had clearly impugned his honour. She had learned to expect the worst in man. George had taught her well. And his cronies. But she was wrong to judge all men by his standards. Particularly this one.

Now where had that come from? At any rate, she could not walk away and leave things as they were. With his honour insulted.

He released the strut and, with his back still to her, tied his cravat, buttoned his coat, then turned to face her, his face impassive. His eyes as cold as a winter night.

A suit of armour could not make him more impregnable. A pang squeezed at her heart. Loneliness. Why did she have to long for closeness with this man?

He bowed with the grace of a courtier. 'I admired your calm last night. Your logic. I decided on this as a suitable course of action. There was no anger involved. I beg your pardon, *madame*. It will not happen again.'

Just as the kiss would not happen again. The memory of that kiss thrummed through her body like a chord struck on a harp, the note lingering in the air long after the strings were plucked.

As he made his way past her, she reached out and caught at his sleeve.

He froze, looking at her hand. 'Claire?' The word was little more than a breath. It grazed her cheek like a sigh. Tingles raced across her skin, tightened her breast. She was so out of her depth with these feelings. These sensations. This man.

'I apologise for mistrusting your intentions.'

The dark gaze lifted to her face. Surprise. Gladness reflected in his eyes. 'Apology accepted.' He lifted her hand from his sleeve, turned it palm up and rubbed it gently with his thumb.

She'd run out without her gloves and the heat of his skin seared hers like a brand. Air seemed in short supply as he held her hand in his large one.

He frowned, brought her hand up to the light and looked more closely.

'These hands have seen hardship,' he said softly. 'It is not something one expects on a woman of rank.'

Shame rushed through her as she realised what he must see. Work-roughened calluses. Scars. Pride came to her rescue. She'd done her best for herself and for Jane this past year and this was the result. She closed her fingers.

But his other hand gently pried them open, once more exposing her palm. 'I admire a woman who is prepared to work for what she wants,' he whispered. 'I should have warned you.'

He bent his head and his lips kissed the centre of her palm. A warm brush of satin lips.

Curls of heat spiralled deep in her belly. She gasped.

Heat. Longing. All the things she should not feel rushed through her. Swamping her will. Weakness invaded her bones, her limbs, her centre. And when he raised his dark head, when his gaze met hers, she stood looking at him. Unable to move. Unable to speak.

His gaze searched her face. Seeing what? Loneliness? Desire? More likely, he saw the trepidation that made her heart beat fast and tremors run through her body. It had to be fear. If it was anything else, this feeling of butterflies and trembles deep in her bones, she was in no end of trouble.

Silence surrounded them, cool air, the mist of their breath mingling above their heads as they gazed at each other, while the touch of his lips remained seared on her skin.

He was just so undeniably lovely. And surprisingly kind. Sweet. Something warm swelled in her heart. Impulsively, she rose up on her tiptoes, one hand inside his pressing into her ribs, the other grasping his shoulder, and kissed his parted lips.

His breath hitched. And then he was holding her, kissing her back, his lips soft and pliant beneath hers, his tongue exploring her mouth. The trembles became shivers of pleasure. A hand at her back pulled her close and his chest pressed against her sensitive breasts. She could feel his desire hard against her belly. Melting warmth trickled upwards invading her limbs, and she moaned low in her throat.

Slowly he pulled away, his dark eyes slumberous. 'Claire.' He spoke gently, almost hesitantly. 'What you said in the library about things being as they are. Would you change them? If you could?'

Would she? 'I don't know,' she whispered, overcome by the sensations skipping through her body.

'You can choose your own path, you know. Decide how you want things to be. People do.'

The words were as seductive as his voice. A seduction she sensed in every breath she took, felt in the ripple of longing across her skin, tugging at her heart. Leading her down a bright new path. But she had chosen once. And made a terrible mistake. She wasn't going to make another one. Not when she had Jane to consider.

Yet she had kissed him like a wanton.

Cheeks flaming, she stepped back, smoothing her skirts. 'Is that what you did? Decided you wanted to be a chef? Decided you wanted to wait on rich people?'

'I will be the best chef in England.'

Her mouth dropped open at his utter arrogance. 'It sounds like a wonderful ambition.' She smiled, but her lips felt stiff and her voice brittle. She felt a brush of resentment that he had his life all planned out, when hers remained so unsure and at the mercy of someone else. 'If determination is a necessary ingredient, I am sure you will be successful.'

His lips twisted wryly, as if she'd said something humorous. 'Thank you. But what about you? What do you really want? Marriage to some elderly country squire?'

How dare he judge her? 'Yes. It is. Jane and I need a safe and secure life. And a good marriage will provide it.'

His head tilted. 'And will you be happy?'

'It is not about happiness. It's about making sure Jane has a future.' Her voice shook.

There was something about his expression that said he didn't believe her. 'Are you sure there isn't another way to achieve the same goal, without selling yourself?'

'You understand nothing about women like me. We marry to please our families, not ourselves.'

'You did not always follow that rule, I think.'

It was like being tangled in a web. No matter which way she turned, how much she struggled, there was always another strand of logic holding her down. 'I think only of Jane. This is my choice,' she said firmly.

'Then I wish you joy in it. I look forward to our meeting tomorrow, to review our plans for the next dinner. *Madame*.'

He bowed and strolled out into the fresh air, leaving her holding the field, but feeling less than triumphant.

'Where is Jane?' Claire knew her voice sounded high-pitched and anxious, but she was too worried to care.

All three occupants of the kitchen rose to their feet—the two kitchen maids seated at the table, a pot of tea between them, and André at his desk in the corner.

A quick scan of the kitchen told Claire her daughter was not present. Her heart gave a painful thump. The small ball of panic in her throat swelled so large she couldn't swallow.

Agnes bobbed a curtsey. 'The young lady was here earlier. After lunch.' She shot André a rather malevolent look. 'Around the same time as them Gypsies were here, *monsewer*.'

'Gypsies?' Claire felt the blood rush from her head. Gypsies were notorious for stealing children.

Becca twisted her hands in her apron and looked thoroughly uncomfortable.

André's expression darkened. He frowned at the young kitchen maid. 'Not Gypsies. Simply people who are hungry and travelling the roads looking for work.' He looked at Claire. 'We keep a kettle of soup hot for those in need. A large group came this morning and a few this afternoon, but Miss Jane was not here at that time.'

Claire turned to Agnes. 'When was she here? Did she say where she was going?'

Agnes's eyes slid away. 'It was just after they was here. She came looking for *monsewer.* He'd gone down to the cellars. I was washing t'floor.'

'She had her coat on,' Becca said in a rush. 'I didn't know if she had just come in or...was going out.'

Going out? The breath left her lungs in such a rush her head spun. 'There was no outing planned for today. The weather. The snow.' Heart pounding, she looked at André. 'What kind people were these that came to the door, if not Gypsies? Were they locals from the village?'

The frown on his face deepened. 'Two of them were soldiers, from London way, I would think, a couple of weavers out of work and their women and children.'

Men from London. 'Did they say where they were going?'

He shook his head. 'Most of them are looking for work. They move from town to town.'

'One of the soldiers mentioned Buxton, madam,' Becca said, bobbing. 'Said they'd be there late tonight if t'snow held off.'

'Buxton?' Claire felt faint. Was André right? That these were simply poor people travelling the roads or had she been discovered? She had never spoken of her past or her family to anyone. But she really feared George might have. In his cups.

'Are you sure she is not in the house somewhere?' André asked. 'It is a very large house with a great many places a small child can hide.'

She swallowed against the dryness in her throat. 'I... No, I am not sure, but I have looked everywhere, including the barn. I was certain she must have come here. I will look again. Thank you.'

Look where? Was Jane hiding somewhere as a tease? It wasn't out of the question, but she usually came when called. She turned to leave, and then turned back to Becca, who had started to sit and now shot to her feet again.

'You said Jane had her coat on. Are you sure?'

The girl nodded. 'Yes, madam. Positive.'

Claire's heart sank. She must have gone outside. 'Thank you.'

She hurried off to fetch her coat. There had been a new fall of snow overnight. If Jane had gone outside, she might be able to see her footsteps. See if she had gone with the people who had come to the kitchen. If there were children, she might have followed them. Jane missed the company of other children. She ran down the corridor.

'Madame Holte.'

André's voice. She kept going. He caught her up in a few steps, walked beside her. '*Madame*, would she really go outside alone?'

'No. I don't know. Perhaps. Before we came here, she played outside all the time, but she was known to our neighbours. I…I was busy. But it was a small place. Safe.' Or she had thought so until she had seen the two men in the market. She had no idea whether they had seen her or not. She'd packed up and run.

André caught her arm.

She looked at his hand on her sleeve, a large but elegant hand with tapering fingers. The hand of an artist. A competent hand. She looked up at his face and saw his concern. 'Give me but a moment to fetch my coat and I will come with you.'

'Oh, I could not drag you away from your work. I am sure she is not far away. Building a snowman, perhaps, or—'

'Shall I ask Lumsden to send the footmen to look through the house?'

Should she? Ask Lumsden to turn the house upside down looking for a mischievous child? Crispin would not be pleased if she set his household on its ears only to discover the child tucked away in a corner somewhere.

'I will speak with Mrs Stratton,' he said decisively. 'She will have the house searched and you and I will look outside. I will fetch my hat and coat and meet you at the door to the stables in five minutes.' His expression was kindly, and his smile gentle, but determined. 'It is better to be safe than sorry, *non*?'

'Yes.' Knowing he was helping made her feel a whole lot better. 'Five minutes.'

She ran upstairs.

The tracks of the group who had come to the back door were easy to follow. They had returned down the drive heading for the lane, the imprint of their coming and going intermingled. André had proved peculiarly adept at identifying who was who. 'There are only two children.'

Claire stared down at the muddle of overlapping footprints. 'How can you be sure?'

'Here. See where one walks beside a woman, the girl, and the other, a bolder stride, a little larger, the boy, marching beside his father. They were a nice family. Respectful. Appreciative of His Grace's generosity. They would not steal a morsel of bread if their lives depended on it.'

He sounded so certain, she believed him.

'And the soldiers? One of them could have carried her.'

He frowned, staring down at the tracks and then looking off into the distance as if seeing that small group of desperate people. 'If they had been alone, I might have concern. There is much anger at the government about the way soldiers have been abandoned after offering their lives for their country. I have heard much talk in the town after the riots. But they had full bellies and I don't see how taking a child would aid them.'

'And no one else came to the door?'

'Not since this morning.'

Then where could she be? The lake. Claire's heart stopped. She had promised to walk to the lake with Jane. When the weather was less threatening. Could Jane have decided to take matters into her own hands? The child had been fascinated by the lake since they arrived. She'd talked about it only this morning as they looked out of the window. Had asked if it was frozen all the way to the bottom as Claire was dressing her hair ready to go down to breakfast.

'I know where she has gone.' Her heart lifted. 'She went to see the lake.'

'Then we must hurry.' André's voice sounded grim.

Claire could only feel relief. The thought of strangers on the property with access to her daughter was far more terrifying than her wandering off to look at an ornamental stretch of water.

Together they strode across the snow-covered grass. As they walked, André scanned the ground, looking for signs of her footsteps.

'There,' Claire said. Seeing small depressions in the smooth blanket of snow.

'Deer,' André replied.

'How do you know?'

'Look at it. There are two very distinct toes. Not the mark of boots. I don't believe she came this way.'

Then he froze, ran ahead. Crouched to look down at something on the ground. Then rose to scan the lake which spread before them, criss-crossed with tracks, some leading out to the island in the middle.

Claire ran to catch him up. 'What is it?'

'There were children here. See. They were playing. Sliding around on the ice.' His jaw above his muffler flickered. 'Very dangerous. The ice is quite thin in places according to Murray when he brought ice to the ice house yesterday.'

'What children? The same children who came to the house?'

'Perhaps. I don't know. If so, they must have left the drive closer to the gatehouse and doubled back. It doesn't make any sense. Hungry children don't run off to play. They are too busy surviving.'

He sounded as if he knew what he was talking about. But it was not something she could think about right now. 'Jane must have seen them from the window. Run out to join them,' she said.

'I don't see how it is possible,' he said. 'There would have been tracks from the house.'

'You missed them.'

His face said he did not believe that, but he shrugged. 'The children are not here now.'

'We have to discover where they went, that is all.'

Now she had a purpose, she felt a whole lot better. She stepped out onto the ice. A crackling sound spread out from her feet.

André grabbed her and pulled her back. 'Not that way. Clearly, it is not safe.'

She stared at him and at the ice, her stomach dipping. 'Don't tell me she could have fallen through.' She looked around wildly, trying to see signs of where the ice had been broken.

'You are not so heavy, *madame*, but the children are lighter. And they did not go on the ice this way. Let us circle around and find where they went on and off. Perhaps then we will discover where they have gone.' He glanced up at the sky. 'It will be dark soon. We must hurry.'

Something tight inside her snapped. 'It is so wrong of Jane

to worry me like this. She will spend the next three weeks hemming handkerchiefs under my eye for giving me such a fright.'

'Yes, *madame*.' His tone was completely neutral.

While they tramped through the snow, Claire seethed. Didn't she have enough to worry about without this? It was better to be angry, to imagine what one would say to one's child, instead of fearing… No. She would not think of that. Of cracking ice and cold water.

'There,' he said. 'The boathouse. Beside the jetty is where they had egress. But I see no sign of them now.'

'Could they be in the boathouse?'

'Perhaps.' He didn't sound hopeful.

All around the jetty and the door into the boathouse were signs of the children. But the silence said they were not here now.

He pulled open the door and entered the darkness. 'Jane! Is anyone here?'

His voice boomed in the cavernous space, but the building which jutted out over the water was clearly empty.

He came out and closed the door with a shake of his head. He strode out onto the jetty, then his steps slowed and he proceeded more cautiously. He dropped to his knees.

'What is it?' she called, following him out.

'Be careful, the planks are icy.'

'What do you see?' she said when she reached him.

'Nothing. We should go back to the house. I think we need more people for this search.'

'You saw something.' Panic closed her throat. Her chest tightened. She struck out at him with her fist. 'Tell me.'

'The ice is broken,' he said.

'No.' She fell to her knees, looking down at the place beneath the jetty where dark water lapped at the edges of splintered ice. 'We have to find her.'

He grabbed her by the shoulders and pulled her up. 'We don't know if it is Jane. We don't know if it is anyone. We need help. We have to go back to the house and get men. Find the children who played here and find out what happened.'

Something howled through her mind. A cold wind. A bitter fear. 'No,' she gasped, lashing out at him. 'We have to find her before it is too late.'

Desperation gave her strength and she broke free of his grip, making for the ladder leading down onto the ice.

He caught her again, holding her, pressing her against him. 'Claire, if she went into that water, it is already too late.'

'No,' she gasped. 'No.' She fought him, but he held her, his hands on her shoulders, gripping tight.

'We don't know she is in there.' He gave her a shake. 'We don't know and I am not going to let you go down there.'

'Let me go!'

He picked her up and carried her to the bank. She fought him, struggled, clawed at him, her mind seeing Jane somewhere below that ice, trying to find her way up, calling to her.

She found herself on her feet and made to run back.

He caught her again, cupped her chin, made her look at him, into his eyes. 'Claire, no!' he yelled. 'You will just make it worse.'

She blinked, his words beating their way into her mind.

'How will it help her if you drown?' he said.

Tears sprang to her eyes. 'She's my daughter.'

'And we don't know she is in the water.'

'She is. I know it. I know. I am her mother. I know.'

Her knees buckled as what she was saying registered in her heart.

He caught her, held her close, patted her back. 'We don't know. We must go back to the house. We must get help.'

'No. We need a ladder. Something that will take my weight. I saw it done with a dog once. On the Thames.'

'There's probably one in the boathouse,' he said instantly. 'I'll get it if you will promise to wait here for me.'

'I promise.'

He ran for the wooden building. Disappearing inside.

She stared at the black hole beneath the jetty. Large enough for a child to fall through. Then he was back at her side, ladder in hand.

He lay it down on the ice alongside the jetty and knelt to crawl. The sound of ice cracking was like shots in the still air.

'Let me,' she said. 'I'm lighter.'

A look of agony crossed his face, but he moved aside. 'Go very slowly, Claire. Take your time.'

She gritted her teeth and nodded. The rails were rotted and splintery. Not in the best condition. Tomorrow she would have a word with the groundskeeper. If there was a tomorrow.

She balanced on her hands and feet, unable to kneel because of her skirts. But the ice didn't make any more of that horrible cracking sound as she inched her way forward, aware of André on the bank tense and ready to come after her should anything go wrong.

'Mrs Holte! Monsieur André!' The shout echoed all around them.

André swung about. 'It is Joe,' he yelled. 'Stay still. Perhaps he has news of Jane.'

She could not take the chance he did not. Frozen inside and out she kept edging forward.

'Claire,' he said. *'Mon Dieu, arrêtez!'*

'Mrs Holte,' Joe shouted still some distance off. 'Miss Jane is at the Dower House.'

Safe. Jane was not in the water, not gone with the Gypsies. She was safe. She couldn't move. Not forward or backwards. And then the ladder was sliding, pulling her back to the bank and André was lifting her to her feet.

He let her go. She felt his hands leave her waist. The loss of his support made her stagger, but somehow she found her balance.

Her heart, which seemed to have stopped beating since she saw the hole in the ice, staggered to life. Joe ran out from behind the boathouse, from the direction of Castonbury. They walked to meet him, but time seemed to slow, as if she was walking through air turned to syrup. She didn't dare hope she'd heard correctly. It would be too cruel to find she was wrong, after all.

Joe halted in front of them, gasping, face red from the chill wind and his run. 'Mrs Holte, Jimmy just brought word from the Dower House. Miss Jane went to visit her cousin. Becca said you'd come out to search for her. I've been looking everywhere for you.'

'Jane is at the house?'

He shook his head. 'Lady Hatherton had a maid put her to bed. She got herself lost in the woods for a while.'

Claire's knees gave way.

André caught her arm beneath the elbow. 'It is all right, *madame.* The child is all right.'

André could scarcely hold her she trembled so hard. Walking half a mile like this was out of the question.

'I must go to her,' she whispered, but it might as well have been a shriek she sounded so distraught.

To see her overcome by all the anguish of her terror now the child was safe shifted walls built one painful brick at a time. Something dark twisted in his chest, wanting to find its way into the light. Clawing at the veil on the past, revealing the stark recollection of crying out for his mother. His fist banging on glass that might as well have been ice for all the notice she took. Or water closing over his head. His knocking had been silenced by the hand of a stranger while he watched her ride away.

Until that moment, he'd basked in luxurious safety, pampered and treasured, or so he'd thought. It had all been a lie.

He slammed the door shut on the grim visage that followed, the brutality and weeks of desperation. Neither memory served any purpose. He lived in the here and the now. Yet deep down he knew what Claire felt.

'*Madame*, you must not go to her until you are calm. You will frighten her.'

He looked at Joe shifting from one foot to the other in the snow. '*Madame* is frozen to the bone.' He gestured to the brick bath house beside the boathouse. 'I will light a fire in here and bring her when she is herself. Have John Coachman ready the carriage to take her to the boathouse. Leave me the torch, *s'il vous plaît*.'

Claire shuddered violently and Joe stared at her. 'Shall I send Mrs Stratton?'

'I do not think it necessary, *mon ami*. I will bring *la madame* shortly.'

The boy touched his forelock, handed André the torch and scampered off.

'Claire,' he murmured softly but firmly. 'Come. Walk a few steps for me. We will have you warm and ready to find Mademoiselle Jane safe and sound, and asleep in her bed.'

'Th-thank you.'

She took a step, but almost fell. He picked her up and carried her into the bath house. So light. So small. Such a very dainty lady. And so very courageous.

Thank goodness for the hearth already set for a fire. He

touched the torch to the kindling and it caught immediately, the flames flickering off the water in the plunge bath and dancing off the blue-and-white tiles that lined the walls.

He sat beside her on the changing bench and she sagged against him, all the strength seemed to have leached out of her. All he could think to do was put an arm around her shoulders and stroke her.

'I thought she was gone.' Her voice was thin and wavering. Her shoulders rose with a deep shuddering breath. 'I thought she'd been taken. And then, when I saw that hole in the ice…I was so sure she was gone. She is all I have.'

Her body shuddered with such force, André feared she might be about to fall into some sort of fit. He held her tighter, willing his strength into her fragile body, cradling her cheek against his shoulder, rocking. 'Hush. Hush. It is all right. She is safe.'

'I can't lose her. I can't.'

'You have not lost her.' He lifted her face with his palms, looking into her eyes, giving her his calm as she had given it to him. 'You heard Joe. She is safe, with her family.'

But he understood only too well that safety could be stripped away in an instant. The thought of what could happen, what had happened to him as a child, brought bile to his throat. Not all families cared for their children. But this woman did. She'd been prepared to lay down her life for her child.

Then she started to cry. Great racking sobs that shook her body, and all he could do was hold her.

'Claire,' he said gently, removing his glove. He tipped her face up and wiped her cheek with the pad of his thumb. 'Tears now, *chérie*? When out there you were so very brave.'

And still the tears fell. He held her close, rocking her slowly.

Letting her cry. 'Hush,' he whispered. *'Doucement. Doucement.'* Gradually the sobs subsided to little hiccups and sniffs.

His mother had walked away. Abandoned him without a backwards glance, whereas Claire would give her life for Jane. Something inside his chest felt too large, too tender. He pretended it was not there. Sought for something to say.

'Hush, now, *ma petite.* It is over.'

When she was finally quiet, he did what any man would do. He mopped her face with his handkerchief.

She lifted her face to his touch, gave him a watery smile and a look of such gratitude he felt like a god among men. She touched his heart in ways that made him long for things he never knew he wanted.

Love. A family. Things he'd always denied were important.

He didn't quite know how it happened, whether he bent to her, or she lifted her face to him, but one moment he was drying her tears and the next their lips met. Passionately. Feverishly. Fiercely. Her lips were hot against his, where her cheeks were cold and damp against his palms.

He wanted to warm her through and through and offer her comfort. And heaven help him take some for himself after the memories she'd evoked. Memories he'd buried as a frightened child.

Her lips parted against his and his tongue swept her mouth, helping him forget the images of that terrible afternoon when his mother had abandoned him to his fate.

She moaned sweetly in the back of her throat and he hardened within his trousers, the fabric tight against his arousal.

Her hands went around his neck and she stroked his tongue with hers, explored his mouth, the little cries in the back of her throat both a wonder and a torment to his heightening desire.

'Claire,' he whispered. *'Ma petite.'*

Her gaze searched his face, looked into his very dark soul

with passion and smiled. 'André,' she breathed. She kissed him at first sweetly and then with fierce demand.

He cradled her head with his hands and kissed her back, nipping at her lips, exploring her mouth with his tongue, tasting the essence of womanhood and wonderful Claire.

His hands roamed her shoulders, brushed the front of her coat, felt the rise of her breasts beneath the heavy fabric. A groan of frustration rose in his throat and she drew back, looking into his eyes. Traces of her tears glistened on her cheeks, but her smile was definitely more than a little wicked.

Hands braced on his shoulders, she twisted around and, pulling up her skirts, straddled his thighs. Her smile, full of bravado, also contained more than a hint of a challenge. Brave girl. Brave to the point of reckless. And thank goodness she was a widow, because there was no way in the world he was going to be careful. He was just too damned aroused to think straight.

While she teased his lips with her tongue, she stroked his face, tickled his nape and his ears with her fingers. He undid the buttons of his falls with one hand and caressed her chilly buttocks with the other.

He had some idea that he should protect her from the chill until the fire could warm the small space, but it was a very vague idea, not fully formed, and her assaults on him were driving him too close to the brink.

And the damned buttons would not undo.

He felt like an awkward boy, all fingers and thumbs, and clumsy eagerness, his knuckles brushing against the hot satiny skin of her inner thigh.

She rose up on her knees with a breathy little laugh at his battle, cupping his face to kiss his lips, open-mouthed and delicious, and giving him better access beneath his coat.

At last, the button slipped through its moorings in the

placket, then the next and the next, and his erection was released from its confines.

With effort, he broke the kiss, breathing hard.

'Claire,' he said, looking into her hazy desire-filled gaze. 'Are you sure?'

She gazed at him, awareness slowly seeping into her expression, while her chest rose and fell with shallow breaths. 'I need this,' she whispered. 'Please.'

The please was the *coup de grâce*. Until that moment, he'd thought he could resist. Be logical. Sensible. Though heaven knew he'd been far from logical in any of his dealings with Claire Holte.

A gentle stroke of her hot damp cleft and her little moan of pleasure in his ear confirmed her permission.

He took himself in hand and guided the head of his shaft against her hot wet sheath, parting the folds gently, caressing the centre of her pleasure with his own hard flesh until she quivered and squirmed. The moment he ceased holding her high, she slid down on him, sheathing him in her heat. His hips rose to meet her downwards thrust and the darkness of passion invaded his mind.

A welcome blackness. A void where only the physical existed, the slide of flesh on flesh. The sound of her encouraging cries. The feel of her hands through his clothes. The deep physical joining of naked flesh.

The abyss drew him on. He pounded his hips hard between her thighs, his hands lifting her, then driving her down on his aching shaft.

The soft sounds of her cries of delight echoed off hard tile and drowned him in the delicious music of lust.

And then he was going over. Too fast. Too hard. He caressed her where they were joined in desperate haste. She uttered a cry. Pleasure, not pain. And the silken walls of her body fluttered and stroked him and he was lost.

La petite morte claimed him. A hot death full of trembling mindless bliss more intense than anything he'd ever experienced.

Deep calm. They clung to each other like the victims of a storm, breathing hard; he inhaled her scent, a fragrance so potent it made him dizzy. She lay with her cheek against his, breathing softly, like a child at peace.

Warily he placed the flat of his hand on her back, wondering if she might reject him now it was over. Steeling himself for righteous horror. Dreading it, even as he knew he deserved it. She'd been vulnerable. Lost. He'd been ignoble in taking advantage.

He hated himself, knowing he'd want it again and again. He'd taken her like a rutting beast. A lady. A noblewoman. He'd been crude and unthinking.

It wasn't like him at all. She deserved so much better.

Slowly she drew in a deep breath and raised her head.

He waited. Expecting recriminations.

Her eyes startled, her expression bemused, she touched a finger to lips reddened by rough kisses. She seemed more surprised than disturbed.

Stunned, perhaps, by the enormity of what they had done.

'Claire,' he said, his voice rough. 'I—'

'Not now,' she whispered. She touched a hand to his lips. 'I must go before someone comes looking. You ordered the carriage, remember?'

Witnesses to his folly were just what they needed. He went hot and cold.

He helped her off his lap, trying not to feel the chill as he lost the heat of her centre. He rose, turning away to fasten his falls, feeling much like a thief in the night.

What the hell had he done? He turned back to find her standing, her skirts in careful order, her gaze directed at the door. 'Jane. I must go to Jane.' She pulled the door open. Cold swirled in around them, bringing with it clarity of thought.

'Give me a moment.' He took a bucket from beside the fire and ushered her out. He scooped up snow and went back and doused the flames, much as reality had doused his ardour. He picked up the torch and they walked side by side back to the house, in silence.

Oddly, there was companionship in that walk, when he'd braced for anger, or even icy contempt. But, after all, he was not the only one at fault and Claire was nothing if not fair.

He just wished he didn't feel so damned guilty.

The carriage was waiting. Caught in the light beside the door, Claire looked flushed and tear-stained and, heaven help him, well-bedded as John Coachman leapt down to help her into the coach.

André bowed as he had been taught as a boy to bow to a lady, in the days when he'd been a gentleman in the making.

'Thank you for your help, Monsieur André,' she murmured, leaning forward from inside. Did he sense more than formality in her tone? Did her gratitude reflect something more deeply personal?

A cold wind whipped across the driveway and André hunched his shoulders against the chill and watched her drive away.

How would she feel about what had passed between them in the cold light of day? Once she was herself again. He saw difficulties ahead.

Eleven

'Why can I not visit Monsieur André in the kitchen, Mama?'

Claire wanted to bang her head against the surface of the library's escritoire. It would be far less painful than the reminder of why neither of them could or should visit Monsieur André in the kitchen or anywhere else. It was bad enough in the daytime. But last night when she had finally sunk into her bed, the rest of the night had been a torture of memories. And the reason they had to be torturous no longer made sense.

'You know why you are not permitted to visit the kitchens for a week.'

Jane, seated on a high stool at the large oak table in the middle of the room, pouted. 'I said I was sorry for going to the Dower House. I wanted to show baby Crispin the kitten and you were busy. Why are you still angry? Every time I mention Monsieur André, you go red.'

Red. Surely her face was vermillion, she felt so hot. Heat, followed by the horrid tight feeling beneath her ribcage. Embarrassment at her wantonness. Her knowledge that she wanted to do it again.

She drew in a deep breath. 'I am not angry, dearest, I promise you. But you broke your promise not to leave the house without my permission. Your behaviour must be punished. Punishment means being deprived of something one enjoys. I already told you how I feel about your adventure yesterday. Now, please, continue working on your letters as we agreed.'

The clock on the mantel struck the hour. Heaven help her, it was only three in the afternoon. The day was crawling by, and he still hadn't responded to her note. Her request to attend her in the library, when he had time.

And then what would she do? What could she say in front of the child? Her heart raced. She swallowed the lump in her throat. He'd looked so utterly devastated when he'd left her at the carriage last night. Once she had seen Jane was safe with her own eyes, his expression had haunted her thoughts, along with the longings.

Glorious wonderful longings that would not leave her in peace.

Last night had been an impulse of the moment. But why should she not have what she wanted as long as she was discreet? Some pleasure, after years of misery with a man who despised her. The future she faced held little more than duty and something inside her needed this. Perhaps it was required to rid her of her attraction. Then she could move on with her life, follow the path she had chosen without regret.

Whatever it was, she did not have the strength to resist it.

Anxiously, she folded the note she had penned into tiny squares. She would burn it. No one must ever see the extent of her foolishness.

Tucking it in her pocket and drawing her shawl close around her shoulders to ward off a sudden chill, she rose and went to look at Jane's work. The child had diligently copied out the passage from the history book. 'Very nicely done.'

'Now can I go and play?'

'Yes. In the nursery. Nowhere else.'

A knock sounded at the door. She would know that sharp firm sound anywhere. He had come. Frozen in place, terrified by the rush of joy, she stared as the door opened.

André. Looking as he always did in his tall white hat and pristine white linen beneath his dark coats. 'You wished to see me, Madame Holte? I apologise for not coming sooner. I went to Buxton this morning for supplies and have only just returned.'

He had not been avoiding her. He'd been busy. With his employment. 'Everything is ready for dinner this evening, *monsieur*?' Her voice wobbled unbearably.

'Yes, *madame*.' He frowned in puzzlement, then smiled at Jane. 'You are well, Mademoiselle Jane?'

'Yes, thank you.' The child dipped a little curtsey, as if he was a gentleman, not a chef. 'Mama says I may not visit you.'

His gaze flew to her face, hurt in the depths of those dark eyes quickly hidden, but there, nonetheless. She had not intended to hurt him.

'As part of her punishment, Monsieur André,' she assured him. 'It is a privilege withdrawn for one week.'

His expressions eased. 'I see.' He bowed to Jane. 'Then I look forward to next week, *mademoiselle*.'

Trembling, she fingered the small square of paper through the folds of her skirts. Dare she? 'Off to the nursery with you, Jane,' Claire said. 'I will be there in a minute.'

They both watched the child leave and close the door behind her.

'May I be of further assistance, *madame*?'

The deep voice did terrible things to her insides. Dare she? Not in a note. It was the height of folly. 'Come to me tonight,' she whispered. 'After midnight.'

Shock blazed a trail across his face.

'Please. We must talk. About what happened.'

His faced closed down, becoming impassive. 'I do not think it wise, *madame*.'

Disappointment flooded through her. And the pain of rejection.

He closed his eyes briefly. 'But yes, I will come.' He turned away, jerkily, without his usual grace of movement, as if he, too, was in turmoil. And then he was gone.

She ran to the fireplace and burned the note. Watched it flare and smoulder until it was nothing but white ash and went to find her daughter.

Twice she changed her gown, finally settling on an undressing robe. So shockingly bold.

A whisper of a knock on the door before he slid inside, not waiting for permission. Wise man. She certainly did not want anyone to hear, unlikely though it was with the other ladies of the house away and the rest of the servants long since retired.

He closed the door behind him, but did not stray from the threshold. He stood looking at her, his eyes unreadable in the gloom, his face still, pale and shadowed.

His hands curled into fists as he waited for her to speak. Did he know he looked ready for battle? But with whom? She had the feeling he was at war with himself.

Was that how he saw life? As a battle to be won. Or was it just her whom he fought. He seemed too kind to be a warrior, too gentle, but she had seen him with Joe and knew he was not.

'I wanted to talk to you,' she said. Her voice was barely above a whisper and it shook more than she would have liked. But then he seemed to have that unsettling effect on her. 'About last night.'

His jaw flickered. His chest rose and fell a little deeper than before, but it was the only acknowledgement he made of her having spoken.

Her heart picked up speed. Pounding in her chest as if she had run a mile. Banging against her ribs. She lifted her chin, gazed at his face straight on, refusing to be shamed. 'I am not sorry.' She plucked at her skirts. 'It was wonderful. Beautiful. I would not have you thinking otherwise.'

'Claire,' he said softly, taking a half-step forward, then halting, his expression a picture of surprise and puzzlement.

She lifted a hand. 'I saw your face, before I entered the carriage. And again today. You think it is something we should be ashamed of, no doubt. But I'm not.'

'Claire.' He closed the distance between them in two long strides. He seized her shoulders in those long-fingered hands of his and gazed into her eyes. 'Claire. I fear I took advantage of you at your most vulnerable. I thought myself better than that.'

'No. No. I took advantage of you.' She licked her lips, wondering how to put what was in her heart and in her mind into words that would not make it sound trivial. 'I do not want you to think you need worry about my saying something.'

A small half-smile touched his lips. 'And this is what you called me up here in the middle of the night to tell me?'

She nodded. 'In part.' She swallowed the sudden dryness in her throat. Heat flushed to her face. Scalding. Betraying. 'All last night I kept seeing that hole in the ice and how I thought she was gone. I didn't dare close my eyes in case Joe was wrong, in case I had dreamed she had been found. Only when I held her this morning was I sure. And even then…' She held out her trembling hands. 'I'm still shaking.'

He held up a hand with a short laugh. 'I also tremble.'

She gazed at him, feeling as if she were another person tonight. Someone she barely recognised. 'I could not bear the idea of being alone tonight.' She shook her head, averted her face. 'I want you.'

For a moment he was still, then his palm came up from her shoulder to cup her cheek and tilt her face upwards. For a moment she resisted the gentle pressure, and for a second moment, she lowered her gaze to his chin, his very beautiful chin, but then something about his tension made her look up into his face.

His expression was tender and full of raw longing. *'Chérie,'* he said in little more than a whisper. 'Darling Claire. Never, ever have I been so tempted.'

Emboldened, she smiled a tremulous smile

He gave a short laugh. 'I find there is an emptiness in me only you can fill, even though it can only be for a short time, an interval, in both our lives.'

'I understand.' She did. And could not turn away. Because yesterday, for the first time in many years, she had felt treasured. Beloved, if not loved. It had soothed some great gash in her heart and she was not ready to let it go. Not yet. Soon she must marry again, and there would be no grand passion. Why should she not take this last chance to experience joy?

André could not quite believe this was happening. Yes, his heart had lifted when she had issued her invitation. And he'd been able to think of nothing else all day. He was lucky dinner hadn't been a total disaster he'd been so distracted, but he kept remembering how he'd used her. He'd taken her in what had been little more than an outdoor shed. Treated a woman he respected like a common female of the street. It had sickened him. She deserved so much more.

And then she'd asked to see him. And he'd admitted his need, when he had never needed anyone. The very idea sent his head spinning like a blow to the temple.

She stepped around him and stood facing the door. She intended to show him out. Confusion filled him. A trace of anger. He didn't like to be toyed with.

She turned the key in the lock. His breath left him in a rush. Anticipation. Understanding.

She spun around to face him, the naughtiness of a school-girl caught out gleaming in her eyes and a shy smile curving her lips. 'We don't need any interruptions.'

The very thought made his blood run cold. An affair with a servant would ruin her completely.

A servant was lower than a gentleman's horse.

'This is not a good idea,' he said.

Her face paled. The brightness in her expression fled. 'You don't want to stay?'

'Yes, I want to stay.'

The relief on her face was painful to see, as if she had expected him to reject her. He could scarcely believe that, but she wore her feelings on her face like the printed words of a recipe. A recipe for disaster. 'It is you I worry for.'

She walked back to him. Her gaze, so open and honest, so clear and direct, spoke volumes. Longing. Hope. Bravery. 'I am no innocent child who needs protection from herself. I know what I want.'

The bold words made his heart race, his breathing hitch in his throat.

She drew in a quick breath and his gaze fell of its own volition to the creamy white skin above the edge of her gown. So smooth. So silken. He wanted to kiss her there. His blood pounded in his veins. He forced himself to look at her face, to make sense of her words.

'I did think my choice should be an informed one,' she said breathlessly. 'That it would be a good idea if we got to know each other a little better first.'

So cautious, his little brown mouse. He wanted to smile, but knew she would take it amiss.

And she was right. What did she know of him? At the moment, he wasn't quite sure he recognised himself. He did know he wanted a chance to make up for last night. The chance to bring her true pleasure as she deserved.

She gestured towards the small sofa beside the hearth, a lovers' couch, a twisted affair where they would sit separately, but converse face to face. An unusual piece of furniture for a lady's boudoir. Beside it sat a small table with a decanter of wine glinting ruby in the firelight and two glasses. So they were to be civilised, when what he really wanted to do was kiss her senseless, and remove the shadows from her eyes, as well as her clothes. He wanted to see all of her.

But he could be civilised. He'd learned the way of it in his youth and if he tried he could remember some of those lessons, though he refused to remember his teachers.

He took her hand, walked her to her side of the chaise, then settled himself on the other with a smile. She poured him a glass of wine and handed it to him over the sofa back.

'To your health,' he said, raising his glass.

'And to yours.'

As toasts went it was pretty innocuous. He sipped his wine and found it a beautiful rich burgundy. The kind of wine he would be proud to serve in his restaurant.

'How did you get Monsieur Lumsden to part with his precious horde of Romanée?' he asked, savouring the bouquet of blackcurrant and leather on his tongue.

She smiled. 'I see you really know do your wines. I asked him for it specifically. I remember it was one of the vintages my father was particularly proud of. How he managed to get it out of France, I do not know.'

A silence fell. Not uncomfortable, or intimidating, and

filled by the crackle of the fire and the faint sound of her rapid breathing. 'It is a great many years since I engaged in any sort of drawing room flirtation,' she said on a deprecating laugh. A strained little sound, and breathless with embarrassment. 'You will excuse me if I am a little rusty.'

He grinned. 'Having never engaged in any at all, I have no means of judging.'

She laughed freely then. Unexpectedly low. A little husky sound at the back of her throat that reminded him of other sounds she had made for him. His groin tightened unexpectedly. He shifted in his seat, looking for easement, hoping she wouldn't notice.

'I never had much practice,' she said. 'My come-out was cut short by my mother's death. I married shortly afterwards.'

'I am sorry for your loss.' The words were much too stilted for the loss of a parent, but he hated discussing parents. His or anyone else's. Tension tightened his shoulders; he felt uncomfortable in his skin. And now the silence dragged on.

It was a game and neither of them knew the rules.

André decided to roll the dice. 'Is there something *madame* would like to know? Feel free to ask anything at all.' But not about his parents. That was one story he would never tell.

'Where were you born?'

'In a very small place in the south of France.' He forced himself to remember the village and not the château. 'Bordeaux.'

'What made you decide to become a chef?'

Surprised, he couldn't speak for a moment. It wasn't that no one had ever asked him that question, they had. On more than one occasion. He just hadn't expected a woman of quality to be interested in such a mundane thing as his work.

'It was a good way to make sure I ate well every day.' His stock answer. It always drew a laugh.

Not this time. She raised a brow, her head tilting as if she thought he might be jesting at her expense. For some reason he wanted her to understand the heart of the joke.

'I grew up on the streets of Paris. There was never enough to eat. And when I joined the army, there was never enough to eat there either. Then I saw that cooks always ate their fill. It took a while, but I learned to make myself useful, discovering I had a talent. I like to eat, yes, but I like the taste, the texture on the tongue, the scents—warm bread, rosemary, spices from the East. And how they blend together to tease the palate.'

'You are an artist, in other words.'

She was charming him. Making him feel wonderfully special as if she cared about him, when they both knew this was only about physical satisfaction. That caring touched a deep place inside him that felt raw and ragged. He tried to retreat. 'Food is hardly art.'

'It is. You create works of art, just like a painter. You have the same kind of passion.'

It was as if she understood what drove him. He laughed it off. 'Except that my art lasts less than an hour before it is demolished.'

'True. But the memory lives on. I can still remember the taste of the pheasant pie you brought me, a perfect blending of flaky pastry, tender meat and delicious sauce and a heavenly aroma that filled the room.'

He gazed at her in awe. 'You are an epicurean. Never have I listened to such a mouth-watering description of something so ordinary as pheasant pie.'

She laughed, as delighted by his compliment as he was by her memories of his food.

Her face sobered. 'It must have been difficult for a boy growing up on the streets of Paris.'

The darkness inside him pushed the door open a crack. The

horror of the guillotine glinting as it descended on a neck he had once put his arms around. His father's. He would never know what had drawn him to the Place de la Révolution that day. The cheers of the crowd. The smell of boiled cabbage and garlic. He'd been as sick as a dog. He slammed the door closed on the memory, because it led to thoughts of his mother. 'They were difficult days. And long gone. The wars are over and a Bourbon king is back on the throne.'

'Will you go back? To France?'

'Perhaps one day. To visit. I am not sure. My home is in England now. I like it here. There are troubles, yes. But not like France.'

A little crease formed between her fine eyebrows. 'You are not tempted to stay here, at Castonbury?'

He was tempted. But only because of her. And that was illogical. He had a future waiting. And it was not here in the depths of the country. It was not the goal he had spent his whole adult life pursuing. 'I leave at the end of my contract.'

'Surely my brother would renew your contract?'

She sounded indignant on his behalf and once more her caring brushed a painful nerve. This was dangerous ground. More dangerous than his presence inside her chamber, and that was practically a hanging offense. Or it would be if she cried foul.

There wasn't another woman in the world who could have tempted him to take the risk they took tonight. He had come here because she had invited him. He trusted her, he realised with a shock. He never trusted women. And worse yet, he cared about her happiness. He swallowed. He had never wanted to feel this way again.

He didn't want to need anyone ever again. Couldn't. But he could make love to her properly. If only she would let him.

He was becoming tired of all this talking. 'My plans take me to London.'

An expression of distaste crossed her face. 'I hope I will never set foot in London again. It is horrid and dirty and full of unpleasant people.'

'Then we differ in our views. To me, London is the heart of England. It is a place where a man can make his fortune.'

'Or lose it.' She shrugged her beautiful shoulders. 'Still, it is your choice.' She sounded so accepting it irritated him. Annoyed him that she did not ask him to stay.

Oh, she really had muddled his mind. He had no wish to bury himself here. He had dreams and hopes. And yet, as they sat talking, he had the feeling he could be happy here. With her and her daughter. And perhaps a few children of his own too.

His gut fell away. She could not marry him. Not a chef. Nor did he want to be married.

He kept his face calm, a mask hiding the turmoil of conflicted thoughts. 'I intend to open a restaurant in London. And then a hotel.'

'Oh,' she said, admiration lighting her pretty eyes. 'How wonderful. An expensive proposition though, surely?'

'This contract paid very well.'

'So everything is in place.'

'Yes.' He barely had enough to get started, but it was all he had lived for these past few years. A way to walk away from a heritage he despised and become successful. Yet now, with Claire, he almost regretted the decision that put them on such an unequal footing.

What? Would he give up all his ideals, his principles, for the sake of a noblewoman? His prick was starting to rule his head, it seemed. 'What about you, Claire? Are all your plans in place?'

'Not quite.'

'But they will come to fruition. You are sister to a duke, still young enough to bear an heir. Old enough to know your own mind. Have you decided who you will choose?'

'You make it sound so cold. So passionless.'

'Is there passion in it?' *Sacrebleu*, why did he ask such a stupid question? Such a jealous question? What she did with her life was nothing to him. Just as he could be nothing to her. This getting to know each other was not such a good idea, after all. He raised a hand. 'I apologise. Please, do not answer what is an impertinence.'

Talking was doing neither of them any good. It was taking them places they could not go, when they should be losing themselves in mutual bliss. That was why he was here. He rose to his feet and drew her up to face him. He led her around the confounded sofa until they stood with a bare inch of warm air between them. Already he could feel the heat of her response. See the gentle flush of her skin. Inhale the very essence of her longing.

He gazed into her eyes and let her see his desire. 'Claire, *ma petite*, we both know why you invited me here. Let us not play with each other any longer.'

'No,' she breathed. 'Let us not play games.'

He placed his hands on her fine-boned shoulders, felt the tremors racing beneath her skin—excitement, fear, longing. 'It is what it is, *chérie*. It can never be more than this. Our stations in life are fixed. We can take this joy for ourselves, but it can never be more.'

'No.'

But as she stared up at him with parted lips, what he saw in her eyes terrified him. Affection as well as heat.

Would she, too, want more than he could give? 'I really am not sure this is a good idea.' He started to turn away.

She caught at his sleeve. 'No. I understand what you are saying. I understand that this is all it can ever be, but I want this. I want to choose this now. Tonight. For once, I want someone to want me—Claire—as a woman, instead of wanting me for my connections. If only it is just this once.' Truth and pain were a bright silver blade in her gaze.

'I don't give a sous for your family,' he murmured.

'I know,' she breathed. 'I know.'

She stood up on her tiptoes and brushed velvety soft lips across his mouth. An irresistible force.

A groan left his throat. Capitulation. Lust. All conscience destroyed by her touch.

He drew her close, buried his face where the exquisite slope of her shoulder met the elegant arc of her neck and inhaled the perfume of jasmine and Claire. He nipped at the delicate flesh and soothed it with a lick of his tongue and felt the bone-deep shudder ripple through her body.

She tasted like manna from heaven. Like nectar from the gods. She tasted of Claire. Delicious. Delectable. A feast for the senses. A feast no hungry man could resist. He'd been out in the wilderness, on the brink of starvation for years, and only now recognised his deprivation.

It seemed that tonight he needed her as much as she needed him. What more was there to be said? One inch after the other—as he tasted her neck, her jaw, her chin, and finally indulged himself with her lovely mouth—he backed her towards the bed. This time he would not take her like a mindless animal. This time, he would please her, and indulge her, and seduce her with consummate skill.

He would hear her beg for him to finish it. He had learned from the best in France. The highest courtesans in the land. She deserved no less.

No. She deserved more, because she never asked for anything for herself.

When the bed brought their slow backwards dance to a halt, he kissed her more deeply, explored the delights of her mouth with his tongue, learning its slick heat and discovering what pleased her from the little hitches in her breathing and the soft cries in her throat.

Those tiny little sounds drove him to madness, his body clenching unbearably with the pain of waiting.

His hands explored the breadth of her narrow back, felt the striation of ribs, the swell of hip and buttock. The picture they drew in his mind was incredibly erotic. And now he would see if his imaginings came anywhere close to the truth.

This time he would make sure he brought all his skill to the table. What had happened at the plunge bath had been a travesty. He owed her his best efforts.

No lying to yourself, André. What went before was a mere taste on the tip of the tongue, an *hors d'oeuvre* compared to the main course tonight would be. The *pièce de résistance.*

He hadn't ceased thinking about what he wanted to do with her since the moment they had parted at the door. And now he would put his wonderfully inventive imagination to the test.

He placed his hands around her waist, surprised by the tiny span of it for a second, enchanted by the urge to feed her up, then lifted her to sit on the edge of the bed. Delighted by the flush of pink high on her cheekbones and the soft parting of her lips, he knelt before her. A supplicant at the altar of a goddess.

The thought made him as hard as granite.

There was something deceptively innocent about the way she looked at him.

In all his vast experience in the cities across Europe, where his good looks had allowed him a sensual education *par excellence*, he'd never discovered such an incredibly arousing combination of innocence and knowing.

Slowly, he sank back on his heels and lowered his gaze, paying homage with his eyes to her breasts, the narrow waist cinched tight by her belt, the shy curve of her bent knee, her small elegant feet.

He ran the back of his hand up her pretty shin bone, parting the robe while he admired the delicate turn of each well-shaped ankle and calf. For a slender woman, she was surprisingly curvaceous. Deliciously moulded.

He couldn't wait to feast his gaze on the rest of her.

First things first though. He removed one slipper, then the other, rubbing each arch with the ball of his thumbs until her toes stretched with pleasure and he felt her relax.

Relaxed was good. He stroked her lovely arch, her ankle, her tender calf, then looked up.

Her eyes were half closed, hazy with sensual pleasure, her mouth sultry. His little mouse had become all purring feline.

His blood fired hot in his veins. The urge to devour her rose like a feral beast. Control slid through his grasp. Shocked, he hauled it back by his fingertips. He would not take her like a common soldier with no thought but to slake his lust and no mind but his throbbing arousal. Not like the last time.

He came up on his knees and pressed his lips to the curve of each knee beneath the satiny robe, the perfume of her desire an aphrodisiac to olfactory senses honed by years of training. But he now had a firm grasp on the reins of his lust. The exquisite torture of waiting would have its own rewards.

As he glanced up at her face, she licked her lips. Again, control slid away.

No. This time he would not allow it. This time was all for her.

'Undo the belt for me, *chérie*,' he said, shocked by the abrasive note in his voice and glad she did not flinch.

Her fingers went eagerly to the knot and he saw that they trembled, not with fear, but with excitement.

Yes. He wanted that for her. Excitement caused by danger and anticipation, and ending in bliss. More than anything, bliss.

The narrow strip of fabric glided away. The cool blue robe parted to reveal her chemise and the start of the valley between her small high breasts, their pebbled peaks visibly thrusting against the white linen. The picture was made more erotic by the practical, modest nature of her undergarment.

A harlot in ruffles and lace could never look so alluring. His breath caught in his throat as his eyes devoured the delectable sight.

Eyelids at half mast she leaned back on her hands, offering a dish as enticing to his palate as it was to his gaze. An invitation to sample heavenly delights.

'Now you,' she said, her voice low and husky.

Blood roared through his veins, his shaft jolted to attention.

Such a wanton, this little brown mouse.

Not a man to deny a willing woman her due, he sprang to his feet.

'You honour me, Claire,' he said softly, ripping free his cravat and shrugging out of his coats. He pulled his shirt over his head and tossed it aside.

Her gaze touched him like flame. It drifted down his body and came to rest at the waistband of his pantaloons. A small smile curled her lips and she raised a brow.

For some reason, he kept forgetting she was a widow. An experienced woman with a child. Most of the time she seemed too unworldly compared to the women he had known. Fresh. Naive.

Yet at the same time, he knew she'd seen hardship and deprivation. The contrasts knocked him off balance, making him lose his place in the proceedings, as if he was some green youth. Strange. Oddly exciting. Hell. Deeply arousing.

Or was it simply the forbidden nature of their congress that had him trembling and eager. Close to losing his mind.

It was without doubt one of the most dangerous adventures he had ever embarked on.

In for a penny, in for a pound, the English said, and now he understood. He kicked off his shoes, pulled off his stockings and peeled the pantaloons down his legs, sending them flying with a swift kick.

Breathing hard, he remained still, kept his distance, letting her look her fill, waiting for her signal that she was ready for his approach. Last time he had been a hurried fool fumbling in the dark.

This time would be a feast for the senses.

Her gaze flicked up to his face and she licked her lips, sending waves of heat through his body. She held out a hand. 'Tonight is ours. Let us not waste it.'

'And to the devil with tomorrow? Is that it, Claire?'

'Yes.' She smiled and beckoned. 'To the devil with tomorrow. Who knows what it will bring?'

But she did know. There was duty and responsibility and he could not fault her for wanting this for herself.

He strode to the bedside, leaning forward to grasp the tops of her arms and bring her to her feet, pulling her against his body, feeling his erection press into the soft swell of her belly with a groan he couldn't contain. He brought her closer with one hand grasping the soft swell of her bottom, while the other eased the robe off one shoulder and took possession of one of the sweetest, firmest little breasts he had ever had the privilege to hold in his palm.

The tightly furled nipple scraped across his skin through the linen. Warmth infused the plump flesh in his hand as she arched into him, offering her bounty and begging for more. He dipped his head and tasted the nectar of her mouth, before trailing kisses across her cheek, her jaw, the column of her neck to lick at the small hollow at the base of her throat.

The thunder of blood in his ears matched the sweet wild pulse he felt against his tongue.

A dish to be savoured slowly, for there were so many flavours to discover about this woman. Sweetness, sharp arousal, creamy skin, dark honeyed places.

He hardly knew where he wanted to start.

But of course he did. One must always start by uncovering

the delights to come. The eyes must guide the feaster to the glory of each exquisite taste.

Drawing on all of his willpower, he released her and stepped back, taking in the wonder of her passion-filled face, the pout of her lush bottom lip. The rise and fall of her pretty breasts still veiled from his gaze by the soft cling of fabric.

A smile dawned on his lips at the thought of his request and the uncertainty he had about her response. He didn't have a clue what she would do. Everything about her mystified. It was a long time since any woman had kept him guessing.

'May I remove this?' he whispered, touching the lace at her neckline.

An answering smile lit her face. Her hand rose to catch his, held it for a moment against the satiny skin, then brought his fingers to her mouth for a swift brush of silken lips.

He drew in a quick breath. Startled and thrilled.

'Let me do it,' she murmured.

'You are bold, tonight, *ma chère*.'

A saucy smile curved her lips. 'I spent years being good. Tonight I feel free.'

Yet soon she would be back in her cage. They both knew it, though did not speak the words out loud as she tugged at the tiny bow at the centre of the neckline, loosened the fabric and gave a little shimmy of her shoulders. The fabric left her bare in one swift slide.

Her beauty swept all thought from his mind. Her breasts were everything he had imagined and more. The nipples pale rose, high and impertinent. The valley between them a gentle swoop to her breastbone. Her belly beneath the clearly defined ribs showed the roundness of maturity and childbirth he found so womanly. Her hips flared in the way of a woman. And at the apex of her slim thighs encased in white silk stockings held up by wisps of blue lace was a light dusting of brown curls damp with desire.

He raised his gaze to her face and found a shy smile curving her lips and the shadow of worry in her eyes.

'Beautiful,' he said huskily. '*Ravissante.* Delicious.'

The shadows cleared. The smile became bolder. She reached for the garters.

He cleared his throat. 'Leave them. Please. I find them… *je ne sais quoi.*'

'Tantalising? A tease?'

'All of that and more.'

She bridled a little, pleased no doubt by the hoarseness in his voice and the harshness of his breathing. It seemed control was held by a thread likely to break at any moment.

'As you please,' she said, and hopped up onto the bed and lay back among the pillows, her eyes gleaming wickedly as she crossed one knee over the other, her hands hiding her breasts with sudden modesty. The curve of her naked buttock pure temptation.

'Do you care to join me?' she asked with a brave little toss of her head.

He swallowed. Yes, he would join her and join with her.

He climbed up beside her and she flung her arms around his neck. 'I want you, André. Inside me.' She tongued the swirl of his ear.

He hissed in a quick breath at her honesty and the bone-deep shiver caused by her tongue in that sensitive place.

Then her mouth, open and hot, found his and he dove into a whirlpool of sensations and tastes.

He feasted on the apple-sweet breasts, nibbling and licking at her nipples, until she cried out from the torture. He explored every inch of her delectable skin with his tongue and his lips, learning the place above her hip bone that made her jump, the spot beneath her ear that made her purr. He found the dip at the base of her spine that caused her to wriggle and laugh breathlessly, then beg for more when he stopped. He teased the little nub at her centre while she writhed like a wild thing beneath him and wound her fingers in his hair, returning her pleasure with sharp tugs of pain. Or strokes of his arms, shoulders and buttocks, tasting his skin, digging her nails in his back, urging him to greater efforts and putting him in torment.

Hot and slick with the sweat of bliss denied, he greedily brought her to the brink of her ecstasy over and over, until she moaned her need deep in her throat and he knew whatever happened after this, he was lost.

Claire wanted the torment to end. Too much unbearable pleasure. Yet she could not resist its allure. Every touch of his hand, every lick of his tongue, took her to new heights, stretched her beyond endurance. Closer and closer by increments, he took her to the edge, but never let her fall, until she was stretched beyond endurance, and ready to shatter. Her mind, her will, were lost in the darkness of sensation, the wilderness of desire. Her ears filled with the sound of pounding hearts and low moans, his and hers, and the rasping unison of their breathing. On her tongue was the taste of his shoulder, his breast, his salty skin and the scent of dark male musk.

He surrounded her with his delicious essence. But she wanted more. She wanted him closer, deeper. She wanted him inside. Now. She brought her legs up around his hips and he stilled on a growl and rose up on his hands.

She grasped the base of his shaft, feeling the pulse of his blood, the heat and the hardness, and guided him to her entrance.

'Not yet,' he said on a half-laugh, half-groan. 'I haven't finished with you.'

But this was her night, her doing, and she wanted him badly. She had been too lonely for too long to be forced to wait.

'André, please, now,' she begged.

She thrust upwards with her hips, guiding him home, seating him deep within her body, offering to bring them spinning into darkness together.

On a shudder, he gave in to her demand and drove deep into her body, slamming into the cradle of her hips with a force that pushed her to the pinnacle of her need and far beyond.

She shattered, light bursting behind her eyes, lava-hot blood racing from the centre of pleasure to melt every bone in her body, followed by bliss so sublime she could hardly bear it.

Vaguely she felt him go rigid in her arms, then shudder. He groaned softly, pulled clear and spilled on her belly.

She drifted languorously on a tide of darkness and heat, aware of the wonderful hot weight of him pressing her into the mattress.

When she came to, she was curled against his body, wrapped within his arms. A most comfortable feeling. His lips grazed her ear, then her throat, then her shoulder.

Farewell kisses. Her heart knew. 'Must you go?'

'*Chérie*, you know I must.'

'Will you come again tomorrow?' How weak she was to ask. Yet the words were out before she gave them thought, and it was too late to call them back.

He let go a long breath. 'I want to.'

The unspoken *but* hung between them.

She had asked, but she was a Montague and they did not beg. Or not very often, for it seemed she was not above it this night. 'I hope you will.'

He slipped from the bed and dressed with as much efficiency as he had undressed. No doubt he was used to such clandestine assignations, slipping in and out of ladies' beds as the mood took him. For surely there wasn't a woman alive who could resist his charm.

It meant nothing, this night of pleasure. Not to him or to her. At the very best, it was comfort for two lonely people, and at the worst, the assuaging of carnal cravings.

She turned on her side and watched him button his shirt and shrug into his coats. So strong. So lithe and handsome. But he was much more than that. He had a kind heart and a gentle soul. She had the feeling that while they had talked a great deal, there was much he had not told her of his past.

Glancing at her, seeing her watching, he leaned over and kissed her lips, just a gentle pressure of his wonderful mouth. 'Claire,' he said softly, his voice full of regret. 'You have given me a gift I shall never forget. *Merci, chérie.*'

Then he snuffed the candles, slipped out into the hallway and closed the door with the softest click.

And that was that. She rolled on her back. He was right, of course, though he had not said the words. This must not happen again. She was seeking a husband. Someone of whom her family would approve and who could keep Jane safe.

But after tonight, after the most unbelievable journey of body and soul, how could she ever let one of the men on her list come anywhere near her? A shudder rolled down her back.

'You sent for me, Madame Holte.'

Claire looked into his eyes and saw nothing but blank politeness as he stepped inside the door.

Beyond the door, she heard the quiet footsteps of Lumsden moving away. One had to listen very carefully to hear the servants moving about.

Inside she was shaking, trembling with gladness at seeing him, longing to kiss him good-morning, to touch his sleeve, to feel the magic of their physical connection. Two days and two nights she had lasted, but finally she had succumbed to her longings.

She smiled politely. 'Yes, thank you, Monsieur André. Please, do come in and close the door. I have some minor adjustments for the menu for tomorrow night.' She gestured at the sheet of paper on her desk.

He strode to the desk, leaving the door open behind him. Carefully avoiding coming close to her, she noticed.

He picked up the paper and glanced down. The moment he read the words she'd spent the best part of the morning composing in her head, he folded the note in half.

I missed you, it said. Such small words with so much import. She clasped her hands at her waist looking at him, the beauty of him, the wide shoulders, the sensual mouth she knew so intimately.

But it wasn't just that. She had enjoyed their conversation. Learning about him, his hopes and dreams, his history. There was so much more to know, if he would let her in.

'Madame Holte.' He shook his head, his mouth tight. 'You risk too much.'

A band tightened around her chest. Apparently he did not feel the same way. And yet she persevered. 'If we are careful—'

His eyes found hers. A gaze filled with regret, or pity. She could not be sure.

'I cannot be that man.' He shot a look towards the door and moved closer, lowering his voice. 'I cannot be your dirty little secret, at your beck and call, while you court a husband.'

The flatness of his voice when he spoke those words stung like a whip's metal point. She had never thought about what they had done in those horrid terms. She'd been too busy living only in the moment, in the joy of it. She could see what others might make of it though. What he had made of it.

His fists clenched. His chest rose and fell with a deep breath. The hard line of his jaw said he had not come to his conclusion lightly. 'Don't make this any harder than it is, Claire,' he murmured softly. 'I cannot be what you want. I am sorry if I let you think otherwise.'

She wanted to plead with him, but instead spun away, gazing out of the window, before he could see her disappointment, or the hot moisture welling in her eyes.

He had clearly made up his mind. And he was right. Their lovemaking was risky. And if he saw it as little more than carnal satisfaction, something he could get on any street corner or tavern, it would be worth nothing. To either of them.

Fear and relief had sent her into his arms the first time. Loneliness the second. How pathetic she must seem.

'Of course,' she said, keeping her voice calm. 'I beg your pardon…' Her voice cracked. 'I did not mean to insult you.'

'Claire,' he said softly. 'You know this is right.'

She turned with a bright smile, patently false but a smile nonetheless. 'The dowager marchioness has indicated that she will not attend our next dinner party so our company will be smaller than usual, but I think we should not change the dishes. Are you agreed?'

'I agree. But—'

'Then there is no more to be said, Monsieur André. I bid you good day. I assume there will be no more little dramas like last time.'

His dark eyes held hers. Unreadable. His expression severe. 'No, *madame*.'

'Very good. You may go.' She sounded every bit the duke's daughter with those words and she held her head proudly in clear dismissal.

'It is for the best,' he said, clearly trying to soften the blow.

'Close the door on your way out.' She spoke coldly, refusing to acknowledge his power to cause her pain. She turned back to the window, looking out blindly, staring at an imperfection in the glass that made the outside ebb and flow in ripples of light and shadow.

It had to be the glass, because she would not cry.

'As you wish, *madame*.'

The silent pause said he'd bowed. The whisper of sound and the click of the door echoed in her ears. She collapsed onto the sofa, the tears she'd held back hot on her cheeks.

She dashed them away. Had she so little pride? No common sense, when it came to this man? This servant? Any hint of such a scandal would lead to utter ruin. For herself, she didn't care about being an outcast. She'd been that for years, but Jane's future hung in the balance. The sins of the parent would not be visited upon the child. She would not permit it.

Oh, why was it so hard to be good? She'd never thought of herself as a bad person. Was she really so starved of affection she could not resist the first kindly man to come along?

What if he bragged of his conquest? Men were prone to talk of their prowess. Her blood turned icy. Should she talk to her brother about sending him away immediately? Or would it look suspicious?

Oh, no, now she was being mean. Acting the woman scorned. He could not have been any more reasonable. And sensible. He must think her ridiculous. Unsophisticated. Foolish.

She'd acted like an idiot. Given in to an impulse of the moment. It was over. Done.

After all, everything hinged on her making a good marriage. Putting right all the old wrongs. She must pretend none of this had ever happened and pray he did not tell Giles.

Thirteen

'John Coachman has the carriage ready, Mrs Holte,' Lumsden said. 'He should be at the door at any moment.' He helped her into her fur-lined cloak.

She dug her hands deep in her swansdown muff and tried to look comfortable. After spending hours primping and preening before the glass, she still didn't feel the slightest twinge of excitement about what was going to be her first assembly in years. She'd much rather curl up beside the fire with a book.

She could escape into a book. Forget the conversation with André by immersing herself in someone else's life and troubles. But Sir Nathan was expecting her. He had even offered a cousin to serve as female companion for the evening, in the absence of Lady Wilhelmina who, along with Phaedra, was not expected back at Castonbury for at least a week.

No matter her own personal feelings about Sir Nathan, she could not let the opportunity slide. Sir Nathan would be as good as any of the others on her list. Perhaps better, given his forceful personality.

'Here is John Coachman now,' Lumsden said, turning away

from the sidelight in the door. 'He's not more than a step or two from the door and the snow is cleared away.'

'Thank you, Lumsden.'

He opened the door and Claire stepped out into the night. Cold air hit her cheeks and filled her nostrils with a scent like no other. The smell of clean crisp country air on a snowy night. Snowflakes stung her face for a moment, then stopped. She glanced up to see clouds scudding across a moonlit sky. Only a flurry. Not enough for concern.

John Coachman, aided by one of the grooms who would accompany them, helped her into the ducal travelling carriage they'd decided to use this evening. Covered in blankets up to her chin and a warming brick at her feet, she would be perfectly comfortable.

The groom climbed up behind and the carriage moved off.

Six months ago, she would not have believed she would ever return to this life. To have been given a second chance was far more than she deserved. She would not let Crispin down again. Clearly she had almost made another fatal mistake with André, once more letting her heart rule her head. And her heart made terrible choices.

It had chosen George, and clearly it wanted to choose André. Thank goodness he had enough sense and the strength to cut the connection.

She hunched deeper within her furs and tried to imagine her upcoming conversations with Sir Nathan. If only his face wouldn't keep melting and reforming into André's.

The journey took little over an hour and she was relieved when the coach finally reached the Great Hotel on the Crescent in the centre of town. The pavement outside the Assembly Rooms bustled with people, carriages and the occasional sled formed a line to let their passengers off. Finally it was Claire's turn. She smiled at John as he handed her down, then turned to greet Sir Nathan, who was waiting beneath the arches. 'My cousin is already inside, Mrs Holte.'

'A good thing too,' she said with a smile. 'It is far too cold out here.'

'But at least it is not snowing.'

'Very true.' The weather. Was there never anything more exciting to discuss than the weather? Would it be like this for the rest of her life?

Sir Nathan led her up the steps and inside where a bevy of maidservants were waiting to take cloaks and boots and help the ladies into their dancing slippers before they went up the stairs to the second floor ballroom. Supported on Sir Nathan's arm, Claire entered the long room, its high magnificently painted ceiling supported by a row of marble columns at one end, its length lit with glittering crystal chandeliers and wall sconces.

The room was already full to bursting and a country dance in full swing on the dance floor. The air reeked of hot bodies and perfume and melded into a kaleidoscope of swirling colour. They edged their way around the dancing and through the crowds congregating along the walls.

'Everyone in the county must be present,' she said.

'With the season in London not yet under way and Christmas all but forgotten, I think people are ready for something to brighten up the long winter nights. And here is my cousin, Jennifer Samuelson.' He made the introductions to a rather severe-looking woman of about fifty. Claire felt as if she was being put under a lens. She smiled bravely. 'I believe we have met before.'

'Years ago.' The woman visibly softened. 'In London. During your come-out. I am surprised you remember.'

She no doubt remembered Claire's scandalous marriage, but

thankfully was polite enough not to mention it. It was water under the bridge. She had been accepted back into the family.

The woman waved her fan in the direction of a lady and a gentleman standing a few feet away watching the dancing. 'Do you remember Majorie? She came out the same year as you. She married Mipton, you know.'

Claire would not have recognised the plump harassed-looking woman as Majorie Goodworth, who had been the reigning beauty, or her portly husband as the dashing Lord Mipton of her youth. It was extraordinary what eight years did to a person.

'She's had six children,' Miss Samuelson said softly. 'All of them girls and none of them lived more than a week.'

'Poor thing.' Claire thought of Jane and felt extraordinarily lucky.

The other woman lowered her voice. 'I hear she's in that condition again. Mipton is determined to get his heir because he can't abide the idea of a cousin inheriting. It is a good thing we know you can bring a child to term.'

Claire tried not to shudder at the thought of how the getting of Sir Nathan's heir would need to be accomplished. She gave herself a shake. It was a small price to pay for Jane's future. Really, it was.

The set ended and the dance floor cleared and then filled again as new sets formed.

'Care to dance, Mrs Holte?' Sir Nathan boomed, holding out his arm, indicating his question was of the rhetorical sort.

She dipped a curtsey and pasted a smile on her face as he led her onto the floor. The mayor's wife, acting as first lady tonight, proclaimed a Scottish reel and people formed themselves accordingly.

Across from her, Sir Nathan bowed and she curtseyed. Then the music began. It was such a lively dance there was little opportunity for talking except when a pair was standing out their turn because of uneven numbers.

'I don't suppose His Grace said anything regarding that bottom land I mentioned at dinner,' Sir Nathan said during one of these moments.

'Not to me. I haven't seen much of my brother these past few days. He hasn't been feeling quite the thing.'

'Got the megrims again, has he?' Sir Nathan asked. 'Hard on Lord Giles, that. The boy is doing his best.'

'Lord Giles is still away.' Claire smiled noncommittally. After all, Sir Nathan wasn't family yet. The more she got to know him the more she thought perhaps she'd do well to wait until she met Mr Carstairs.

But her heart wasn't really in it. If only André wasn't so unsuitable. If only she hadn't made that promise to Crispin.

She smiled up at Sir Nathan and he visibly preened.

She just wished she could like him.

The Rothermere Arms seemed unusually dull to André staring at his bumper of brandy. Perhaps he should have gone to Buxton, after all, and pounded the punching bag for an hour or two. Or better yet gone a few rounds with the owner of the salon, the toughest bruiser in the county. In the past, the anger burning in his gut had sustained him, now it seemed to have flickered and died. Two glasses of brandy had done nothing to fill the emptiness.

Life was so damned unfair. Just when he thought he'd got it all planned out, when he thought everything was in order, something unexpected came at one with a left hook.

Not that he should be surprised. Life had dealt him many blows. But this one, this vague sense that if he had remained a member of the aristocracy things might be different with Claire, had knocked him to the ground. He knew the *ancien régime*, what it had done to the people of France, and he had turned his back on it. He had sworn never to claim his title.

He sipped at his brandy.

Edie waggled her bottom as she walked by. A perfectly lush round bottom offering a promise that turned his stomach.

He should never have let himself be tempted by Claire. Never have forgotten his purpose in coming to Castonbury. Everything he had ever wanted was within his grasp. He would not let a woman divert him. Particularly not a woman of nobility who wanted to use him for a bit of fun.

Yet there had been hurt in her eyes when he had told her the hard truth. Somehow her disappointment had been the most painful thing he'd ever experienced. Ever? He smiled wryly at himself. Now he was being dramatic.

And he'd be a fool to believe it. Women like her, women like his mother, were very good at pretending what they did not feel.

Edie plonked down beside him. 'Finally cheering up, love? For the past half hour you've been looking like you lost a crown and found a penny.' She nudged him with her elbow. 'I know how to put a bigger smile on your face if you wants to wait 'til I'm done here.'

Damnation. She must have thought his smile was for her. *'Milles pardons, mademoiselle,'* he said. 'I must return to Castonbury.'

She pouted. 'Don't be like that. There's an assembly tonight in Buxton. We could sneak in at the end. I love a trip round the dance floor, I do.'

He knew all about the assembly. Claire was going. Probably already there. He hadn't been to a ball since he'd left France. Balls were in his past. Like noble ladies.

'Eeh, lad, there's that look on your face again,' Edie said. 'What is the matter, love?'

André looked down and saw he'd finished his brandy without even knowing. He forced a grin. 'My glass is empty, what else would it be?'

She patted his cheek. 'You can't fool me. You've lost yer heart to some hard-hearted lass. Well, she's a fool if she won't have ye and no mistake.'

'Edie,' the tavern owner yelled from his place at the bar.

She bounced up from her seat. 'Oops, talk to you later.'

Lost his heart? Lost his head more like.

And if he didn't leave now, he'd be hard put to escape Edie's well-meaning offer of a bed without insulting the girl. He half pushed to his feet when a stocky man of around André's age slipped into the bench, cutting him off. 'Excuse me,' André said. 'I am leaving.'

Instead of getting up, the man surprised him by shifting on the bench so they faced each other. His florid skin did not go well with his red hair. 'You're the famous French chef from Castonbury.' He had the cultured accents of a gentleman.

Surprised, André raised a brow. 'I am.'

'Hugh Webster,' the man stuck out a hand. 'Late of His Majesty's army.'

André was not about to trot out his own military pedigree. 'André Deval.' He shook the man's damp rather languid hand. 'I am about to depart, *m'sieur*.'

'What! I was going to offer to buy you a drink. Girl!' he shouted at Edie. 'Two more of the same.'

The man's obvious insistence piqued André's curiosity so held he himself still, waiting for what might come next.

'And how is the old duke?' Webster said heartily. 'I hear he is about to cock up his toes.'

'Well enough, the last time I saw him.'

'I hear they are in financial trouble, the Montagues.'

'Do you?'

Edie delivered their drinks and Webster raised his in toast before taking a deep swallow. André left his on the table. He did not want another drink. He did not like this Webster. The man wanted something and he was too sly to come out with it directly.

'I heard some new woman arrived. Some sister or other. Looking for money, no doubt?'

André bristled. Was Claire the reason for his sudden *bonhomie*? 'If you mean Mrs Holte, I know nothing of her reasons for visiting her brother.'

Webster put down his glass and smiled ingratiatingly, but behind the smile lurked menace. Cleverly disguised, but André hadn't survived the war without recognising the kind of officer who would step on his comrades to get to the top.

'Come now,' Webster said. 'We both know those below stairs know everything. What is she up to? They say she's been in trouble with the old duke in the past. I hear she brought along a child. Squeezing him dry, is she? Lining her pockets?'

The questions sent the hairs on the back of André's neck standing straight up. This man represented danger for someone, and it seemed it was Claire. Was this man from her past? The secret she hid? The thought of this man touching Claire sparked his anger.

'*Mon ami*, if you are looking for gossip you chose the wrong man. Please excuse me, I have an appointment.' He'd changed his mind about a quiet evening in his rooms. Instead he would visit his friends at the boxing saloon.

Webster looked ready to argue. 'Just making conversation, old fellow.'

André bunched his fists and stood with a challenging smile. He wouldn't mind a nice round of fisticuffs this evening.

The other man's lips tightened as he took in the signal, his shoulders tensed, then he grimaced and rose. 'No need to fly up in the boughs.'

André gave him a puzzled look. 'I think you will see that my feet are firmly on the ground, *m'sieur*.'

'Idiot Frenchman,' Webster muttered.

Better to be thought an idiot than talk to an enemy. He gave Edie a wave and a half-bow and stumbled out into the night. Cold air drove up his nostrils, shocking him. He shook his head to clear away what felt like cobwebs floating around in there, too much drink and not enough food. Claire's fault. Or rather his fault for thinking about her too much. He buttoned his redingote tight.

Feathery light touches landed on his face. They felt like cold kisses. He blinked and looked up, watching snowflakes flutter and swirl in the light from the lamp beside the door.

Snow. So far only a light dusting. And it wasn't too late to be heading to Buxton. The more he thought about it, the more he didn't like this man Webster and his questions.

He headed for the stable.

When André entered the ballroom many eyes turned his way. While he was dressed much as the other men in the room, apart from the military men in their red coats, the glittering order on his chest pronounced him to be someone of importance. One look at him and none of the servants downstairs had questioned his right to be there. He still didn't quite believe he was doing this, but it was the only way to see Claire right away.

He glanced around the crowded room and found Claire on the ballroom floor stepping lightly in the star formation of an English country dance.

She looked lovely in a gown whose colour mystified him. Not pink, nor red, perhaps the colour of burgundy wine mixed with water. The colour of a stormy sunrise. It showed off her delicate shoulders and milk-white skin, and matched the glow in her cheeks. Even at this distance, he could see that her eyes sparkled blue tonight. She had never looked more lovely. Or more tempting.

She was enjoying herself. A pang twisted in his chest. Guilt at spoiling her evening? Or something darker, like jealousy. He squeezed his eyes shut to regain his sanity. Claire was not the woman for him. She never could be. Noblewomen did not go into trade, not willingly, and he would not join the ranks of nobility. At least, not permanently.

He could not prevent the stir of excitement in his blood as he watched her small form move lightly through the figures of the dance.

He half wished he had not said what he had this morning. Even if it had been the right thing to do. The honourable thing. He still wanted her, more than he'd ever wanted any woman.

The man she was dancing with, Sir Nathan, he knew because he had seen him in Castonbury village. Not that the man would recognise him. Men as full of their own importance as Sir Nathan never saw servants, even if they tripped over them. Tonight he looked as proud as a peacock as he galumphed heavily down the set with his arm about Claire's waist. Beside Claire, he looked decidedly brutish. André's hands curled into fists. She deserved so much better.

He resisted the urge to rip her out of Samuelson's arms and leaned against one of the columns supporting the ceiling. He need not have come upstairs, of course. He could have waited in the hallway below to tell Claire of the change in plan. But truth be told, he had as much right to be here as any of the other men present.

A dark-eyed young miss in white caught his wandering

gaze and peeped over her fan at him, fluttering her lashes. The blonde beside her, a lady of the overblown English rose variety, gave him a come-hither tilt of her head.

As a colonel in Bonaparte's army, he'd attended plenty of soirées and received lures enough at balls to recognise signs of female interest. The only female in the room who had not glanced his way, it seemed, was Claire.

The music drew to a close and her partner escorted her to an older woman seated nearby.

'The next dance is a waltz,' said a buxom matron passing by on the arm of a sweating man. 'You do know how to waltz, do you not?'

The man mumbled something under his breath.

A waltz. What could be more private? As he approached Claire, his heart picked up speed. He had taken many risks as a soldier, but would she out him right away? Call him a fraud?

He knew the moment she saw him. Her eyes widened, her lips parted, her cheekbones flushed a delightful shade of pink.

'Madame Holte,' he said, bowing low. 'We met once before. The Comte du Valière.' He smiled at the other two members of her party, managing to look down his nose while at the same time appearing perfectly affable.

Bosom rising and falling, she stared at him. For a moment he thought she would call his bluff. *'Monsieur le Comte,'* she said breathlessly. 'This is Sir Nathan Samuelson and his cousin, Miss Jennifer Samuelson.'

André bowed with just the right amount of condescension of a nobleman introduced to a mere knight. 'Madame Holte, will you do me the honour of this next dance? A waltz, I believe.'

Panic entered her gaze, then relief as she realised this was the perfect way to get him away from her friends and take him to task for his impudence. 'Thank you, *Comte*. I should be delighted.'

Samuelson frowned as André placed her hand on his sleeve.

'Damned émigrés,' Samuelson muttered to his cousin, clearly intending his voice to be heard. 'Flouting titles of no value at all.'

The insult didn't bother him one little bit. Indeed, if asked yesterday for his opinion, he would have completely agreed. Yesterday. Tonight though, the title served him well.

He led her onto the dance floor and smiled down at her. She opened her mouth to say something and he gave his head a quick shake. 'Wait until the music starts, *madame*. Then you can berate me until your heart is content.'

'Unconscionable,' she whispered.

He chuckled. And felt her little shiver. A tremble of her hand. A tremor of the ribbon in her hair and at her breast, as if some stray breeze had set them stirring.

André knew better. It was her racing heart that set them in motion. Her excitement. He could taste it on his tongue. And it spoke of promise. A promise he must not let her keep.

Nor would she want to when she knew why he was here. Frustration roared through him. But he remained determined to do what was best for her and ignore the beast of lust pulling at its chain.

The orchestra commenced the introduction. 'I hope you know what you are doing,' she said. 'It is years since I danced a waltz and only once or twice then.'

'Follow my lead, *ma petite* Claire,' he said for only her ears. 'I will not let you down.'

And then they were dancing, twirling and gliding around the floor, and she was in his arms, mere inches away from his body, her skirts twining around his legs on the turn in a most seductive fashion, her face tilted proudly, her gaze meeting his.

He couldn't remember when he had been more enchanted. Or had so much fun. The devil inside him felt very smug indeed. It began to have wicked ideas about how he would like to spend the next few hours.

'Well, *madame*. What did you wish to say?'

Claire's heart was pounding so hard in her chest she could hardly feel the beat of the music. But her feet wanted to skip and her lips to smile. It was ages since she'd danced a waltz and he was a wonderful partner. But a count?

The brazen enormity of it had left her speechless. The sheer daring had stolen her breath. And now she was in his arms floating around the room as if the floor was made of thistledown and she was a girl of eighteen again.

His touch, despite their gloves and the maintenance of the correct distance between them, seared her with heat. Inside and out. Her blood leapt to the feel of his hand on her waist, the way he guided her around the floor and swung her into the turn. Life coursed through her veins. It was him. Every time she was close to him she felt more alive than she had for years.

She glanced at the faces whirling by. None of them looked shocked or startled. The only people following their progress were young females with decidedly green eyes.

It was all just too delicious to relax in his arms and let the music carry her along as if this was something real. It was wrong. So very wrong. 'How could you?'

While his mouth remained grave, his dark eyes smiled. 'How could I what?'

A pang twisted in her heart. Desire and longing tangled with regret for what could not be.

'Pretend to be a count? Impose on all these people?' she asked in a voice barely above a whisper.

'Ah, that.' He sounded not the least perturbed. 'You think it is a problem?'

Was ever a man so infuriating? How could she answer that without being thoroughly insulting? 'You know it is.'

His boyish grin at her sharp reply made her heart falter in her chest. He swung her around in a wide turn at the end of the dance floor. 'I will admit there is a certain amount of dislike amongst the local populace for émigrés.'

She winced at the obvious reference to Sir Nathan. 'You lied to my friends. What if you are caught out?'

He shrugged. 'I will worry about that when it happens.'

'And me? I went along with your deception.'

'You will tell them you didn't remember me at all and were just being polite.' He grinned. 'Deny all knowledge.'

'You are my brother's chef,' she said, exasperated and laughing at his lack of concern all at once.

'No one expects you to recognise a servant out of his proper place.'

The truth was a bitter taste on her tongue. 'You are mad.'

'Mad for a chance to waltz with you. Just once.'

She couldn't stop herself from laughing. The man certainly knew how to knock down her defences.

'Dancing wasn't the only reason for my coming here this evening, however.' His eyes became intense.

Heat flashed through her body. Her stomach gave a little hop of excitement. Foolish, foolish stomach. He was altogether much too charming. Too tempting. She must not let his allure lead her astray again. She'd come to terms with his earlier rejection. She really had. She knew nothing about the man and she knew to her cost how deceiving appearances could be. Still, she could not prevent her body from shivering at the thought of why else he might be here masquerading as a French count.

He whirled her around with amazing skill. Keeping her on tenterhooks quite deliberately, she thought. When she was back in his arms, his face was once more completely calm, his smile charming. 'I was worried.'

Her heart dropped. 'Is it Jane?'

His eyes narrowed. 'No. Not Jane. At least, I think not.'

She tensed. 'You think?'

'The moment the music ends, I need to speak with you in private.'

She didn't want to be private with him. It only led to temptation. The temptation to kiss. The temptation to engage her carnal desires. He'd been right in what he had said; she'd convinced herself he was, no matter how miserable it had made her feel. 'We can't.'

'But I insist.' He spoke coolly. 'It won't take more than a moment or two, I promise. And you will not be sorry.'

She ought to be sorry she'd ever met him. But she wasn't. 'Very well. Just for a moment. Outside in the hallway.'

He nodded.

Slowly the music drew to a close. She hated the idea that they would never do this again. Must never. She fanned herself briskly with her fan and let him lead her outside into the corridor.

Private, but not alone. All around them, people were coming and going from the ballroom to the withdrawing room and the card room.

He led her to a niche with a sofa at the end furthest from the ballroom.

She swung around to face him. 'Was it not you who indicated we should not meet again? It seems, sir, that you are not very constant in your opinions.'

His lips twisted wryly. 'You see it is snowing.'

It had been snowing lightly when they left Castonbury. 'So?'

'So John Coachman will not want to take the carriage out again tonight.'

'Oh.' She frowned. 'Then I am to stay overnight? At an inn? Is that the message? I hate to leave Jane alone. She will be worried when she awakes and finds me gone.' The knot in her stomach tightened.

He gave her a long hard look as if there was something he wanted to ask. Then he shrugged. 'You could stay overnight at an inn, or you can let me drive you home in a sleigh.'

She stared at him. 'We don't have a sleigh.'

'I borrowed one. From a friend. The owner of the boxing saloon.'

Her choices? Leave Jane at Castonbury with only Crispin and the servants for who knew how many days, or risk travelling home with André. A small cracking sound made her glance down at her hands. Bother. She had snapped the shoulder of her fan. In that second she made up her mind. 'Very well. I will go with you. Give me a moment to make my farewells and I will meet you outside.'

He looked as if he might protest and stay at her side, but then he nodded and strode off. She hurried back into the ballroom. Hopefully, Sir Nathan would understand, but if he did not it was really too bad. She had promised herself that she would never leave Jane alone, not until she was sure Pratt could do her no harm, and it was a promise she would keep.

Pratt, she really had to deal with him soon. She couldn't keep feeling so constantly fearful and not have it show.

Fourteen

At first, Sir Nathan was inclined to protest her departure. The supper had not yet been served, but Claire's statement that because of the approach of inclement weather one of Castonbury's servants had been sent with the sleigh to fetch her trumped his objections.

'Do not worry, Sir Nathan, I shall be quite safe, I assure you. Thank you and Miss Samuelson for a wonderful evening.' The other lady gave a regal incline of her head.

'I will send you an invitation to the hunt, Mrs Holte,' Miss Samuelson said.

'When Giles returns, I'll have you both for dinner,' Sir Nathan said. 'My Derbyshire cook is as good as any French chef, I can tell you.'

'I am sure you are right.' She sketched him and Miss Samuelson a curtsey and squeezed through the ballroom and ran down the stairs. It did not take her but a moment to retrieve her coat and her boots. Fortunately, because it was early, the servants were able to help her right away.

A footman opened the door. Snowflakes whirled around

outside and the wind sent them flying indoors. 'Is your carriage waiting, madam?' He looked gloomy at the thought of venturing out to find it.

'I believe so,' she said.

He stepped out into the shelter of the portico and opened an umbrella.

'Is that it, madam?' The footman sounded almost shocked.

Claire peered into the street and then gasped. Instead of the kind of sleigh she expected, a heavy affair with dray horses plodding in front, there was this light-bodied thing, a racing curricle with runners. André stood in the driver's seat while one of the grooms employed by the Assembly Rooms fought to hold the head of an excitable-looking horse.

'Oh,' she gasped. 'Yes. I suppose it is.'

He started down the steps. The wind tore at the umbrella and he struggled to hold it over her head.

She slipped him a coin. 'Don't bother.' She ran down the rest of the steps.

'Hurry,' André said, his teeth gleaming white in the lamplight. 'As fast as we can travel in this, the roads will be impassable before long.'

Another liveried groom helped her up into the high-bodied oversprung equipage and quickly disposed several warm fur lap rugs about her legs and shoulders, and pushed a hot brick beneath her feet.

'Let him go,' André yelled. And they were off. Racing through the night.

At first the streetlights at the centre of Buxton lit their way. Then as they left the town, it became completely dark. It was like being in a cocoon of black, travelling at breakneck speed. For some reason once they were moving, the snow seemed to pass over them. André remained standing, looking out at the road intently.

'How can you see your way?' she yelled above the noise of the wind. 'Surely this is far too dangerous.'

He flashed a quick grin like a boy caught in mischief. A string plucked in her heart, painful and sweet all at once.

'The mail is just ahead of us,' he said. 'I am following their tracks. Look carefully and you will see them.'

She squinted into the dark, and then she could see the dark impression of wheels and horses' hooves. She relaxed back against the seat and pulled her blankets up to her nose. It seemed he knew what he was doing.

What manner of man was he, this chef? He seemed more like an adventurer than a servant. He spoke like an educated gentleman, mingled with people he should see as his superiors as if he was their equal and he boxed like a ruffian.

The only thing she knew for certain was that he was a puzzle. And Jane liked him.

Jane didn't like everyone, though she had seemed happy enough since they'd come to Castonbury. But she really liked André.

They had been travelling for some time, when the clouds began to break up and the wind to die down.

At first the stars glimmered here and there, then the moon floated free of the clouds.

'It seems the worst of the storm is over,' André said, sitting down beside her, slowing the horse to a walk. 'Perhaps I was a little precipitous in whisking you away.'

'I would not have been happy leaving Jane alone all night.'

'Why?'

She shifted in her seat to better see his face, he sounded so serious.

'Why?' she repeated, her mind scrambling, looking for plausible explanations.

'What do you fear, Claire?'

Her stomach tightened. 'Jane doesn't like to be alone.'

'Nonsense. A child who can walk all the way to the Dower House by herself is not afraid of being alone. And besides, you left one of the maids with her. Claire, you might be fooling everyone else, but there is something or someone you fear.'

She swallowed. A shiver ran down her spine. 'I don't know what you mean.'

He gave a shake of his head 'There was a man asking questions about you and Jane at the Rothermere Arms.'

'What? Who?'

'See. This is what I mean. You look behind your back.' He shook his head. 'That is not right. Your shoulder, you always look behind your shoulder. When Jane went missing, you were terrified that she had been taken.'

Was it really so obvious? Or was it just because he knew her too well? 'Who was this man asking about me, André?'

'A man called Webster. He works for Sir Nathan, he says.'

'A red-haired man?'

He tensed. 'Yes.'

'I saw him at the Rothermere Arms too, the day the horse bolted. I do not know why he would be asking questions.' He was not the henchman she'd seen with Pratt in the market, nor did he seem like the sort of man a criminal would employ.

'But still you are worried. Tell me what you fear, Claire. Perhaps I can help.'

She clasped her hands together inside her muff. It would be so easy to tell him all of her problems. To unburden herself to him, when she had said so little to Crispin because she knew he would be horrified. Dare she trust André with something so important?

'I swear that whatever you tell me, I will keep to myself.'

Could he read her mind? Dare she trust him? Yes, he was charming. Exciting. He made her feel young again. Giddy.

And that was the problem. She'd felt this way about George and look how he'd failed to live up to expectations.

She'd been little more than a child then. Lonely. Swept off her feet. She was a child no longer and she had decided on her own course of action. Made her own plan. And until she'd become involved with André, she'd been perfectly happy.

Well, if not happy, then content.

'I cannot,' she said.

She felt his disappointment like a live thing. She also felt him distance himself. Shutting her out.

'Not for myself,' she added swiftly. 'For Jane.'

He shrugged. 'Then we must say no more, *n'est-ce pas*?' He stood up and looked around. '*Tiens*, we are making good time. I expect we shall soon see the lights of the village.'

She nodded. But his coolness hurt. As she had hurt him. Always his French became more noticeable when he felt some deep emotion. He'd been wounded by her lack of trust. He cared more than he had said. And heaven help her she did not want him feeling that pain.

'I need a great deal of money.'

His hands went slack on the reins and the horse faltered. He gathered the animal, then turned to look at her. 'You have debts?'

'My late husband had debts.'

'I see.'

He didn't see. No doubt he thought she had been living high above her means. Nothing could be further from the truth and now she was talking about it the words just wanted to flow.

'The night before my husband was struck down by a carriage, he confessed he owed a large sum of money to a criminal.' A bitter laugh erupted from her throat. 'He'd been gambling, despite a promise to stop, and lost far more than he could ever repay. He feared for his life. He warned me that if anything happened to him, anything at all, I was to take Jane and run. Use a false name and go as far away as possible.'

Beside her, André remained silent, listening intently, only the muscle in his jaw telling her he did not like what he heard.

The shock of that night returned in full force. Her husband's trembling voice. His scared eyes. He'd dipped deeper and deeper, he'd said, until he had no hope of recovery. But what he said next had terrified her. 'We rented a small house in a mean part of London, but I had been making ends meet by taking in mending. George said this man was ruthless. That if George didn't pay up, he would get his money another way.' She took a deep shaky breath, the terror drying her throat and making it hard to speak. 'The man had told him that Jane and I would work off the debt.'

André muttered a curse. '*C'est incroyable.* Your husband would allow it?'

'He was in a panic. Terrified of this man. He was trying to borrow from friends. We'd fallen so far by that time, I knew none of his old friends would help. And all his new friends were no better than Pratt.'

'And the next day, he died?'

She shuddered, still unable to believe they had escaped. 'We were lucky. One of my neighbours brought the news. She was in the street when it happened. When I mentioned Pratt, she practically fainted. He is infamous for punishing anyone who bilks him out of money. And he bribes officers of the law to make sure of it. Jane and I ran.' She put her hands over her face as all the horror of that day came rushing back.

André put his arm around her shoulders, strong, so warm and comforting. 'Hush, *ma petite*. You are safe.'

She shook her head. 'I will never be safe until he is paid.'

'You think this man still looks for you?'

'We moved to Rochester. A year passed and I felt sure he must have forgotten us.' Her body started to tremble.

He gripped her tighter, his gloved hand on the reins clenching.

'I saw him,' she whispered. 'Him and some brutish bully in the marketplace. They were searching. For us. I know it. We ran again. Here. But I fear he will never stop unless I pay him.'

'*Mon Dieu*. Can the police do nothing? Or your brother? Your husband was murdered.'

'I have no proof. And how can I burden my brother when he has so many troubles?' She tried to pull herself upright away from him, but he kept her close and she relaxed against him.

'So you will make a marriage. But how does it help?'

'His Grace will ask a high price for my hand. I hope it will be enough to pay off the debts.'

André cursed. 'When you say a large sum, how much are you talking about?'

'Three thousand pounds is what George told me.'

He let go a long breath. 'Claire, I really think you should go to your brother and have him talk with the authorities. He is a powerful man.'

This time she did pull away. 'I brought a great deal of pain to my family the first time I married. This time I will do my duty. But more importantly, I cannot risk him finding Jane and if I talk to the authorities he will. You promised to say nothing of this to anyone. I trust you to keep your promise.'

'You extract a hard bargain.' He sounded angry. He sat silent for a moment. 'I still do not understand why this villain did not immediately look for you at Castonbury.'

'Because George was constantly running close to the wind with the law, we changed our names all too often. I had no wish to further embarrass my family and George promised he would never reveal my family connection to anyone.' She twisted her hands together. 'But I cannot be sure. He was weak. He drank. He might have said something.'

A long silence ensued. As if he was having trouble taking it all in. She wasn't surprised. It had the makings of a gothic novel.

In the distance she saw a light, then another. The village of Castonbury. In a few minutes, they would be home.

Surprisingly, she felt calmer, less fearful than she had for a very long time. She put a hand on his arm. 'You don't know what it has meant to me, to tell someone about this.'

She did indeed feel lighter, as if part of the weight had been lifted from her shoulders. More than that, she was certain she was doing the right thing.

'And you don't think this man Webster is looking for you?' He sounded so fierce, she could imagine him seeking the man out.

'If so, he would have taken us when we met him at the inn.'

'Then why the questions?'

'I don't know. But I thank you for coming to warn me.' Impulsively she rose on the seat and kissed his cheek at the same moment he turned his face towards her. His mouth brushed hers, velvet soft, scorching hot against her numb lips.

He gave a soft groan. Then they were kissing, his tongue plunging inside her mouth. The sensations were indescribable. Exotic. Like eating ice cream for the very first time.

She pulled her hands free of the muff and the covers and threw her arms around his neck, kissing him with all the fervour of a desperate woman.

He held her gently, carefully controlling the kiss, tasting every corner of her mouth with his tongue, savouring her with such tenderness she thought she would go mad.

Then his hands began stroking her back, caressing and shaping her breasts and the heat low in her belly exploded with need and want.

With a moan of longing she sought his mouth again, kissing him, nibbling at his lips until he opened his mouth and she plundered the hot dark depths with her tongue.

Their breaths mingled around them, the beat of their hearts thundered together. She was lost. Yet she felt completely at home.

Finally breathless and utterly undone, they broke apart.

The horse shifted in its poles, and whickered a protest. Sometime in the past few moments it had stopped in the middle of the road and was pawing at the frozen earth as if to raise some grass from beneath the snow.

André sighed. 'I promised myself I would not succumb to this again. It seems I have no control when it comes to you.'

'Me neither,' she whispered.

He looked about them with a sort of desperation, then gave a short laugh. 'There is nowhere for us to stop here. I will not make love to you outdoors in the cold on the seat of a sleigh and risk being seen. Even I have some standards. We must return to Castonbury.' He clicked his tongue and the horse started forward. 'I will report this man's questions to Lord Giles, I think.'

Disappointed about the veto on the lovemaking, Claire nodded. 'Can I ask you something?'

'Bien sûr.'

'Where did you get that French order you wore on your chest?' It was odd that it troubled her, but it had looked so right on his chest, as if it belonged there.

'From a pawn shop in Paris.'

When she said nothing, he set the horse in motion. Her body ached, her blood hummed. But there was nothing to be done about it. The kiss had been an accident. Another one that must never be repeated.

She supposed she was fortunate the man had so much honour. He could easily have taken advantage. She didn't feel fortunate. She felt frustrated. And the future seemed bleak.

They passed through the gates and up the drive in silence. When they stopped outside the front door, he leapt clear, helping her down carefully, but keeping her at a distance. As he should. According the rules.

The front door opened and there was no time for anything, not even words. She scuttled inside the house.

'That's a fancy rig you came home in,' the footman said.

She handed him her cloak. 'Yes. It was.' André was full of surprises. But, she realised as the footman handed her a candle, she knew no more about him now than she had when they'd first met, because she'd been too busy telling him all of her troubles. Perhaps that was part of the attraction. His mystery. 'Goodnight, Mark.'

'Goodnight, madam.'

It would not be a good night. Because she would be thinking about André, and that kiss. And wishing things were different.

Fifteen

Jeremy, a huge man, with dark twinkling eyes above jolly fat cheeks and an enormous belly, arrived the morning after the assembly. Determined to end the affair with Claire, André had written to him days before. Jeremy had agreed to exchange positions for the last two weeks of André's contract. They had worked together at Grillons and had liked each other on sight. Now André would take his place back at the famous London hotel.

After a tour of the kitchen and cellars, it was time to introduce him to Claire. Time to tell her he was leaving. Much as he regretted it, this was the right thing to do. As they took the stairs, Jeremy began to puff loudly. André adjusted his pace. 'You need to lose some of that belly, *mon ami*.'

Jeremy patted his paunch. 'Creams and sauces of the very finest distinction put that there. My sauces. So stow your criticism.' He gave André a considering glance. 'You look as if you haven't eaten properly in weeks. Do they run you ragged?'

'*Non, mon ami.* You will see it is all very simple. Just one dinner party planned for tonight, then nothing but the family. Though I understand Lord Giles, Mrs Landes-Fraser and Lady Phaedra are expected in a day or so.'

Jeremy raised a brow. 'And Mrs Holte?'

'Madame Holte and her daughter eat like birds.'

Jeremy's sharp eyes looked at him for a moment, then he shrugged. 'The plans for your hotel proceed well?'

Glad of the change of topic, André slapped his friend on the shoulder. It was like striking a mountain. 'Another month and everything will be in place. I just need to firm up one or two more investors.'

'I have no doubt you will do it. It is good to see a man achieve his dream.'

'Thank you.' André paused on the stairs. 'And thank you for agreeing to assist with my plan for this evening.'

'We'll find out who is ruining these dinners. Don't you worry about that.'

'I hope so. It is important for the *madame* that the evening goes well.'

Jeremy raised a brow. 'It seems you have more than a passing interest in what Mrs Holte thinks.'

Was he actually feeling heat in his cheeks? 'Nonsense. What makes you say such a thing?'

'Your voice. The look on your face. You had it the first time you mentioned her too. Don't tell me you have fallen for your employer's daughter. Is she the reason for your hasty departure?'

His friend saw too much. 'Now you are being more ridiculous than usual. She is his sister and I have grown fond of her child.'

'Her child?' Jeremy's astonishment was palpable. André had expressed his dislike of families on more than one occasion. The big man narrowed his gaze. 'You like her. Does she know who you are?'

She did, but she hadn't believed it. He shrugged. 'What would that serve?' He started walking again.

Jeremy hurried after him. 'Life is about more than getting on in the world, you know. The right woman can make it all worthwhile.'

A spurt of anger heated his blood. A woman could also destroy. Look at Marie Antoinette. Or his mother. He clung to that anger, took strength from it, took a deep breath and gave a careless chuckle. 'So speaks the man who's been courting the same woman for five years.'

'Exactly my point. And she'll come around too, when I have something to offer.'

'There are enough women in London that I don't need to settle on one.'

Jeremy gave him a long look. 'Ah, but a wife, now that's different. And a family. If you like her child, think how you will feel about your own.'

His own children. With a woman like Claire. She would protect her child with her life. But she was a rare woman. He'd never imagined himself married. He'd always lived for himself, at first for survival and then for his goals.

'I don't want a wife. I don't need one.' In the past the thought of marriage had made him feel ill, yet somehow he could imagine a life with Claire.

No. Casual relationships. That was all he had ever wanted. He would never settle on just one woman. Never become too attached. Women were fickle. They abandoned you when you needed them most. His heart stilled as a vision of his mother's face swam in his mind's eye. Her beauty. Her gay little smile before she galloped away. Damnation, why would the past haunt him now, when he'd scarcely given it a thought for years?

He'd seen it with his mother and he'd seen it happen to friends. Better to enjoy and move on before things got painful.

It was not his concern that Claire was shouldering this burden alone and in such an unacceptable way.

There was nothing he could do for her. Not even if he claimed his birthright. The title was worth nothing. And besides, he would never do that. Not for anyone.

Their arrival at the drawing room door put paid to his uncomfortable thoughts.

When her voice bid them enter, his gut clenched. He wasn't sure if it was because he thought she would not like the news of his departure, or because she might be indifferent. Or because he knew he was being cowardly using the presence of his friend to prevent any personal discussion.

He ushered Jeremy in. She wore a soft dove-grey gown that matched her eyes, which widened at the sight of Jeremy. Such a modest gown that only hinted at the swell of her breasts where lace lay against her creamy skin. He didn't need to see their form to recall their shape or their weight in his palms, or the feel of her satiny skin. All those memories were seared into his soul.

Her cheeks flushed as if she guessed at his thoughts, but her gaze moved on to his companion, a question in her eyes.

'This is Chef Jeremy, Madame Holte,' André said swiftly. 'He is replacing me for the last two weeks of my contract.'

She swallowed her gasp of surprise, but her shock was there on her face, along with dismay and hurt. Why had he expected anything different? He should never have seduced her. He'd let her think there could be more, even though he'd tried to warn her.

He watched her pull herself together, bravely adjust to what his words meant, with a sick feeling in his gut. He kept his face impassive. For her sake. For his own.

'Leaving?' She took a little breath, shook her head slightly. She looked first at Jeremy, then at him. 'And dinner tonight?'

'Chef Jeremy will assist me. We will find out who is spoiling the food before I leave.' It was the best he had to offer. To make sure all would go smoothly for her. 'I have an idea. If you would permit?'

She rose to her feet and drifted to the window, looking out. Her shoulders rose and fell as she fought for the calmness he admired so much. Finally she turned to face them. 'Tell me your idea.'

She'd come to terms with his news. He could still see the hurt in her eyes, and some stupid part of him was glad that she cared enough to feel hurt. While another part was furious he'd let it get so far out of hand. But whatever he was feeling, what he was doing was right.

Jeremy held out the paper they had worked on together. 'We will serve the meal *à la Russe*.'

'The way they do in Russia,' André added. 'It controls the food coming to the table. I saw it when I was with Napoleon.'

'And we did it at the Pultney in 1814 for the tsar's party,' Jeremy added. 'Let me explain.'

Claire looked paler than usual. The soft candlelight shone gold in her hair, but tension lurked in her jaw and around her mouth. She was suffering. And it was all his fault.

Hell, he wasn't exactly enjoying watching her entertain this Carstairs, a man of ruddy complexion, fair hair and a suave tongue. A man she might marry. There was something too smooth about him. Too charming. Hands curling into fists as he stood beside the sideboard, he wished he'd let Jeremy serve in the dining room and remained in the kitchen. Except that Lumsden would never have accepted Jeremy's presence in his domain. He was barely accepting of André.

And besides, he had promised Claire he would be the one to make sure nothing went wrong this evening.

For once, His Grace was present at dinner. On any other occasion, André would have been pleased. Tonight not so much. Not when they were trying something so very different.

So far the duke hadn't seemed to notice anything and was sipping at his mushroom and leek soup with relish.

'Well, Carstairs,' His Grace said after a few mouthfuls, 'what news from Town? What are the latest *on-dits*?'

Carstairs beamed. 'They say Princess Charlotte is once more engaged in the happy pastime of trying to produce an heir.'

Claire glanced at her brother, who seemed oblivious to the racy turn of the conversation. She glanced at André and he saw that she was stifling a giggle. He raised a reproving brow, and kept his face blank.

Reverend Seagrove, who had come alone, cleared his throat. 'I am sure we will all be very glad of an heir to the throne. The regent and his brothers are terrible fellows. I hadn't liked the idea of a foreign prince, but this Leopold chap seems sensible.'

'I heard he had the princess firmly under his thumb. And she looks the better for it,' Carstairs said.

His Grace lowered his brows. 'And the disturbances in the countryside?'

It was something every great landowner should be concerned about, André thought morosely. If they didn't find a way to employ all these starving people, Britain might well find itself following in France's footsteps. Bitterness burned in the back of his throat. No one would be safe if that happened. Not women. Not children. As he knew from firsthand. His gaze once more sought Claire's face and a surge of protectiveness gripped him.

If things went bad, he would come to her aid. Married or not. Men like this Carstairs, soft men who had everything handed to them on a platter, had no idea how to deal with the mob once they went on the rampage.

'There is talk of spies and infiltrators. But I cannot tell how true it is. My main reason for being in Town was to attend a lecture on fossils at the British Institute.'

Fossils, when there were such important matters at hand. André felt his lip curl and pulled himself together. The conversation was nothing to do with him. The duke had finished his soup and it was time to bring the next course. André signalled to the footmen to start clearing the plates.

'You are a scientist, Mr Carstairs?' Claire asked.

'I dabble a bit,' Carstairs said. He frowned as the footman whipped his plate away. 'I say, is dinner over?'

Claire smiled sweetly. 'We are following the new fashion,' she said. *'Service à la Russe.'*

'Never heard of it,' Carstairs said grumpily. 'I wanted more soup.'

The duke frowned and looked at Claire.

'It is the service used by the Russian imperial family,' she said. 'I thought we might try it. I hear it is all the rage in London. The next course will be along immediately.'

The next course was the meat and fish course. André watched its arrival with an eagle eye. Some of the platters were placed on the table for the guests to help themselves. The footmen offered the others down each side of the table and then to His Grace at the head and to Claire at the foot of the table. The duke looked confused. 'Are we supposed to all eat the same thing at the same time?'

'That is the idea,' Claire said with an encouraging smile.

'How odd. I always said these Russians were a barbaric lot.'

André frowned, losing track of the conversation as he counted the dishes, the ones on the table and the ones being served by the footmen. Something was missing.

Claire was also looking around. She glanced over her shoulder at the door as if she was expecting another dish. When she caught André's eye, she gave him a speaking look and then glanced at Carstairs.

The jugged hare. It had not arrived. This was the course during which they had agreed it would make its appearance. Early in the proceedings. As a safeguard. Had Jeremy forgotten it, or had something happened?

He bowed, though no one noticed beside Claire, and slipped from the room.

A grim-faced Jeremy was waiting just outside the door. 'We have your culprit,' he said.

'Who?' André tensed, fearing it would be Joe Coyle and the lad would be turned off at once.

'The scullery maid, Becca.'

'What?'

'I'm afraid so. I can't get a word out of the stupid woman—she is bawling her eyes out.'

'Send her to her room and lock her in. We will deal with her later. You have sent for the replacement?'

'Aye, it should arrive from the Dower House kitchen at any moment.'

André clapped his friend on the back. 'Then we will take it with the next course.'

Jeremy nodded and went puffing off back to the kitchen. André returned to his place in the dining room. The course was well under way and, as before, the duke had set down his knife and fork. The man was eating more, but not a great deal more.

André would give the others a little more time, in order for the jugged hare to arrive, but not much, for the duke was looking around for something else and he had already sampled everything from this course.

He felt Claire's gaze watching him. Wondering what was happening. Wondering about the dish that had not arrived. But there was nothing he could do or say. Not in front of the guests. He shot her a flicker of a smile and hoped she took from it that everything was under control. Hoped that she trusted him to make sure all went well this time.

Her tiny nod of acknowledgement was all that he needed. In spite of everything, it seemed that she trusted him in this. He could only watch in admiration as she played the perfect hostess, pointing out dishes that might have been missed by her guests, encouraging each guest to participate in the conversation by gentle questions. She was a lady. This was where she belonged.

He could not give her this life. He was right to leave.

Yet his skin crawled and his fingers tingled every time he looked at the florid Carstairs.

'Your Grace sets a sumptuous table,' Mr Carstairs said with obvious relish as he helped himself to a *vol au vent* of salt fish.

'So I should hope,' His Grace said. 'Too bad the man won't stay, but you know what it is with these Frenchies. High strung, the lot of 'em.'

Claire's cheeks went pink. André wanted to hit the duke over the head to make him realise the Frenchie he was talking about was standing behind him. He glanced at Lumsden, who gave him a blank stare in return. Of course. What else could he do? They were servants.

'Monsieur André plans to open his own restaurant and a hotel,' Claire said.

André wanted to kiss her for rushing to his defence. But really she shouldn't be saying anything.

Carstairs stared at her in surprise. 'Aren't there enough hotels and restaurants already?'

'I gather this one will be particularly fine,' she replied

calmly. 'You will want to keep it in mind next time you travel to London.'

Carstairs was too busy with his venison to reply. The venison was cooked to perfection and the burgundy mushroom sauce was André's own recipe. The man's obvious enjoyment should please him. It didn't.

He gestured to the footman to clear the table. Before Carstairs could blink, his plate was picked up and the platters were on their way out of the door.

André caught Claire's startled expression and winked. She shook her head at him, but he could have sworn there was a smile lingering at the corner of her mouth.

The next course arrived and was served as before. In pride of place came the jugged hare, the guest of honour's favourite dish. André would have preferred to put Carstairs in the jug and let the hare run free.

But the meal was almost done. The torture of watching Claire woo this man with his food would soon end and he wouldn't have to go through it again.

'I hear you have a grandson, Your Grace?' Mr Carstairs said. 'I gather he arrived out of the blue.' There was an odd note in his voice.

'A very pleasant surprise too,' Claire said defensively, as if she, too, had caught something unpleasant in his manner.

'Not for Lord Giles, I'll be bound,' Carstairs said, looking at Reverend Seagrove. 'Thought he had it all wrapped up nice and tight, I'll warrant. Must have been a bitter blow.'

The reverend coughed into his napkin. 'A bone,' he said red-faced.

'Nothing of the sort,' His Grace said. 'Giles would give his right arm for his brother's return. His heir is the next best thing.'

Reverend Seagrove sent him a look of gratitude while Claire blinked, obviously surprised by the duke's forceful manner.

'Well, that may be what *you* say, Your Grace,' Carstairs continued, tucking into his hare. 'But it ain't what they are saying down at the Rothermere Arms.'

'What who are saying?' the duke said with emphasis.

Carstairs must have realised he'd gone a mite too far, because his eyes widened in innocence, but there was still that sly sort of twist to his lips. And Claire was looking so horrified, André had the strong urge to knock the man's teeth down his throat.

'The locals, Your Grace,' Carstairs said. He leaned back in his chair. 'Gossip says Lord Giles is trying everything to prove the boy ain't his nephew.'

Reverend Seagrove put down his napkin. 'It's a damnable lie.' He coloured. 'I beg your pardon, Mrs Holte, but I cannot sit here and listen to the maligning of my future son-in-law. Next you will be saying my daughter put him up to it.'

'Gentlemen,' Claire said. 'Really, the question is moot. Jamie has an heir. Lord Giles will no doubt assist in training the boy to his position in life and then return to his career in the army. If I am not mistaken, it was what he wanted above all things. Let us not concern ourselves with what the gossips say.'

Reverend Seagrove smiled at her. 'Indeed. You are correct, Mrs Holte.'

'Well, why isn't he here, then?' Carstairs asked. 'I heard as how he'd gone off in a pet.'

'Heard from whom?' Mr Seagrove asked.

'That new chap of Sir Nathan's. Met him on the road the other day. Webster. A military chap with red hair.'

Webster. What an earth did he know of anything? The man was becoming a positive menace.

Claire's shoulders were stiff with outrage. It seemed she

was well able to manage without his help. 'Lord Giles is accompanying Lady Phaedra on an important matter of business,' Claire said.

'I'm feeling tired,' His Grace announced. He looked exhausted, grey-skinned and breathing hard. He struggled to his feet. 'I think I'll retire.'

André felt desperately sorry for the old man. He had taken the death of his heir very hard, but had been on the mend, according to Smithins. This verbal sparring with Carstairs seemed to have set him back on his heels.

The ever vigilant Lumsden leapt forward to offer the duke his support.

Reverend Seagrove pulled out his watch. 'Dear me, is that the time? I promised to visit one of my parishioners this evening. She is not well. Not well at all.'

Mr Carstairs feigned surprise. 'Was that the last course?'

'No,' Claire said. 'However, I think the evening is finished, Mr Carstairs. Monsieur André, will you put a selection of fruit and pie in a basket for Mr Carstairs to take with him, please?'

'Gladly, *madame*,' he replied, wondering, as he saw just how upset Claire was, if he could find anything in his kitchen that would cause Mr Carstairs a very nasty belly ache the following day.

'Say what?' Carstairs's eyes bulged.

'You and I can hardly dine *tête-à-tête*, Mr Carstairs,' Claire said with an icy smile. 'However, I would not wish to deprive you of some of the finest delicacies this side of London.'

He snorted. 'I'm not some beggar who needs a parcel of food to take home. Are you telling me you are throwing me out on my ear?'

André wanted to show him what being thrown out on an ear really meant. Claire shot him a warning glance. 'Certainly not.'

Reverend Seagrove raised his eyebrows at Claire, then turned to Mr Carstairs. 'Did you bring your carriage, Carstairs? Perhaps I could trouble you for a ride home. Save asking His Grace to turn out his coachman.'

André smothered a laugh as Claire cast the vicar an appreciative smile. 'What a good idea, Reverend.'

'Not at all,' he said, his eyes twinkling at Claire.

The reverend was a good man. Unlike this *cochon*, Carstairs. André could not believe Claire would lower herself to taking a man with such a cruel tongue. He would make a most unpleasant husband.

Yet if the duke insisted, would she have a choice? He began to feel very uncomfortable inside. Frustrated that he could do nothing to help. He had no right to interfere. Yet he could not bear the thought that she would marry this man, or one like him. He clenched his fists at his sides, desperate to show nothing on his face. He was a servant. Whatever happened in this room, or in the lives of his employers, was none of his business.

He'd already made his decision in that regard. He was leaving. Leaving her to her fate.

A glowering Carstairs pushed to his feet. 'Come along, Reverend, I'll walk you to the door. I want to know what happened to all the money that was collected for repairs to the church roof. I've been hearing some troubling things about the funds.'

Reverend Seagrove's shoulders stiffened. 'Have you indeed? Perhaps you would like to view the church accounts?'

'Perhaps I would,' Carstairs said, following him out of the dining room. 'When I have time.'

Claire sagged against the chair back and looked at André.

The footmen were milling about the place, clearing plates, picking up glasses. Lumsden also looked at André. 'I don't think we will be serving dinner in that manner again, *monsieur.* His Grace was most distressed when he left.' He turned to Claire. 'Will you take tea in the drawing room, madam?'

'No.' She forced a tired smile. 'No, thank you, Lumsden. I think I will retire also.' She pushed slowly to her feet. She did not look at André, and he tried hard not to look at her. Lumsden was no fool. André would not risk the old butler seeing what must not be seen, and yet the dispirited way she left the room was hard to ignore. If only there was something he could do to cheer her.

But what? And would she even permit it?

'Will there be anything else, madam?' Daisy asked.

Claire, brushing her hair, smiled. 'No, thank you.'

The maid slipped away. Claire looked wistfully into the mirror. Carstairs was such an ass. If she hadn't wasted her youth and what little beauty she'd been born with on a wastrel like George, she wouldn't now be faced with the prospect of marrying someone like him.

But she'd been headstrong. Wilful. Impulsive. She could still hear Crispin's voice in her head. He'd been strong back then. But she'd been lonely too. Afraid. What if no one would marry her mother's daughter, even if her father was a duke? Her portion had been very small.

The mistakes were all hers. If she must now devote the rest of her life to a man for whom she had no affection, for the sake of her own daughter, she probably deserved it. She sighed. She would suffer anything for Jane's happiness. She looked over at the connecting door, got to her feet and went into her daughter's bedroom.

As usual all that could be seen of Jane was the top her head. She had always liked to burrow deep within the covers.

She returned to her chamber and closed the door softly. A soft rap on her door made her heart leap into her throat.

The door opened. A mouth-watering scent filled the room.

Chocolate.

André stepped over the threshold balancing on one hand a round silver tray containing a small custard cup.

Her heart stuttered and stumbled. She had not expected him tonight, or any other. She rose to her feet. She could not go through any more of this. 'What are you doing here?'

'Dinner was a success, *n'est-ce pas*?'

'The food was.' She managed a smile. 'Thank you.'

'Am I permitted to say that your sense of style is *magnifique*? The decorations in the dining room were stunning. It made my food seem all the more appetising.'

The compliments surprised and pleased her. She had taken special care with the table this evening and Lumsden had followed her orders to the letter. 'I'm glad you approve.' She *was* glad. His opinion mattered more than it should.

He glanced down at the tray. 'You did not have dessert. I made you something special.'

'Hot chocolate.' She swallowed the flood of moisture to her mouth.

He shook his head. 'Not quite. It is something new. I would value your opinion.'

More flattery. Yet his gaze was so sincere. But she wasn't sure she could bear any more talk or discussion this evening, she was feeling too low in her spirits. Because of Carstairs. Because André was leaving, even though she had tried her best not to think about his departure. 'It smells wonderful. Please, leave it and go.'

'It must be eaten right away.' He stepped into the room and set the tray on the table beside the hearth. He unwrapped a spoon from the napkin and gestured for her to sit. He flashed her a boyish smile full of appeal.

What could she do against that smile? With a frown, she sat and he moved the table in front of her and spread the napkin over her skirts. The little cup was full to overflowing.

He stepped back. '*Madame*, you are served.'

She shook her head. 'You really are quite mad.'

'This is true. Eat.'

She dipped the spoon in and the concoction collapsed around it, the chocolate scent rising up in a cloud of deliciousness. 'Oh, my.' She filled her spoon, tested the temperature with her tongue—not to hot, not too cold—and then filled her mouth.

Heavenly flavour burst on her tongue. 'Mmmm,' she managed as she savoured the pudding. 'Sumptuous,' she breathed when she could speak. 'Decadent. Smooth like velvet. Light as air. And sweet as honey. Seduction on a spoon.'

He cracked a laugh and looked extremely pleased. 'Your words make it seem better than it is. I should write them down.'

'What do you call it?'

'Soufflé. It will be a signature dish in my restaurant.'

'And you made it especially for me?'

'I did.'

Two more spoonfuls and it was gone. 'I have never tasted anything so glorious.'

He grinned. 'I am glad you like it.'

'You will make a great name for yourself,' she said softly, hoping he heard only the praise and not her sadness.

He shrugged modestly but could not hide his pleasure. Not from her.

As she licked the last taste from her spoon his eyes watched her with hunger.

A ripple of anticipation careened through her body.

He crouched beside her on his haunches, bringing his face level with hers, his dark eyes searching her face. A fingertip traced the line of her jaw. 'Not so thin any more.'

'Thanks to your cooking,' she whispered.

'I thought you a little brown mouse the first day I saw you,' he murmured, those eyes so intense, so mesmerising, she could not move or breathe. 'Now I know you for a tigress.'

Embarrassed, she laughed. He smiled back and her stomach flipped. He always looked handsome, but tonight he seemed younger, more vulnerable.

Something inside her, something strong and maternal, wanted to hold him, to offer comfort. But the moment was lost as he pushed to his feet. Perhaps he had sensed her intention and wanted to put her at distance.

A distance she felt as keenly as the sharp winds off the dales. It was the right thing to do, of course. She stood up, trying to keep her smile. 'Did you come only to feed me?' she asked, cursing the hope spreading in trickles of heat up from her centre.

He took a deep breath. 'Two things, besides feeding you, when once more you ate very little at dinner. I wanted you to know our saboteur is discovered and will never strike again.'

'Who is it?'

He gave a rueful shake of his head. 'Mademoiselle Becca.'

Claire frowned. 'Her reason?'

'She thought to rid me of my rivals. For you.'

'What?' Claire gasped, recoiling. 'She knows? About us?'

'She knows nothing,' he said quickly. 'Except my attraction. My fondness for the child.' He grimaced. 'She is a strange *petit chou*. She feels. She does not know. I have put the idea out of her head. Now she weeps on Mrs Stratton's shoulder.'

'Poor thing. It sounds as if she is in love with you.'

He frowned deeply. 'She almost ruined my reputation.'

She smiled. 'Love is strangely unselfish, isn't it?' She spoke thoughtfully, hardly knowing where the words were coming from, but feeling their truth. 'If one loves, one will do anything to make that person happy or safe or whatever is needed.' Her voice broke a little as she thought of what she would do for her daughter.

He stared at her. Clearly nonplussed.

She brushed her words aside. 'I really hope Becca will not be required to leave. Little harm has been done, fortunately.'

'It is up to Madame Stratton, of course, but I asked her to forgive.'

'I am glad.'

'No doubt she will consult with you, since you were the one most harmed.'

'Then she will be forgiven.' She bit her lip. 'And the other thing?'

'I had to bid you *au revoir*, Claire. I will miss *la petite* Jane very much, also.' He held out a package wrapped in brown paper tied with ribbon. 'This gift is for her.'

'As the food was for me.'

'A culinary farewell. All I have to offer.' The ache in his voice brought a lump to her throat.

She inclined her head. 'It was something I will never forget.'

'The more memories we make, the harder they are to forget, *non*?'

He sounded as if he spoke from bitter experience.

She could only look her fill, take in the angles of his hard set jaw, the bleakness in his dark eyes, the determination of his mouth.

A groan broke free of his wonderful lips and in one quick stride he was so close she could feel his heat through her gown.

His fingertips—light, too light—formed a cage for her face. 'Claire,' he said softly.

She placed her hands flat on his chest and felt the tremors racking his body. The storm inside him. His head lowered and his beautifully sensual mouth brushed her parted lips. She closed her eyes overcome by the pleasure of his touch.

Then he tore himself away and was gone.

She blinked back the moisture in her eyes and gazed at the tray and the dish on the table.

He'd brought her all he could offer. Food from the gods.

Something inside her cracked open and heartbreak leaked out; she sank down onto the sofa and let the tears fall.

'But why did he have to go?' Jane whined.

Claire really didn't want to talk about this any more. It was like being pricked all over with pins. Painful torture. She wanted to scream. She forced herself to calm. 'Monsieur André had business in London, I am told.'

Jane closed the atlas. 'Then we should go to London and find him.'

'No, we shouldn't.'

The small girl flounced from the chair, her face moody. In that moment, she had the look of her handsome father when crossed. She was going to break hearts when she was older. 'He was my friend. He left without saying goodbye.' She kicked at the carpet.

'Saying goodbye can be painful to all concerned. You know that.' Jane looked up at that. 'He left you a gift, did he not?'

Jane touched the glittering star on a ribbon around her neck. 'I'd sooner have him than some silly old star. I thought you liked him.'

Another one thinking to matchmake? Or had Becca filled her head with these ideas?

Claire carefully arranged her expression into a motherly smile of indulgence. 'Perhaps one day when we visit London, we will go and find him at his hotel.'

Jane brightened. 'Can we?'

'Perhaps.' It wasn't a promise. Not really. Since Claire was unlikely ever to go to London. She daren't. And not only because of Pratt. She didn't trust herself to be sensible around Monsieur André. 'Where is that cat of yours? He is usually underfoot.'

An impish grin curved her daughter's lips. 'Visiting Chef Jeremy. He hates cats so Tiny visits him every day.'

Claire laughed. The small sound hurt in her chest, but she had become used to the pain and ignored it for Jane's sake. And for her own. She would not sit around moping for something that could never happen. Remember George, was her mantra. Remember what a disaster he had been. But it didn't ring entirely true. Because André was not George. André was good and honourable and kind. And she knew that in her heart and this time her heart was not wrong.

But André didn't want her the way she wanted him. Their worlds were too different.

'Well, if you have finished your map, perhaps we should start on your letters.'

Jane groaned, but went to fetch her slate.

'Aunty Claire!' A brisk voice said. The door swung back with a bang revealing a tall young woman energetically removing her gloves. She tossed them at the hovering footman. Her fashionable bonnet followed suit, revealing long thick dark honey hair. Her grey-blue eyes were alight with pleasure.

Claire rose to her feet.

'When Lumsden said you were in the library, I had to come right away.'

'Phaedra,' Claire said, smiling. 'Dear Phaedra. Is it really you all grown up?'

They hugged. Just as they had hugged when Phaedra was a schoolgirl.

Jane stood watching them from large eyes, a hopeful smile lurking on her lips.

Phaedra, seeing her, crouched down. 'And this is your daughter?' She held out a hand. 'Good day to you, Cousin Jane. I'm Phaedra. Do you ride?'

Jane took her hand gravely and dipped an awkward curtsey. 'I don't know how to ride.' She glanced up at Claire. 'But I would like to learn.'

'Then you shall,' Phaedra said, bouncing to her feet. 'Come along, we'll go to the stables and see about a mount for you.'

Jane took her outstretched hand.

'Any excuse to get back to the stables, sister,' said a tall grey-eyed, brown-haired gentleman strolling into the room.

'Giles,' Claire exclaimed, taking him in. He'd filled out and matured since she'd seen him last; his pace was leisurely, perhaps even measured. Remembering him when she had left, she thought he looked a little too careworn for a man of his age.

'It is good to see you,' she said a little tentatively, unsure of how he would feel about her return.

He grinned and looked more like his old self. 'And you, Claire. Or should I be calling you "Aunty" now?' The tease in his smile and his voice reminded her of when they were young.

Claire immediately felt at ease. 'Claire will do just fine. And this is my daughter. Jane, bid your cousin Giles good day.'

Giles bowed with a twinkle in his eyes. 'I am pleased to meet you, Cousin.'

Jane bobbed a curtsey. She gave him a measuring look.

'Mama said I have lots of family here, but they are all growed up. Don't you have any children?'

Claire muffled a gasp. That was something one did not ask a single gentleman.

Giles lips twitched. 'Sadly not yet. But I certainly hope I will.'

Jane looked disappointed.

'But then there is Phaedra,' he said, his lips twitching. 'Half the time I think she is no more than ten.'

Phaedra laughed. 'We are off to the stables.'

'Go quick, then, before your aunt Wilhelmina is done changing, or you will find yourself plying your needle in the drawing room instead.'

'A fate worse than death,' Phaedra muttered. 'Don't worry about Jane, I will take good care of her.' She whisked the beaming child away.

Giles strode up to Claire with a fond smile and took her hand. 'How are you, really, Claire? Smithins wrote of your arrival. I have been dying to see you after all this time.' He tucked her hand under his arm and they strolled the perimeter of the room together. Cosy. Comfortable.

'I am well. Glad to be home. Amongst family. I hope you don't mind?'

'I could not be more glad.' He stopped at the windows and looked down into her face as if searching for information. Probably seeing how much she had changed. 'I was furious with Father for casting you out. So was Jamie.'

His voice caught on his brother's name.

She touched his sleeve with her free hand. 'Oh, Giles, I am so sorry.'

He shook his head as if words were too painful. 'We looked for you, you know.'

'It is water under the bridge. Your father did what he

thought was right. He did more than he should have, in truth. I learned only when I came back that he gave Holte money.'

He looked out over the park. 'You speak of him with disdain.'

'You and Jamie and Crispin were right about him. His will was weak, his charm only a thin veneer. But he gave me Jane and she is my life.'

'And you are home now.'

'Yes. I am home. For a while at least.'

He started walking again, his steps a little sharper than before. 'Smithins says you came seeking money.'

She looked up startled. 'He told you?'

'At Father's behest. It is a cursed nuisance, but Father trusts the man, so what can we do? Claire, I wish we could help you. If this issue of Jamie, his death, was settled, if his son had not shown up, we could have been of more assistance.'

'Finding an heir is a good thing, is it not? You never wanted the title.'

'Goodness, it couldn't be better from that respect. If he really is Jamie's son. But until we can prove Jamie's death, the money is all tied up in Chancery. Damned lawyers and judges.' He halted and squeezed his eyes shut. 'Claire, please, say nothing to the others, but I honestly fear we will go bankrupt.'

'Oh, Giles.'

'Kate is fine. She married a rich American. But there is Phaedra to think of. And Harry.'

'And yourself and Lily.'

'I'll be fine. As long as I can get back to the army soon. I know what Father promised, and I will do my level best to meet it, but it will be touch and go, I'm afraid.'

'I expected nothing, Giles. Really. But can I stay? For a while? Until I have my situation in hand?'

He took both his hands in hers and smiled. 'Need you ask?

This is your home. Stay as long as you wish and know you are welcome. If anything changes on the financial side, I will be the first to let you know.'

'And in the meantime, I will continue to find a suitable husband. I will make the family proud this time.' And pray Pratt didn't find her before she managed to land her fish. And hopefully Crispin was right and one of these men would be willing to pay for the privilege of marrying a Montague.

Her stomach tightened into a knot.

Claire had forgotten just how much of a martinet Aunt Wilhelmina could be and had spent the past week trying to head her off from Phaedra and Jane.

Fortunately Jane didn't spend much time in the kitchens any more; she was too busy in the stables with her cousin, when she wasn't at her lessons with Claire. A situation which did not please Aunt Wilhelmina.

'Every girl needs a governess,' she pronounced over the top of her embroidery frame.

'All in good time.' Claire smiled sweetly and drove her needle through the handkerchief she was hemming. 'When she feels comfortable here, I will employ a governess.'

'Spoiled,' Aunt Wilhelmina said. 'You were spoiled. Look where it got you.'

Claire took a couple of deep breaths. 'I am sure you didn't mean to be rude, Aunt Wilhelmina.'

The older lady looked up surprised. Then visibly wilted. 'I apologise,' she said gruffly. 'I am too used to speaking my mind. I will ring for the tea tray.' She set her frame aside.

Claire jumped to her feet. 'Let me.'

'I thought Phaedra would have joined us by now.'

'She is giving Jane a lesson, I believe.'

'She should be here, plying her needle.'

'It is no good wanting Phaedra to be different, Aunt Wilhelmina. She is as she is. And she will join us when she is ready.'

Wilhelmina sniffed, but said no more as Lumsden wheeled the tea tray before her. 'The post, madam. It finally arrived,' he intoned.

There were quite a number of letters on the tray. The older lady shuffled through them. She frowned. 'There is one for you, Claire.' She turned the note this way and that as if the outside would reveal the contents. 'Not like you to receive mail.'

No, it wasn't. Claire's stomach dipped. No one apart from the family and the locals knew she was here at Castonbury. Her pulse started to race. She held out her hand for the letter.

The seal was plain and she didn't know the bold black handwriting, yet she had an odd feeling of recognition.

She split the seal with her thumbnail and heard Wilhelmina give a tsk of disapproval.

As she unfolded the note a dog-eared stained slip of paper fell out into her lap. The note was blank. Was it some sort of horrid jest? She picked up the piece of paper and gasped.

IOU E. Pratt the sum of three thousand pounds—George Harrowgane Holte

Diagonally across it were printed the words *Paid in full. E. Pratt.*

Blankly she stared at George's vowels. Returned by whom? Pratt? It hardly seemed likely. Did this really mean he was paid?

Only one person knew about this debt. But surely he could not have paid off such a large sum?

'Is it bad news?' Aunt Wilhelmina asked. 'You've gone as white as the cup in your hand.'

'No,' she said, feeling giddy. 'Not bad news at all.' She glanced at the note again, her heart filling with joy. 'It is the freedom to choose.'

Aunt Wilhelmina's jaw dropped open. 'Are you ill?'

'Excuse me, I must speak with Giles right away. I must seek him out.'

'You gels, always dashing about on some mad start or other. It wouldn't have done in my day. You need to send him a note by way of Lumsden. Wait for him to invite you to his office.'

Claire picked up both pieces of paper and rose to her feet. 'I think Giles needs to hear about this right away.' She fled for the study.

Freedom. The word buzzed around in her brain like a trapped bee behind the curtains on a summer day. Before she dare let it out, she had to be sure she had read it right.

'For a man reduced to chopping onions for a living, you seem remarkably cheerful,' Jeremy said, his hands on his hips grinning at André. 'Though I must say Grillons is lucky to have you back.'

'Thank you, *mon ami*,' André said, chopping at full speed. The sooner he was done, the sooner the tears would stop. The heavy weight on his chest, however, would remain. Yet he wasn't sorry for what he'd done.

A few bouts in Jackson's saloon and he would soon feel like his old self. He really wished he believed that.

'So what happened to all your big plans of a hotel and a restaurant?'

'A question of money.'

'Investors let you down?'

'Something like that.'

'I would be willing to join you. If you would care for a partner. I've a bit put away.'

Rely on yourself. Trust no one. Don't get involved. It was the creed he'd lived by since he was ten. A creed he'd already broken. And yet he felt more content with himself than he'd felt for years. Not happy, but a sense of knowing he'd done the right thing. 'We will discuss it over a bottle when we are finished here.'

Jeremy grinned. 'I'd like that.'

The rest of the night passed in a blur of orders from the *maître d'*. Finally they found themselves back in the room they shared on the top floor of the hotel. It was no different to the room he'd had at Castonbury, except it had two beds instead of one. A stark reminder of his reduced status.

Weary, but elated at the compliments he and Jeremy had received throughout the evening, André pulled a bottle of *vin ordinaire* from under his cot.

He opened the bottle and poured two glasses. 'Thank you for putting in a good word for me with the head chef.'

'Thank you for the holiday at Castonbury,' Jeremy said. 'And for filling in here in my absence. Sorry I had to come and take my old job back.'

'I thought they might keep you at Castonbury.'

'They would have. It was just too flaming quiet. Not one dinner party in two weeks.'

'But Mrs Holte remains in residence.'

'She does. And Lord Giles and Lady Phaedra arrived a day or two after you left.'

'Did you see Mademoiselle Jane?'

He pulled out his pipe. 'A couple of times. Looking for you.'

André felt impossibly sad. 'She liked coming to the kitchen.'

'Ah, but Lady Phaedra is giving her riding lessons, I'm told.'

The right thing for the niece of a duke to learn. The child

would soon forget him. She was female, wasn't she? Somehow the realisation made him feel worse. 'The lady will need to keep an eye on that young miss—she will wander where she is not supposed to go.' Perhaps the new husband would keep her in order. As long as he wasn't harsh. The child was bright, it would be a shame to squash her spirit. And Claire. How would she feel about a man interfering in her child's upbringing?

He didn't want to think about it.

Jeremy chuckled. 'She went missing the day before I left.'

André felt his heart beat a little harder against his ribs. Anxiety. 'But she was found, of course.'

'Up a tree. Trying to see into a bird's nest.'

André laughed at the image.

'They needed a ladder to get her down.'

'I expect her mother was frantic.'

'Apparently not. She was laughing so hard she had to ask Joe Coyle to climb up the ladder in her stead.'

André felt a glow of pride. It seemed Claire had been able to put her fears to rest. 'Is she engaged yet?' he asked casually. Too casually, apparently, because Jeremy raised a brow.

Sacrebleu, why had he asked? He did not want to know.

'If so I never heard anything of it.'

Time to change the subject. 'And the other servants. Mademoiselle Becca?'

'All still the same.'

They subsided into the silence of old friends.

'I see you've been through the mill a couple of times recently.' Jeremy jerked his chin at André's face and then gave his knuckles a pointed glance.

'A little argument with a bully.' Who had wanted to keep him from seeing an ugly customer named Pratt. 'It is nothing.' It had felt good to teach Pratt and his man a lesson they would not forget. Once he'd paid them their money.

'So what about this partnership, then?' Jeremy asked.

André grimaced apologetically. 'It will be a good while before I have enough money, but if you would care to wait?' He shrugged.

Jeremy sucked on his empty pipe and put it down with a glower of disgust. 'You didn't gamble it away, did you? I don't hold with gambling. It takes a man down too far and too fast.'

'I had a friend who needed help.'

'Will he pay you back?'

'No.' He didn't want repayment. Being able to do something, one small thing for Claire, had eased some of the pain he'd felt at leaving.

'So how long will it take, do you think?'

'Two, three years, if I work hard. I will find a good position with one of the political hostesses perhaps. Find a patron.'

'All right. I'm in.' Jeremy stuck out his hand.

André shook it and poured them both another glass of wine, which they downed in one swallow. A gentleman's agreement, they called it in England.

'Now, if you don't mind, I'm going to have a puff of me pipe out in the alley before I turns into bed. I know you don't like the smoke so I will take it outside.'

'I appreciate your thoughtfulness, *mon ami*.'

Jeremy put on his coat, wound a scarf around his neck and left. André looked at the half-drunk bottle. When he was busy, he didn't feel so bad, but when he was alone, the pain of loss returned. What had she said? Love is a selfless thing? Did he love her? He wasn't sure he could love anyone, but he did know he couldn't have felt happier than when he paid off that villain Pratt with money and his fists.

And if Claire was laughing at her daughter's antics, then it seemed he'd made a good choice, whatever it was called.

And for some reason he was happy about deciding to take Jeremy on as a partner when he had never wanted any permanent attachments in his life. Perhaps it was the dark void inside him he was trying to fill.

Perhaps he'd filled a corner.

Seventeen

Giles glanced up and down the alley at the back of Grillons Hotel, and kept a firm hold on Claire's elbow. 'This is no place for a lady. Let me go in and bring him down to you. You can meet in the carriage.'

As sorry as she felt for putting Giles in this uncomfortable position she was not going to let him change her mind. 'Your presence will make things difficult. He will feel constrained. Perhaps even obliged. I don't want that.'

He muttered something unflattering under his breath. 'I think I am a damned fool. I will give you five minutes, then I will come up and find you.'

'Ten.' If she could not get her business done in ten minutes it would not get done at all. 'You've done your part, Giles. You settled things with His Grace, and you found Monsieur Deval. This is my part to play.'

'It was little enough. I simply looked where I found him in the first place.' He rubbed at the back of his head, knocking his hat askew in his concern. 'You always were a stubborn woman, Claire. I can only hope you are not making another mistake.'

She hoped so too. She pulled her arm free.

The back door to the hotel opened to discharge a huge man, who huddled against an alley wall to light a pipe.

'Chef Jeremy,' Claire called out, recognising his face in the glow of the tobacco.

The big man turned towards them, his body tense. 'Who is there?'

'Lord Giles Montague,' Giles announced, stepping between Claire and the taut Jeremy. Protective. He just couldn't help himself.

Claire stepped around Giles's bulk. 'It is Mrs Holte. Can you tell me where I can find Monsieur Deval?'

Jeremy came closer, eyeing her warily. 'Good evening, madam. A bit late to come calling, isn't it? Is aught amiss?'

'I simply wish to have words with him.'

Chef Jeremy looked at her, then at Giles still bristling defensively at her side. 'I'll fetch him down, then, shall I?'

'No.' She spoke too sharply for he recoiled. 'Tell me where to find him and I will go up. Alone.'

The man's jaw dropped, folding his many chins in creases. 'No women allowed in the men's rooms.'

'I told you,' Giles said.

'I won't be but a moment. Tell me where to find him.'

The fat man's face split in a grin. 'It won't be the first time a woman found her way up to the men's quarters.' He winked at Giles, who glowered. 'Third floor, first door on the left.'

Finally. She had begun to think she would have to send Giles up for him, after all. 'Ten minutes,' she said to Giles, and passed through the door Chef Jeremy held open and climbed the stairs.

André stoppered the wine bottle with a regretful sigh. Oblivion tonight, headache tomorrow. He needed all his wits about him if he was to move up through the ranks again. He would have to work hard to recoup enough funds to move on, even with a partner.

Once the pain of missing Claire left him, everything would go as planned. And wine wasn't going to help with that.

He knelt to slide the bottle under the bed. The door opened behind him. 'That was fast, *mon ami*. The wind is too cold, *non*?'

'André?'

He spun around on his knees, not sure he believed what he was hearing. He did believe his eyes. 'Claire?'

She stood in the doorway, lovely, doubtful, unsure. 'Oh, my word, what happened to your face?'

'Qu'est-ce que c'est?' He shook his head at his foolish tongue. 'What is wrong? Is it Jane?"

She clasped her hands behind her back, looking small and vulnerable and as if she had not slept well. 'Jane is fine. I wanted to thank you. For what you did. It is such a weight off my shoulders.'

He rose slowly to his feet. He had not anticipated her seeking him out. He had not thought he would have to say goodbye to her again. He did not want this. 'I don't know what you are talking about.'

'The money.'

He shook his head. 'I beg your pardon, I do not understand. Please go. You should not be here.'

Her lovely grey eyes darkened like storm clouds over the peaks. 'I am not a fool, André. You spoke of buying a hotel, of owning your own restaurant, yet here you are back working for someone else, while I am debt-free.'

He'd been right. She was a tiger and right now she had her claws out. He fought for control. 'Your family would not approve of your coming here.'

'They know where I am.'

'And Jane?'

'She is at Castonbury with her cousin, Lady Phaedra.' A small smile tugged at her lips. 'I didn't dare tell her I planned to see you. She would have insisted on coming with me. She misses you.'

Something hard and hot squeezed up behind his nose and made his eyes want to water. He turned away from her, staring at the stark white wall above the head of his cot. 'So, now you have thanked me you can go.'

'Why?' she asked softly. 'Why did you give up all your grand plans to help me?'

How did one put the emotion that had urged him on into words. *I felt sorry for you?* That would make her angry. And it really wasn't true and she would know. 'You deserved it,' he said finally. 'It was what you said. Your unselfish love for your child deserved its reward.'

'And you? Don't you deserve your reward?'

A jolt when through his body at the thought of the form such a reward might take. He tamped it down. This wasn't about sex. It had gone far beyond that. Too far for him to feel comfortable.

'I don't need a reward.'

'Not if the reward was me?'

Another searing jolt. He turned to face her with a frown.

She shook her head. 'That did not come out the way I meant. André, you gave me the freedom to choose for myself. What if I choose you?'

He stared at her, dumbfounded, then laughed, to hide his shock and the leap of longing in his heart. The thoughts of a home and a family. The old fear twisted in his chest. The fear that it wouldn't last. The painful landing was almost too much to endure, yet he somehow managed to raise a brow. 'Now who is mad?' he said, not surprised to find his voice raw and hoarse. 'I am a chef. I would not put you in the position of sinking so low, or going against your family.'

'And if they approve?'

It was like being a fish caught on a line twisting and turning, trying to break free. Only a very clever fish could do that. 'They wouldn't.'

'They would approve if you were a hotelier, with prospects. I could help you. I am not afraid of hard work.'

Help him? When all he had wanted was the privilege of helping her? How could he allow her to stoop so low? 'There is no hotel.' He gestured around the bare room, fought to gain control of the longing that interfered with his thoughts and his reason. 'And I am quite content with this. I have women aplenty and no ties or responsibilities. As long as I have my knives, I can take my skills anywhere I wish, because I have no one to hold me back. I do not want a wife. I have never wanted a wife. We had a liaison. It was very nice. It is over.'

He turned away from the hurt in her eyes. Fought to control the shaking in his body. Tried to find the anger in his heart that had always shielded him from such powerful emotions when it came to people. She'd carved her way through the barrier to the stupid softness inside. The part that had cried when his mother left him. The part he thought he had eradicated.

This past week he'd made a good job of repairing the walls, he could not let her break them down again.

'What are you so afraid of, André?'

The whispered question drove the breath from his body. An accusation of cowardice. A sly blow from his blind side. She was wrong. He was afraid of nothing. It was not possible to be afraid when you lived by your wits. And living by his wits was what he did best.

'Tell me, André. Surely I deserve to know?'

A vision of his mother riding away to screams of a mob out for blood filled his vision. He'd needed someone once, desperately. He'd called out. She'd heard him, but never glanced back, and then she'd spurred her horse onwards. His mother had abandoned him to strangers when he'd needed her most.

She hadn't cared if he lived or died.

Later, when he had recovered from the shock, from the betrayal, he'd understood she'd been afraid too. She'd feared for her life and had done what she felt she needed to do. The *curé* who whisked him away in the dark had said almost those very words. *She did what she must.* He never forgot them or the lesson he'd learned.

From that day to this, he hadn't needed anyone. He took care of himself. By paying off her debt, he'd given her completely the wrong idea.

'I'm sorry,' he said. 'I think you misunderstood.'

The silence, so full of hurt, almost killed him. He wanted to call back the words and lie. He wanted to hold her close and forget in her arms. But if he did, his whole world would turn upside down and he would be lost.

He heard the door open and close and when he looked over his shoulder she was gone. Only the lingering scent of her perfume remained to prove it wasn't all a dream. A figment of his imagination.

Just as his mother's departure hadn't been a dream, though he had dreamt of it every night for years. Cried out in his sleep too. And the terror that he'd done something wrong had left him paralyzed. Until he'd realised she was the one to blame, not him, and anger had replaced the hurt.

He sank down on the edge of the bed and put his head in his hands. Clenched his fists and felt the welcome pain of the tug of his fingers in his hair.

The door opened and hope rose in his throat. He let it go with a grunt when he saw Jeremy.

The big man peeled off his coat and hung it on the hook on the back of his door, then started on the buttons on his waistcoat. 'She said she would wait at the White Hart for three days. Then she will be returning to Derbyshire.'

'She might as well leave now,' André said coldly.

'What the hell did you say to her, Deval? She looked so happy when I told her where to find you. Now she looks crushed.'

'You should not have sent her up here.' He reached beneath the bed and pulled out the bottle of wine.

Why on earth had she said she would wait three days? He wasn't coming. She'd always been perfectly clear theirs was a fling. He'd been happy with the arrangement. Why had she thought things had changed?

Yes, he was charming. Seductive. But he was another man who never settled long in one place. Clearly, her heart had made another terrible choice.

At least she hadn't made a complete fool of herself and told him she thought she loved him. How ridiculous of her to think true love could be found in the space of three weeks.

Now poor Giles was champing at the bit to get back to his Lily. It wasn't fair of her to drag him away from the woman he loved after already being away for weeks with Phaedra, and then make him wait around for something that would not happen. They should leave. Now. Today. But what if André came tomorrow? The stupid hope he might change his mind wouldn't leave her alone. The hope he might feel something for her.

No, that wasn't it. He cared for her. She knew he did, or he would not have paid off those debts. She also knew it from the way he had looked at her when she'd walked into his room. In that unguarded moment she had seen his joy at her arrival. Only then he'd retreated.

That was what she did not understand. That was the question she wanted answered. She'd thought about going back and trying again, but Giles had vetoed the suggestion. He'd made her feel a bit of an idiot, asking her if she had no pride.

It reminded her too much of what had happened when she'd ran off with George. He was right. This was stupid. They might as well leave today.

She left her chamber and went in search of him in the private parlour they had rented on the ground floor. He was reading the paper and looked up at her entrance.

He rose to his feet. 'Claire. How are you doing?'

'As well as might be expected.'

He looked at her with understanding. He'd told her some of the rocky road he had faced courting Lily, so she knew he understood. Somewhat.

He and Lily had worked through their differences.

It seemed she was doomed to spend the rest of her life a widow. She certainly wasn't going to marry again, now she didn't have to. Thank goodness she had Jane. Jane needed her and would for a good long while.

'Would you like coffee or tea?'

She shook her head. 'I've decided we should go home.'

The look of utter joy on his face tugged at her heart. 'I am so sorry for keeping you away for so long.'

'No. Really, Claire. I was glad to be of service. I am just sorry—'

'No sense in being sorry. It is time to move forward.'

He nodded. 'I'm glad you see it that way. There are lots of very eligible gentlemen in Derbyshire.'

'I think Jane will be quite enough to keep me busy. I'll

find a cottage. I can earn a living taking in sewing. I've done it before.'

'You will not.'

'Really, Giles. I will not be a burden on the family. Don't worry, I will make sure I am far enough away that the Montagues won't be embarrassed by their poor relation, but I am really quite determined.'

'We can talk about it on the way home.'

It sounded like the threat of an argument, but she was more than a match for her nephew. And a good discussion would while away the weary hours and keep her mind off André.

'I'll have the horses put to,' he said, his eagerness making her smile.

'Would you also ask our host to send up the chambermaid to help with the packing?'

'Glad to.'

They parted ways at the bottom of the stairs and Claire climbed back up to her room. She glanced at the mountain of stuff she'd brought with her thinking she might stay for a while.

She sighed.

No. Enough pining. It did no good at all. She must focus on what she needed for the journey and what should go in her trunk. Her fur-lined cloak would serve as a carriage blanket as well as keep her warm when tripping out to the necessary or when they put up for the night. Hopefully Giles would remember to order hot bricks for their feet. Her best bonnet she would not need. She opened a hat box and popped it inside.

A knock at the door. The maid. 'Come in.'

'You can start on the gowns in the clothes press,' she said, folding the ribbons neatly into the box so they would not become unduly wrinkled.

'That's the oddest request I have ever had.'

She swung around. Her heart practically jumping out of her chest and she pressed her hand flat against her ribs to make sure it stayed in place. 'André?' The bruises on his face had faded a little, but there were dark smudges beneath his eyes.

'Are there other gentlemen you let into your bedroom?' His eyes danced. His charming smile made an appearance. She didn't trust it.

But her heart was beating hopefully.

She turned, pressed the lid on the hat box and set it on the floor. 'So, you came, after all. I had quite given you up.'

'You are leaving.'

'Yes.'

'You gave me three days.'

She turned and sat on the edge of the bed, giving him a knowing smile and a sultry glance. She'd practiced it all day the first day, when she had hoped he would come to her. 'It was very foolish of me. If you did not know your mind within the hour of my leaving you, then it was obvious you were not going to come.'

'I am here now.'

She tapped a finger against her chin. She'd seen some very naughty ladies flirt in this way with their beaux. It seemed to work well for them. 'Better late than never, I suppose. But why have you come?' She held her breath.

He tossed the gloves resting in his hat, like a pancake in a frying pan, watching them rise only to fall back into the depths of his hat. 'I owe you an explanation.'

Her heart sank to her shoes. Justification for his actions was not what she had hoped for, even now, even as she was preparing to give him up.

She shrugged. 'There is no need.' She slid off the bed with a cheerful smile. 'On your way out, could you please see what has happened to the maid?' She opened the dresser drawer and busied herself sorting ribbons she couldn't see for the blurring of her vision.

'Claire, I'm sorry.'

'What? Is it beneath your dignity to check up on a maid? Then I will ring the bell.'

'I don't mean that. You know I don't.'

'All right. You are sorry. And I am sorry. But there really is no need for it. We both agreed it was nothing.'

'It wasn't nothing,' he said softly. 'Not to me.'

She turned and leaned against the table edge, feeling the wood digging into her hips. 'Then what was it?'

He swallowed as if his mouth was dry. 'It was wonderful.'

Wonderful was good. But not good enough. Only all or nothing was good enough now.

'There are some things you don't know about me,' he muttered, his cheekbones staining red. 'Things I should tell you.'

Oh, there went the whole dipping sensation again, only this time it was her stomach. 'Tell away.' She knew she sounded hard, brittle, but she couldn't let him see she was hurting, not if all he had for her were explanations. She'd gone to him, placed her heart at his feet—well, almost—and he'd kicked her offering aside. She wouldn't do it again. Not lightly.

She folded her arms across her chest, and almost jumped when she felt how hard her nipples had become. Anticipating a romp on the handy bed no doubt. What a wanton. Well, it was not going to happen.

He set down his hat and gestured to the two chairs in front of the hearth. 'Might we sit?'

'I really don't have long. The maid is due to arrive at any moment.'

'I will be fast.'

She sauntered to the upholstered chair and sat down, primly

crossing her ankles. He eased into the wooden armchair opposite.

'The title I used at the assembly,' he said.

Goodness, he was probably involved in some sort of scheme to con people. He probably used it to part gentlemen from their money at the gambling table. George used to do it all the time.

'It really is my title.'

She laughed.

He met her gaze steadily.

She gasped. 'You mean you really are a French count?'

He nodded.

She felt ill. 'So all that talk about being a lowly chef was a lie?'

Horror filled his face. 'The title is an empty shell. The land went back to the people.' His face spasmed with distaste. 'My family was obscenely wealthy. They didn't deserve all that for themselves. No one does.'

'So why tell me about it?'

He glanced at her face and then away. 'When I was old enough to understand the abuses of the *ancien régime*, I wasn't sorry to see it gone. But I didn't believe in the killing. Not of my parents or any of the others. My parents weren't bad. They had instituted many reforms. Not enough, but more than some others.'

'The reign of terror.' Her chest tightened. 'You were lucky to escape.'

'Yes, I was one of the fortunate ones.'

'You hid? You were spirited away by some faithful servant? You know émigrés have been dining out on those tales for years.'

'I had the help of a priest. I didn't know him. And he died protecting me before we could get wherever it was he was taking me. He showed me how to hide in plain sight and I lived on the streets just like so many other street urchins of the time. Stealing. Drinking. Running messages. I was picked up by a soldier and dragged off to dig latrines.'

She wrinkled her nose.

He gave a wry laugh. 'Actually, it was the best thing that could have happened. At first I did menial tasks. I was big for my age and some of the soldiers liked to pick on me, so I badgered the company prizefighter to teach me how to box. I even won a couple of matches. I also wormed my way into the good graces of a cook and discovered I had a talent. That lasted until the troop captain learned I could read and write and ride a horse after a fashion. Then I was back to fighting. I worked my way up to the rank of colonel. But I spent all my spare time with the cooks. I hoped when the war ended it would be something I could do. That or box. The great Carême took me under his wing for a while. I think he saw something of himself in me. I left France when the emperor abdicated. I had heard good things about England. The best of it, that it was peaceful and French chefs were in demand.'

'You weren't tempted to go home when Napoleon returned?'

He shook his head. 'I had established myself as a chef at Grillons.' A wry smile twisted his lips. 'I never agreed with the republic of France having an emperor. It was not what the Revolution intended.'

She leaned back in her chair. 'But what has all this to do with me? With us? Indeed, your title might have made you an eligible *parti*. Had you thought of that? Or are you only thinking of it now that you have spent all your money on me in some fit of madness? To which you seem prone, by the way.'

A quick rueful smile curved his lips. Heavens, she loved those smiles, but she wasn't going to let them worm their way into her heart so easily. It was already too sore from his earlier rejection.

The muscles in his jaw worked. He was clearly having trouble forming his words or his thoughts. It didn't bode well. He leaned forward, resting his elbows on his knees, staring down at his boots as if he wished they would grow wings and fly him away.

Claire folded her hands in her lap and waited.

'I'm not a marrying man.'

Ah. 'I see. Well, that certainly puts the whole in a nutshell.' She started to rise.

A gesture of his hand held her still. 'I have always lived alone. I'm not like you. I am selfish. I go after what I want. Once I have it, I move on to the next thing.'

'Or the next woman, I suppose.'

His expression darkened. Then he sighed. 'In the past, yes. Claire, it is not that I don't care for you, but you deserve someone who knows how to love. You know how to love, I see you with Jane. I saw Lord Giles with Miss Lily too. I never had that.'

'You don't remember your family?'

'I try not to.'

Shock rippled through her. Horror. 'They were cruel to you?'

He frowned. 'I was a spoiled little prince as far as I recall. Dandled on my papa's knee, cosseted by my mother. I had nurses and governesses who petted me. I even remember a pony. Never do I remember anyone hurting me or denying me anything.'

'Then they loved you.' She couldn't see what more he could have wanted.

'A mother does not leave the child she loves to the fury of the mob.'

He spoke so matter-of-factly, with so little emotion, she could only stare at him.

'Would you leave Jane to save yourself?' he asked harshly.

'I hope not,' she whispered, seeing the hurt in his eyes, the bleakness in his heart, the loneliness in his soul. 'Really though, I can't be sure what I would do in such terrible circumstances.'

'I can. You would never leave her behind. I needed her, and she left me.'

'But you survived.'

'I wish I had died with her.'

'Oh. She died later?'

'No.' He shook his head and a shudder ran through his body. 'They followed, ran after her down the drive with pitchforks and shovels. They caught her at the gate. Pulled her off the horse. She disappeared beneath them. And then we were running. Out of the back of the house. Across the fields. Days. Nights. I barely remember how long we ran.'

'You must have been terrified.'

'I was angry. Angry that she left without me. Angry that she died. She did what she had to. That's what the *curé* said. I needed her, but she left me. To save herself. But she died. Why didn't she wait and come with us?' Agony scarred his features alongside the anger.

The thought of him as a small boy deserted by his mother, losing everyone he knew, twisted a knife that seemed to have lodged itself in her ribs. It hurt to breathe.

'André, when your mother rode away, did all the people follow her?'

'All of them,' he said bitterly. 'She sat there on her horse, the sunlight in her hair, taunting them till they ran at her foaming at the mouth like dogs scenting blood. She whipped them into a frenzy of hatred, then rode off.' Bitterness twisted his lips.

Claire pictured it in her mind, only she was the one on the horse. She nodded. 'Yes, that is exactly what I would do too.'

He raised his head and stared at her, fury flashing in his eyes. 'You would never leave Jane.'

'I would,' she said, her throat thickening, her eyes blurring until she could scarcely see him. Her voice broke. She sniffed. 'I would. If I thought I could lead them away from her.'

Eighteen

'No.' The word exploded from his lips like cannon shot and left a smoky haze in its wake. The images he'd avoided for so long wavered and changed. He could no longer hold them in place.

'No,' he said again. 'She left me. I stood at the window peering behind the curtains, the priest's hand on my shoulder, watching her go.'

'And then you ran the other way.'

The gentleness in her tone, the clarity of her eyes, made it all seem so simple. So logical. And his world turned on its head. 'I remember the way she sparkled on that horse in the sunlight. She was wearing all her jewels. She must have known they would come after her.' His stomach roiled. 'She was twenty-two.'

'Where was your father?'

'Not there. Later I saw him guillotined in Paris. I couldn't understand why she kept hugging me earlier that day, holding me when all I wanted to do was play.' A groan left his lips. 'She must have known they were coming. The priest must have warned her. She was saying goodbye.' The pressure of tears burned behind his eyes. He clenched his fists, willing them back. 'I kept trying to think what I had done wrong. Thinking if she had loved me, she would have taken me with her.'

And then Claire was holding him, her small arms around his shoulders. He pressed his face against her sweet breasts and, heaven help him, he cried. Sobbed like a child. Shed tears he'd buried for so long beneath his anger. The rage and the pain that she'd left without him.

Slowly the storm inside him died away, leaving him drained, but not empty. He was full of a warm kind of light. A quiet kind of peace. The old need to strike out at the world was gone. 'Oh, Claire,' he breathed. 'I never understood.'

She stroked his hair back from his temple, her smile soft. 'You were her baby. She loved you. She did what she must. What any mother must. She gave you a chance at life.'

'Damn it all.' He pulled out a handkerchief, blew his nose and wiped his eyes. '*Mon Dieu*, what happened? I feel such a fool.'

'No. No. There is no reason to feel foolish. Hush.' She kissed his cheek. 'I think the little boy who was lost just found his way home, that's all.'

She stroked his arm, patted his back. Nothing sensual or arousing. Just comfort. And he let it wash over him and through him while he tried to find himself.

Finally she got up and poured him a glass of wine. 'Only sherry, I'm afraid,' she said as she put it in his hand.

He took a sip. 'It is perfect.' He swallowed a mouthful. 'Not as perfect as you, but excellent, nonetheless.'

She laughed. 'Thank you, kind sir.' She bobbed a curtsey that reminded him of her daughter's funny little efforts and he smiled.

'Can you forgive me?' he asked, suddenly wanting to say

the things that were bubbling inside him, but not sure he had the words.

She tensed. 'Forgive you? For what, pray?'

Curse it, what had he said? What did she think he was talking about? '*Chérie*, come here.' He held out his hand and drew her down on his knee; he looked into those clear grey eyes and felt like a new man. 'Claire, *chérie*,' he whispered, 'without you, I am hollow.' He'd lost his English again. He wasn't making any sense. '*Je t'aime.* I love you, Claire.'

'You do?' She sounded so doubtful it pressed down on his chest like a heavy rock. He deserved her doubt. He'd treated her abominably.

'I came here tonight to explain why it could never be. Why you deserve so much more than me. And you do.' The truth seared his soul. 'Until tonight I was afraid to admit I needed anyone. When my mother left me, I told myself I was better off alone. Better to be alone than to be betrayed by someone you love. You freed me from a hell I didn't realise held me in thrall. I can never express the gratitude in my heart.'

'André, it is all right, you don't owe me anything.'

'That isn't it.' He opened and closed his hands, staring at knuckles still raw from his bout in the ring the day before, seeking the words he needed. It was so much easier to express anger than love. He took her face in his hands, looked into her eyes. 'I need you, Claire. I need your generous heart. I need you more than I need air to breathe. You cannot know how scared that makes me feel inside. But it makes me feel free too. You gave me that freedom. The freedom to love again. It doesn't matter if you can't love me back. I will always love you.'

'Oh, André,' she sighed, reaching up to clasp her hands at the back of his neck. 'We both have our dragons to defeat. My heart knew you were the right man for me the moment I saw you and Jane in your kitchen. But my heart has been terribly wrong in the past.' A smile lit her face. 'It is not wrong this time. I love you, André.'

Joy filled his heart and flowed over and he kissed her until he was dizzy with longing and the bed beckoned, but there was more to tell and tell it he would.

'Oh, *chérie*. What can we do? I don't have the money to support a wife. I may not have it for years.'

'Because you used it to save me.'

'Because I could not bear to see you unhappy. Will you wait for me?'

'For ever, if need be. But, André, dearest, it won't be necessary.' Her eyes gleamed with a wicked light.

'What plot are you hatching?'

'Crispin wrote to the regent telling him about a new hotel he planned to invest in and wishing he could let the prince be a part of it, but that all the shares were taken up.'

He couldn't grasp her meaning. 'What hotel?'

'Hotel du Valière. The prince insisted on putting up three thousand pounds, for a tenth of the profits.'

'What? Are you jesting?' It was the amount he needed. The amount he had given to pay Claire's debts. 'You never said anything of this before.'

'No. Giles would have written and told you. After we returned to Castonbury, if you had not come today.' She hesitated. 'I did not want you to feel obliged. I wanted to know what was in your heart.'

'And now you do.'

'Yes,' she said, smiling. 'I do. Your title will give our hotel great cachet with the *ton*.'

He groaned. 'I swore I would never use it. That I would make it on my own merits.'

'Now that's just plain silly.'

He started to speak but she put up a hand. 'If that is what you want, then it is up to you.'

What he wanted was to make her as happy as she had made him. 'If you think it will help us, then I will be a count.'

She looked surprised. 'You would take my advice?'

'*Bien sûr.* Why would I not if it is good advice?'

'André, you make me feel very happy.' She pressed a hand to her breastbone. 'In here.' Tears glistened in her eyes. 'Truly. You will let me help you with your hotel too?'

'*Chérie*, I can't think of anything I want more, except to relieve this overwhelming need to kiss you.' And he did, most thoroughly until she could scarcely remember how to breathe.

A knock sounded on the door and he cursed.

She laughed. 'It must be the maid come to help me pack.' She made to jump up.

He held her fast with a grin. 'You are not the only one with secrets. Come in.'

It was Giles who walked in. He frowned at them.

André laughed when Claire wriggled on his lap, trying to stand up. 'You find your aunt compromised, my lord. There is nothing for it but for us to marry.'

'Is that a proposal, André?' Claire asked, nudging him with her elbow.

He kissed her cheek. 'It is.'

'I accept.'

Giles gave them a comical look. 'And I suppose you now expect me to inform my father.'

'If you wouldn't mind,' Claire said.

'I suppose it is the least of my worries.'

The man sounded so harassed, André felt a pang of guilt. 'I am sorry to impose on you.'

Giles drew in a deep breath. 'No. I'm only too glad to see Claire looking so happy at last. She deserves it.'

'That is what I have been telling her.'

She gave his arm a squeeze. 'You too.'

Giles rolled his eyes. 'A little decorum please, Aunty Claire. You need to set an example.'

Claire's laugh made him glow inside. He kissed the tip of her nose. 'I must go. It seems I have a hotel to organise and you have a daughter who needs to know you are getting married in seven days' time.'

'Seven days!' Claire squeaked.

'I'm sorry, but that is how long it takes to get a special licence.'

'Only a week? Oh, my goodness. We have to get the house ready. Send out invitations. I need a dress.'

This time André let her get up. He didn't want to. He would far rather keep her there, close, where he could be sure he couldn't lose her. But he knew he could trust her and he had to let her see that trust.

He followed her up.

'I'll walk with you to Doctor's Commons,' Giles said.

'Because you want to make sure I keep my word?'

'No. To keep you two apart until after the wedding. We have enough scandals to keep hushed up without another one on top. Claire, be ready to leave when I get back, please.'

André kissed Claire's hands one at a time and then her lips. 'I will be at Castonbury before you know it.'

'And it will still seem too long.'

'Yes, but it will be worth the wait.'

He turned to Lord Giles. 'I wanted to talk to you about a man named Webster. He was asking questions about His Grace.'

'He is Sir Nathan's man,' Claire said.

'I know of him,' Giles said. 'He's been hanging around the Dower House.'

'Did you know he was interested in the state of your father's finances?' André said. 'At first I thought he had something to do with Claire's debts. His questions were very pointed.'

'Really.' Giles ushered him out of the room. 'What did he want to know?'

Epilogue

The wedding breakfast was a small affair, only family and servants, held in Castonbury's downstairs entrance hall, where harvest home was celebrated with the tenants. The mood was exceedingly cheerful.

A wedding from one's own home was far more enjoyable than a nightmare dash to Scotland, Claire decided, looking about her.

While they were missing many members of the family, Phaedra was there, sitting beside Jane looking beautiful. On her other side, wearing her most magnificent turban, Aunt Wilhelmina was tucking into the dinner prepared by Jeremy. Lily sat further along with her father. She would make a lovely bride herself in a few months and her love for Giles was clear in her eyes every time their glances met. Which they did often.

André had arranged for men and women from the local inn to wait on them and so the servants were all sitting down at one end of the table. Becca looked nervous. Agnes beside Joe Coyle was whispering and giggling. Daisy had baby Crispin on her lap, while his mother conversed with William Everett beside her.

Lumsden and Smithins sat opposite each other, competing to look the most patriarchal and keeping a close watch on the other servants' behaviour, while Mrs Stratton cozed with the new cook, a woman from the village.

'A toast,' the duke said from the head of the table. He staggered clumsily to his feet. Giles put out a hand to steady him.

The company rose to their feet. All except Claire and André.

'To my dear sister, Claire, and her bridegroom, the Comte du Valière,' Crispin said. The title had gone a long way to settling the duke's concern about their marriage. Not that André would use it every day. 'The happy couple.'

'The happy couple,' everyone chorused.

'To my mama and Monsieur André,' Jane said, coming in rather late, but her little voice ringing clear in the huge room. She took a sip of the champagne her uncle Duke, as she called him, must have poured for her, and screwed up her face with a shudder to much laughter. The star on the ribbon around her throat caught the light of the overhead chandelier with myriad pinpoints of fire.

Claire stared at it.

André rose to his feet, glass in hand. Claire felt so proud of him. He was just so handsome. He exuded confidence and charm and seemed somehow able to include everyone in his smile. He glanced down at her and grinned. The shadows were all gone from his eyes. Every last one.

'Your Grace.' He bowed, elegant and courtly as always. The duke inclined his head, his smile broad as if he, too, had forgotten some of his sorrows on this happy occasion.

'Lords, ladies, *mesdames et messieurs*,' he continued. *'Et mes amis.'* Some of the servants groaned.

'In English,' Joe Coyle shouted, and received a repressive look from Lumsden.

'My friends,' André said, acknowledging the boy. 'Thank you for attending what is the happiest day of my life. I wish all of you the same happiness *et bonne chance*.' His grin broadened. 'Good luck for those of you not fortunate enough to speak French.'

More groans.

He raised his glass. 'To my wife. My dearest heart. My Claire.' He leaned down and kissed her to the sound of cheers. Then sat down hard when she pulled on his arm. He laughed and she laughed with him.

The servants began clearing away and an orchestra began setting up at one end of the room.

'There will be dancing?' Daisy asked, her face lighting up.

Talk and laughter rippled up and down the table. Claire took advantage of it, leaning closer to her new husband. 'André, is that star you gave to Jane set with real diamonds?'

'Yes.'

'You said you bought it in a pawn shop.'

'I did. It was my father's. Sold off by one of the mob who destroyed my home, no doubt. It was an act of providence that I found it at all. It was grimy and labelled as tin.'

'Providence indeed. But it is a family heirloom, surely?'

He looked at her, his expression soft, his eyes full of love. 'Jane is my family.'

She threw her arms around his neck and kissed him. Not done, of course, really not done in the best of circles, but they were not in the best of circles, were they? They were with their family.

Cheers and the drumming of hands on the table and feet on the floor lasted as long as their kiss, which lasted a very long time.

* * * * *